M000191581

ANGEL FALLS

Copyright © 2016 Babette de Jongh
Published By Tranquil Dragonfly Press

ISBN: 978-0-9979398-0-4
ISBN: 978-0-9979398-1-1
All rights reserved. Except for use in any review, the reproduction or
utilization of this work in whole or in part in any form by any electronic,
mechanical or other means, now known or hereinafter invented, including
xerography, photocopying and recording, or in any information storage
or retrieval system, is forbidden without the written permission of the
publisher.

This is a work of fiction. Names, characters, places and incidents are either
the product of the author's imagination or are used fictitiously, and any
resemblance to actual persons, living or dead, business establjshments, events
or locales is entirely coincidental.

Printed in the USA.

Cover Design and Interior Format by

Angel Falls

Angel Falls Series
BOOK ONE

BABETTE DE JONGH

Babette de Jongh

This book is dedicated to my first ballet teacher, Susanna Smith, who taught me to love ballet and gave me a firm foundation that set me on my path as a dancer, and later as a small-town ballet teacher. Without her guiding influence in my young life, this book would never have been written.

Note from the Author:

The town of Angel Falls and its inhabitants are all entirely fictional, though anyone who knows me may notice similarities to the small town where I grew up and then taught ballet for almost a decade. I started teaching in an upstairs studio very much like Casey's—but not nearly so nice because I didn't paint the walls or refinish the floors, though maybe I should have.

My studio was accessed by steep metal stairs sandwiched between two downtown buildings. Pigeons roosted on the steel support beams in the stairwell, so it always smelled like pigeon poop. If the music wasn't too loud, we could hear the pigeons cooing, and watch them through the windows while we did our barre work. I later moved the studio to a space adjacent to the town's newspaper, but alas, no one like Ian Buchanan worked there.

I still remember many of my ballet students by name. While none of the characters in this book are modeled or named after them, a little bit of everyone I taught is in there. I also had many wonderful "ballet parents" through the years, and each is in the character of Meredith. Students and parents who were so good to me, I love you all. This book is for you, too.

I have taken many liberties with the location of Angel Falls. There is no way any place could be simultaneously as close to Gulf Shores, Tuscaloosa, Birmingham, or in fact any of the real towns I mentioned, as I have created Angel Falls to be. It's a fictional world quilted from every place I have lived, and others that never existed.

I hope readers will enjoy Angel Falls, and come back to visit again.

Chapter One

IT WASN'T THE END OF the world. Just the end of *my* world. And that was close enough.

A warm breeze teased the hem of my sundress, but my leotard and tights sucked at my skin in the late-August humidity. Lizzie, my awesome Australian Shepherd, walked beside me, tongue lolling sideways in a doggie grin. Happy in the heat, as long as she was with me.

I wished I could be as happy with life exactly as it is.

So I'll get happy. My never-ending mantra since I moved back to Angel Falls. *I'll trade the stage for the studio and get happy in the small town where I grew up, where nothing ever changes. I'll get happy teaching the kids of my old friends, my old enemies, my first lover.*

I'll get happy teaching the kids who might have been mine, if I'd made different choices.

I slapped myself upside the head. *Get happy, dammit.* Not a mental slap. A real slap. A get-happy-dammit slap.

Lizzie turned blue eyes up to mine, questioning. I ruffled her speckled gray fur and we crossed the street to the sidewalk in front of the newspaper office.

I glanced inside and saw a man so gorgeous, so sexy,

so perfect, I forgot to walk. I forgot to breathe. Struck stupid, I forgot to do anything but stare.

Here was someone I wouldn't mind getting happy with.

He was beyond beautiful. Gerard Butler's Attila but modernized, civilized, realized in physical form—in my century and my zip code. A sublime tower of sculpted brawn in blue jeans and white button-down shirt, with short dark hair and smoldering eyes—were they gray? He was smiling an indulgent and very sexy smile, looking down at Grace Lambert, Old Man Shaw's elderly secretary. He put a gentle hand on her narrow shoulder. His left hand. His unadorned, ringless left hand.

My heart did a crazy little twirl that ended with a splat on the sidewalk in front of me. I knew better than to get excited from a glimpse through a window. But if any man on earth could make me forget about Ben, this one could.

He'd probably come into the newspaper office to have his photo taken for the article someone must be writing—*Rare Eligible Man Sighting in Angel Falls*. I hadn't seen a desirable man—desirable according to me, anyway—who wasn't taken or gay, or both, since I moved back home.

My heart ooched back into my chest and collapsed. What was this Prince of Perfection doing in Angel Falls, Alabama, our dinky little deep-south town on the backside of nowhere? He didn't belong here. Though neither did I. Yet here we were. Gerard Butler's twin and me—displaced daughter of the old south, back on home soil, but still unrooted.

Unrooted, because back-home looks a lot like hell, where I'm forced to watch my old boyfriend and my once-best-friend share the happy-ever-after that should have been mine. We'd been the Three Musketeers throughout childhood, and Melody had been happy for us when Ben chose me to be his high school sweetheart.

I couldn't say the same about my feelings when he chose her to marry.

After months of witnessing Ben and Melody's happiness, months of being steeped in jealousy—then mired in guilt for feeling so jealous—I craved a true love relationship of my own. But Holy-Mary-Matilda, I'd happily settle for a true lust diversion. How long had it been since I'd felt a man's arms around me, since I'd wrapped my legs around—

Too long. That's how long.

Pickings were slim around here. Since coming home, I had so far avoided settling for the town's only halfway hunky bachelor, Ken Kelley, the Kar-Wash-King. If I could think as much of him as he thought of himself, I might be tempted, because being alone was sometimes, well, lonely.

Lizzie, the best dog ever, trotted to the pressed-metal staircase sandwiched between the Angel Falls Informer and the Gulf States Bank. She turned and sat on the first step, waiting for me to follow. I couldn't. I stared through the window of the newspaper office, afraid if I blinked, this mirage of masculinity would disappear. But I blinked, and he was still there.

He turned toward me as if he felt my presence. Caught staring, I should have felt embarrassed, but when a slow smile carved dimples into his lean, tanned cheeks, all I could do was smile back and keep on looking at him while he looked at me. The two of us, suspended in time.

The editor's ancient secretary was patting his arm, trying to get his attention. He took his hand—his ringless left hand—off the old woman's shoulder and held up a hang-on-a-second finger.

Then he came outside.

Onto the sidewalk.

With me.

He took my hand in his, and I nearly hyperventilated. His appreciative glance devoured me from my skimpy sundress and the leotard I wore beneath it, to my ballet tights, to my Keds, then back up to my face. His eyes weren't gray, as I'd imagined before. They were the light amber of well-aged whiskey.

"You must be Miss Alexander, the ballet teacher." His voice was deep and rich as double-dark chocolate, threaded with a Scottish accent as smooth and sweet as butterscotch caramel. The sexy voice matched the sexy rest of him.

"Please, call me Casey." Breathless, I sounded like I was having an asthma attack.

"All right, Casey." My name sounded exotic and beautiful with those deep Scottish tones wrapped around it. "Glad I caught you on your way upstairs so I could introduce myself. I'm Ian Buchanan."

Ian Buchanan. A sexy name to match the sexy voice to match the sexy rest of him.

It's fantastic to meet you, I'd like to go out with you, I'd love to get naked with you… All those possible responses raced across the ticker-tape scrolling through my mind. Thank God none of them made me open my mouth. Instead, I came up with an uninspiring but appropriate reply. "Hello."

The door to the newspaper office opened. "Mr. Ian." Wilson, the beefy young guy who ran the presses, stepped outside. His blond hair and liberal use of hair gel made him look like a peroxided rooster. "Mr. Shaw asked if you'd come into his office now."

Ian gave my hand a little squeeze and let go. "We'll talk later." Then he followed Wilson back inside. What we'd talk about was a mystery. How he knew me was less of a mystery, because not only did everyone in this town know everyone else, everyone knew everyone else's business, too. And they didn't seem to mind talking about it. There wasn't much else to do in a small southern town.

Lizzie and I raced up the narrow flight to the second floor studio. At the top of the iron landing, I unlocked the Capezio-pink door, and we ran inside.

I leaned against the wall and figured out how to breathe again. Lizzie spun in circles, nails scrabbling on the wood floor. I clapped my hands. "Woo-hoo! We just found the Holy Grail!"

Lizzie stopped spinning and sat poised in front of me, vibrating.

I stroked her silky head. "Lizzie girl, that's my new boyfriend."

Based on one look? My mother's voice invaded my head. *You don't even know the man. Ring or not, he might be married.*

"Shut up, Mom. At least he's not married to my best friend."

Lizzie panted agreement. She didn't care what my mom thought, either. She knew I was right.

It was past time for the Universe to toss something good my way, and maybe this was it. Maybe he was interviewing for a job at the newspaper office. Maybe my long months of abstinence and awkwardness and angst were at an end. "Lizzie, I'll bet you a dog treat he's—"

At the magic words—dog treat—Lizzie zoomed into the classroom and gave a little yip, meaning, "I can't reach the treat jar by myself."

"Don't pitch a conniption, I'm coming." I followed

Lizzie into the sunlit studio. She waited by the vintage stereo cabinet, where the treat jar lived. I handed over the bone, and her stub tail gyrated like a fluffy helicopter propeller. She took it to her pink paisley ottoman under the windows, then settled down to munch.

I glanced around the room I'd spent the summer scraping, sanding, and painting, and now my ballet studio—Casey Alexander's School of Dance—was ready for its first fall-semester.

Pearl gray walls made the big classroom look even bigger. High-gloss white trim shone like satin ribbon. The double row of wooden barres beneath the windows gleamed like honey. Framed dance posters hung between tall narrow windows, and the mirrors on the opposite wall sparkled from yesterday's scrubbing. The faded, wide-planked floor still smelled faintly of the lavender scented floor cleaner I'd mopped with. It was almost as pretty as any New York studio.

Lizzie yipped, announcing an arrival.

"Casey," a small voice chirped. "I'm a ballawina now!"

I knelt down and braced myself for impact, arms wide to catch the three-year-old hurtling toward me. Dressed in head-to-toe pink, her blonde ringlets swept into a tiny bun, this child twisted my heart into a knot that made every beat hurt.

I kissed her cheek and inhaled her strawberry baby shampoo scent. "Hey, Amy."

She should have been mine.

I closed my eyes, not sure where the insidious, jealous thought had come from. Children weren't at the top of any to-do list I'd ever made. But when I was still young enough to think I could have everything, I had dreamed of a faraway future of making babies with this child's father.

"Hello-o." My once-best friend Melody followed her daughter into the room. Melody looked like a fashion ad in a mommy magazine, with her expertly cut-and-dyed dark sable bob, a red-striped formfitting tee—bought from the front of the store, not the clearance rack—and curvy denim jeans. Shiny pedicured toenails peeped from the open toe of stacked espadrilles.

"I know we're a little early. Amy was so excited about her first day of ballet, she wouldn't take a nap."

"Girl after my own heart." I dredged up a fake smile, then stood and gave Melody a hug. Best friends were more important than boyfriends. We'd both been raised on that wisdom. It must be right, because here we were, still close.

Just not as close as before.

Melody patted my back. "I know you're still disappointed. But I'm glad you decided to take over for Ms. Daphne instead of going back to New York. Now you'll have a new career, still doing what you love."

I lifted a shoulder and let it drop. Teaching little girls to dance isn't the same thing as being a prima ballerina. But it wasn't like I had a choice, and the timing had been perfect. I was lucky Ms. Daphne had decided to retire when she did, after twenty years of teaching ballet in her converted garage. Lucky I had months back home to find a suitable studio space I could renovate in time for fall semester. Lucky, lucky me.

Melody stepped back. "What you need is some retail therapy. This Saturday, I'm taking you to the mall. I'll treat you to an appointment with Valerie." Melody plucked a long strand of hair off my leotard. "She can add highlights, make it blond again."

The sunny hair I'd had as a child had darkened to not-quite-blond. "I can't. I have to—" but I couldn't think of anything I had to do.

Melody pounced on my hesitation. "I'll even stop at every yard sale along the way. Please say yes. You'll love Valerie. She'll make you look like a movie star."

"I'm sure looking like a movie star will improve my mood." Not that I cared all that much; I kept my hair in a bun most of the time anyway. But I knew better than to argue with Melody. She looked like a cream puff, all soft curves and sweet smiles, but she had a backbone of titanium. She was determined to reclaim best-friend status. If I refused to let her, everyone would know I still had a thing for Ben after all these years. "Your car or mine?"

She looked sideways at me with salon-shaped eyebrows raised. "Are you serious? I wouldn't travel more than walking distance to anywhere in that old hag."

"Hey, don't talk about Dame Margot like that. She's a classic." But I didn't take Melody's rejection personally. The 1980's hatchback rattletrap I had inherited from my ex-apartment-mate was like a giant, messy purse. Traded for my furniture and named after the famous ballerina I had idolized in childhood, the old car had been sitting in a garage for over a decade. Margot had to be towed home, where my dad finally got her running again, after he finished fussing at me for trading my worldly possessions for a clunker.

Melody's SUV was newer, cleaner, and more comfortable, and the drive to the mall took a whole hour. "Okay. You drive, I'll buy lunch."

Just as well, since Margot had developed a tendency to overheat—hot flashes, probably—and the highway outside Angel Falls wasn't the best place to have car trouble. It undulated along the river like a mean black snake, twisting and turning through tiny bridges, cut-through hills, and built-up blacktop with no place to pull over.

Melody started inching toward the door. "I'll make your appointment with Valerie when I get home."

Amy hugged Melody's legs. "Bye, Mommy. See you after ballet."

"Bye, Sweetie." Melody took Amy's face in her hands and kissed her little pursed lips. "Dance pretty for Aunt Casey."

"I will." Dismissing her mom and me for a better deal, Amy skipped to Lizzie's ottoman and draped herself across my exceptionally tolerant dog.

I walked Melody out, then stood on the landing and greeted the parents arriving with their preschoolers. At the bottom of the long flight, a little girl started up, hitching herself up the steep stairs one slow step at a time. Danielle Carlton, by herself, no parent to hold her hand or make sure she made it safely into the studio.

"Dani, wait." I slid a wedge under the entry door and galloped down the stairs, passing a few parents bringing their kids up. "Y'all go on inside," I said. "I'll be there in a second."

I knew Dani's mother. I knew she could read. But she clearly hadn't read the note I mailed to the parents who didn't bother to come to orientation. If she had, she wouldn't have sent Dani up these stairs instead of bringing her into the studio. I hoisted Dani onto my hip and started back up.

"Miss Casey." Dani wrapped her arms around my neck. "My mommy has a new baby growing in her tummy."

"She does?" She already had more kids than she could handle in this little package I was carrying. "I'm sure you'll be a great big sister."

"Did you know babies grow inside their mommy's tummy?"

"Yes, I did." In the studio, my other students gathered around Lizzie's bed, their ballet bags strewn around her like roses at a ballerina's feet after a performance. I ushered a few lingering parents out the door and thanked God for Lizzie. Without her, I'd have had at least one crying child who didn't want her mother to leave.

I put Dani down and took her hand. "Time to get started. Let's hold hands and make a circle."

We made the circle with a minimum of pulling, and no one fell down on purpose or tugged hard enough to pull anyone else down. "Criss-cross applesauce," I instructed, showing them what I meant. Everyone sat cross-legged in the circle for beginning exercises.

"Babies grow in their mommy's tummy," Dani yodeled to her classmates. "Guess how they get out."

"How do they get *in* there?" Amy's voice was a hushed whisper of awe, disbelief, and a hint of horror.

Lord, help me. I could just hear the phone calls I'd get tonight from mothers asking why I was teaching about the birds and bees instead of ballet.

"I'm going to be a blue butterfly." I moved my arms in a slow flutter. "What color butterfly are you going to be today, Dani?"

I spent the next hour leaping, hopping, spinning, swaying, teaching ballet technique to a dozen preschoolers through creative movement and imaginary play. We were butterflies, then trees, then frogs, then horses. I even managed to slip in the correct terminology.

The preschooler's hour ended, and after a hectic flutter of coming and going, the first-grade class began. Then came second-and-third grades, then fourth through sixth. After that, classes were grouped by ability rather than age. In the interest of simplicity, I had followed Ms. Daphne's schedule from last year, so my last session every

Monday would be the most advanced. The girls wowed me with their barre work, and before I knew it, I was hurrying to fit in one more combination. I turned up the music then ran to stand in front of the teenage girls.

"Spread out so you don't bump into anyone when you do the *tour jete* to the back." I demonstrated the correct form. My injured ankle didn't allow professional perfection, but I could still do this. "Roll through the foot and bend your knee for a soft landing. If I hear a smack or a thud, you're not doing it correctly."

I danced the combination with my students, watching in the mirror and calling out corrections. "Mandy, step back-side-front on the *pas de bourre*. Alison, point your foot! It looks like a dead fish hanging off the end of your leg."

A shrill ring cut through the music. I flapped a hand for my students to keep practicing and ran into the foyer to answer the studio's landline. Leaning over the U-shaped counter that embraced the desk and a rolling chair I would probably never sit in, I snatched up the receiver. After a brief struggle with the type of curling cord I'd forgotten existed until I found the ungodly-expensive office phone with an un-losable handset, I answered. "Dance studio."

"Miss Alexander?"

All the oxygen in the room floated up to the ceiling. It was *him*—Ian Buchanan, the handsome hunk I'd met downstairs. He was talking, but with the music blaring in the studio and the girls' feet pounding on the wood floor in the lively *sauté, jete, pas-de-chat* combination, I could barely hear him. I put my finger in my ear to drown out the sound. "Excuse me?" Had he said, *new editor*?

"Excuse you?" Ian drew out the word *you* so it had about fifteen vowel sounds. "No, pardon *me*," he roared.

"I was hopin' you could turn down the music, but I hadna realized ye taught ballet to the *hard o' hearin'*."

I took my finger out of my ear. Yes, the music was loud, and the thump-thump of the girls' leaps vibrated through the old wood floors. "I'm sorry, but Mr. Shaw said the newspaper closes before my advanced classes begin."

All summer long, when I'd been up here scraping and sanding, painting and polishing to get the studio ready for fall classes, the newspaper office had been locked up and deserted every day by five. But apparently, Mr. Shaw had hired an editor who liked to work late, a late-working editor who wasn't happy about the noise.

"Good God Almighty, the noise is the least of it. The ceiling is about to come down! Are those wee ballerinas up there, or is a herd of elephants leaping about?" His accent thickened as he spoke, and the word *about* sounded like *aboot*. "If ye canna make 'em stop jumpin', can ye at least turn down the music?"

Even pissed-off and shouting, his voice made me shiver—and not with fear. A hormonal surge made my stomach rise up against my diaphragm like a loose helium balloon, made my pores prickle with the rush of blood to my skin. I wanted to run downstairs and rub up against him like a cat in heat. I knew it was just my months of abstinence, since I'd left my friend-with-benefits back in New York. But the anticipation swirling in my belly had begun to curdle like blinky milk. My potential prince wasn't very charming, and he wasn't calling to ask me out. He was calling to complain.

Fortunately, nobody's anger can stand up for long in the face of a well-trained southern belle. If I kept my cool, I could help him regain his. "Mr. Buchanan," I said in a homemade whipped cream voice, "I'm sorry if it inconveniences you, but dancers have to *jump* sometimes. Mr. Shaw said it wouldn't be a problem."

"Well, o' course he did." Ian's voice had calmed down a notch or two. "He's a nice old fossil, and deaf as a chunk of petrified wood. But the fact is—"

"It's after five-o'clock—"

"Lass, sheet-rock dust is falling from the ceiling. I'm surprised the building is still standing."

I ignored whatever he was saying about the overhead light fixtures swaying down there.

"It was nice talking to you, but we'll have to continue this conversation later. My class is waiting for me. Have a nice evening. Goodbye."

The girls had gathered at the classroom door to eavesdrop, so I put the receiver into the cradle as gently as if it were a sleeping baby. Then I sailed past and turned the volume down.

But wait. Did I really want to reward the annoyed Scotsman downstairs for the pissy phone call that interrupted my class? No, I didn't.

Man of my dreams, ogre of my nightmares, either way, he might as well learn his lesson now. I turned the music up a click and danced the final combination with my class, then led everyone in a curtsey and dismissed class. My students changed into their street shoes and shoved pointe shoes into their ballet bags. I stood on the landing at the top of the stairs until my last student waved from below when her parents arrived to pick her up.

The whole time, my mind churned right along with my stomach. I had faced-up to the reality that my hopes and dreams were burned to ash, and there would be no phoenix rising. I had come to terms with the possibility that I'd end up just like Ms. Daphne, the town's last ballet teacher, a lifelong spinster who'd never quite managed to fit into the small town landscape. I had swallowed my jealousy, pretending it didn't bother me to see Ben and Melody together, living the fairytale life I'd given up to be a ballerina. I had restored Melody to best-friend status in all but the deepest depths of my wounded heart, hoping that time would turn that tiny white lie into truth.

Couldn't the universe cut me some slack? Give me a break? Toss me a bone? Couldn't Ian Buchanan turn out to be the Prince Charming I imagined him to be?

Lights from the newspaper office illuminated the sidewalk at the foot of the stairs. Ian Bloody Buchanan—who'd better not continue to be an asshole—was probably down there brooding over the noise level of a ballet studio and wondering how to get me to break my lease.

Thank God Mr. Shaw owned the building. His family had known mine for generations, and ties like that matter in a small town. He wouldn't kick me out, even if I got crossways with his new editor.

Back in the studio, I popped the *Nutcracker Suite* CD into the player and selected the Turkish number. Immersed in the slow, sultry strains, I danced, releasing Ian Buchanan's irritation, my ruined career, and the fact that I might never find the kind of love Ben and Melody shared. The kind Ben and I had known, before he threw it away.

The last notes eased into silence. The abrupt sound of applause erupted. My heart fluttered like a startled bird, its wings beating against my ribs. He stood in the doorway, as if my thoughts had conjured him. "Ben..."

Chapter Two

"I'M SORRY I SCARED YOU." Ben came closer, his footsteps loud in the quiet studio.

"Surprised," I said. "Not scared." He and I seemed to avoid each other by unspoken consent. Melody must have sent him. Sure of herself, sure of him, sure of me.

She might not be so sure, if she knew how hard it was for me to look into Ben's blue eyes and hide the longing that had imprisoned me in heavy chains for the last twelve years.

His face looked the same as always. Kind eyes, perfect nose, sweet smile, the front tooth that overlapped its twin just slightly. His expression, the polite disinterest of a stranger, gave those chains a sharp, cruel twist. Afraid to look into his eyes, because that would let him look into mine, I focused on the slight cleft in his chin.

He stepped close enough for me to tell that he'd washed his hair with Amy's strawberry baby shampoo. He held out a folded piece of paper. "September tuition for Amy and Maryann. Melody said she's been meaning to give it to you since orientation but keeps forgetting."

I reached for the check, careful not to touch his hand. For the space of a breath, we stood connected by the slip of paper. Then he let go, and his hand dropped to his side. I folded the check again and closed my fingers around it. "Thanks."

Lizzie, the traitor, padded up to sit beside Ben.

He reached down to stroke her head. "I haven't seen you dance in a while. It was nice."

"I'm glad you… um… liked it." Was he remembering that time in New York? The time I danced for him, right before he came back home to Angel Falls never to return? If we were both remembering that time, we needed to put some space between us, and fast. "I need to finish…" I had no idea what I needed to finish.

"Okay. Well." Ben swallowed. The smooth muscles of his neck flexed. He shifted his weight a couple of times, acting like he wanted to run but couldn't remember how.

I made myself look down, and realized I had folded Melody's check into a thick square about the width of a quarter. Feeling exposed, I glanced up at him and caught a flicker of emotion in his eyes I wished I hadn't seen.

He angled his body toward the exit. "I'll see you later."

His tennis shoes squeaked on the wood floor, and I watched him walk away. I took a shaky breath and sat to untie the knotted ribbons of the stiff pointe shoes I had just begun breaking in. I took the shoes off and peeled my tights back, easing my blistered, bleeding toes through the hole that converted tights to leggings.

While I bandaged my toes and slipped on a soft pair of socks, Lizzie leaned against me, reminding me that I had plenty to be thankful for. I shoved Ben out of my head and tried to think of sunny beaches and soft kittens and the precious, bitter smell of puppy breath. But my thoughts swung wide instead, latching onto Ian Buchanan and his pissy phone call. Was he going to be a jerk about the noise again tomorrow? And the next day? And every blessed day of ballet classes for the rest of the year?

I folded in the heels of my pointe shoes and wound the ribbons around them, tucking the ends under to keep them in place. "Come on, Lizzie." I put my Keds on and followed Lizzie down the narrow stairs. Even before I turned the corner onto the shadowed sidewalk, I knew the newspaper office lights were out.

Good. He was gone.

But as I reached the darkened windows, a light clicked on behind the slatted blinds.

"Jeez!" I leaped sideways, tripped over Lizzie and nearly fell, saved only by a quick-footed two-step from curb to asphalt. A twinge in my left ankle reminded me to be more careful. Thank God I hadn't injured myself— or Lizzie.

I stepped back onto the sidewalk. Lizzie gave me a wide berth, keeping close to the building wall, in case I decided to surprise her with another brilliant move. "It wasn't my fault," I told her. "The Newspaper Nazi startled me."

Lizzie shot a worried glance my way, obviously not convinced.

I could tell the peaceful coexistence I'd imagined with the newspaper office was ending before it began, by the surge of adrenaline that zapped through me at the thought of Ian Buchanan.

I took a calming breath and lifted my face to the sky. The night air settled on my skin like a soothing balm, thick with humidity and the intoxicating scent of the sweet olive tree at the edge of Miss Lula's yard. The slow walk home took my worries and left them behind, step by step.

Serenaded by the choir practicing *Rivers of Babylon* in the Methodist Church down the street, I walked up the sidewalk of my Victorian farmhouse-turned-duplex feeling better, looking forward to a glass of wine and a hot bath.

The cute little yellow clapboard house with its wide front porch belonged in the middle of a twenty acre farmstead. But it did fine here, too, at the corner of an old-fashioned city block halfway between downtown and the river. The place suited me, and renting out the other half gave me a financial safety net—about the size of a minnow net, but when every drop of money mattered, even minnow nets counted.

I walked through the beveled glass front door into the entry hall both apartments shared, then unlocked my door. I tossed my ballet bag on the hall table—though there wasn't a hall, just the living room with the shabby chic tables and overstuffed couch and chairs I'd found at yard sales. I was glad I'd traded all my New York furniture for Margot. Glass and chrome and modern sectionals wouldn't have worked in a yellow farmhouse.

On my way to the kitchen, I gave a passing head scratch to the fat Siamese making like an overly yeasty loaf of bread on the back of the couch. "Hey, Chester. Hard day waiting at home?"

Chester purred and drooled. Lizzie spread herself belly down on the kitchen's white tile floor. I popped a frozen dinner into the microwave, poured a glass of wine, and sat at the oak farmhouse table I'd scored for twenty dollars at a junk store. The faint sound of my neighbors talking leaked through the kitchen wall.

My serenity evaporated. It seemed that everyone else in the world had someone to share their lives with, while I had no one.

The microwave dinged, but I wasn't hungry any more. I poured the rest of my wine down the sink and tossed the overheated food in the trash. Lizzie looked up, her gaze sliding toward the garbage can.

"Don't even think about it." I turned off the kitchen light and slumped into the bathroom. I brushed my teeth furiously—enamel erosion, receding gums, tooth sensitivity, I didn't care. I scrubbed my teeth as if they'd done something wrong then went to bed.

On Friday, with the first week of classes behind me, I dressed in laddered tights, a strappy leotard, and Homer Simpson boxer shorts, then walked to the studio. Lizzie had declined to come with me. She had her dog door into the fenced back yard, so she could do what she wanted.

At the studio, with my iPod playing *One Republic*, I cleaned, I sang, I danced. Because having every Friday off is something to be grateful for.

When the studio sparkled, I rewarded myself with a relaxing stretch. Sliding into a split, I held the arch of my pointed foot in both hands and pulled gently to increase the tension. Sweat rolled between my breasts and down my back. My muscles were blissfully wrung-out, warm and elastic. Even my left ankle felt strong yet pliant. No matter what was wrong with my life, this, at least, was right. Life is good, I told myself, even if you're not having sex with anyone other than yourself.

"That's gotta hurt." Ian's voice, the deep rumble, the lovely purring sound on the 'r', shot goose bumps through every follicle. My nipples drew into hard little points that poked into the floor. I turned my face toward the velvety sound.

He prowled the room like he owned the place, marking his territory just by walking around with all those X-filled pheromones. He'd already done this to me over the phone. Even after the call, I'd felt him sending invisible waves of testosterone up through the floorboards. In person, all that in-your-face manliness was ten times more potent. And oh, goodness gracious, he was a sight to behold. Who cared what a dick he'd been on the phone?

Hoping to affect him at least as much as he affected me, I pressed my palms against the floor and eased into a center split, both legs straight out to the side. Showing off, yes, I'll admit. And showing a complete lack of maturity, to boot. But I didn't care. I hoped he was imagining how good I'd be in bed. I hoped he ached with disappointment because unless he sweetened up a little, he'd never get a chance to do anything but wonder about the incredible sexual positions my extreme flexibility would allow.

And I really did hope he'd sweeten up so we could be friends. Or more than friends. Maybe friends-with-benefits friends.

"Mr. Buchanan." I said his name in a voice like day-old iced tea without a bit of sugar. "What can I do for you?"

He slid his hands into the front pockets of his jeans—easing some strain? I hoped so.

"I'd like to apologize for being a little testy on Monday." His voice was low, deep, cajoling. Just short of seductive. "I shouldn't have called to complain. I hope we can start over." Leaning down, he extended a hand, expecting me to shake it. "I'm Ian Buchanan. Your new landlord."

Say what? "You mean, you own this building?"

"Yes." He sounded almost apologetic. "I bought the

newspaper and the building from Mr. Shaw. All part of my plan to save the *Informer* from drowning then drag it up onto the shore of the digital age."

"Oh." No wonder he acted like he owned the place— he did.

The Southern Belle Handbook demanded I sit up and slip my hand into his. But I knew that if I raised up, my sweat-soaked leotard would be see-through, and my bra-less boobies would point straight at him. Already, I hoped he hadn't noticed that the floor had a sweat-imprint, an embarrassing chalk outline of my torso, including two tangerine-sized boob prints. But a southern belle is nothing if not polite. I sat up and put my hand in his. "You're forgiven."

My breasts were magnets his eyes couldn't resist. He looked down, a tiny flicker I might have missed, if I hadn't been so aware of him. Then he turned away and made a big deal of examining the studio, looking at the framed ballet prints on the walls, running a hand along the polished barres. Giving me a chance to recover my dignity, I thought.

Until he spoke. "Nice studio. Lots of natural light, incredibly low rent, utilities included. Sweet deal."

I wasn't stupid. I knew where this was headed. My rent was way below the going rate so naturally, he would want to raise it. I hugged my knees to my chest, hoping my leotard would dry sometime soon.

"I realize my rent is a bit on the low side. But this place was a dump when I moved in. It only looks nice because I made it look nice. I cleaned, I sanded, I painted. All summer long." The brick on the south-facing wall took six whole gallons of paint. All those tiny crevices. I thought I'd never finish.

He shrugged. My elbow grease didn't enter into his

bottom line. His bedroom eyes burned a path from my ratty ballet slippers, laddered tights, and too-thin leotard to my face. "I'm sure you worked hard, lass. But your rent hardly covers the cost of utilities."

"I'm sorry if the cost of my utilities causes a problem. Not too much of one, I hope, because I just signed my lease for a whole year."

My polite way of saying F.U.

He squatted next to me, close enough to touch. Jeans molded to muscular thighs. Rolled-back shirtsleeves strained against wide shoulders and powerful arms. I imagined the kind of strength all those muscles indicated.

I imagined all sorts of things I shouldn't be imagining.

I wanted so much to like him, but I wasn't sure I could. My body wanted his body, sure. Falling in lust with him would be easy. But I'd need to like him, to have the friend part of friends-with-benefits.

A tiny smirk lifted one corner of his mouth, as if he'd read my mind. He stood. "I'll let you get back to what you were doing."

I struggled with the impulse to leap up and walk him to the door. But my nipples were still trying to pop out of my leotard, and I didn't want him to think they were excited to see him. So I stayed put.

"It was nice meeting you," I said, hoping it kept me from seeming completely rude. Polite F.U.'s were acceptable. Bad manners were not.

He gave me a my-work-is-done-here nod. "Feel free to call if you need anything."

His body, in my bed, came to mind. "I will, thanks."

Chapter Three

ISNAGGED ONE OF THE OVERFILLED shopping bags Melody was about to drop, and tried to remember where we'd parked. I hoped it wasn't far. "Jeez-o-Pete, Melody, I guess you invited me to go shopping so I could help carry your hundred pounds of loot." Five dresses from three different boutiques, two nearly-identical pairs of strappy sandals in a Buy-One-Get-One deal, jeans and blouses and chunky jewelry from one store after another after another.

"It isn't my fault you didn't buy anything." Melody pursed her lips in the trademark pout she'd perfected when we were teenagers. "I know you're mad about the mix-up with Valerie, and I'm sorry. I could have sworn I made that salon appointment."

Scanning the parking lot in the evening gloom, I spied Melody's midnight blue SUV parked under a security light that was just beginning to flicker on. I started walking in that direction. "I'm not mad." I'd just forgotten that I hate shopping, and that outings with Melody were always all about Melody. "I'm sure God wants me to have mousy hair."

"I'll make an appointment for you next weekend."

"Can we forget about it? I'm happy with my hair the way it is." Not quite blond, not quite brown was fine with me.

It was almost dark when we loaded the shopping bags and secured them behind the cargo net. By the time we reached the twisting highway that had been built-up along the river, the only scrap of light in the universe came from the car's headlights. The feeble glow swept brush strokes of gray-green onto the forest of pine trees.

Melody turned the lights to high beam. "Have you met Ian Buchanan yet? I heard he bought The *Angel Falls Informer* from old man Shaw."

"God, yes." I pounced on the subject, telling-all about his irate phone call. "I haven't decided whether he's an asshole or not."

"He seemed nice to me," Melody said in her sweet little Smurf voice. I was one of the few people who knew some of that sweetness wasn't real sugar. "And besides..." She sighed like a teenage groupie. "He's so handsome." As if she didn't have her own handsome husband waiting at home, keeping their kids so she could spend the day shopping.

"No, wait. I've decided. He's an asshole whose good looks only make him more dangerous."

Melody glanced my way. "It sounds like you're enjoying the challenge. It wouldn't be fun if it was *too* easy to wrap your sexy new landlord around your pinky finger."

Says Mel, an expert at wrapping. Such an expert, she wrapped *my* boyfriend tight enough to turn him into *her* husband. I picked at a hangnail on the pinky finger that had never held onto a man for long, much less wrapped one. "Wow, Mel, you didn't tell me you'd gotten a degree in psychology. Congratulations."

"My Mrs. Degree qualifies me to psychologize, didn't

you know?" Mel laughed a birds-singing-in-the-trees laugh that climbed up my nerve endings.

But her high-pitched laugh wasn't the problem. My rotten attitude was the problem. She might have stolen her Mrs. Degree from me, but the statute of limitations on that crime had long since expired. After keeping the title for twelve years, she'd earned the right to claim it. The dank smell of sour grapes in the air was coming from me. I had no right to sit in judgment on the quality of Mel's sweetness.

"Why don't you put in a CD?" Melody opened the center console and handed me a CD, since I'd failed to punt the conversational ball down the field.

I glanced at the title and put it back. "Don't you have anything approaching real music?" I rifled through the country twang collection. "Nope," I answered my own question. "You've gone over to the dark side."

The headlights flashed on mile marker twenty three. We were half an hour from home. Much too long to listen to country music. I turned on the radio and dialed through bands of static. "Reception out here is pathetic." I plugged my phone into the car's USB port and scrolled through my Spotify playlist.

Melody made a strange choking sound. "My God!"

I looked up. Headlights pinned us through the windshield, first from one side of the road, then the other. A huge truck loomed in front of us. My lungs quit working. I dropped my phone and grabbed the dashboard. Those two yellow headlights expanded until they were all I could see. My heart raced and my insides buzzed with fear. We were going to die.

Melody screamed, slammed on brakes, and jerked the wheel.

The car skidded off the blacktop. The tires plowed

through soft dirt then dug in, lifting the driver's side off the ground. The car balanced on two wheels, and I had all the time in the world to contemplate our fate. We would roll down the embankment. Sink into the swamp with the water moccasins and alligators and flesh-eating-bacteria.

The car dropped to the blacktop with a *whoomp*, right in the path of the oncoming truck. Its bulldog hood ornament was close enough to—

The airbag exploded, burning my arms, punching me in the face. My bones smacked together. Glass spewed, pelting my skin. Smoke stung my eyes and clogged my throat. My head spun. No... we were spinning. Backward, screaming down the highway, a tin-can billiard ball hit with too much English. CDs and cell phones ricocheted like bullets; an umbrella whacked me in the forehead and whirled through the broken windshield.

"Shit, shit, shit!"

We hurtled down the embankment and rolled toward the black water below. The roof smashed into something and crumpled. Metal groaned then settled. The car rested on the driver's side.

Movement stopped, time slowed.

I hung sideways, my chest and ribs smashed by the seatbelt, my heart going haywire. Arms and legs dangling, hair in my face, I coughed up the taste of smoke and blood and dirt and glass.

One by one, my senses came back online, but a foggy sense of unreality stood between me and my brain. The dashboard wavered like it was under water. Mel's face was a pale blur below me.

"Melody?" My voice sounded hoarse. "Melody, are you all right?"

No answer. But I heard her breathing. Harsh rasping

inhales, soft huffing exhales.

She was hurt. I had to help her. "Hang on, I'm coming." I pressed my feet against the dash to keep from falling on top of her, and tried to unbuckle my seatbelt. But something stabbed my arm. I looked down, expecting to see a chunk of metal sticking out of my left bicep.

My arm looked fine, but when I moved it, pain blazed through me like fire. I felt lightheaded, and realized I was breathing too fast, a breath away from hyperventilating. "Fuck, fuck, fuck!"

Muttering curse words didn't help. Fucking fabulous. "Melody, I think my arm might be broken. I can't get my seatbelt undone. Are you okay?"

Her gasping breaths had slowed. "It hurts to breathe."

"You probably cracked a few ribs. But we're still alive. We'll be okay."

"I can't... I can't breathe." She was panting, short, shallow breaths. "Help me."

Hanging sideways by the seatbelt, I felt myself spinning through a memory, springing hand to hand to foot to foot, cartwheeling through fifth grade with Mel's hands at my waist. She taught me to cartwheel, and I rewrote her incoherent essay on Beowulf in high school. She dyed my hair orange—not on purpose—and I showed her how to wax her legs. Then she somehow managed to get her legs stuck together and ended up in the ER.

We had always helped each other, or tried to, at least. And I had allowed the one time she hurt me to cancel out all that helping. In a flash of gratitude-induced insight, I let go of my long-held resentment and promised God that from here on out, I'd be a for-real best friend to Melody. She couldn't change our past, but I could change our future. "Are you hurt anywhere else? Can you climb up to the road?"

She didn't answer. Her struggle for breath was all the answer I needed. I had to do something, but my brain was having a hard time coming up with a plan. My heart pounded in my head and behind my eyes. My chest hurt from hanging by the seatbelt. My throat felt dry from breathing in the smoke. My sinuses stung from the smell of gasoline—

Holy shit! What if the car caught fire?

I had to get us out of here.

I pushed my legs against the misshapen dash, curved my spine into the bucket seat, and locked my knees to get my weight off the seatbelt buckle. I tried again to unfasten my seatbelt. It popped loose, flew up, and whacked me in the forehead. I fell, hit the steering wheel, and landed in a heap on the driver's door, practically in Melody's lap. I touched her face. Her skin felt cold, clammy. She coughed, a wet, rumbling sound. Dark foam trickled from her mouth.

Her breathing sounded... bubbly.

Sparks of panic exploded like firecrackers under my skin. "I have to call 911." My cell phone still dangled from the USB cord. "Thank you, God." I punched in the numbers.

"911 Dispatch," a woman's voice answered.

"Help." My voice shook. I took a breath. "We need help."

"What is your emergency?"

"Accident. C-C- Car..." I couldn't get enough air to speak. "Car accident."

"Calm down, ma'am. What is your location?"

"Highway 80." I saw again the headlights' flash on the glowing mile-marker. "We just passed marker twenty three on the way to Angel Falls."

"Is your car on the road, or—?"

"No. We've gone down the embankment—on the river side."

Mel's breath in my face smelled like blood, like someone had just opened a package of raw, bloody meat. I realized then that her ribs weren't just cracked, but broken. Maybe broken enough to puncture her lungs.

"My friend is really hurt. You've got to send someone."

"I'm dispatching police and ambulance services right now."

"Tell them to hurry."

"They're on the way. Stay on the line until they get there."

The cell phone made a low-battery-hiccup, then died in my hand.

Melody coughed, spewing blood, making a choking, retching sound. Jesus, help us. She was drowning in her own blood. With my right hand, I pulled up the hem of her shirt and used it to clean her face. A thousand white-hot lightning bolts shot up my left arm with every movement, even though I held it close to my side.

"Casey." She turned her head toward me. The moon had risen, and we could see each other clearly. "Am I dying?"

My teeth chattered. My hands shook. My skin erupted with goose bumps. "Of course not, Mel. You're just scared."

She made a sobbing sound, then choked. "I don't want to die."

"You're not going to die. I won't let you." My voice sounded far away, muffled by the blood rushing in my ears, the pulse pounding in my head. "Help is coming. Just hang on."

She sucked in air that seemed too thick for her to take in. "If I—" Her exhale made an awful, horrible gurgling sound. "If I die…" Her hand clutched mine. "Take care…" Her fingernails stabbed me like tiny knives. "…of my kids."

Jesus, Christ. She couldn't die! Not like this. "You're gonna be okay."

"I'm sorry…"

"Don't apologize. You're not going to die."

"I stole Ben…"

My body flooded with heat, as if I'd just been caught in a lie. Had she known all along that I still loved Ben? That I still wanted him? But not like this. Never like this. She could keep him forever and I'd be happy for it, if she'd just keep on breathing. I wiped her face again.

"Take," She choked, then managed a rattling inhale. "Take him back." Her voice was a whisper, almost more thought than sound.

"Jeez, Mel. Would you please stop yacking and breathe?" She couldn't get any air, and there was nothing I could do to help her.

Her lips moved. "Promise."

"Okay, I promise." I'd promise anything to make her shut up and breathe. "But you've got to…"

Her eyes rolled back in her head. Her body went limp.

"Dammit!" I tilted her head back, put my mouth over hers, and tried to force air into her lungs. Her cheeks puffed out. Her lungs didn't expand. "Don't you die!" I tried chest compressions, but with only one hand, it wasn't enough. I tried breathing for her. None of it worked. "Dammit, Mel, please don't die."

After what seemed like forever, I stopped trying. Shivering in the night air, I held her limp body close, as if by holding tight I could keep her from leaving this world. "Please, God," I whispered. "Don't let her die."

But she was already gone.

Chapter Four

TIME STOPPED.

It could have been minutes, it could have been hours. It felt like a lifetime that I clung to Melody's lifeless body and shivered so hard my teeth chattered. My ribs ached and my injured arm radiated a throbbing pain all the way up through the top of my head, all the way down to my knees. After an eternity, I heard voices yelling. "They're down here! Down here! Hurry!" Lights arced through the night, enormous light-sabers flashing across the dark sky.

At first, I fought against the arms that pulled me away from her and lifted me out of the wreckage. I was vaguely aware of soft words and gentle hands, of being lifted from the car and strapped down to a flat surface. "Wait, no! Wait!" I flailed around, grabbed the metal sides of the basketlike contraption and struggled to sit up. "You've got to help my friend." I knew Melody was dead, but some part of me hoped something more could be done to save her.

"Ma'am, you've got to be still." Hands pushed me back down, straps pulled tight.

I struggled. I couldn't let myself be taken away from

her. Couldn't leave her all alone in that crumpled mass of metal. "No! Wait. Please."

"Hold up a minute."

I recognized the Scottish accent before I saw him. Then my hand was in his, and I finally let myself relax. "Ian, don't let them leave her here."

Ian glanced at one of the medics, eyebrows raised in question. Then his lips tightened. He squeezed my hand. "Wilson is here. He helped me find you. He'll stay with your friend, and I'll go with you. Deal?"

Everything that happened after that was couched in a hazy blur of light and sound that never quite reached me. Carried up the hill, lifted into the ambulance, I felt wrapped in a protective layer of cotton batting, so nothing could really touch me.

Except him.

Even when the paramedics tried to push him away, he held onto my hand, stubbornly staying with me no matter what anyone said he was allowed to do. He never let go, as if he knew I would go spinning off into the void that loomed just beyond him. In the ambulance, his wide shoulders shielded me from the flashing lights and featureless faces. In the emergency room, his presence protected me from the bustling people and beeping alarms. His touch was the only thing I felt, until someone stretched my right arm out, holding it down firmly.

Cold fluid rushed into my veins, numbness chased the pain away, and I surrendered to it.

It seemed like days later that I opened my eyes in a hospital room, but in reality it was just the morning after the accident. Memories of the accident and its aftermath, the emergency room ordeal of X-rays and examinations, all seemed hazy and dreamlike. I wished for someone to tell me it had all been a terrible dream, but there was only my mother, sitting in a chair by the bed. Her sad eyes and the tight resignation of her mouth told me it wasn't a dream.

I would not be able to breathe a sigh of relief and get back to living my life as it had been.

I would have to begin to live with this horrible thing I couldn't even bear to think of. "She's dead." I said the words out loud, two sharp jabs straight into my heart.

My mother dipped her chin just once in an almost-nod, an I-can't-bear-to-say-this nod, and blinked back tears. "Yes."

The bright, avaricious voice of a talk show host blaring from the television set on the wall seemed obscene. How could anyone, anywhere in the world, remain unaffected? Everything I'd ever worried about, obsessed over, loved or hated, seemed miniscule compared to this.

My ruined career, bah.

My crappy love life, so what?

Why had I spent a moment crying over the loss of my stupid dream, or Ben, or anything my life was lacking? At least I *had* a life.

And somehow, the knowledge that I still had a life only made me feel worse.

"Turn the television off." My voice sounded as beaten and scarred as I felt.

Mom reached for the remote control attached to the bed rail, and with a click, the room went silent except for the faint hospital noises beyond the bare walls.

Mom tried to fill the void by talking. "The doctor said your left arm is badly bruised but not broken, unless there's a tiny hairline fracture too small to see on the X-ray. That's good news, right? You'll have to wear a sling for a couple of weeks, or after that if it starts hurting, but you can..."

Mom's chatter went on but I tuned it out. I hurt. God, I hurt. Every inch of skin, every muscle, every bone. My left arm, broken or not, throbbed. My chest, bruised by the seat belt, ached. My blistered skin, burned by the airbag, stung. And I was hot, sweating underneath a forced-air heating blanket. "Ugh." I tried to kick the thing off.

"Are you hurting?" My mom put her cool fingers on my forehead.

"Yes. Everywhere."

But none of those physical discomforts hurt as badly as the pain of Melody's death.

I couldn't even spare a thought for Ben, or for Melody's children, left now without a mother. I could see them all standing outside the wall I'd built around myself. But I couldn't let them in. I couldn't bear their grief on top of my own.

Mom put something in my hand. "Push the button if you need more medicine for the pain."

She must have pushed it for me, because I felt an immediate softening. I still hurt, but I didn't care. Turning away from Mom's soft, concerned face, I closed my eyes and tried to go back to sleep. The pain medication buoyed me up, and for a while I floated just out of reach of my hopeless thoughts. Then the hospital sounds faded and I escaped into a dreamless sleep.

When I woke again, I was alone.

The orange vinyl chair was empty. I could tell it was daylight outside because shards of light pierced the closed blinds and slanted across the walls. Even when I closed my eyes, those lines sliced across the inside of my eyelids.

I wanted to cover my eyes to block out the light, but even my good arm felt like lead, so I turned my face away from the window. In the shadows, a man sat in the ugly orange chair's green twin. I widened my eyes, then narrowed them to focus. Ben?

He sat forward into the dim light thrown from the slatted blinds.

No, not Ben.

Ian. Recognition and awareness collided in my brain. I remembered his strength shielding me, his hand holding mine. "Ian?"

"Lass...." His deep voice was soft as a sigh. He rose in one smooth move, lowered the bed rail and sat facing me. One of his long legs aligned with mine from hip to knee.

I moved my right hand to rest on his jean-clad leg, surprised at how weak I felt. How much effort it took to move even that little bit. "You found us."

He covered my hand with his. "I heard the dispatch call on the scanner in my office. Wilson and I went to help with the search."

"I'm glad it was you." Why I said it, I don't know, maybe the painkillers talking. But it felt right, and I didn't mind letting the words lie there between us.

He squeezed my hand. "I'm glad, too."

"I wish..." A sob threatened to escape, but I swallowed it down.

He brushed my hair away from my face, gently touched a butterfly-sutured cut on my forehead, trailed his fingers down the swollen, bruised flesh between my left shoulder and elbow. "How's your arm?"

"Bruised, not—" Without warning, my throat closed up. Tears rose like hot lava from a burning pit of regret inside me. I swallowed them down, turned my face away and closed my eyes. Ian's hand covered mine where it lay on his hard muscled leg.

"Your parents are in the cafeteria."

I couldn't bring myself to speak, afraid that if I opened my mouth I would begin to howl and scream, and not be able to stop. I clamped my lips together and nodded, and he seemed to understand it was the best I could do. I felt him shift his weight on the bed. Then he took my hand in one of his. He smoothed my hand out straight against his palm, threaded his fingers through mine and stroked slowly down to my fingertips. Over and over again his hand caressed mine, until, with his body blocking the harsh slats of light from the window, I was able to fall asleep.

The day of Melody's funeral was the most beautiful autumn day I had ever seen. I didn't know whether to be thankful or angry. Melody deserved sunshine on the day her loved ones told her goodbye, but part of me wanted the sky to weep with us, to be as dark and cloudy and turbulent as my thoughts.

Only a few wispy white clouds floated, phantom ships in a cerulean sea, past the ancient Mimosa trees that towered over the open grave.

Melody's white casket had shiny gold rails along each side. Pink roses covered the smooth polished lid. Their powerful, sweet scent reached me where I stood on the spongy cemetery grass, lost in a sea of mourners.

Ben and the children sat in the first row of chairs by the dark abyss that would swallow Melody and take her away from us forever. Melody's parents sat beside them. Lois's nose was red from crying. Herb stared ahead, his expression stoic, his shoulders hunched, his arms around Amy, who sat in his lap swinging her legs with impatience.

I could tell Lois had dressed the children and made sure their hair was neatly combed. I wished someone had done the same for Ben. His dark blonde curls stood unruly and wild around his dazed face. Ben's parents sat directly behind him. His dad kept one hand on Ben's shoulder.

Ben and Melody's two oldest kids sat on each side of Ben. Jake, the twelve-year-old who'd been born the year I moved to New York, kept his mouth set hard between his teeth. Maryann, born the year I danced my first solo, held Ben's hand, but leaned against her Grandma Lois's shoulder and cried quietly. Amy squirmed to get down from her Grandpa Herb's lap, bouncing, wiggling, wanting to run and play. Too young to know what was happening.

What *had* happened.

I dragged my eyes away from Mel's family and noticed the tall, still figure standing several yards away, near the edge of the crowd.

Ian.

He looked at me, and even from that distance I could see the compassion on his face. The tears I thought I'd conquered once again filled my eyes.

A handful of police officers in dress blues held their hats over their chests, heads bowed. Jack McKenzie, a classmate and one of Ben's best buddies, glanced up. Sunlight made his buzz-cut blond hair look almost white.

Jack had come to see me in the hospital. He had questioned me about the accident then told me that the guy driving the truck had apparently suffered a heart attack and lost control of his vehicle. Jack hadn't asked whether Melody had died right away, or slowly, in agony and despair. He had patted my hand, then sat by my side in the hospital room, watching some stupid reality show until I fell asleep.

That all seemed so long ago, as if Melody's death had catapulted us into some time warp that would make this new, horrible reality last forever.

After the service, I walked back to my parent's car with my mother on one side of me and my father on the other. Halfway there, I was nearly tackled from behind as two little arms flung around my thighs.

Grateful for Amy's small body pressed against my legs, I turned and knelt down.

Amy slung her arms around my neck. "I have new shoes," she said, her breath hot and damp in my ear. "My mommy died, so I have new shoes to wear to the foo-neral." Her little baby voice strangled my heart, and I struggled not to cry as she held her foot up for me to see one of her shiny new patent leather shoes. "Won't she love them when she comes home?"

"Your mama loves *you*. Forever and always." I kissed her bow-shaped mouth, her rosy cheeks. The familiar smell of strawberries and little girl wrapped around my heart and squeezed. I tucked an errant blonde curl behind her ear. "And I love your new shoes."

Amy planted a sloppy kiss on my cheek then turned to Ben, who'd been trailing behind her. He picked her up, and she laid her head on his shoulder. It had been a long day, and I knew it was way past her nap time. She would probably be asleep before they reached the car.

And she'd wake to a world without her mother.

A surge of guilt made me flush like I'd been slapped with a handful of stinging nettle. I knew I hadn't made this happen, but if Melody and I hadn't gone shopping…

I looked at Ben, and sorrow swamped guilt. My guilty feelings made Mel's death all-about-me, when I'd secretly accused her of being self-centered. Mel's death wasn't about me, at all. It was about her children, her husband, her family, and their loss.

Ben cleared his throat. "You're coming to the house after... after..."

I wondered if this was a polite way of asking me not to come. Maybe my cuts and bruises would be a painful reminder of how Melody had died. "Do you want me to?"

Ben gave a jerky nod, like the person working his marionette strings had forgotten to do the job for a second. "Of course."

Then someone touched his arm. Ben turned away, and my mother took my hand. The next thing I knew, Daddy was driving us away from the cemetery, down familiar streets that suddenly looked foreign and strange to me.

Too soon, he parked in front of Melody's house.

"Mom," I said from the back seat, "I don't think I can go in."

She looked over the seat to pin me with her pale eyes. "You have to."

Daddy held my arm on the way up the sidewalk, as if I might do a runner if he let go. I wished I *could* run away. But Mom was right.

I had to do this.

Guilt, jealousy's red-headed stepchild, held hands with my regrets. Together they skipped round and round in my head in a continuous loop I could only escape when I slept. The accident's every detail haunted me, even some I hadn't noticed then but remembered now. The chirping of crickets. The whine of a persistent mosquito. The stench of rotting vegetation and mud wafting through the broken windows.

My daddy tapped on the front door, but it was just a

formality before walking inside. Mom added her famous chocolate pound cake to the huge array of tragedy foods already on the dining table. Someone gave me a gentle hug. Someone else drew me toward the kitchen and pressed a red plastic cup of iced tea into my hand.

"Can I fix you a plate, hon?"

I looked up to see Grace Lambert, Ian's secretary, a compassionate smile creasing the loose folds of her sweet, elderly face. I wondered whether her ever-present black wig made her head hot, or if it itched. I wanted to tell her she'd be beautiful without it, even if she didn't have a hair on her head.

"No, thanks," I roused myself enough to say. "I'm not hungry."

Grace patted my shoulder. "You've got to keep your strength up. You've got to be strong for Melody's family. They need you." She filled a plate and directed me to the couch, where she set the plate on a TV tray then drifted back to the kitchen. The mother of a ballet student was sitting on the couch talking to a big, muscular man with scruffy blond hair and a beard. They scooted to one side to make room, and the man waited for me to sit, then slid the TV tray in front of me.

"Hey, Casey." His voice was deep, quiet, comforting. A confidence-inspiring voice like the one on TV that made me want to buy Allstate Insurance. "I'm Cole Sutton, and this is my wife, Meredith. You teach our daughter, Jennifer."

"Oh, yes. The intermediate class on Tuesday." I put my iced tea on the tray. The woman, lean and leggy with a mane of wavy brown hair, reached around her husband to squeeze my hand. "We're so sorry for your loss. I know you and Melody were very close."

"Thank you." The words almost stuck in my throat,

and I took a quick sip of my tea then made a face. I was one of the few people in the deep-south who hated sweet tea.

"You want unsweet?" Meredith hopped up and grabbed my cup. "I'll get you some."

I was trying to figure out how Meredith had read my mind when Cole spoke. "Our daughter, Jenn, is in Jake's class at school. We've known Ben and Melody since our kids were in kindergarten."

Cole's kind blue eyes and soft tone were soothing. But I had lost my ability to make small-talk, and a ready response didn't pop into my head. I wished Ian were here, even though I knew he wouldn't have been invited. He was new in town, and hadn't known Melody or Ben. "I'm sorry. I'm not..." I waved my hand in a vague gesture. I'm not ready for this.

"I understand. Ben told me that you were with Melody when she died." Cole's voice was neutral, stating a fact without being condemning or curious. "I'm sorry you had to go through that."

Meredith glided back with a blue plastic cup and handed it over.

I realized then—color-coded cups. "Thanks."

"You're welcome." Meredith didn't sit back down; she patted her husband on his wide, muscle-bound shoulder. "Honey, we should get the kids from your mother's before she feeds them enough sweets to put them into diabetic comas." She turned back to me. "Give me a call sometime. I'd love to take you to lunch when you're feeling up to it. I know we'll both be missing Melody, and maybe we can help each other."

Meredith's sincere offer made my eyes water. "Thank you. I won't forget."

Cole and Meredith left, and Jake plopped down next

to me. "Aunt Casey," he whispered. "I can't stand this. When are all these people going home?"

I stroked Jake's blonde-streaked curls away from his face. "Oh, honey. I don't know. They may stay all evening."

"Nooo." He managed to insert a decent whine into the whispered word. "I hate this! All these people feeling sorry for us…"

"Shhh." I shushed him, though when I glanced around I realized I was the only one able to hear him above the other conversations.

"Can't you give me the key to your house? I could ride my bike there."

"Oh, Sweetie, I don't think your dad—"

Jake took my hands in his and squeezed his desperation into my skin. "Please, Aunt Casey. Please, please..."

His eyes trapped mine, the chocolate brown iris so much like his mother's, while his lanky pre-teen frame and the loose, blond-brown curls of his hair reminded me of Ben. "Aunt Casey, I swear, I'm gonna explode."

"Why don't we go for a walk?" I didn't want to be here, either. "You and I could walk around the block."

"Noooo. I want to leave and not come back until all these people are gone."

"I'll talk to your dad and see what we can work out. But I can't promise anything."

Jake's body relaxed, and I could tell how tightly he'd been holding himself. "I knew you'd come through."

"I'll try." I stood and scanned the room for Ben.

Jake's red-rimmed eyes were full of hope and despair. "Thank you."

"Have you eaten anything today?" I asked.

"Nah, I'm not hungry."

I nodded toward my untouched plate. "You eat this,

and I'll see what I can do."

He shrugged and picked up a chicken leg, studying it without enthusiasm. "Okay."

As I threaded through the crowded rooms, sad, subdued voices hummed around me like clouds of invisible smoke. I found Ben in the kitchen, leaning against the counter nursing a cup of iced tea while his mother and mother-in-law bustled around him. He seemed to be hiding out, and my hopes rose that he might take pity on Jake.

"Ben, can I talk to you for a minute?"

He looked up. "Yeah, sure."

"Casey, hi." Ben's mom, Irene, put gentle arms around me. "I didn't realize you were here."

"I've been in the living room."

"Thank you for coming." She hugged me for a long time. "I was so glad when Ben told me that you're staying in Angel Falls. It makes me feel a little better about John and me being all the way up in Birmingham."

Mel's mom, Lois, came up behind me and put a hand on my shoulder. "We're all so thankful you're here for this family in their time of need." Lois always sounded like an itinerant preacher, the way she worded things.

"Mom, Lois," Ben interrupted, "I think Casey wants to talk to me about something." The kitchen door stood open, and he reached past his mom to open the screen door. "Let's go outside."

Irene kissed my cheek and turned away. Lois patted my shoulder. "You kids go on."

As we stepped out into the back yard's humid September air, I hugged myself against a sudden chill that had nothing to do with the weather.

Here I was, doing exactly what Melody had wanted me to, and it seemed everyone expected it. "Ben." I cleared my throat and looked away, focusing on the clutch of men who stood near the metal swing set, smoking cigarettes. "Jake wanted me to talk to you. I think he's had about all he can take of... of..."

"Yeah?" Ben, too, looked toward the circle of men and the cloud of smoke that wreathed their heads. "I can relate."

"He wants to go to my house. Stay there until everybody goes home."

"Can I go, too?" He was trying to make a joke, but it fell to the trampled grass beneath our feet. He watched it fall and kept his eyes on the ground. "It's probably best that he isn't alone right now." The sounds of family and friends talking tumbled through the open kitchen door. "Isn't that why they do this when someone..." He swallowed audibly, "when someone dies?"

"I want to come through for Jake." I wanted to feel I'd been able to help at least one of them make it through this horrible day. Not because of my guilt, or my sadness, or because of the promise I'd made to Melody, but because I loved Ben's kids. In a different world, they would have been mine, too. "What if we take him to my parent's house when we leave? Lizzie will be there. You know how much Jake loves Lizzie."

Ben's head came up, and his shoulders relaxed, just a fraction. I pressed my advantage.

"He could hang out by the pool, talk to me or my parents... Maybe he needs a little quiet time, a dog to cuddle, somebody to talk to without the crowd around. I'll bring him back after dinner, on my way home."

Ben met my eyes long enough for me to watch him make his decision, then gave a brief nod of agreement. "Okay."

"Thanks." I wanted to hug him, but held myself back.

We were both holding it together by the skin of our teeth, and the slightest amount of comfort given or received could tear into our hard-won composure.

And then there was the ambiguity of our relationship to each other. Without Melody standing between us, without the jealousy and guilt—and let's face it, bitterness and resentment—that I had used to build the wall between Ben and me, what were we? Friends? Ex's? Or something new?

I spoke to my parents, quietly told Jake to get a swimsuit and a change of clothes, then went to find Maryann and Amy to tell them goodbye. Maryann hugged me, sniffing back tears. I stroked her dark hair. "I'll see you soon, sweet girl," I whispered. "Call me if you need me. Anytime, day or night. Promise?"

"Promise." Her voice sounded muffled because her face was pressed against me. Poor girl. I'd have to make a point of taking her out with me to get pedicures, haircuts, and all the other girlie things Melody had done with her. I wasn't big on girlie things myself, but I could learn.

I found Amy in her room. Ben's dad was rocking her to sleep. He looked up and put a finger to his lips to signal me to silence. I turned to leave, but in the uncanny way of sleepy three-year-olds, she sensed my presence and turned in her grandpa's lap so she could see.

She wiggled down and ran to me. "Rock me, Aunt Casey."

I knelt down in front of her. "Oh, baby, I was just about to leave."

She clutched the shoulders of my black dress. "You have to stay. Stay with me until my mommy gets back."

Amy needed me to stay as badly as Jake needed to leave. I looked up at Ben's dad, who had stood so I could take over rocking-chair-duty. He shrugged an I-can't-help-you shrug.

"Okay, Amy. I'll stay."

"Good." Amy took my hand and pulled me toward the rocker. "You rock me now."

Ben's dad turned to leave; I caught his eye. "Tell my folks and Jake to go on without me. Daddy can come pick me up later."

He nodded then closed the door softly behind him.

I cradled Amy in my good arm and rocked until she fell asleep, then kept on rocking until my arm fell asleep, too. My bruised-not-broken bone wasn't up to lifting Amy. Even if I could, I wouldn't be able to transfer her to her toddler bed. If I called out for help, she'd wake up, so I held her soft weight and rocked while needles of numbness skittered from my fingertips to my armpit and back again.

After what seemed like hours, Irene opened the door and peeked in. "Oh, honey." She came into the room and gathered Amy into her arms. "Why didn't you holler?"

I wiggled my fingers and winced in relief. "I didn't want to wake her."

"You sweet thing." Irene settled Amy into her toddler bed then turned up the ceiling fan before leading me out the door and closing it softly behind us.

And there was Ben, standing in the hallway staring at a framed photo of Melody.

He looked... beaten. Defeated. Past enduring anything else. I put my hand on his shoulder, and he turned and wrapped his arms around me.

It was the first time we had touched like this in a dozen years.

Meredith and some of the other ballet moms had set up a phone tree and canceled all my classes after the wreck and through the week of Mel's funeral. They'd offered to cancel through the whole month of September, but I couldn't afford to lose a month's tuition. I had worked out the math. Every penny I didn't need for survival, I had to save to get through the summer months when I'd have no income.

My first day back the next Monday was tough. At the end of the day, I felt limp, physically and emotionally drained. Even though I had worn a sling, my left arm throbbed, and the bruised, swollen area was hot to the touch. I'd have to ice it when I got home.

Maryann and Amy hadn't come to their ballet classes. I hadn't expected it, but I decided to give Ben a call from the studio phone to see how they were doing.

No answer.

I called Melody's mother.

"The kids are staying with us," Lois said, a shade of exasperation in her voice. "Ben has taken time off work, but he isn't up to caring for himself, much less his children."

The guilt that lived in my gut rose up to choke me. "I'm so sorry, Lois." Tears stung the back of my nose as I struggled once again with the beast that wouldn't die. Its sharp scales scraped against my insides. "Is there anything I can do to help?"

A mean, small voice whispered in my brain. *Yes, Casey. Offer to help. You can help and help and help, and soon enough, Ben will be yours. But you'll be his second choice. You'll always be his second choice.* I didn't want Ben to be mine by default.

"Thank you so much for asking, honey. I could use a little help with some of the driving. Picking the kids up from school and such—I mean, whenever we can't do it. It would be great if we could add you to the kids' emergency contact lists at school. We have an extra car seat for Amy that you can keep in your car."

"Sure. That'll be fine."

Lois sighed, a sound of exhaustion and relief. "I don't know how to thank you."

"No thanks necessary, Lois."

"Let me make you lunch tomorrow?"

"That's really not necessary." The last thing I wanted was be alone with Lois and Herb and Melody's ghost. I still hadn't told anyone about Mel's last moments, that she had died in unimaginable pain, drowning in her own blood, terrified for her life, worried for her children, begging me for help I couldn't give. No one had mentioned it, but I knew they all wondered whether Melody had suffered. No one had asked—yet—but I had a sneaking suspicion Lois had conjured up this lunch idea for exactly that purpose.

"I insist, honey. It's the least I can do. Come at twelve-thirty."

"Lois, really—"

"You could pick Amy up at preschool on your way. I'll remind Ben to leave that extra car seat at the daycare. Lunch will be on the table when you get here."

Well, hell. "Okay, Lois. I'll pick Amy up tomorrow and have lunch with y'all." I hung up, wondering why I'd called in the first place.

Well, I knew why.

Apparently, I was just plain stupid.

On the walk home, Lizzie seemed to sense my mood,

and reflected it in her own posture as she slumped along beside me. She pushed her nose into my hand, and I patted her head, thankful for her quiet company. "Such a good dog."

She raised her face, her eyes shining with adoration.

I gazed at the cool, starry sky, instinctively turning toward the river instead of heading straight home. Maybe the unconscious decision was a good one. I was tired in soul as well as body, and the river offered its own comfort.

I rolled my aching shoulders and tilted my head side to side, trying to relax my knotted muscles. We walked past the town square, where the halyard banged rhythmically against the flagpole in the evening breeze. It had been clanking like that for years, a steady clink-clink-clink that never ended, even as people lived and died, and those left behind picked up the pieces and went on. The flag was taken down every evening and put up again each morning. But the halyard kept up its relentless chant, no matter what happened.

What would I tell Lois tomorrow when she asked me about Melody's last moments? Part of me wanted to lie, to say Mel's death had been easy. But I knew that if I told the lie once, I'd have to keep telling it to everyone, forever.

I didn't know if I had the strength to keep the truth to myself without it eating me up from the inside. "Help me," I whispered out loud, but I didn't expect an answer. I felt as if a veil separated earth from heaven. I was pretty sure God was watching but not planning to get involved.

The thick, earthy smell of the river rolled toward us on the wind, and Lizzie's nose lifted to sniff the air. I breathed in the scent of freshly mowed grass, tannin-rich water and the faint, elusive scent of peace.

Stepping off the paved road onto a wide grassy field where picnickers spread their blankets on sunny days, we walked through the damp grass toward the river's edge. Years ago, the city had poured a concrete footpath along the water, with park benches bolted to it every hundred feet or so. I trudged to the nearest bench and sat, draping my good arm over the armrest so I could reach down and caress Lizzie's ears.

I hadn't been sitting there five minutes when a sleek car slid to a stop at the road's edge. I knew it was Ian even before I looked over my shoulder to see him illuminated by the glow of the interior light. I could hear the faint beep-beep of the alarm until he slammed the door and strode toward me.

A little thrill of excitement fizzed through me.

Chapter Five

IAN STOOPED TO GIVE LIZZIE a pat and sat next to me on the bench, one arm draped across the back. "Not planning on drowning yourself, are you?"

"No." I gave him a weak smile.

"That's just as well." He stretched his long legs out in front of him. "I'm wearing my good shoes and wouldn't want to have to fish you out."

A huff of laughter escaped me, and I immediately felt ashamed. I couldn't believe I had actually laughed, when Melody was no longer alive to laugh as well.

Ian touched my shoulder. "It's not disrespectful for you to get on with your life."

I couldn't think what to say to him, so I clamped my mouth shut and stared out over the night-dark water that whispered before us. He seemed content with the silence, and eventually I was the one who broke it. I said the thing that had been sitting in the back of my mind for days, a sharp-toothed thing waiting to pounce. "It should have been me. Melody had so much to live for. So many people to live for. I should have been the one to die."

"It's not your place to judge which one of you should

have lived." His voice was low, soothing, reasonable. For some reason, that quiet tone made me want to hit him. A tidal wave of antagonism came flooding into me, and I embraced it. It was the one emotion I could feel without it tearing me apart.

I wanted to make him as angry and hurt as I was.

I wanted to make him hate me as much as I hated myself.

I wanted to show him the darkness inside me and make him so disgusted he would walk away and leave me to my misery. "I was jealous of Melody," I said out loud for the first time. "I wanted what she had."

He sat there looking at me with that same compassionate expression on his face.

"Did you hear me?" I shouted. "I wanted Mel's husband. I wanted her kids. I wanted her life."

I realized that tears were streaming down my face when Ian quietly handed me a handkerchief—the real deal, a soft cotton square of comfort.

I wiped my eyes and took a shuddering breath. "Ben was my boyfriend first; did you know that?"

Ian shook his head but didn't speak, giving me the time I needed to barf-up the whole damn hairball that had been stuck in my throat for twelve long years.

"We were high school sweethearts, but I was determined to be a ballerina, so I auditioned for City Ballet then moved to New York. Ben stayed back home and we talked on the phone every day, but it felt like I was losing him, you know?"

Ian nodded.

"I convinced Ben to apply to NYU, and when he got accepted, he came to New York and we picked out an apartment in Greenwich Village. He went home to pack his shit, but he didn't come back right away—one excuse after another—then I got the sorry-Casey-we-didn't-mean-to-hurt-you phone call. That was twelve years ago. Twelve! A dozen years, and I still couldn't forgive her. Him, yes. But not her."

"I'm sorry that happened to you."

"For Ben's sake, and the sake of my own stupid pride, I pretended to forgive her. I pretended she was still my best friend. I pretended so well, I think even she believed me. I pretended so well, I started to believe it myself. But all the time I've been her *best friend*, I wanted him back. I wanted him to be mine instead of hers."

Ian didn't draw back in horror. His face didn't turn cold with disgust. His soothing tone didn't even change when he responded to my tirade. "So, you lured her on a shopping expedition so you could crash her car into a truck and drive it off a ravine?"

"Of course not. You know I wasn't driving."

He took my face in his warm palms and pinned me with his amber gaze when I would have looked away. "So help me figure this out. How, exactly, is her death your fault?"

"I wanted..." I squeezed my eyes shut against the burn of tears that felt like a hard knot behind my eyeballs. "I loved Mel, and still I wished..." I had yearned for the impossible, to have what she'd taken from me, without taking anything from her. But I hadn't wished for her to die. My jealousy hadn't made this happen.

So why couldn't I get out from under the crushing rock of guilt I carried everywhere?

"Wishing doesn't make things like this happen, Casey." Ian stroked my hair, then my cheek, with a touch so tender it made my lips quiver, made the tears flow even faster.

He had uncovered a soft, scared part of me that didn't

want to be dragged into the light. I sprang up, clutching his handkerchief, wanting to run but rooted to the concrete beneath my Keds.

"Shhh," he said.

I hadn't said anything, but I guess he knew I was screaming inside.

"Sit back down."

He grabbed me by the hips and pulled me back. I put out a hand for balance, and his wide chest under my fingertips emanated more BTU's than a space heater. When I was sitting beside him again, he relaxed, like a lion relaxes, in a way that still makes a gazelle keep its distance.

I tried to relax too, but all my nerve endings were buzzing in Ian's presence. "I seem to have lost the ability to be around people."

"It's all right." His voice turned warm and rich as melted butter. "I understand what it's like to be afraid—"

"I'm not afraid."

"Yes, you are." His tone lowered to a confiding whisper. "You're afraid that if you let go of feeling guilty, you'll be free. And freedom is a very scary thing."

"I'm not afraid." I was way past being afraid.

"Prove it."

I channeled my inner Black Swan, the powerful seductress archetype I used to give myself confidence and courage when I had none. I turned toward him, tucked my injured arm in its sling between our bodies, and leaned in close. I let the fingertips of my right hand caress his lean, tanned cheek and trail down his strong neck, then come to rest on his broad shoulder. I lowered my lashes. My mouth dropped open as I came in for the kiss, and I watched his gaze follow the movement.

I was going to kiss him until he couldn't breathe.

I was going to kiss him like he'd never been kissed before.

The moment our lips touched, all thought ceased and pure sensation took over. The inside of his mouth was hot, wet, sweet. He slicked his tongue along my teeth, then into my mouth, lightly teasing. I tried to keep the upper hand but the seducer had quickly become the seduced. My nipples tingled where they brushed his chest, and other parts of my body wept with wanting.

He stroked my back, pushing the thin straps of my leotard aside. Finally he broke the kiss and pulled back to look into my eyes.

I hoped the moonlight wasn't bright enough for him to see how dazed I was.

I showed up at Melody's mom's house just after noon the next day. Amy had fallen asleep on the way, so I had a struggle getting her out of her car seat then hoisting her onto my hip one-handed. But I managed.

Lois answered the door. The raw grief in her eyes confronted me like a punch in the face. Her eyes were dark, like Melody's, but now they were deep pools without color, deep pools of endless pain. Her hair had been tortured into an old woman's over-permed salt-and-pepper cap of curls. She'd been doing her hair this way for years, and it had always looked carefree and casual. But now, the dated style made her look old.

"Casey, honey." Lois took Amy from me, transferring her easily from my shoulder to hers. "You shouldn't be holding Amy like that. Your arm won't heal right if you don't let it rest." She turned her face away to hide the sparkle of tears I saw anyway. "I'll put Amy down for her nap. You go on in the kitchen."

Walking into the old house, I felt like a teenager again, enveloped in the familiar smell of furniture polish and disinfectant overlaid by the aroma of roast beef and Lois's famous red velvet cake. I wouldn't have been surprised if Melody had come bouncing down the stairs, seven years old and wearing the hideous brown shift we'd been so proud of as Girl Scout Brownies. Or maybe she'd be fifteen, in her orange and white cheerleader outfit, her dark ponytails tied with matching ribbons.

I walked through the cedar-paneled den to the large, bright kitchen. Ran my hand along the top of a ladder-back chair, remembering how the scratchy cane bottoms always left an imprint on the backs of our bare thighs in the summer.

The dark mahogany table was set with vinyl placemats edged in a bright strawberry print. I lifted the edge of one in particular, and peeked underneath to see if a pale oval of bleached-out varnish still marred the dark wood.

"It's still there." Lois came into the kitchen. "I swear, I wanted to kill that child when—" She choked on the words, swallowing the thought too late.

"It wasn't just Mel," I reminded her. "We were both painting our fingernails." We'd set the bottle of polish remover directly on the wood table, never imagining that the liquid dripping down the sides would collect along the bottle's rim and eat away the varnish on Lois's new dining table. We'd tried to wipe it away, compounding the problem, leaving a big smear instead of a small one.

"I know, honey." Lois patted my shoulder. "It was never just Mel, or just you. Everything y'all ever did, it was both of you, together."

Like loving Ben. Even that, we'd both done together.

"Lunch is ready." Lois took plates down from the cupboard. "It's just the two of us. Herb had something else he had to do."

"That's okay." I knew what else Herb had to do, because he'd left the garage door open, and his bass boat wasn't there. I couldn't blame him. I didn't want to be here, either. It was just too painful. Unfortunately for me, without Herb here, I knew Lois would take the opportunity to ask about Melody's death.

"I'll finish setting the table." I knew where everything was in this kitchen. I gathered napkins, forks, spoons, knives, wondering if I'd be able to eat anything with the dreaded conversation about Melody's last moments looming. Before coming here, I had made the decision to lie, to say that she hadn't suffered. I had also made the decision to save Lois from asking the question, by giving her the answer first.

But the words hid behind the flimsy wall of my good intentions and refused to come out.

We both filled our plates with comfort food—mashed potatoes, roast and gravy, corn, green beans, homemade yeast rolls. But as Lois and I bowed our heads to say grace, I knew that none of it would bring us the least bit of comfort.

"Dear Lord." Lois took my hand. "We give thanks for the bounty spread before us. Most of all, we are thankful that You saw fit to spare the life of this beautiful child, Casey, so she might continue to live in Your service, and provide a loving light to those of us who must now survive the darkness without our beloved Melody." Lois squeezed my hand then released it. "Amen."

"Amen," I echoed by rote, then sat there staring blindly at my plate.

Was Lois right? Was I spared so I could light the darkness left by Melody's passing? Was my only purpose in life now to atone for her death? Not because of my jealous thoughts. I knew, realistically, my thoughts hadn't killed Melody. But our shopping trip had been contrived for my benefit. She'd have been safe at home, with her husband and children, if not for me.

"Casey." Lois laid her cool fingers on my arm. "Honey, are you okay?"

"I'm fine. I was just—"

"I know. It happens to me, too." Lois withdrew her hand and pushed the plate of yeast rolls closer. "Something reminds me of Melody, then I'm reliving the past, and it becomes more real than what's happening right now."

I tore my warm yeast roll in half, but couldn't imagine putting the delicious bread in my mouth, much less chewing and swallowing it. "Lois, can we talk before we eat? I just don't think I can eat a thing until I get this done."

"I'm not sure what you mean." Lois turned her chair toward mine, and gave me an expectant look of hope mixed with fear. The unasked question shone in her eyes.

"Lois..."

She leaned toward me. "Yes, honey?"

"When we had the wreck..."

She scooted closer, her chair scraping on the linoleum floor. "Yes?"

"The truck that hit us..."

Lois bit her lip and blinked rapidly. "Go on."

"We only saw it for a second. It came up over a hill, and it was just... there."

Lois nodded, a desperate, I-hate-this-but-I-have-to-know nod.

"It hit us before we knew what was happening. The

impact knocked Melody out. What I'm saying is..."

"Yes, go on..."

"She didn't feel any pain. She didn't have time to be afraid. I think all she had time to feel was a second or two of... surprise."

Lois crumpled, and pitched forward into my arms. "Thank God." She squeezed me tight. "Oh, Casey. You don't know how relieved I am. I was so afraid she might have been frightened or in pain...."

"She didn't feel a thing, I promise." Liar, liar, pants on fire.

Lois released me and sat back, dabbing at her eyes with her napkin. "Are you sure? Because at the hospital they said something about her lungs...."

I couldn't make up for Mel's death, or for my jealous thoughts, but I could do this one thing for Mel's mother. And later, I'd do it again, for Ben. I had never been good at lying, but I could do this.

Even though it meant that I could never tell another living soul the truth about what happened that night. I looked Lois straight in the eye, without blinking. "She didn't die from that first impact, Lois, but she never regained consciousness after it. Her breathing just got slower and slower until it stopped. I tried to breathe for her, but I couldn't... I couldn't."

Lois took my face in her hands, kissed my cheeks tenderly, and enfolded me in her arms again. "You did everything you could, Casey. I know you did. Sometimes God's will is hard to understand, and He just decided He needed Melody more than we do. I'm just thankful we still have you. I love you like a daughter, you know. Always have."

I released a sigh of relief and returned her embrace. "I love you, too, Lois."

Thinking I'd done what I came here to do, I relaxed, clueless that I was about to be enlisted for something much more difficult. I shoveled-in a forkful of the delicious food, then noticed that Lois was sitting there as still as a little bird, watching me, her hands folded in her lap.

Chewing, I raised my eyebrows in question.

"Casey, I hate to ask, but I need you to do something."

I swallowed. "What's that?"

"I need you to talk to Ben. No one else has been able to get through to him. You may be the only person on earth who can stop him from self-destructing."

I didn't have time to go to Ben's house after lunch because I had an afternoon of teaching ahead of me. But before noon the next day, I stood on Ben's front porch. I soon gave up ringing the bell and pounded on the door Melody had painted such a rich, dark red.

Red for luck.

"Ben, I know you're in there," I screamed, ignoring the twitch of the curtains in the house next door. Mean old Edna Fitzpatrick, unable to mind her own business. "Open the door, Ben, or I swear I'll throw this damn bench through the window!"

As if I could lift the heavy wrought-iron bench one-handed, I dragged it toward the window to show I meant business. It made a hideous screeching sound as its legs scratched a white line across the concrete porch. I was sweating like a pig despite the cool breeze, and my hair clung to my neck in strings.

I stood to give my back a rest, and noticed the front door stood open.

But I hesitated to go through it.

What could I say that would bring Ben back to his children? How could I help him when I couldn't even help myself? I had no idea, but I walked inside anyway. Lifting damp strands of hair off my neck, I shivered in the dark, air conditioned house. Every curtain closed, the place looked like a cave. A dirty, messy cave.

"You're a damn pushy little chick, you know that?" Ben's slurred voice reached me from the shadowed den. I followed the sound, and stepped on something that crunched underfoot. I picked it up—a framed photo of Ben and Melody—and started to put the picture back on the piano where it belonged.

"Leave it!" Ben's voice sounded like the snarl of a wild animal.

Lowering the shattered frame back to the floor, I looked around, now that my eyes had adjusted to the dark. He had swiped every horizontal surface clear of picture frames, vases, knick-knacks, and memories, then crushed them underfoot. The place smelled of rotting food and spilled liquor.

On the coffee table in the den, a bottle of Wild Turkey sat surrounded by a mishmash of paper plates, pizza boxes and crumpled napkins. Ben lay sprawled on the couch, a tumbler of bourbon in his hand.

Not his first.

I sat on the edge of the cushion next to him. I had never seen Ben act this way. But then, he'd never had a reason to.

"Have a drink." He gulped back half a tumbler full of the nasty stuff. "Oh, I forgot. You only drink wine." He drew out the last word obnoxiously, making it sound like "whine."

"Ben, you're being an asshole." I don't know if I said

it because I was finally getting as angry as he was, or because I thought it might provoke a reaction.

It did.

He lunged at me and pushed me against the back of the couch with his hands hard at my shoulders. I yelped in pain but he didn't seem to notice.

"My wife is dead!" He yelled through clenched teeth. His blue eyes were cold and his jaw stood out rigid in his face. "My wife is dead!" He shook me once, hard, then released me and sat back to cover his face with his hands.

"I'm sorry," I said, knowing how inadequate it was. "I'm sorry."

"God, Casey, I'm the one who's sorry." His red-rimmed eyes made the blue seem even bluer when he looked at me. "Did I hurt you?"

"I'm okay. You're the one everyone is worried about. Are you okay?"

He didn't answer, just pulled me to him and hugged me hard, and I let him hold me. When I felt him begin to shake with tears, I reached up to smooth the silky curls of his hair, just as I would have done with any of his children. "I know you're hurting." I patted his back. "But your kids need you." I kept talking, hoping to get through to him while I had the chance. "Ben, I know this is going to sound harsh, but I'm telling you this because I love you, and I love your kids. You have to get over yourself and take care of your children."

He sniffed and sat back, wiping his eyes. I took a napkin off the coffee table and handed it over. He blew his nose, then made a face. "Ugh. You gave me one that smells like rotten pizza." He tossed the wadded napkin onto the messy table.

I shrugged. "Sorry. But in case you haven't noticed, this whole room smells like rotten pizza."

Ben looked around, then winced. "I guess I've been a little out of control."

"You needed some time to wallow in grief. It's understandable. But now you've got to bring your kids back home and get on with your lives. It's what Melody would expect of you."

"I know you're right, but I can't seem to pull myself together, and I don't want them to see me like this." He gave me a sad smile. "If you can tell me how I'm supposed to get over myself anytime soon, I'll listen."

"Ben, I don't have a good answer for you. I wish I did. But maybe putting that bottle back in the cabinet and cleaning up this mess would be a good start. Do you need me to help you?"

He gave me a bleary-eyed glare. "I'll do it myself. Tomorrow, when my head isn't about to explode from an ongoing hangover. Thanks for the offer though."

"And you'll pick up your kids from Lois sometime this weekend? They need you, and you need them. Besides, having them around might force you to pull yourself together."

He grimaced. "I guess I should thank you for giving me a kick in the behind."

I stood and patted his shoulder. "Anytime."

A week later, I sat in my living room with a glass of Merlot, huddled in my favorite reading chair. I loved the big overstuffed chair even more because I'd found it at a thrift store for next-to-nothing. Someone had upholstered it loosely in antique quilt fabric, patched-over in even more quilt fabric, making it the comfiest chair on earth and the next-best thing to being in bed.

The book I couldn't read lay face down the chair arm, so I finally gave up and set it on the lamp table. I saw my reflection in the hall's full-length mirror, and wondered for the hundredth time why I didn't look different.

Lois's face was ravaged by grief.

Ben looked like a different person entirely.

But my face looked the same. Sadder, maybe, more solemn than usual, but the same face I was used to seeing. What was wrong with me, that I didn't show the pain outwardly like everybody else?

My mind floated back to last week, to the park bench, to Ian's kiss. Maybe my pain wasn't as bad as it should be, because I had a handsome Scot to distract me from my grief. But should I allow myself to fall for Ian? Did I have any business letting happiness into my life when Melody's family was just beginning to suffer?

My cat jumped into my lap, and I ran a hand along his arched back, sending a flurry of cat hairs floating through the air. Absently petting Chester and admiring his dark Siamese markings, I absorbed comfort from his thick, nasal purr and his warm bulk in my lap.

Lizzie lay on the floor beside me, her soft snores adding to the quiet chorus.

I should call Ben, see how he and the kids were doing. I was reaching for the cordless phone when its shrill ring made me jump out of my skin and made Chester dig his claws into my thigh. "Ow, dammit," I yelled into the receiver. "Hello."

My tone may have been less than pleasant.

"Casey, lass." Ian's voice was sexy and deep. "It's so nice to hear your lovely voice."

I figured he was being sarcastic, so I responded the same way. "Well, I know you're not calling because the music's too loud, so..."

His rich chuckle rumbled across the phone line. "I'm calling to ask if you'll come to dinner with me on Saturday. Please don't say no."

"No." But a shiver of anticipation made my shoulders twitch.

"Come, now. Remember our conversation?" His voice was intoxicating as a whole bottle of Bailey's Irish cream. "What are you afraid of?"

Pretty much everything.

Closing my eyes, I stroked Chester's thick brown fur, entertaining visions of Ian's kiss the week before.

I shouldn't say yes.

I shouldn't say yes.

I shouldn't say yes.

I held my breath and imagined myself doing a swan-dive off the limestone cliffs of Angel Falls—and doing a belly-flop into the water below. "All right. I'll come. What time?"

Chapter Six

PROPPING MY CHIN ON MY hand, I looked out over the dark river. The Riverboat Restaurant's windows projected bars of light that floated like snakes on the rippled surface. My own image stared back at me from beyond the glass, a cameo hologram in space, my black velvet dress disappearing against the water's inky backdrop.

Shifting my gaze, I could see Ian's reflection, too. He leaned back in his chair, stirring his after-dinner coffee. The spoon made slow clinking sounds inside the cup. In black jeans and an even blacker linen shirt, he looked like a magazine advertisement for something very wicked and very, very expensive. I still didn't know exactly what it was, but I knew I wanted it, hoped I could afford it.

I fiddled with my almost-empty wine glass, twirling the stem in my hand.

Ian's golden gaze settled on me. "You look lovely, as always. But tired, too. Are you not sleeping well?"

"No. I close my eyes and all I can see is..." I folded the big cloth napkin in my lap, in half and then in half again.

"It will get better." His voice was low and soothing. "I promise it will."

"How do you know?" There was more than a trace of bitterness in my voice but I couldn't keep it out, even knowing he was only trying to help.

"I've lived through it myself."

"Your best friend died in a car accident right before your eyes?" I regretted my words the second they left my lips. Regretted them even more when I saw his sad smile. A smile that hinted at a deeply-embedded pain that still stung. I leaned across the table and covered his hand with mine. "I'm sorry. I didn't mean that."

"That's all right." He turned his palm up and threaded his fingers through mine. "It was a long time ago."

"What happened?"

"My wife committed suicide."

"God, Ian! I'm so sorry. I shouldn't have said—"

"You're angry. I understand. I remember the anger, too." Ian looked down at the table while he spoke. His voice was flat, emotionless. "I wanted to kill Maeve even though she'd already done it herself."

"Why would she—" I stopped myself. This was none of my business. But still, I wanted to know. "If you don't mind telling me, I mean."

Ian gracefully picked up the ball I'd fumbled. "She'd been diagnosed with bipolar disorder and depression, and whenever I went on assignment she'd stop taking her medication and threaten to kill herself. I convinced myself she was making threats to manipulate me. I told her she could do what she wanted, and I went anyway." He glanced up, guilt and grief reflected in his eyes.

"Why didn't she want you to do your job? That seems a little selfish."

"As a journalist, I was often sent to political hot spots, and she worried. A certain element of danger was expected. I was willing to take the risk, because I knew it would advance my career. I didn't realize it was Maeve's safety I was risking. Not until it was too late."

"Oh, Ian."

"She waited until I was on my way home from the airport. I don't think she planned to die. I was supposed to arrive in time to save her. But a colleague who was on the same flight asked me to meet him for a beer on the way home, and I said yes." Chagrin curled the corners of his mouth. "I was furious at her, at myself, at the whole world."

"How long—"

"It was more than ten years ago."

"Does it still... Does it still bother you? I mean, how do you get over..." my voice trailed away as I struggled to find the right words.

"Feeling like you've failed someone you love in the worst way possible?"

His quiet tone held an underlying bitterness I couldn't miss.

The waiter placed a leather bill folder on table edge. Ian pulled his hand from beneath mine and dealt with the bill while I stared out over the water.

"Shall we go?" Ian stood and offered me his hand.

"Yes, but..." I put my hand in his, waiting to hear the answer to the question he'd helped me ask. But his face had a shuttered expression, as if the door he'd opened to me had just slammed closed. I knew he had revealed all he meant to. But I'd glimpsed a sensitive, caring man hidden behind the tough façade.

And I wanted to see more.

He unlocked the car and helped me inside. Then he got in, and I realized that something between us had shifted. He'd let me see inside his heart, even though it was only a quick glimpse, and I felt connected to him in a way I hadn't felt with anyone in a very long time. My breath started coming faster—that testosterone thing he'd done to me already—and I parted my lips to breathe through my mouth.

His eyes dropped to my lips, then back up again to meet my gaze.

He leaned toward me.

I leaned toward him, across the car's console. Our breath mingled. He wrapped gentle fingers around my shoulder and pulled me closer. I could taste the warm heat of his mouth even before we kissed.

And then, we kissed.

We kissed.

Oh, my God, we kissed. The sweetest of kisses—soft, shallow, but soon becoming deeper and more meaningful. My eyes closed without my even being aware of it, and when I opened them again, I saw that his eyes were closed, too. Dark crescents of thick black lashes swept his cheek. I ran a hand up along his arm, sliding over his shirt. The contrast of hard muscle under the soft fabric did something to my insides.

His eyes opened slowly, trapping me in a pool of sparkling amber. He cranked the engine. "Let's get you home."

Butterflies of anticipation somersaulted in my stomach. Neither of us spoke as he drove the few blocks to my house. The riverside restaurant was so close we could've walked there and back if we'd chosen.

The Methodist church was having some event, so the curbside space in front of my house was taken. He parked down the block, and on the walk to my house, he paused to pluck a wild climbing rose from the trellis that arched over old Mrs. Mercer's sidewalk. He stripped the leaves and thorns from the short stem and tucked the fragrant bloom into my hair.

Then, we were standing on the sidewalk in front of my house.

The white planks of the old Victorian farmhouse glowed under the streetlight. The facets of the antique beveled glass front door sparkled in welcome. Chester roused from his spot on the porch rail and meowed, arching his back and rubbing his face against the upright post. Dimly, I heard the dog door bump as Lizzie entered the house from the side yard, ready to meet us at the front door.

Ian turned me toward him and linked his hands behind my back, holding me loosely in the circle of his arms.

I licked my suddenly-dry lips. "Would you like to come in?"

"Only if you want me to."

I could have kissed him good night on the sidewalk and gone safely inside. But instead of "Good night," the words that jumped out of my mouth were, "Come in."

Lizzie gave Ian the grand tour, unimpeded by her inability to speak English. "Here's my dog bed, here's my toy basket, here's my treat jar, on the hall table."

Ian ruffled Lizzie's fur and looked at me. "Can I give her one?"

"Sure. Make yourself comfortable. Pick out a CD. I'll go pour us some wine."

Then I stood in my kitchen, wringing my hands.

Holy Shit. What had I done?

Well, I knew what I'd done, and that's what had me wringing my hands. I had just invited a handsome almost-stranger into my house with the unspoken intent of having sex with him.

My fingers shook as I took down two fishbowl crystal wine glasses and set them on the counter beside an unopened bottle of Cabernet and a corkscrew. I looked at all the familiar items spread before me, but my mind and my hands weren't communicating because the rest of my body was yammering on about something else entirely.

The CD player came on in the living room—Dave Matthews, of course, because who can listen to Dave without wanting to have sex?

Taking command of my fingers, at least, I opened the bottle. I measured almost exactly the same amount of Cabernet into each glass, then took a sip from the glass I'd overfilled by just a tad.

Ian came up behind me. "What an incredibly sexy backside."

What an incredibly sexy voice.

Ian reached around me from behind. His arms bracketed me for a moment then curved to hold me close. With my sexy backside cradled by his sexy front side, I was surrounded by his warmth, his spicy scent, and some mysterious, magical pheromone. I let my head drop back onto his shoulder. He kissed my neck, then turned me around.

He lifted me up until I half-sat on the edge of the kitchen counter. I wrapped my legs around his waist, hooked my ankles together, and rested my thighs on his hard, muscular forearms. My you-know-what was right up against his, and the iron-hard blast-furnace of his erection just about melted my panties.

My body responded without consulting me. My arms wrapped around his neck, my lips parted, my tongue slipped into his mouth.

He opened to me, hot, wet, delicious. His tongue skimmed the roof of my mouth, raising goosebumps on the back of my neck. I was hardly aware of it when he carried me out of the kitchen.

He took his lips off mine. "Where?"

I pointed to the bedroom door with my foot and slipped my tongue back into his mouth. He spread me across the quilt, lifted my dress over my head and tossed it aside. His kisses burned a trail—eyelids, cheeks, jaw, neck—then paused to feast on my collarbone. My skin tingled with static electricity.

"You're so beautiful." He caressed my bare breasts. "Your nipples are like little raspberries. I wonder do they taste..." His whispered words trailed away as he nipped lightly then sucked.

"Lord God." I moaned, and felt his smile against my heated skin.

He chuckled, then moved up to kiss my lips. "I hoped you'd remember my name by now."

"Ian." I loved the foreign sound on my lips. "Ian."

"That's better." With a fingertip, he conducted a lazy tour of my body. From my neck... to the tip of one breast... across ribs... across belly... then lower. "I've wanted to do this since the moment I first saw you."

I couldn't help but squirm under his hand. "You have?"

He didn't answer, but knowing what I needed, brushed lightly at the edge of my panties. Up and down, up and down, he ran a finger along the thin elastic barrier, finally pressing the edge aside, sleeking his finger inside where I wanted it to be.

He propped his head on one hand while the other continued its lethal caress. My eyelids fluttered down, my hands fell limp at my sides.

"Casey."

"Ahhh," I said. But it wasn't exactly in response to what he was saying.

"Casey, do you have any protection?"

"Hmmmm?" I mumbled vaguely. Protection? My parents had encouraged me to keep a handgun, but I refused to have anything like that in my home. Too many children would have access to it. Lizzie would be a much better protector than...

"Sweetheart."

"Mmmm..." I liked the way he said sweetheart. The long E sound was drawn out and the R had a slight burr.

He took his hand away and adjusted my panties back into place.

Reluctantly my mind began to clear.

"Are you on the pill?"

"Well no, because I haven't had sex in..." and then I realized. The fact that I hadn't had sex lately didn't matter, because I was for damn sure about to. I brought my legs together and sat up. Here was my chance to back out. I could come away unscathed and almost uninvolved. But my body was still under his control, including, apparently, my mouth. "I think there might be something in the bathroom closet."

Naked except for a scrap of damp panties, I scrambled off the bed, ran to the bathroom, and yanked open the closet door. Standing on tiptoe, I could see it—The Pink Box—perched on top of a pile of stuff at the very, very back of the top shelf.

Dimly aware that Ian had come into the room behind me, I dragged out the step-stool and climbed on. I could hardly reach The Pink Box, but I managed to knock it down. It bounced off my shoulder, and Ian caught it.

"Contraceptive Sponges," he read aloud. "Expiration date... about three years ago."

"*No*," I wailed. Taking the box from him, I read it for myself. "The ink's a little faded. Could be an eight instead of a three. Do you think...?"

"I wouldn't chance it, lass."

"Don't you have anything?" I punched him on the shoulder. What kind of man takes a girl out to dinner without bringing along a just-in-case-condom?

He gave a humorless laugh and laid a consoling hand on mine. "If yours is out of date, mine has turned to dust by now." That got a desperate laugh out of me as we stood there in my bathroom, more than an hour away from the nearest all-night drug store.

"I hate small towns," I whined, slowly becoming aware that I wore only a small bit of skimpy lace and elastic, while he was still fully clothed.

"I know exactly what you mean." He caressed my shoulder.

I slapped his hand away. "Weren't you ever a Boy Scout?"

He laughed and put his hand right back on my shoulder. "If I'd been prepared, wouldn't you have thought it a bit presumptuous?"

"I'd have been hopping mad and thrown you out." I wouldn't have even noticed, as we both knew very well. But I appreciated his effort to save my pride.

"I could give you some relief," he offered gallantly.

"No, thank you." I tossed the dusty pink box into the bathroom trash. "It'd just be torture for both of us."

Sunday morning, I woke with a headache. The headache, I could handle. What threatened to kill me was the overwhelming case of unrequited lust.

I felt incomplete.

Desperately... unfinished.

I was familiar with the standard remedies for this ailment. Most left me more frustrated than ever. The only things I could count on to relieve my condition were those that left me too tired to do anything but pass out from exhaustion.

With this goal in mind, I dragged the lawn mower from the shed and gave the back yard its weekly crew-cut. Then I hauled out the hedge trimmers and attacked the red-tip photina along the back yard fence.

In the early afternoon, I picked up the last pile of severed branches and staggered toward the heap of limbs already stacked at the curb. A cloud of glowing floaters hovered just in front of me. I was about to pass out, but that was okay, since the remedy was working. I walked into the house to guzzle a few glasses of water and some iced tea with lemon, congratulating myself for a job well-done. I had hardly thought of Ian at all during the last twenty feet of shrub trimming.

Shit. I'd just thought of Ian. And sex. And lack of sex.

After Ben, I'd only had one sexual partner, a fellow-dancer-friend-with-benefits, and I hadn't seen him in months. My heart might not be ready for sex with another person, but my body was way past due.

It was time for another form of distraction.

I called Lizzie away from the rabbits she was chasing in her sleep. We were going to my parents' house, where I could count on chocolate, cherishing, and cheering-up.

And if that didn't work, my mom had Valium.

When we got there, the driveway was empty. I parked at the curb so my car wouldn't block the drive, and went in the always-unlocked back door. Lizzie splashed into the swimming pool before the gate clanged shut, and I decided to do the same.

Being human, I had to locate a swimsuit first.

Tossing my keys and purse on the dryer—the closest horizontal surface to the back door—I went into my old bedroom and rifled through the dresser in search of the raggedy bathing suit I'd been wearing for years. I found it, but it seemed to have aged since its last wearing. Stretched-out leg openings, wavy waistband, dry elastic that had lost the will to snap back. I should have bought a new one when Melody and I...

My knees quit working. They didn't give one shit when I fell to the plush pink carpet beside my old canopy bed.

Stupid, selfish, over-sexed bitch.

Guilt and shame twined in my stomach and climbed up my throat.

I'd forgotten.

For hours, almost a whole day, I had forgotten Melody was dead. A reservoir of tears bulged behind my eyes. My skull felt like a dam about to burst. I made desperate choking sounds that I heard in a strange, detached sort of way as my mind tried to hold onto the last thread of sanity. I could see myself going completely crazy, losing it totally. If I really let my hurt have its way, I might never find my way back again. I realized now, the wave of grief that had knocked Ben to his knees was just now hitting me. "I'm sorry."

But being sorry wasn't enough. Not nearly enough to stop the suffering I knew I deserved. The tears were stronger than I could ever be, and they burst out, coming so fast I couldn't stop them or even wipe them away.

I heard Lizzie barking in the back yard. She'd heard me keening and wanted to come inside and make sure I was okay. But I couldn't move, trapped in an undertow that wouldn't let me surface.

Headlights lit up the walls of my old room as my parents' car pulled into the drive.

When had it gotten dark? I wiped my eyes with the back of my hand and pulled against the bedpost to stand, unlocking muscles gone stiff from sitting so long on the floor.

Mama met me in the dark hallway and flipped on the light. "Oh, my dear." She pulled me into her embrace. After a few moments, she led me into the kitchen and dosed me with half-a-Valium and a huge slice of chocolate pie with cream cheese and coconut frosting.

Lizzie had already been let into the house and fed a plate of leftover stew, so she had no objections when Mom insisted we stay the night. I took a warm bath, and Mom brought hot tea for me to drink and wet tea bags to put on my swollen eyelids. I knew the tea bags wouldn't do much good, but I used them anyway.

It was nice to be pampered for a while, and I knew I needed it, though I didn't deserve it. After my bath, I put on a T-shirt of Daddy's and one of Mom's big velour zip-front robes. In the living room, Daddy stretched out in his recliner, the remote control clutched to his chest, sleeping to the sound of the television blaring loud enough to wake the dead.

It was good to be home.

"Lizzie was filthy." My mother came into the room behind Lizzie, who smelled strongly of peppermint shampoo. Lizzie splayed her feet and shook, leaving her damp fur standing up in spikes—and startling my dad from his before-bedtime nap. "Don't you ever bathe her?"

"Huh?" Daddy fumbled for his glasses and snapped down the footrest on his easy chair.

"I bathed her last week, I think."

"Hello, mangy old dog," my dad greeted Lizzie in his usual way, absently petting the top of her wet head. Lizzie was only two when I got her from the pound shortly after moving back home. She was neither mangy nor old, but that was Daddy's form of endearment for all canines.

I grabbed the remote and turned off the TV. "How can you hear yourself think with all that noise?"

My dad stood. "Come on, Lizzie. Let's go to bed."

Mom planted a kiss on his mouth. "See you in a little while."

"G'night, Daddy." I gave him a hug.

"G'night, baby girl." He returned my hug then patted mom on the butt. "Don't stay up too late. Come on, dog," he commanded to Lizzie.

Lizzie looked back at me once then followed him down the hall.

"Your fur's too wet for you to get on the bed, you know." He held the bedroom door open for Lizzie to pass through. "You'll have to sleep on the floor until..." And the door clicked shut on their one-sided conversation.

Mom sat in her recliner and I sat in Dad's. "So," Mom said, "tell me what's going on."

My feelings were so complex I hardly understood them myself. "I feel so bad for Ben and the kids. I wish I knew what to do for them."

"Why do you have to do anything?"

"Of course, I have to do something." Couldn't she see that?

"Well, it's a sad situation, I agree with you on that. But I still don't see why you feel—"

"If Melody hadn't come with me that day, she'd still be—"

Mom sat forward, making the recliner squeal. "Well, now, you correct me if I'm wrong." Her face had tightened with something that looked almost like anger. "But it was my understanding that *you* were going with *her.* She was the one driving, was she not?"

I just looked at her. She knew the answer to that question.

"Sweetheart." Mom's voice softened. "You're always trying to save the world. Just don't lose yourself in the process."

"Mom..." I wanted so badly to tell her about the accident. The part I hadn't told anyone. The way Melody had died, her last request, and my promise. But if I told even one person, I ran the risk of everybody finding out.

"What, Casey?"

"Nothing." I looked away so she couldn't read my face. "Nothing."

We sat for a moment in silence. Then Mom stood and turned out the lamp. "Let's go to bed. Things will look better in the morning. Do you need the other half of that Valium?"

"No." I still felt sad, guilty, and desperate, but thanks to the Valium, my feelings sat a few feet away, just looking at me instead of trying to poke my eyes out.

I slept all night and most of Monday morning in my old bed. Classes didn't start till two in the afternoon, so I could afford to be a slug. Mom served me breakfast at lunchtime, then disappeared into the laundry room. I sat at the kitchen table, looking out the bay window at Lizzie lounging by the pool. My sadness, guilt, and desperation sat beside me, small, quiet companions much more easily managed than the night before when I'd lost it over a stretched-out swimsuit.

My cell phone broke through my thoughts.

"Casey, your purse is ringing!" Mom yelled from the laundry room. She carried my brown leather bag into the kitchen by its long strap, bringing with her the comforting aroma of fabric softener.

I answered the call and listened with a sinking heart. "I'll be right there." Disconnecting, I dug through my purse for my car keys.

Mom handed them over, and I remembered I'd tossed them on the dryer the day before. "That was Amy's preschool. Ben was supposed to pick her up. He's AWOL, and Amy's hysterical."

"What about Herb and Lois? Can't they—"

"Apparently they're both at a doctor's appointment for Lois, and I'm next on Amy's emergency contact list."

Minutes later, I parked in front of the preschool, left Lizzie in the passenger seat with the car running, and rushed into the office. Amy catapulted into my arms and buried her hot, tear-streaked face into my neck. "Nobody..." She gulped, sobbed, started over. "Nobody... came... to get... m-m-me."

"Oh, my darling girl, I'm here." I hugged Amy and forced my roiling thoughts down into a deep place, so she wouldn't feel my anger at Ben and think it was directed at her.

I would fucking kill Ben the second I saw him.

I would kill the goddamned bastard.

How could he forget this precious child? "I'm here, baby girl. I'm here."

Amy hiccupped. Her breath came in hitching sobs. I hugged her close and patted her back, willing her heart rate to slow down, willing mine to do the same. "Should we go to McDonald's for lunch?"

I exchanged looks with the preschool director over Amy's head. This isn't the first time, the woman's eyes said. I tried to forgive Ben, or at least put him out of my mind. "Amy, does McDonald's sound good to you?"

She nodded against my neck and said "umm-hmm," in

a whimpering, trying-to-stop-crying voice.

I buckled her into the car seat Lois had said I could keep, noticing that Amy's hair—and her teeth—probably hadn't been brushed in days. My irritation at Ben simmered, a slow rolling boil I kept from erupting into outright anger. We went through the drive-thru of McDonald's, and had a picnic at the park.

Amy ate most of her food, and Lizzie dutifully finished the rest. When Amy ran off to play, I left a curt message on Ben's cell. "I'm at the park, babysitting the daughter you forgot about."

While I had my phone out, I checked for any texts or messages from Ian, but there weren't any. Had I given him my cell number, or did he only have the numbers to my home and the studio? I tried to remember if he'd—

"Aunt Casey, Look at me!"

"I see you, sweetheart," I yelled. Tucking the phone into my purse, I gave her my complete attention. "I see you."

I watched Amy go down the slide, and my sadness for Ben deepened while my anger at him grew. *How could he*? How could he forget for even a moment that this child waited for him? What in the world was he doing?

I watched Amy slide down again, smiling and waving. A hand touched my shoulder and I looked up to see Ben standing beside me. I realized then that Amy had been waving at Ben, not at me.

"Casey, I'm so sorry."

"Tell that to your daughter," I snapped. "She probably thought you were dead, too." I lowered my voice as Amy ran toward us. "How could you do that to her when she needs you so much?"

Amy grabbed Ben around the legs, and he rested a hand on her tangled hair for a moment before lifting her up. "I'm so sorry," he repeated, only this time he was saying it to his daughter.

Chapter Seven

BACK AT HOME, I SLAMMED the front door with enough force to break the heavy leaded glass. It didn't break, but it scared the hell out of my neighbor. Angela leapt out into the entryway our duplex apartments shared, her brown eyes alarmed. Even her frizzy red hair looked alarmed. "Oh, Casey! It's you. I wasn't sure what was going on."

"I'm sorry, Angela." I opened the door to my half of the house. Lizzie, poor dog, scooted inside to avoid any further slamming that might occur. "I'm in a horrible mood."

"Me, too." Angela stepped back and opened her apartment door a little wider. "Come on in. I'll make hot tea, and we'll be in a horrible mood together."

"I can't stay long. Ballet classes start in an hour." Would Ben remember to bring Amy or Maryann to class? I doubted it. I followed Angela into her place—almost an exact mirror of mine—and moved a rocketship-looking-thing made of Legos from a kitchen chair so I could sit. "How's Ray doing in school?"

"Loves his new teachers, thanks for asking. How's everything with you?" Angela put the kettle on the stove and turned the burner on.

"Ben is being an idiot. I guess he's entitled, but when he drops the ball, someone else has to pick it up. I feel so sorry for those kids. They've lost their mother, and their father is emotionally absent. Lois is trying, but..." I shook my head. "They need more than that."

Angela got out mugs and put in sugar and milk while the water heated. "It's so sad."

I twisted a lock of hair around my finger, absently searching for split ends. "So what's got you in a mood?"

Angela leaned against the counter and crossed her arms over her chest. "Carl wants to give Ray a hunting rifle for Christmas."

"Ray's only ten years old!"

"Well, he's eleven, a year younger than Jake, remember? But I agree with your sentiment." Angela stirred milk and sugar in the bottom of the cups. "Ray is way too young to be going out into the woods at the butt-crack of dawn to shoot Bambi's mother."

"The whole practice of hunting should be outlawed until somebody figures a way for the animals to shoot back."

Angela didn't comment. She knew my views on hunting. She shared them, but couldn't express herself freely without pissing off her husband or his family. She wasn't from around here—meaning she wasn't born here—and living in Angel Falls for the last fifteen years wasn't enough to qualify for permanent citizenship. "English Breakfast, or Earl Gray?"

"Earl, please."

Angela dropped a tea bag into each cup and poured boiling water over them. I accepted the warm mug she handed me, and we sat across from each other, stirring our tea bags round in the milky, sugary elixir. I despised sugar in iced tea, but loved hot tea prepared the English way.

"You know..." Angela looked up briefly from her stirring then looked down again.

"What?" I took out my tea bag with a spoon and used the string to squeeze out the last few drops.

"I know how you could take care of Melody's kids."

The look on Angela's face made my scalp prickle. "What do you mean?"

"If you and Ben got together."

My guilty conscience pounced, landed in my stomach, tried to claw up my throat. "Angela. I..." I had no idea what to say, so I just stopped talking.

"I'm not the only one who thinks it's the perfect solution. I saw Melody's mom, Lois, the other day at Caroline's Big Hair Salon, and she said you and Ben used to date in high school. Even she—"

"Ben made his choice," I interrupted. "It wasn't me." Astonished that the whole town was apparently planning my life for me, I pushed my chair away from the table. "I have to get ready for class." Even though it was unbelievably rude, I ran out of there and escaped into my apartment.

But wasn't Angela's suggestion rude, too? I couldn't decide. Since the wreck, I lived so much in my own head that interacting with anyone seemed like a convoluted maze of do's and don'ts.

I went back to my bedroom and dressed for class. Then Lizzie and I walked to the studio, where teaching ballet, at least, was simple. Not easy, but simple.

Amy didn't make it to ballet, but I hadn't figured she would. If Ben couldn't remember to pick her up after school, he was sure to forget ballet. I didn't expect to see Maryann in class, either, but she stormed in when we were working on *developpes* at the barre. Stifling sobs, she slammed her ballet bag against Lizzie's ottoman, and stood with her back turned to her friends.

I hurried to give her the hug I knew she needed.

She swiped at her tears with first one hand, then the other. "My daddy is so stupid!"

"Aww, baby, no." I patted her shoulder. "He's doing his best."

"Well, his best is horrible. Look what he did to my hair."

I smoothed back the tangled mess that had been inexpertly scraped back into an off-center ponytail. "It's not so bad."

"I tried to put it in a bun, but Mama always did it for me, and I couldn't get it right. The pins kept sliding out and the bun kept falling down. I asked him to help, but he doesn't even know how to make a stupid ponytail!"

"I'll do it for you. No problem."

The music ended, and another track started. The girls at the barre stood waiting for instruction. "Do y'all remember the combination for *frappes*?" I took the hairbrush off the stereo cabinet and brushed Maryann's thick dark hair, a shimmering mahogany fall that reached the center of her back.

"No, Ma'am," a few of the girls responded. Others leaned against the barre and started whispered conversations.

"Okay." I switched the music to a long, slow track. "Go ahead and do some stretches at the barre."

"Can I come live with you?" Maryann asked in a small, trembling voice.

"Sweetheart," I whispered, "how do you think that would make your daddy feel?"

"He wouldn't care. We stay at Grandma's half the time,

and when we're home, he doesn't pay any attention to us. All he ever does is work on the computer, talk on the phone, and sit in the den like a big fat slug."

Damn. Maybe Ben wasn't up to taking care of his kids after all. Maybe I shouldn't have pushed him to take them back so soon. "He hasn't gone back to work yet?"

"He's working from home now, except when we're in school. So he can take care of us, he says. But he totally forgot about ballet, and I had to remind him. Amy's probably still crying because she didn't get to come. She didn't know she'd missed her class until I started getting ready for mine."

I wrapped a covered band around her hair and started twisting the ponytail into a tight bun. "Would you like me to talk to him?" As if that would help any more than it had before.

Maryann shrugged and wiped her cheeks. "I dunno."

"How about you plan to come to class a little early from now on," I suggested, "and I'll do your hair until your daddy can learn how."

"What if he's too stupid to learn?" Maryann wasn't quite ready to abandon her anger.

"You don't think I'm a good enough teacher to show a dumb old man how to make a ponytail?" I started poking in hairpins.

"Maybe you are." A tiny, unwilling smile turned up one corner of Maryann's mouth. I could see it in the mirror, could feel the tension seeping out of her as I pushed the last pins into her bun. "And you know; you're old enough to put your hair in a bun all by yourself. There are a few tricks to it, but I'll teach you."

"Okay."

"Shall we dance?" I turned her toward her classmates.

"Yes," she answered, her confidence bolstered for the

moment. She walked to the barre, and I chose music to combine *plies* with low *developpes*. Then I led the class in a combination designed to help Maryann get warmed-up before we moved on to *Grand Battements*.

Lois picked up Maryann after ballet, but Ben called me not too long after I got home. "I hear my daughter is coming to live with you."

"I didn't tell her that."

"I know." Ben sighed. I could envision him running his fingers through his hair as he often did when something wasn't going right. "I'm calling from work. I had to go back in to catch up on some things, so the kids are having dinner with Lois and Herb. Can I stop by your place on my way home? I really need to talk to... to someone." His voice sounded nasal, kind of stuffy, and I wondered if he'd been crying.

"Sure. What time?"

"Is right now okay?"

"Yeah. Now's fine."

Ben co-owned a small company that designed and installed communication systems for big corporations all over the southeast. Phones, internet, special internal servers, stuff like that. His office was across town, but in a town our size that was only five minutes away. I rushed to make myself decent.

I had already dressed for bed, and was only wearing a big T-shirt and panties. I put on an almost-clean pair of jeans and rummaged in the bottom drawer for a pair of socks. I had painted my toenails bright red for my date with Ian, and somehow the sight of those ten shining beacons peeping out from under my jeans made me feel guilty. My best friend was dead, her husband and children struggling to pick up their lives without her, and I had painted my toenails a cheery vermillion. I pulled the socks carefully over the new blisters I'd picked up in the last pointe class.

Ben knocked. Lizzie ran to the door and gave a sharp bark.

My heart squeezed when I opened the door and saw Ben's face. I was right. He'd been crying. His eyes were glassy and bloodshot. The tip of his nose was red, and his mouth seemed puffy. I wanted to hug him, make him feel all-better, like I'd have done with any of his children. But Mel's ghost whispered in my ear. What Ben needed now was tough-love, not coddling.

"Come on in." I took his arm and led him inside, because he seemed inclined to stand in the entry hall. "Sit down," I ordered, pointing to the overstuffed couch. "I'll get you a drink."

In the kitchen, I peered into the refrigerator. "What do you want?" I called out. "I have wine, beer, coke, water."

"Beer," he yelled back. I opened the bottle and poured it into a tall glass. The stereo came on, but I could tell Ben hadn't chosen a CD, he'd just hit the play button.

I cringed. Dave Matthews' sexy love songs wouldn't have been my choice for this moment. I resisted the urge to go in and change the music. Calling attention to Ben's non-choice would be worse than enduring it and changing to something less provocative later. I set the beer on the table in front of him, and curled up in the fat-quilted reading chair with my wine. Leaning back against the cushions, I tucked my feet under me and took a sip. "How are you?"

Ben slouched against the couch, drained a third of his beer in one gulp. "As well as can be expected, considering I've lost my wife and am in the process of losing my children as well." He took another long drink of the beer and looked up at me, his eyes shining, but maybe not so much from tears as I'd first thought.

"Ben, have you been drinking—I mean, before this beer?"

His only reply was a slight smirk. "Amy cries and clings to Lois every time I go there to pick her up. Maryann claims she wants to live with you." His eyes flashed a brief accusation and then fixed again on the beer glass in his hand. "Jake spends all his free time at Nicky's house next door." Ben took a swig of his beer and set the glass aside. "Melody was the glue that held us together, and now that she's gone, my family is falling apart."

I felt sorry for him. But my feeling-sorry wasn't going to help him. I remembered Mel's legendary back-bone-of-titanium, the way she'd ordered her life and everyone else's around her. I tried to use a little more of that and a little less of my need to single-handedly save the world. "I'm glad you finally realize your family needs you. Now what are you planning to do about it?"

"Do?" He looked shocked at my lack of compassion.

I was kind of shocked, myself, but it didn't stop me from saying what Mel would have wanted me to say. "Yes, Ben. Do. What are you going to do? I'm sorry if this sounds harsh. I know you've lost your wife, but your children have lost their mother."

Ben hung his head, but I refused to feel sorry for him. Well, at least, I refused to show it.

"They've needed you to grieve with them, and you've been completely absent. You've farmed them out to their grandparents and the neighbors, and now you wonder why they don't want to come home? How can they trust you to be there for them, when you've been unavailable since their mother died?"

Lizzie whined and pressed her nose under my hand.

For a second, I saw myself as she must, perched on the edge of my chair, all-but yelling at Ben.

Hell, I *was* yelling, as if I had any right to chastise anyone. Maybe I'd taken just a little too much of Melody's backbone-of-titanium. She knew how to balance it exquisitely with her Smurfy-sweetness, while, clearly, I didn't. Instantly ashamed, I moved to kneel on the floor in front of him.

He dropped his head into his hands. "You're right." His voice was muffled. "I've been selfish. I only cared about myself. I couldn't stand to see my kids because I knew they wanted me to make it better... to fix it the way I've always been able to fix everything before."

He sniffed a few times. I went into the kitchen and spun a few paper towels off the roll. I dropped the loosely-folded wad onto the couch beside him. "I don't have any tissues."

"Yeah, you'd make a better bachelor than a housewife." He tore the towels into neat squares and used one to blow his nose.

I sat beside him on the couch and put an arm around his shoulders. "Hey, don't be any more of a jerk than you have to, okay?"

"I'll try not to. But tell me, Miss-know-it-all. What am I going to do about my kids?"

"You might not like everything I have to say."

He cut his eyes over at me, and I saw a little of the Ben I'd once fallen in love with.

"Hit me."

"Okay." I leaned back into the corner of the couch, and thought about the things Melody had always done for their children. "Are you taking notes?"

He nodded, and I began ticking off items.

"One, pick your children up at school on time, every

day, Monday through Friday. Maryann said you were working from home most of the time now, so I know you can do it. Put it in your phone's calendar, and set alarms if you can't remember. Your children's schedules are just as important as any of your business meetings. I'll bet you don't forget *them*."

He winced. "What else?"

"Two, make sure they do their homework before supper."

"They have homework?" As if he didn't know.

Of course I ignored him. "Three. Cook supper, and sit with them while they eat it."

"But I can't—"

I held up a hand to stop his excuses. "You can make macaroni and cheese, can't you?"

He said, "Yeah," in a sheepish tone.

"Four, make sure they have a bath and brush their teeth every night. Make sure they wash their hair every couple of days, and for God's sake, help them brush out the tangles afterward. Maryann's hair was an absolute mess the other day at ballet."

He shifted uncomfortably and looked toward the door. "Is that all?"

"Is that about all you can take?"

"Yeah." He grinned the ghost of his old grin. "I think that's enough to start."

"Okay. Go pick up your kids, take them home and get started."

He stood. "What do I do when Amy cries and doesn't want to leave Lois?"

"Promise her you'll read her a story when you get home." I took our glasses into the kitchen and set them on the counter. He followed and put his wadded paper towel into the trash. "*Goodnight Moon* is one of her favorites. Promise her that one." I walked with Ben onto the porch. He gave me a hug, but released me the second I started to wonder what the hug meant—if it meant anything more than thanks to an old friend.

"The part you mentioned about cooking supper..."

"The macaroni and cheese part? It comes in a blue and orange box—"

His mouth lifted into an almost-grin, and he punched me lightly on the shoulder. "The kids would love if you'd come over some night and, well..."

"Cook something besides macaroni and cheese?"

Ben smiled a real smile for the first time that night. "Yes, please. If you wouldn't mind."

"Only if you promise to watch and learn while I cook."

"Deal."

"Go get your kids. It's almost their bedtime."

"Slave-driver." He went down the steps to his car. I'd already turned to go back inside when he yelled, "Casey."

I turned to see him standing in the open car door with his arms crossed on the hood. "What about tomorrow night?"

"Ben, I'm busy all this week, and your kids need you to themselves."

"Okay, okay. What about Friday? Come cook dinner for us on Friday. We'll all be sick of macaroni and cheese by then."

I wondered if instant capitulation would constitute backsliding, but couldn't find the will to say no. "All right. I'll come on Friday." I felt as if I'd caved in, but I missed the kids, especially Jake, whom I'd hardly seen at all since... God, I could hardly think the words. Since Melody's death, just a month ago.

A chill wind touched my shoulders, reminding me. More than a month. Melody had died the first week of

September and it was now halfway through October.

Chapter Eight

I GOT HUNG UP IN THE not-so-fast lane of the grocery store when the woman ahead of me pulled out a wallet full of coupons instead of cash. I showed up to Ben's house late, carrying two heavy-duty canvas shopping bags that each weighed as much as a medium-sized goat.

Ben opened the door before I'd figured out how to knock without using my hands or making another scuff mark on the red door. He took the bags from me and pretended to stagger. "Damn. No wonder you're late."

"The checkout lane was a nightmare. I couldn't decide whether I felt sorrier for me, the checkout girl, or the lady who was holding up the line with her gazillion coupons."

"I'm glad you made it here in spite of complications." He led the way to the kitchen. "The kids threatened to run away from home if I made them eat hot dogs again, so thanks."

"You're welcome." I'd brought enough food—the kind Melody would have wanted them to have—to break the shelves in the refrigerator.

"Aunt Casey!" Amy skidded down the polished wood

foyer and into the kitchen, her bunny house slippers making shushing noises as she skated along. "Look at me! I'm dusting!"

Maryann came in behind Amy and burrowed into my side for a hug. "Dad made us clean the house. We tried to tell him you weren't company, but he wouldn't listen."

Ben put the grocery bags on the kitchen counter and started unpacking everything onto the kitchen table. "I'm doing everything you said."

Maryann was still hanging onto me. "He made us finish our homework before you got here, so we can watch a DVD after dinner."

I gave Ben a thumbs-up sign.

Jake slumped into the kitchen from the living room and gave me a quick hug. "What's for dinner?"

"I thought I'd get your daddy to cook steaks on the grill, and y'all can help me make a salad, boy-scout potatoes, and—"

"We're gonna eat boy scouts?" Amy stuck her thumb in her mouth and leaned against Ben's leg.

"No, Punkin." Ben reached down to ruffle her hair. "Boy-scout potatoes are like mashed potatoes, cooked and mashed-up but not peeled."

"I *hate* that kind, Aunt Casey," Maryann whined. "Mama never made that kind of potatoes."

"No problem." I patted Maryann's back. "We can make regular mashed potatoes, but you get to peel them."

"No." Ben pinned Maryann with a severe stare. "We're going to eat whatever Casey has planned, and we're going to be happy and polite about it."

Maryann pulled away from me and crossed her arms, grumbling something too quiet to understand. Jake slid past her, delivering a sly pinch. "You get what you get, and you don't fuss a bit!" She slapped his hand away but didn't rise to the bait.

"Young lady." Ben's voice was low and slightly threatening. "What should your response be?"

Maryann's "yes, sir," was barely audible.

"I don't think I heard you." Ben snapped the edges of the big shopping bag and folded it with sharp motions.

"Yes, sir," Maryann yelled over her shoulder then flounced from the room.

Jake sniggered maliciously. "Welcome to paradise."

I moved closer to Ben, close enough to feel the waves of irritation coming off his body. Amy's warm little hand slid into mine, and I clasped it firmly, taking comfort from her innocent touch.

"Jake..." Ben's voice held the restrained fury of a man on the edge of physical violence. "Your sly comments are not allowed in this house. If you can't control your mouth, please go to your room."

I put a hand on Ben's arm, doing my best to infuse his rigid muscles with a calm I didn't feel myself. "Let it go," I whispered.

Ben shrugged off my hand and lowered his eyebrows at Jake. "You will answer politely, son, or I'll tan your hide."

I turned away and started putting things into the fridge. If I were Melody, I'd have intervened. But I wasn't Melody, and I needed to remember that. I devoted all my attention to shifting the contents of the refrigerator to make room for a six-pack of yogurt. But of course, even with my head in the fridge, I couldn't help but hear the desperation in Ben's overly-controlling tone when he kept hammering away at Jake. This autocratic attitude wasn't like him at all. It had to be attributed to his grief, and the stress of raising these kids alone. I felt like sitting them all down in a circle and insisting that we sing a round of Kumbaya.

"Yes, sir." Jake's tone was filled with sullen resentment, his posture as stiff and unbending as Ben's. "May I go to my room now?"

"Go on." Ben crossed his arms over his chest and leaned his butt against the kitchen counter, releasing just a hint of the aggravation that held his body so tense I could feel it from three feet away. "I'll call you when supper's ready."

I closed the refrigerator door and waited for someone—Ben—to say something. Amy stood in front of me and lifted her arms, so I picked her up. She wrapped her legs around me and snuggled her face into the crook of my neck. "You smell good, Aunt Casey."

My gaze flew to Ben's. "It's just soap, honey." I didn't want Ben to think I'd put perfume on for him. Because I hadn't.

She stroked my hair, sifted it through her fingers. "Your hair smells good. And it feels good, too." Amy was oblivious to the nervous energy shimmering in the air. I carried her to the table, pulled out a chair and sat with her in my lap. She snuggled close, bringing her clasped hands up between my breasts, pressing her arms there as if she missed the softness of a woman. "You don't come to see us anymore." The quiet plea in her whispered voice twisted around my heart. "I miss you, Aunt Casey."

"Oh, honey." I kept my voice low, trying to spare Ben from hearing our conversation as he took the steaks out of the package and put them in a dish to marinate. "I'm sorry. I promise I'll come more often."

"You didn't just love our mama, did you? You love us, too, right?"

I squeezed Amy a little tighter. "Of course I love y'all."

"Daddy too?" Amy's voice was quiet, but not quiet enough. I looked up to meet Ben's level blue gaze. Amy tugged at a lock of my hair, turning my attention back to her. "Do you love my Daddy, too?"

I hugged Amy, and looked over her shoulder at Ben while I gave her the only answer I could. "Of course I do, honey."

The confession brought no joy, no comfort, no peace along with it. I felt only a crushing weight, even heavier than the weight I'd carried all the years Ben had been married to Melody, all the years I had struggled alone with the shame of my love for him.

I doubted there would come a day when I didn't love Ben. But I couldn't derive any joy from a love so burdened by guilt.

"I'm glad you're here." Amy cupped my face between her small hands. "You're gonna come back a lot, right?"

I smoothed a blonde curl behind her ear. "I promise, sweetheart. I'll come back."

Her smile blossomed. "I love you, Aunt Casey."

The back door closed with a soft click, and I heard the squeal of hinges as Ben opened the top of the gas grill. I tore my gaze from his broad shoulders, slightly hunched as he reached down to turn on the burners. Amy puckered her lips, and I did the same, planting a quick kiss on her pursed little mouth. "I love you too, baby girl."

That night, I rolled in my twisted sheets like a plucked bird skewered over a roasting fire. The leaves had already turned on the redbud trees, but a warm front had invited summer weather to rot the jack-o-lanterns on the town's porches. I got up and tinkered with the thermostat, but still slept badly, waking to dreams of twin yellow headlights that turned into the amber eyes of Ian Buchanan.

Toward morning, I was walking into a college Algebra class only to realize that I hadn't attended class all semester, and was about to flunk the final exam. Naked.

The classroom bell rang.

I woke in a panic and catapulted out of bed. The phone rang again, and I snatched it up. Blinking in the garish mid-morning light, I answered. "Hello?" My voice sounded thin and breathy. I put a hand to my heart to slow its skipping.

"I'm sorry I woke you, lass."

I'd forgotten how much deeper his voice was than Ben's. Something about it softened my insides like caramel heated over an open flame. "You didn't," I lied, as if sleeping late on Saturday was a crime. "I was awake."

His chuckle sounded like sin and sex, like warm chocolate and cold whipped cream drenched in Godiva liqueur. "Liar. You're still in bed. I can tell by your voice."

I quit trying to convince him otherwise and stretched out across the sheets. "Okay. I was asleep."

"I wanted to catch you before you left the house."

"Well," I said, the last of the word lost on a jaw-cracking yawn. "You've caught me."

"Already? I thought you'd be much harder to get than that."

"Where are you, anyway?"

"I'm in South Carolina at the moment, looking at some…" there was a tiny pause, "investment property."

"Oh," I said brilliantly. "When are you coming back?"

"The end of the week, I should think. Thursday or Friday."

"Oh, good." I wanted to bite my tongue the minute

I'd said that. I had no business implying that I missed him, or that I wanted him to come back soon.

"Could I persuade you to save some time for me this weekend?"

Hell, he could persuade me to do anything, but I didn't want to sound too eager. Ian was entirely too sure of himself as it was. "Sure, I guess. How much time were you thinking?"

I heard a muted sound on the other end of the line, a door opening, maybe, and a quiet sound muffled by Ian's hand over the receiver. Then his smooth voice came back on the line. "I'll call you in a day or two, all right?"

"Okay, sure," I chirped, trying to replace my disappointment with a nonchalant tone. But my tone didn't matter at all, because the line was already dead.

For the week of Halloween, I wore my usual costume, black leotard and tights and a tattered skirt I'd made by tying long strips of black tulle to an elastic waistband. I didn't bother with a witch hat. My own hair, braided the night before and brushed out into a cloud of frizzy waves in the morning, looked witchy enough.

The week's parties went well until my first class on Thursday, Halloween day. I should have suspected a downward spiral was about to begin when the mother who'd offered to stay and help with the preschool-class party bowed out. She sent a dozen chocolate cupcakes and juice boxes instead. Things were going okay, though, in spite of my lack of assistants.

I managed to get the bunch of ballerinas, fairies, princesses, and witches seated in a fairly organized circle on the studio floor. I doled out cupcakes. I stuck tiny straws into juice boxes. I cleaned up the mess from one little witch's discovery that a juice box, if squeezed hard enough, could shoot a delightful stream of liquid through the straw.

Sticky orange mess notwithstanding, we made it through the party-half of class very well. Then we moved on to the Halloween dance. I had choreographed one for every class, just a simple combination of well-known steps set to spooky music and repeated twice. Parents had been told to come early to pick up their kids, so they could see the dance performed at the end of class.

We'd gone through the steps a few times, and I was standing at the stereo cabinet working on a slight glitch with my iPod, when Amber, hopped up on sugar and excitement, asked if she could go to the bathroom. I didn't even look up, just waved my hand in a shooing motion to give permission. I knew better than to deny a four-year-old the right to go to the bathroom.

I started the music again, and we were on the second repeat when Amber came running into the classroom, panic-stricken.

"Miss Casey, the toilet's overfloating!"

"Oh, Lord." My outburst was more prayer than blasphemy. I ran toward the bathroom with eleven little girls behind me, doing the calculations—what part of the newspaper office was below the studio bathroom?

Think quick.

Think quick.

Think…

Holy shit. If I couldn't unclog the drain quickly, toilet water would drip through the ceiling and onto Ian's desk downstairs.

Just as things were going so well, too. Ian had called

twice more while he was out of town. We'd talked of everything and nothing, phone-date conversations designed to ramp up interest and expectation. I'd given him my cell number, and he'd texted this morning that he'd be back sometime today.

This was not a good time for toilet water to pour onto his desk.

I encountered a lake just outside the bathroom door. "How many times did you try to flush this *overfloating* toilet?"

Amber stood beside me, eyes wide, thumb in mouth, innocent.

"Back up," I yelled to the excited, curious crowd. "Don't step in the water." I took off my ballet slippers and tossed them across the foyer into the doorway of the dressing room. I rolled up my tights, waded into the bathroom, grabbed a mop from the utility closet, and pushed a path through the deluge.

A double-sized roll of toilet paper lay like a pufferfish at the bottom of the bowl. And hadn't there been *two* extra rolls on top of the tank earlier today? I shoved my sleeves up and reached into the bowl, causing another tidal wave to gush onto the floor. The waterlogged mess came apart in my hand, and thin strips of toilet paper floated wraith-like in the water. I dug the wad of gummed-up paper from the pipe it had been partially sucked down and threw the mess in the trash. But I wasn't rewarded by the glug-glug sound of a cleared pipe.

I worked the plunger, and even more shreds of paper swirled up through the yellowish water like some demon version of egg-drop soup. "Amber!" My voice rose to a screech. "How many rolls of toilet paper did you stick down the toilet?"

Amber blinked wide, innocent eyes and sucked harder

at her thumb.

Bet she didn't wash that thumb, either, I thought, with just the tiniest bit of malice.

The studio phone rang, but I didn't answer, being too busy pumping the plunger into the toilet like a person possessed. It was either that or hit the child over the head with it, and I didn't think her parents would appreciate that, no matter how much she appeared to need it or some similar form of correction.

The phone stopped ringing, and moments later I heard footsteps on the stairs. The door at the top of the stairs opened and shut, and a chorus of excited voices informed the visitor, "The toilet overfloated! It overfloated! Miss Casey stuck her hand in the potty water!"

I blew out a sharp breath, shook my head to get the wildly waving hair out of my face, and stood to confront Ian. Holding the plunger in front of me like a sword, I warned him: "Don't say a word. Not one word."

Chapter Nine

I AN STOPPED IN THE MIDDLE of the studio foyer and held his hands up in surrender. "I know better than to confront an armed and angry witch."

I wilted in relief, because he wasn't angry even though his desk must be soaked. He came close, pushed the toilet plunger aside and took me in his arms. "This has been a horrible day," I muttered into his shoulder. "And it's just barely started."

He cupped the back of my head and caressed the base of my skull with his thumb. Oblivious to the crowd of little girls surrounding us, or the fact that we were standing in almost an inch of potty water, I closed my eyes and leaned into him.

"I'll take care of this," he offered with a light kiss on my forehead. "You go back in and teach your class."

"Thank you," I whispered. I stepped back, near tears.

He rolled his shirtsleeves back, revealing tanned, muscular forearms that would have made my mouth water if I weren't about to dissolve into a pitiful crying heap.

"Go on," he urged, taking the plunger. He seemed to know that the least amount of comfort would have me blubbering like a fool, so he turned away, tossing the last comment over his shoulder. "I'll see you later tonight."

"Okay." I sniffed back my silly tears and herded the girls back to class. "Make a circle, and sit criss-cross-apple-sauce. I'll be back in two seconds." I ducked into my private dressing room, washed my hands and feet, put my ballet slippers back on, and made it back into the classroom in one-point-five.

At the end of class, parents collected their children, and while I had a quiet word with Amber's parents about the recent *incident*, the next set of girls trickled in. Leaving a trusted ballet-mom in charge for a minute, I peeked out into the foyer. The floor was dry. I ventured to the bathroom door. The floor in there was clean and dry, too, and the air smelled faintly of bathroom cleaner. I flushed the toilet, and watched the water swirl right down.

At the end of my last class, I felt Ian's presence and looked over to see him standing in the doorway with shower-wet hair, butt-hugging jeans and a flimsy sweatshirt. I ushered all the stragglers out the door, then stopped in front of Ian feeling tentative and unsure of myself in a way I never had before. "Hi."

He drew me into his arms, drew my tongue into his mouth and sucked, as if he was unbearably thirsty and I was the drink he craved. His kiss was hot, hungry, possessive. His hands roamed my back, slid down to cup my backside, then pulled me up against the hard bulge in his jeans. He didn't stop kissing me until my lips were swollen and tingling, my mind incoherent.

"I've missed you," he admitted, just like that.

"I'm glad you're back," I responded, offering a truth of my own. "Do you want to come to my house for dinner?" What I would cook, I had no idea, but I didn't want to wait through an entire evening at a restaurant just to have him to myself.

"Oh, yeah," he answered in a pretty good imitation of a southern drawl. "You could tempt me with food... or anything else you've a mind to tempt me with." He smiled, and I was speared once again by his movie-star good looks. This guy was gorgeous, and before the night was over, I'd have him in my bed.

I knew it because of the confident sexuality that radiated from him.

I knew it because I wouldn't be able to resist him even if I wanted to.

I knew it because the sparkle in his eyes warned me: this time he'd be fully prepared.

"What are we waiting for?" I rubbed my hands up his strong arms, twined one leg around his legs, unable to behave like anything other than a cat in heat. I went up on tiptoe, squashed my breasts against his chest and slid my tongue along the seam of his sensuously curved lips.

He kissed me again, hard and quick, then looked over at Lizzie—whose presence I had completely forgotten. "Come on, Liz." He snapped his fingers, and Lizzie moved faster than she'd ever moved at my command. Ian rewarded her with a quick caress, and she gazed adoringly at him all the way down the stairs.

I was just as enthralled as she, both of us completely taken in by him.

Ian drove us home and waited in my living room with Lizzie and a glass of Cabernet while I took a shower. Though I'd washed my hands (and my feet) after the toilet escapade, I still felt nasty from stirring around in the potty and couldn't wait to wash myself from head to toe.

Okay, that's not strictly the truth.

Ian smelled wonderful, and I wanted to be clean and good-smelling for him, too. Because I knew tonight would be our first night together. Because I wanted him to be at least as bowled-over by me as I was by him. I showered, dried, and doused myself with honey dust, an expensive edible powder Melody had given me for a birthday years ago. Tonight was the perfect time to take it out of the closet, because it smelled divine, but tasted even better.

The doorbell chimed, and Ian called out from the living room. "A bunch of ghouls and goblins are trying to get inside. What should I do?"

Shit. I'd forgotten. It was Halloween. "Candy's on top of the refrigerator. Help, please."

His laugh was low and erotic. "Do I get something in return?"

"Take a chance. You might be rewarded beyond your wildest dreams."

I heard him mumble something about playing with fire, then the rustle of a plastic bag tearing open and the squeal of the front door hinges.

I dressed in Hollister sweats that were old and casual enough to make him think I'd just pulled on the first thing I could find, but thin and cut to perfectly caress every curve. I didn't bother with underwear.

When I joined Ian in the living room, he was closing the door after giving out another handful of candy.

"Thanks for handling the trick-or-treaters."

He tossed the bag of mini chocolates on the hall table and put his arms around me. "I'd rather handle you."

"Mmmm." I slid my hands up under his sweatshirt to feel the firm muscles along either side of his spine. "I'd like that, too."

"You smell delicious." He kissed the curve of my neck and opened his mouth to suckle lightly. Groaning, he hugged me closer. "Good Lord above, you taste even better." He pulled away and looked down into my face, not hiding the passion and need that tightened his features. "Forget about food. Forget about trick-or-treaters. Let's go to bed." Grinding his hips against mine, he persuaded with a ravenous kiss, lifting his lips just enough to deliver the coup de grace. "Please, lass. I'm dying for you."

The doorbell rang again, accompanied by a chorus of childish, screeching voices. "Trick-or-treat!"

I gave him a consoling kiss but pushed him away. "They know I'm home."

He grabbed my arm and kissed me again. "Can't your next-door neighbors supply the neighborhood with candy?"

I wriggled away. "Angela and Carl are taking Ray trick-or-treating. They'll probably stop by here soon."

He pouted hopefully. "We could turn off the lights. Pretend nobody's home."

I smiled at his sad-little-boy expression. "Ian, our cars are parked out front."

The doorbell rang again, and one brave little boy yodeled, "Trick-or-treat, smell my feet, give me something good to eat!"

Ian slumped in defeat and shoved his hands into the pockets of his jeans, pulling outward discreetly. "Answer the door, then." He turned away and ducked into kitchen. "When you're done handing out candy to this lot, you might as well come in here and cook something for me to eat. I'm starving."

I grinned at his grouchy statement. It was just the sort of insensitive, sexist remark I might have expected from the Ian I'd first met over the phone. Coming from the Ian I knew now, I didn't find it irritating at all. Actually, I found it sort of cute.

The doorbell rang again, several times in quick succession. Obviously the natives on my porch were getting restless.

"I'm coming," I yelled, taking the bag of candy off the table.

"Not yet, you're not," I heard Ian mumble from the kitchen as I answered the door.

We shared a thrown-together meal of spaghetti and canned sauce (not my finest culinary hour) then tortured each other on the couch between waves of trick-or-treaters. I expected Ben to show up with his kids at some point, and wondered how I'd handle an introduction between Ben and Ian.

Let-go-and-let-God, I decided. Either the kids would be all excited and ready to move on to the next place, or they'd come at the end of the evening and Ben would expect to hang out for a few minutes and drink a beer while the kids surveyed their loot.

If that happened, well... I hoped that wouldn't happen.

Around seven-thirty, a car pulled up at the curb. I was rinsing the plates and loading them into the dishwasher when I saw the lights through the kitchen window. Ian stood behind me, his mouth on my neck, his hands on my hips, his erection at my backside, teasing.

Wondering how much could be seen through the windows, I watched a tall man get out of the car, taking his time to unbuckle a small child from the booster seat while two older kids ran up the sidewalk.

I pushed Ian away under the pretense of backing up to slam the dishwasher door. "Somebody's coming."

I rushed to the door with the candy, ready to toss out chocolate and quick excuses about why I couldn't invite Ben and his kids inside.

Why did I feel so guilty? I didn't owe Ben anything. Did I?

I opened the door.

It wasn't them. One of my ballet students and her family, but not Ben. I handed out candy and wondered how soon it would be appropriate for me, the town's ballet teacher, to turn out the porch light, signaling the end of my participation in the Halloween tradition. Maybe Ben and his kids weren't coming. Maybe they'd gone to the haunted house instead.

I hugged my student and her siblings, waved goodbye, went back inside. My fingers felt magnetized toward the porch light switch. Was it too early to bow out of my Halloween duties? I'd give it another few minutes, I decided. I plopped down on the couch, and Ian joined me there a second later. With the soft whir of the dishwasher running and the kitchen light off, Ian took my feet into his lap and kneaded my instep.

"Ahhh, that feels so good." It felt incredible to be on the receiving end of a little TLC. It was all I could do to keep from purring. Seconds ticked by, followed by minutes. I began to relax.

"God, what a horrendous day this has been." I sighed away the last bit of stress I'd been holding onto and reached for a mini-chocolate bar.

Ian grinned, but his eyes were heavy-lidded with a promise for later. "It seems to be ending well."

I was almost getting used to his deep voice and devastating accent. Almost. "I have a feeling it's about to get even better."

"I think Halloween is officially over." He leaned back to see the kitchen clock through the doorway. "It's almost eight-thirty, and the last bunch was just after eight o'clock." Sliding one hand under the hem of my sweatpants, he gripped my calf lightly and tickled the back of my knee with a finger. His other hand tunneled under the hem of my sweatshirt.

"You might be right." God, I hoped so. I ran a hand down his hard-muscled forearm. My insides tingled with shooting-stars of anticipation. "Should we turn off the porch light to discourage any stragglers?"

"Then you could keep the rest of the chocolate to yourself." His questing finger brushed the underside of one breast. "Might be an idea..."

I scooted toward him to allow a couple more inches reach. Part of me was astonished at my shameless behavior, but I couldn't help it. This man aroused me by his presence alone, and when he touched me, I was powerless to resist. Whatever he wanted, I was all-in.

He flicked a finger across one peaked nipple. My eyes slid closed, my mouth dropped open, and with a sigh, I surrendered to the boneless heat his touch infused. He tweaked my nipple again, and leaned across my belly to give me a hot kiss on the mouth.

Then he stood, leaving a wash of cold air in his place. "Hold that thought..."

I kept my eyes closed against the lamplight, trying to retain the feeling of abandon.

Holding on to the liquid heat of him until he returned.

I kept track of him by sound as he turned off the porch light, locked the doors and closed the blinds. Then he turned off the lamp with a click, and I opened my eyes to darkness, with only the shine of his eyes to show me the way.

He led me into my bedroom then stood beside my neatly made bed, watching my face in the dim glow that slipped through the closed blinds from the streetlight. "Is this what you want, Casey?"

"Yes," I whispered. My hands roamed the dips and curves of his muscular arms and shoulders. Boldly, I cupped the hard bulge that pressed against his jeans. "I want this." I nipped at his mouth with my teeth. "I want you."

I laid my cheek on his chest and slipped my hands into the waistband of his jeans—one in front, one in back. He was like a big, muscular, living, breathing teddy bear. He felt so good, and smelled even better. I felt the vibration of his voice through the hard wall of his chest, and realized he was saying something. "Huh?" I breathed.

He stilled my exploration by backing away from me, taking my hands in his and holding them between us, clasped as if in prayer. "Are you sure?"

No way, answered the tiny flicker of my rational mind I could still hear. What was I doing, starting something with Ian when a big part of me felt obligated to Melody's family? I went up on tiptoe and kissed his sexy mouth. "I'm sure."

He nipped at my lips. "This time, I came prepared."

"I know. I'm still sure." I slid my hands out of his, and turned away to peel back the quilt and the top sheet. The smell of fabric softener floated briefly in the air, reminding me of Maryann, when I showed her how to run a load of laundry.

Which reminded me of Amy, when she put her arms around my neck and begged me to come more often.

Which reminded me of Jake, when he added a whole stick of butter to the mashed potatoes when I wasn't looking.

Which reminded me of Ben, when he brought steaks from the grill, holding the plate high and trailing his free hand along my waist.

Then Ian touched my shoulder, and thoughts of anyone else floated away like dandelion seeds on a gentle breeze. He turned me toward him. His wide palms skimmed along my ribs, under my sweatshirt. I raised my arms, and he pulled the shirt over my head and tossed it to the floor.

He cupped my breasts. His thumbs rasped against the distended nipples and shock waves of pleasure rocked through my chest and belly. "You're beautiful," he whispered. "So beautiful it makes me ache to look at you."

I ran my hands under his sweatshirt, up the hard plane of his abdomen to his chest, learning the textures of his heated skin and crisp hair. He let go of me just long enough to take off his sweatshirt and unbutton the top button of his jeans.

I reached down to help.

Ooh, mama. He was wearing button-down jeans. My appreciation of his sex appeal soared another notch. I'd always thought button-down jeans were sexy—the one-by-one loosening of buttons prolonging the anticipation—and on this man, they were almost unbearably so. I popped the next button loose, then another and another. I felt him grin against my mouth, and a second later his jeans fell to the floor.

My sweatpants followed. I moved back to step out of them, and got a good look at the naked man standing before me. My hands dropped to my sides.

I was used to seeing men with perfect bodies. I had danced with plenty of them. But Ian was more than just a beautifully formed body. He exuded a raw masculine grace I was sure God intended to be the ideal for his sex. Everything about him turned me on, both the things I could see, and the intangible essence of him I could only feel by the answering response within my own soul.

"Casey?" His deep voice was tentative, questioning. I realized I'd been standing like a zombie, staring at him.

"You're beautiful," I whispered.

The sound of my voice released us both, and we lifted our hands, each to touch the other's body. My fingertips grazed his chest, drifted down the arrow of hair that led to his impressive erection. I closed my fingers around it. "If I had any sense," I joked, "I'd be terrified. Think it'll fit?"

Ian made a sound that might have been a chuckle or a groan. "I hope so. God, I hope so."

We tumbled backward onto the bed, a tangle of entwined limbs and exploring tongues. The brush of cool sheets ignited my sensitized nerve endings, setting me on fire for him.

I kissed his neck then sucked lightly, not enough to leave a mark. The scent of his bare skin sent an image through my brain of the night he'd found us after the wreck. But the image blended with my passion, infusing a sense of safety and comfort. He had saved me then. He was saving me now.

His lips touched mine. His fingers slid between my legs. "Ahh, Casey," he murmured. "You're so hot, so wet."

I sighed into his mouth, but couldn't speak.

He stroked me with a slow, deliberate rhythm, setting off fires of wanting that sparked and swelled and swirled through me. "Come inside me." I dropped my trembling knees open against the cool sheets. "I've waited so long for this... so long for you."

His hand stilled for less than a heartbeat. I sensed a slight pulling away, a distancing of what had felt like a soul-connection between us.

Then he kissed me, and his masterful lips almost per-suaded me that I had only imagined the disconnect. I kissed him back, kept my hands moving along the hard planes of his shoulders and back while he put on a condom. But I felt an invisible wall grow between us.

If I'd known him better, I would have insisted we talk about my intuition that I'd said something frightening enough to make him pull away. But it had been more a feeling than an overt action, something I might not be able to put into words, something produced by my vivid imagination rather than anything Ian had done or felt. I closed my eyes and concentrated on tactile sensations.

The silky-rough surface of his tongue stroking mine.

The sweet slide of his fingers over my breast and down my ribs.

The hard strength of his hairy knees nudging my thighs.

"Open to me, love," he crooned, and I realized he wasn't the only one who'd closed himself off. I had brought my legs together, stiffening against what felt like an invasion. The mutual bond I imagined had melted away to reveal what we really were—two almost-strangers exchanging comfort and gratification with each other.

Ian slid a gentle hand down my arm in a soothing gesture. His body was poised above mine, the powerful arm that supported his weight trembling with restraint. "Let me love you."

I allowed my limbs to open, to loosen, to accept his weight. "Come inside me." I draped my arms around his shoulders and relaxed into the exquisite pressure of his body opening mine wide.

His arms shook as he kept his weight above me, but not on me. Sweat slicked his skin as he stopped short of impaling me with his full length. "Sweet Jaysus," he breathed, "you're tight. Am I hurting you?"

"God, no." I dug my fingers into his firm backside and pulled his hips to mine, taking joy in the fierce ache of having every inch of him inside me. "You feel like

Heaven."

He shifted, brought one knee higher until our bodies fused, seared by the heat of our passion. Then slowly, slowly, he withdrew until only the tip of his sex touched the opening of mine.

"Please, Ian." I clutched his buttocks, trying to drive him fully home again. "What are you waiting for?"

He resisted. "Let's take our time."

"Please." I dug my nails into his back. Every nerve ending sparked and sizzled and cried out for release. He pressed into me slowly, so slowly. I whimpered and pleaded for him to hurry, hurry, hurry. Please, God, I'm about to fly apart.

He teased, torturing me with his maddening restraint. He pulled out until all I could feel in the whole world was the broad tip of his penis opening the swollen flesh between my shaking legs. He kissed me, his lips teasing my mouth the way his body teased mine down below. "Tell me what you want."

"I want you inside me." I bit his lip. "I want it hard and fast."

And he gave it to me. Oh, God, did he give it to me.

I lifted my hips to meet his hard thrusts, pumping and pushing against him until sweat poured off us both and my animal-like whimpers joined his rasping breaths. I felt consumed, burned by passion, scraped raw by the unbearable friction that cracked me open, exposing me body and soul. An aching void inside me tightened like a hard fist clenching the distended nub he brushed against with every stroke.

Something desperate and frightened and unbearably vulnerable spiraled up inside me, warring with a physical ecstasy more intense than any I had ever known. I felt something within me reaching, reaching, almost but not quite touching the unattainable prize.

He slipped his fingers down between us and touched me... *there*... sparking an electric response that made me buck beneath him. I shoved his hand away, pumping my hips to recover the frenzied rhythm. I didn't want time to think about what would—or wouldn't—happen in this bed tonight, or outside of it tomorrow. I didn't want time for either of us to think.

"Slow down, love." He brushed my damp hair away from my face, his amber eyes turned deep chocolate in the dim light that filtered through the closed blinds. "Let me make you come first."

I held him tight, my arms like manacles around his back. I ground my hips against his and claimed his mouth with mine, sucking his tongue in an imitation of the heated rhythm we'd just abandoned. "I don't want it slow."

With a sigh that turned his bunched muscles fluid for an instant, Ian drove hard into me, his hips slamming against mine. He held himself still for one trembling instant. "If you want me to stop, you have to say—"

"Don't stop." I roamed my hands across the sweat-slick terrain of his back and shoulders. "Don't stop. Don't stop."

He planted both hands flat on the mattress beside me, and his flesh slapped against mine in a steady, driving beat. "God help me...." he groaned. His Scottish accent grew stronger by the word. "Ye're turning me inside-out."

"Come." I grabbed his butt and held on in case he got some crazy idea about pulling out. "Come now. Come as hard and fast as you can."

His muscles went rigid beneath my hands, his handsome features tightened into a grimace of fierce pleasure.

We struggled and strained with some elemental force that had us in its grip, shaking and shaking until we collapsed together on the damp twisted sheets. Ian shuddered, and I smoothed my hands down his back, feeling goosebumps erupt under my palm.

"Jaysus Christ." He turned his back, tossed the used condom into the wastebasket and grabbed an edge of the quilt we'd shoved into a rumpled heap on the floor. "If I live, I swear I'll ne'er again come before you do."

"It's okay." I put a soothing hand on his shoulder. "I wanted you to. It was good for me, even without—"

Ian hooked an arm around my waist, dragged me against him, and tossed the quilt over us both. "Good's not good enough."

"It was better than good." I backed up close to absorb a little of his heat. "It was amazing. It was—"

"Hush." Ian took the sting from the word with a soft love-bite at the nape of my neck. Spooning me into the curve of his body, he hugged me close. "You'll get yours in the morning, I promise. Now go to sleep."

I sighed, releasing every frustration, every care, every worry, along with any tension that dared to remain in my exhausted muscles. Surrounded by Ian's protective strength, I let go of all but the moment's bliss.

Chapter Ten

I KNEW THE INSTANT IAN WOKE. The hand that cupped my breast began a lazy caress, arousing the sleeping nipple then moving leisurely across my chest to give similar attention to the other side.

A thought drifted through my mind. *I think I love this man.*

Stupid, crazy thought.

His arm tightened around me and pulled me closer. His penis strained against the cleft of my buttocks. I wiggled backward, pressed more firmly against him, and was rewarded by a low groan and another hot kiss on the back of my neck. The barrier I'd sensed between us last night had melted away, as if by mutual consent our bodies had worked out any resistance between us while we slept.

Several times during the night I'd been aware of Ian's body sheltering mine, of him adjusting his position to accommodate the times when I shifted my own. Sometimes he kissed me or stroked my skin lightly.

Or maybe it was just a dream.

"I must have died during the night," he rumbled in a sleep-rough voice. "Because this has to be heaven."

"We might be in heaven," I murmured. "But I have no intention of behaving like an angel." I slid my hand along his firm buttocks to his hard thigh. The sense of being blanketed by him, enveloped in his strength, was the most delicious feeling in the world.

Or so I thought, until he made good on last night's promise. He rolled me onto my back and knelt above me, kissing one breast and caressing the other while his fingers slid inside me. Then he moved down, kissing all the way down, all the way down to….

Oh, my… Oh… His mouth, heated from sleep, felt like a furnace when his lips closed onto my….

Oh, my.

Moments ago I'd been resting in his arms, now I twisted and writhed, completely at his mercy. I cried out at the bombardment of sensations. My back arched, my knees came up as the incredible climax I knew was coming began to build.

My hands were free to caress him in return, but I was powerless to lift them. I clutched the sheet in one hand and the solid strength of his arm in the other. I gave myself up to his touch, his hands, his mouth, and let the powerful feeling come. He was giving, but I had to give as well, in order to receive his gift. Trust, I thought, maybe. Trust was what I had to give… then the feeling took over completely.

I whimpered, cried out…. Dimly, I heard the noises I made, but I didn't care. I surrendered all, and the climax shattered around me like a burst of stars until I fell back to earth, and the stars went out one by one.

"God, Ian… God." I tried to scoop together my scattered thoughts.

"No…" He smoothed the sweat-damp hair away from my face. "It's just me."

"My heart," I panted. "I think it's going to explode."
I took his hand in mine and placed it on my chest. He
spread his fingers against my skin and left them there.

Neither of us moved or spoke for a moment.

"I should go." He drew out the O in that Scottish way
I loved even though I hated what he had to say. "It's
almost dawn, and my car shouldn't be in front of your
house when people drive by on their way to work."

"I know. But, Ian... couldn't we..." I fumbled the words
and had to swallow and start over. "Could we go somewhere, together?" I took his hand and wrapped it around
mine, bringing it to my lips and pressing a kiss onto the
rough skin between his thumb and first finger. His hand
smelled like sex. It smelled like me. "I have the day off,
and I'm not ready for this to end."

"Well, I don't have the day off, but I'm willin' to take
it anyway." He glanced ruefully down at his still unsat-
isfied erection. "Because it would appear that I'm not
ready for this to end either." He bent gingerly to retrieve
his jeans from the floor. "Would you allow me to kidnap
you for the whole weekend?"

"You wouldn't mind?" I asked, beginning to feel a little self-conscious.

"I'd be honored." He scooped up my discarded sweats
and dropped them onto the bed. "Get your beautiful
naked body covered, so I can have a hope of getting my
jeans buttoned."

I started getting dressed. "What should I pack?"

"Nothing. Anything. Whatever you like." He pulled
up his jeans but didn't button them. "I'm taking you to
my house, so you can go naked all weekend if it suits
you."

I threw some things into a duffel bag. "I've got to fill
the food dispensers for Lizzie and Chester, then I'll be

ready to go."

"Doesn't Lizzie want to come too?"

At the sound of her name, Lizzie tipped into the bedroom and looked up at Ian, then at me. She had very sweetly elected to spend last night in her living room dog bed, and I wanted to reward her by letting her come along. At the same time, I didn't want to impose on Ian quite so soon in our relationship.

"She'll be okay here." I knew she'd be lonely, but she wouldn't lack for food or water and the dog door gave her freedom to spend her time indoors or outdoors as she pleased.

"She'll be okay at my house, too. We'll take her for a walk in the woods behind my house."

If I hadn't loved him before, I did now. The three of us loaded into his car just as an orange glow lit the eastern sky.

I slept late on Sunday, cradled in Ian's arms in the center of his massive four-poster bed. Lizzie slept on top of the silky soft comforter that was crumpled at our feet. A wash of cold air signaled Ian's departure, but I rolled over and snuggled back down until he tossed an armful of Sunday papers onto the comforter and climbed in beside me. He was sexily rumpled, his cheeks darkened by the night's growth of beard.

I turned toward him. "You read all those?" There had to be at least a dozen different newspapers there.

"Not in detail, no." He stacked a couple of pillows and leaned against the headboard, then unfolded the *Angel Falls Informer* and scanned the front page. "I like to compare our paper to others. See what we might do better. We could go with more of a magazine format, or—"

"I thought you said y'all were going digital. Online, I mean."

"Yes, but we won't stop the print version. We'll have both."

I scooted close, draped one leg over his midsection and laid my head on his chest. While he read, he sifted through my hair in an idle manner. I snuggled, adjusting my position until I felt the promise of subtle movement under my thigh, but after a moment he dropped a casual kiss on top of my head. "I know someone sent you to kill me. There's no use denying it."

I moved my thigh away from his vital organs. "Don't worry. I'm so sore I wouldn't dare instigate anything."

'Hmmph." As Ian rifled through the paper, I played with his chest hair. He placed a quelling hand over mine. "Sweetheart, you're driving me crazy. Why don't you read one of these? There are plenty to choose from."

I moved away and leaned over the edge of the bed to reach my duffel bag. Good thing I'd thought to bring a book. I was reading *Outlander* for the third time—Ian's Scottish accent had prompted me to take the book off my keeper shelf and get to know Jamie Fraser again. "I'll just read my book, thanks." I stacked my pillows as he'd done and leaned against the headboard on my side of the bed.

"You're welcome to read a newspaper," he said in a slightly puzzled tone. As if the news   could compete with Claire Beauchamp and Jamie Fraser.

"That's okay." I opened my book to the page I'd turned down. "I don't read the newspaper."

"You don't?" He said this as if I'd just declared I didn't believe in brushing my teeth. "Why not?"

"I just don't." I wasn't about to apologize. Lack of interest in current events is not a crime.

"You have to have a reason."

"I have a multitude of reasons, but I doubt you'd be interested in any of them." I wasn't reading my book, but I turned a page as if I was.

He folded the paper and crossed his arms over his chest. "Try me."

"Okay." I put my book aside, picked up his hand and turned it to the light. "Look at this. Your fingers are covered in newsprint. Doesn't that drive you insane?"

Frowning, he studied his hand. "I've never noticed it."

"Well, I do. I can't even touch newsprint without getting the shivers. That coarse paper all covered in ink."

"We use soy ink these days, completely safe and doesn't transfer like—"

"I don't care." I shuddered. "Touching that rough newsprint is worse than fingernails on a chalkboard."

"You're kidding." His tone was incredulous, exactly as I figured it would be.

I picked up a newspaper and slid my hand down a page, then held my arm up for his inspection. "See?" Every hair on my arm stood on end. "And besides that, newspapers never finish an article on the page it started. You always have to hunt for the rest of it."

"That's because—"

"Yeah, yeah. I know all that. But I still don't like it."

"Okay," he conceded. "I guess you watch the news on TV."

"I hardly ever watch television. I'll read a news article online every now and then, but I find them extremely frustrating. All headline and no meat. I end up with more questions than answers."

"How do you know what's going on in the world?"

He looked at me as if I were a strange breed of animal he hadn't encountered before.

"Unless it happens to you or somebody you know, the news is just another soap opera. Same shit, different names." I knew this was sacrilege to a newspaper editor, someone whose very life was based on relaying day-to-day happenings to the rest of the world.

So we were different. Maybe even opposite polarities coming together like magnets. I wasn't interested in resisting our differences. So I pushed the mound of newspapers aside and covered his mouth with mine.

Much later, I drank my coffee and wandered around Ian's house while he showered. Lizzie had been outside for her morning potty, but being in a new place, wasn't eager to leave my side. Her toenails made tipping sounds on the hardwood floors as she followed me from room to room.

The house was big, substantial, blocky, built of stucco-over-brick and oak timbers. In the enormous den, a grouping of leather furniture crouched before a stone fireplace. Crowded bookshelves hugged the room like welcoming arms. I could see myself living here. But he'd have to ditch a few of his moldy old leather-bound books—*Moby Dick, War and Peace, Crime and Punishment*—to make room for *Spy of the Knight* and *Border Lord* and *Outlander*.

With a guilty glance around to see if Ian was watching, as if my face would give away my thoughts word for word, I chastised myself for my mental leap from almost-casual sex to walking down the aisle. I had given myself to Ian, and the part of me that believed in fairy-tales wanted it to mean forever.

And this was a lot of house for one man—not at all suitable for a bachelor. Had Ian bought it with future plans for a family in mind? After everything we'd just done together, it shouldn't be hard to ask him, but I knew I wouldn't. Ruthlessly, I beat back my little-girl dreams of happily-ever-after. Maybe we would talk about the future sometime.

But not today.

I heaved a sigh, releasing my Cinderella fantasies like so much carbon dioxide. Back in the kitchen, I poured the dregs of my coffee into the chipped enamel sink and made a fresh cup. Bored with following me around, Lizzie turned circles before collapsing in a cubby space under a small built-in desk. Outside the window, a pair of cardinals flitted past, and two deer stepped into the yard. A young buck with a small set of antlers stood guard over a smaller doe as she nibbled gardenia leaves. The scene was so peaceful, so perfect, I sighed with contentment.

Ian, bigger than life and damp from his shower, put his arms around me from behind. "Planning on venison for dinner?"

I ignored his stupid comment and leaned my head back against his chest. He felt hard as a brick wall, safe and substantial. "I haven't thought about dinner. I'm wondering if the injuries you've inflicted on me are permanent. I'll definitely be walking funny for a while."

Ian laughed. "Lass, you're not the only one." He rocked me against him, his arms around my middle. "I hesitate to ask, but... aside from any physical trauma, are you okay about what happened between us this weekend?"

That depends on what happens next, my heart shouted. I wanted to know if there was any chance of this becoming a forever kind of thing. But I didn't want to scare him. I had tried to think of this as almost-casual sex, but I knew in my heart that sex could never be casual for me. The fact that I'd allowed him inside my body wasn't as damning as the fact that I'd let him into my heart.

"Casey?" Ian held his breath for a moment. I could feel his chest go still against my back.

I watched the birds take cover in the trees when the young buck picked his way to the concrete birdbath at the center of the large unfenced yard. "I guess you knew when you saw the dusty pink box in my bathroom closet, I don't tend toward weekend flings. So this is... new for me."

Ian took a deep breath and let it out. "I've told you about my wife." His arms tightened around my ribs, preventing me from turning toward him. "I'm afraid you'll want more than I'm capable of giving."

I watched the buck sip rainwater from the birdbath though he stayed on full alert, his eyes scanning the yard for predators. "Ian, what happened to Maeve was not your fault."

"I don't know what to tell you, Casey." He hugged me tight, the strength of his muscled arms so different from the wounded little boy I sensed inside him.

The earth-mother in me shoved Cinderella aside. I turned around and went on tiptoe to kiss his chin. "We don't have to figure anything out right this minute. Let's just take it easy and see where this goes."

"Christ." His voice was weary and low, the voice of a sinner at confession. "I meant to help you through your grief, and now I don't know what I'm doing. I might be hurting us both more than we've ever been hurt yet."

"I'm responsible for my own safety, and I'm not ready to run yet. At least for now, I'll take what you have to offer and be happy for it."

He released his breath in relief, and I knew I'd said the right thing.

Monday afternoon, I got to the studio early. I'd been trying out new choreography and was spread out on the classroom floor doing the splits and making notes in my choreography notebook.

Lizzie gave a short bark of recognition, and I looked up. Ben came in carrying Amy, her head lolling sleepily on his shoulder. She wore the red tights Melody had probably bought to go with her Christmas dress last year—I remembered them from the family Christmas card—and the same leotard she'd had on last week, now smeared in back with grass stains.

I closed my notebook and walked to them. Lizzie hopped down from her ottoman and sat in front of Ben, expecting her share of admiration.

"Amy's still sleepy." Ben leaned toward me, preparing to hand over his burden. "I didn't get her down for a nap early enough, I guess."

"That's okay." I held my arms out. Ben transferred Amy to me. She snuggled her face into my shoulder. I hugged her close, watching an elusive stream of emotions wash across Ben's face. He rubbed a hand down Amy's back, and we stood silent for a minute, connected like beads on a string.

He broke the connection by kneeling down to ruffle Lizzie's fur.

"How are y'all doing?" I asked.

He scratched Lizzie under her chin. "Better." He

looked up at me with his shy smile, chin tilted in the endearing, boyish way that had once tugged at my heartstrings. In a way that still made me feel swollen inside. "We'd like it if you'd come over and cook dinner for us again. Macaroni and cheese is wearing a bit thin."

Thanks to Ian, I had moved beyond thinking of the accident as my fault. Maybe I *was* meant to be with Melody on that fateful day, so she wouldn't have to die alone. Maybe I *was* meant to help Ben put his family back together again, just not in the way Melody had expected. "I guess I'll have to give you a recipe file for Christmas."

"Don't bother unless the recipes are simple." He stood, hands in pockets, and bumped his shoulder against mine the way he'd done a thousand times before. "No more than three ingredients. That's about all I can handle."

Something in me loosened, the tension defused by his familiar gesture. "You idiot."

"Oh... I almost forgot." He brought a hand out of his jeans pocket and opened his palm to reveal a bunch of hairpins and a rubber band—the thick purple kind that come on bunches of broccoli at the grocery store. "Here's the stuff for Amy's hair. So you can fix it. That's why I brought her early."

I grabbed a covered hair dooley off the stereo cabinet, carried Amy toward Lizzie's tuffet and motioned for Ben to sit. "Come here."

Ben sat, and Lizzie jumped up and curled herself around him. Ignoring Amy's sleepy protest, I lowered her feet to the floor, stood her in front of Ben, and handed him my hairbrush. "It's about time you learned to make a ponytail."

That night, I started reading *Sacred Contracts*, a book Melody had given me years ago but I'd set aside without reading past page twenty-five. At the time, I'd thought she was absolving herself, sending me the message that stealing Ben from me was part of some spiritual contract between the three of us. Now, reading further, I wasn't so sure.

The phone rang. Distracted by my thoughts, I picked it up, but only said, "hmmmm?"

"I need you." Ian's words sent a shivery little thrill through me. I set the book aside, along with the philosophical conundrums it presented.

"You do?" Huddled in my big reading chair, I picked polish off my toenails and held the phone against my shoulder. I pretended indifference, though my insides were swirling with anticipation. "Would it be foolish to ask what you need me for?"

He chuckled, a low, devilishly attractive sound. "Among other things, I'd like you to be my date for an awards banquet on Friday, in Birmingham. I'll book a hotel room for the weekend. If we leave early, we'll have time to change clothes," his voice lowered suggestively, "or something... before the banquet. Then we'll spend the rest of the weekend doing whatever we want in the big city."

"Oh, Ian." Fuck the indifferent tone. I couldn't wait to spend the weekend with him. "That sounds wonderful."

"It's not. At least not the banquet. But the rest of the time, I'll make it up to you."

"I can't wait."

"Now..." His voice got all sexy and deep, and I pictured him leaning back in his office chair, the lights turned down low. "Since I'm stuck here at work until Wilson finishes the print run, why don't you make me miserable. Tell me what you're wearing."

I looked down at my oversized mustard yellow T-shirt, holey and paint-smeared but soft and clean—one I wore to sleep in now that I'd ruined it for anything else. "Well, I have this red satin nightie with black spaghetti straps..."

On Friday, I was packed and ready by two. Angela had agreed to look out for Lizzie and Chester, and to let them come inside her apartment to visit if they seemed lonely. I'd brushed my hair, twice. I'd put on lipstick, again. My nails were done. My fanciest dress hung in a garment bag across the back of the couch. I was rummaging in the refrigerator in search of anxiety food when the phone rang.

"Casey."

Expecting Ian, I got Ben. My pattering heart tripped and fell. "What?"

"Thank God you're home. I'm stuck in a meeting with new clients in Gulf Shores. The meeting's almost over, but even if I left now, I couldn't get home to pick up the kids on time. I need you to get Jake and Maryann from school, and Amy from Marina's. You know Marina's mom—"

"Yes, I know Marina's mom. But I can't—"

"I need you to take them all home and hang out until I get there."

"Ben." I spat out his name like a bad piece of meat. "I'm going—"

"Casey," Ben begged, "I'm all out of options. Lois and Herb are out of town. I'd have called my parents in Birmingham, but by the time I realized I was in a bind, it was too late. You've got to. I promise, I—"

"Dammit, Ben." Exasperated to the bone, I pounded my fist on the back of the couch. "You can't do this to me."

"I wouldn't ask if there was any other way. I've got nobody else to call."

"What about Cole and Meredith? Couldn't they—"

"I asked. Meredith is on her way to a real estate seminar in New Orleans, and Cole's driving to Meridian to pick up some rich guy's horse."

"He's what? I thought Cole worked construction."

"He does, but he also trains horses on the side. Anyway, their kids are going on some long-weekend thing with Cole's parents. So I'm out of options. If you can't help me, my kids will be sitting on the sidewalk come three-o'clock."

"Okay, fine." My shoulders slumped in defeat. "I'll go get them."

"Thank you so—"

"But," I interrupted, "I am taking them to my house, not yours. And you had better be here to get them no later than four o'clock. Do you hear me?"

"Yes, Casey, yes. Thanks a bunch. Listen, I've got to go. I'll see you in a little while."

"No later than four o'clock," I yelled, but he'd already hung up.

"Well, hell." Feeling defeated, I hung up too.

Just in time to see Ian's car pull up out front.

I walked onto the porch and leaned against the rail, watching him get out of the car. Even such a simple act, he performed with the powerful grace of an athlete. From thirty feet away I could see muscles bunch and lengthen as he moved. My heart did flip-flops in my chest, trying to run toward him while I stood still.

He walked toward me smiling that sexy-as-hell smile of his. "You look so good. We may not make it any farther than your bedroom."

Not even that far. I put my hands on the broad muscles of his shoulders. "Is there any way we can hang around until about four o'clock?"

He grinned a grin that would put the devil to shame and slid his hands into the back pockets of my jeans. His long fingers cupped my butt cheeks and squeezed. "What did you have in mind?"

"Unfortunately, not what you think." I explained the circumstances and watched the charming grin fade from his face. He knew I often helped Ben out with the kids. But this was the first time my involvement with Ben's family had directly affected our plans.

"Ian, I'm so, so sorry." I found myself using Ben's words, though I knew they didn't sound any better to Ian than they had to me. "If there was any other way..."

"Yeah, okay." His voice was stiff. He turned away and stomped up the porch steps. "I understand."

But it was pretty clear he didn't. I followed him across the porch to the swing, rubbing his shoulders as I kept pace behind him. "I told Ben he had to pick the kids up no later than four. We can still make it in plenty of time, can't we?"

"Yeah, sure." Ian dropped into the porch swing. "Plenty of time."

"Hey, now." I sat beside him and scooted up against one of his wide-spread legs. "Ben called me, being pitiful to get his way. Don't you start, too."

Ian turned his lips down in an exaggerated pout, then allowed an unwilling smile. "All right. I'll try to be a big boy about it." He looked down at his watch. "Shouldn't you be on your way to get them?"

I took his wrist, turning the watch face toward me. "Not quite yet." I leaned against the swing's slatted back and cuddled up to Ian, just for a few minutes.

Chapter Eleven

BY FOUR THIRTY, I HAD emptied the contents of my refrigerator into the stomachs of Ben's offspring, and he still hadn't shown. His cell phone connected directly to the message center every time I called. By quarter-to-five, Ian was fuming. He stalked to the front door. "I have to leave now to have even a hope of getting there on time."

"I'm hungry," Amy whined. "I'm tired of eating this yucky old popcorn!"

"Amy, go watch TV." My voice rose in frustration and tears stung the backs of my eyes. "I will fix you something else in a minute." Even though I'd already emptied the fridge and started in on the pantry to satisfy the bottomless pits Ben had foisted on me.

"Ian." I put a hand on the taut muscle of his forearm. I could feel the tension vibrating through him. Noting the kids watching us from their spots in front of the television, I took Ian's hand and led him out onto the porch. "Please don't be mad."

He shook off my hand. "How am I supposed to feel?"

I crossed my arms in front of me. "You know I couldn't leave those kids sitting outside the school. Ben didn't have anybody else."

"You know, that's the problem." Ian's anger brought out his accent. "He doesna have anybody else, so you come runnin'. Have you ever thought if you didna come runnin' a time or two, he'd soon find somebody else?"

"Ian, that's not fair. I'm not just doing this for Ben. I love those children, and I'm doing it for them more than anybody."

"Aye," he said, his voice calming a fraction. "I know that. I do. But I think maybe you've forgotten, those children in there, much as you love them, are not your children. And they're not your responsibility. With them, just like with their father, you'll always be a substitute for the real thing."

Ouch. That hurt, but part of me accepted the truth in it. Another part fought back. "Ian, that's mean. Even if it's true, it's not okay to say it."

"It's not okay to point out a truth you seem blind to?"

"I'm only trying to help. I'm not—"

"I have to go." Ian started down the steps. "Just be careful you don't give so much of yourself to Ben and his children that you've nothing left to give to anyone else."

He drove away, and I stood on the porch for a full five minutes before going back into the house.

Ben finally showed up just before six o'clock. Madder than I've ever been in my life, I met him on the sidewalk. Car keys in one hand, overnight bag in the other, I shot him a look that made him take a step back. "Your children have been fed. Lock the door when you leave. I'm going to see if I can get Ian to forgive me for standing him up tonight."

"Who?" Ben shook his head as if he hadn't heard right. And maybe he hadn't heard at all, but I didn't care, and I didn't wait to discuss it. I left him standing where he was, got into my car and slammed the door.

I peeled away from the curb, slowing down only when I reached the first stop sign. I forced myself to stay under the speed limit until I'd navigated the narrow streets through town. Then I hit the long snake of Highway Eighty and floored it.

The speedometer bounced at the right edge of the display. The whole car rattled and shook. About ten miles outside of town, where fishing camps and trailers scattered along the river bank like tin cans thrown from a car window, the *Check Engine* light came on.

I slowed down a little. This had happened a few times before, but only in stop-and-go traffic when I drove up to Tuscaloosa or Birmingham, or down to Gulf Shores. I hadn't driven much since the accident, and then only for short stretches in town, so it hadn't been much of an issue.

Until today.

About fifteen miles out of town, near the River Road turnoff where teenagers and college kids congregated on weekends to party, the engine lurched. Smoke billowed from under the hood. Margot chugged forward, had a few little seizures and lost momentum. I was just able to make the turnoff and pull over into the weeds when the engine sputtered, gave a sad little hiccup and died.

I pulled out my cell phone. If I was lucky, Ian would answer his phone. I wasn't hoping he'd come and rescue me, but I wanted him to know I'd tried to catch up with him.

But he didn't answer. I left a stupid, rambling message that probably didn't make any sense, and the mailbox didn't give the option of a do-over. The automated voice said a cold good-bye and ended the call about halfway through my stumbling attempt to make things right.

I refused to cry.

I considered it, but in the end, anger won out. Anger at Ben, anger at my stupid, stupid, car, but most of all, anger at myself. I don't know why, because I still couldn't think of any way I might have done things differently. I mean, I could've said no, but then where would that have left Ben's kids, whom I loved too much to leave stranded? Maybe I should've said no. But I couldn't imagine doing it, even to teach Ben the lesson he needed to learn.

For my inability to be callous and ruthless enough to stand up for myself and what I wanted—what I needed—I was so angry with myself, my skin could hardly contain the rage.

I thought about calling my dad to come and get me, but neither he nor my mother liked driving at night, and it was already nearly dark.

I might have called Ben. After all, this mess was his fault, and he'd have been happy for a chance to right it. But right now, if I had to look at him, I'd kill him. Or at least, say something that would damage our friendship beyond repair. So I walked toward the river, toward the faint sound of car radios playing and teenage laughter tumbling through the air.

The skunky smell of burning marijuana reached me long before I spotted the group of cars parked near the deserted boat ramp. The headlights formed islands of light in a sea of darkness. I walked up to the car closest to me, where a handful of teenage boys stood, bopping absently to the sound of music coming from another car's ramped-up sound system. "Hey—"

"Holy shit!" The blunt they'd just lit flew into the bushes.

"We was just…" A tall, gangly youth who looked vaguely familiar moved into the shadows, his voice fading away even before he did.

The boy who'd just thrown probably ten dollars' worth of weed into the bushes stepped close enough to see me, then even closer so he could identify me. "I'm sorry... Miss Casey? The ballet teacher? What are you doing here?"

I didn't know any of these boys—well, either of them, because all but two had melted into the darkness to blend into other groups standing beside other cars—but odds were that some girl they knew took ballet, so they definitely knew me.

"What are you...?" The kid who'd thrown the blunt touched my arm. His wide eyes searched mine in the dim light thrown by the confluence of headlights where local fishermen parked boat trailers in the daylight. "Are you okay?"

"My car broke down. I need a ride home, if y'all don't mind. I'm sorry to interrupt your party."

"Oh, no ma'am. You didn't interrupt. It isn't really a party. We're just about to... um..." he looked around and noticed that his one remaining friend had also absconded. "I was just about to leave anyway. I'll be happy to take you home." He waved a hand toward his vehicle, a low-slung, beat-up convertible with racing stripes that glowed white in the darkness. "Hop in."

In the car, my newfound friend—who didn't seem stoned yet, so I felt safe getting into his car—introduced himself. Kyle Kelley—nephew of Ken Kelley the Kar-Wash-King, the over-confident entrepreneur I had declined to date. Kyle dropped me off at the curb in front of my house with a wave and a double-beep of his convertible's tinny-sounding little horn. I ran inside, fed Chester and Lizzie, then took a bath. I powdered-up and slipped-on the sexy red nightgown I had packed to wear tonight.

Because I didn't need Ian—or any man—to enjoy the feel of satin on my skin, did I?

No, of course not.

Smelling fine and dressed like God's gift to any man, I opened a bottle of wine and turned on the TV as the nightly news began. Not that I was planning to watch, because I wasn't. I don't watch TV. In particular, I don't watch the news. Especially not the nightly news. Especially when everything about it was disturbing. Especially when—

The phone rang.

Miffed over my lost weekend with Ian, depressed by the nightly news, I didn't plan to be Miss Mary Sunshine for anyone. I didn't check caller ID before I snatched up the receiver and snarled a curt, "Hello."

"Lass, I'm sorry. I was wrong to get my knickers in a twist. Forgive me?"

My anger dissolved. I was mad about what? I couldn't quite remember. "Oh, Ian, I'm sorry, too."

"I've decided not to stay in Birmingham. Do you want some company?"

My butterflies started fluttering. "Yes, please."

"I'm on my way, but it'll still take me a couple of hours."

"Be careful driving." I thought about that treacherous stretch of highway between him and me. "Take your time. I'll wait."

"Okay, love." His voice was a warm caress. "See you soon."

After an eternity, headlights projected a kaleidoscope of colors onto the living room wall, and I looked out to see Ian's car at the curb.

I ran to the bathroom, had a quick pee, washed hands, glossed lips, brushed hair, and made it to the door before he did. I tossed the hairbrush on the couch and opened the door before he could knock.

"Mmmm…" It was all either of us said, too occupied with kissing for conversation. It was cold outside, and his leather jacket chilled my fingers, but underneath the jacket, his body was warm. Ian turned the deadbolt and dropped his overnight bag with a thunk. He walked forward with me in his arms, until the backs of my knees touched the arm of the couch. We tumbled back, his hard, muscular body on top of mine.

Hallelujah, my body sang. Everything was right with my world now that he was here.

"Ow." He looked down, found the hairbrush and sent it clattering across the floor. "Thought I'd put my knee down on a hedgehog."

"How was the awards banquet?" I asked. "I'm so sorry I missed it."

He put a finger over my lips, shushing the apology. "Boring as hell." He scooched us around until I was on top of him. With his hands caressing the silky fabric covering my backside, he started to kiss me but pulled away before our lips touched. "Hey, where's your car? It's not out front."

"I left a voice message." I kissed him, since he hadn't quite managed to kiss me. "Didn't you get it?"

He shook his head. "Bad connection, too garbled to understand."

Thank God. "I had a little car trouble on my way to Birmingham.… I was going to try to catch up with you."

"You were." He trailed a finger along my cheek. "How sweet."

"I made it as far as River Road before Margot—my car—decided to give up the ghost. Smoke was pouring from the hood. I thought for a minute she'd catch on fire."

Ian snorted. "Probably be a good thing if she did. So what did you do? Did your father come and get you?"

"Nah. It was dark already, and he doesn't like to drive at night."

"Ben, then?" Ian asked, the caution in his voice cooling a little of the passion between us. His hands on my backside went still—a bad sign.

I hurried to correct his mistaken assumption. "I got a ride from a kid who was down by the river partying."

Ian stood, dumping me onto the couch. "You *what?*"

Uh-oh. I realized too late that I'd only made things worse. "You heard me, Ian Buchanan." I hoped to ward off the impending argument by going on the offensive. "And here I am, safe and sound. No harm done."

He jumped in with both feet, about how I was too trusting, irresponsible, taking unnecessary risks, all sorts of stuff. If I'd ever read the newspaper, I'd know that strangers couldn't be trusted, and even in small towns, teenage kids abducted women and yada yada. I stopped listening after that, but he yelled a bit more before he wound down enough for me to get a word in edgewise.

By this time, I knew he was right and I was wrong, but of course I still got back in his face, about how I was a grown woman who'd been getting along just fine all this time without him telling me what to do. Lizzie whined and pawed at my leg, sending worried looks between us. I got up and flounced out of the room with my slinky nightgown billowing out behind me. I turned off the bedroom light and climbed into bed to wait with my arms crossed over my chest.

Lizzie hopped up onto the bed and put her head down on her paws, looking out into the hallway. I heard Ian walking, his steps slow and measured on the wood floor outside my range of vision. I couldn't tell where he was, exactly.

Was he leaving?

No. He was coming down the hall. I let out the breath I'd been holding. I heard the bathroom door close, the sound of water running... And then the silhouette of his strong body blocked the bedroom doorway, his muscular shoulders and arms silvered in stark relief from the hall light.

I folded back the covers. "Come to bed."

He stopped beside the bed, and when he spoke, his voice came deep and serious. "Promise me you'll never to do anything like that again. Even in small towns, terrible things happen. Even in Angel Falls, there are bad people who do bad things. That was dangerous, and you know it."

"I'll try not to." I had the feeling my light tone wasn't doing any good. "Okay?"

Ian growled at my stubbornness, but got into bed anyway. "Tomorrow morning, I'll take a look at your car."

"Okay." I turned toward him.

"Your toes are like ice."

I stuck my feet between his legs. "Warm them up, then." I slid my hands around his ribs. "And my hands, too, while you're at it."

"Bossy lass," he complained, his voice gruff. "Come closer."

And I did.

In the morning, we swung past the fast-food drive-through for breakfast muffins and bitter coffee. I don't know why, but a canned energy drink didn't appeal to Ian, and it was the only thing left in the refrigerator. We were standing in front of my car before the sun had a chance to burn the dew off the grass. I stood back as

Ian lifted the hood and peered inside. He made a tsking sound, and I figured I was about to get fussed at.

"Casey." His voice was quiet, but I wasn't deceived. He looked over his shoulder at me. "When's the last time you looked under the hood of this car?"

Yep. I was right.

I sniffed, trying to dredge up a little Black Swan. "I never look under the hood of a car if I can help it."

"And I'm guessing you're about to explain to me why that is?"

I licked my lips and thought fast. "What good would it do? I wouldn't know what any of that stuff under there is supposed to look like anyway. How would I even know...?"

"Well, I'll bet you could figure this one out." He motioned me toward him with one grimy hand.

This was some sort of trick, I could tell. "I'd rather stay back here." My view of his jeans-clad backside and muscle-filled T-shirt was much better from this distance anyway.

"Get over here and look at this," he growled.

I eased forward, cradling my Styrofoam coffee cup as if it offered some protection. Then I peered down into the black and gray mass of metal and hoses under the hood of my car.

Ian stepped back, the long fingers of his grease-smeared hands spread on his lean hips. "You tell me what's wrong with this car."

"Um..." Feeling like a murder suspect about to receive a life sentence, I leaned forward and took a closer look. "That fan-thingy in front isn't supposed to be hanging by a wire?"

He clapped his hands once, really loud, and I jumped like I'd been shot. Not life sentence after all; death sentence by firing squad. "You win the prize. That 'fan-thingy' is what keeps your engine from overheating." His voice had an over-exaggerated patient tone that made me want to find the nearest hollow log and crawl into it. "And no, it is not supposed to be hanging by a wire."

Ian stared me down, his warm whiskey eyes colder than I'd ever seen them.

Boy, he could be scary when he wanted to be.

"This is a vintage car, Casey. You can't take its care and maintenance for granted. How long have you been driving it like this?"

I shrugged, staring down into my cooling coffee. Now was probably not the time to stand up to him. I should pick my battles, and this was one I couldn't win. "You mean, exactly?"

"How long has your car been overheating?"

"Only when I drive a long way in stop-and-go traffic," I said, oozing meekness.

"For how long?" he thundered.

"About... I don't know, a couple of months." More like four, but I wasn't going to tell him that.

Ian spun around to stare out through the trees. "Do you ever check the oil? The water? Anythin'?" His back was to me, his Scottishness rising, his voice just barely under control.

"Sometimes my daddy checks it for me."

Ian looked heavenward but didn't say anything. He walked to his car, opened the trunk, took out an old rag and wiped his hands.

"We're going to the auto parts store." He slammed the hood and checked that the doors were locked. "This may take a while."

"Come on, girls, get up." I clapped my hands to perk up my advanced students. "I know it's Monday, and I'm ready to go home, too. But give me a break. If you take too long getting your pointe shoes on, your muscles will get cold."

They hustled to finish taping blisters and wrapping toes in wool batting or gel pads before shoving them into the torture box. "Victoria, if you put one more bandage on your toes, they won't fit inside your shoe. Enough, already!"

"But my toes hurt." She wiggled her toes at me and whimpered. "The blister on my baby toe is bleeding already, and we haven't even done anything on pointe yet."

"They'll get numb once we get going." I turned toward the stereo. "Let's do a quickie at the barre and then we'll go right on to the center combination we did last week."

Quiet giggles erupted behind me, and someone said "whoo-eee" under her breath.

I turned to see Ian leaning in the doorway, his arms crossed over his chest. He wore those button-fly jeans that made me want to jump his bones, an ink-stained tee ripped at one shoulder, and a lopsided little grin that made it impossible for me to look away.

But I did it anyway. "Keely, please get the music going—the third selection, for *tendu* and *degage*." I gave quick directions for the combination. "Facing the barre, you'll do *echappe, echappe, releve, sauté*. If you're up to it, substitute *entre-chat-quatre* for the *sauté*. After four repetitions, follow with the *coupe, sauté, coupe, sauté, pas-de-bourre over, pas-de-bourre under* combination we did last week. Got it?"

"Got it," they replied in unison. Keely started the music, and I could hear the familiar thump-swish sounds of the class going through the combination. I walked toward Ian and tried not to seem overjoyed to see him.

He leaned close and whispered in my ear. "I'd like to do a quickie at the barre..."

Heat spread up from my chest to consume my face, but even in my embarrassment I could appreciate the way his eyes crinkled at the corners when he smiled.

"Come to dinner with me tonight." I could smell the tantalizing spice of his skin, feel the heat of his body reaching out to mine.

I looked at the clock above the mirror, noting my students' reflections as they executed the simple pointe warm-up.

"I have another half-hour of class." Less than twenty minutes, really, but it would take time for the girls to get their things together.

"I'll wait."

"I'm not dressed for dinner."

"I'll take you and Lizzie home and wait while you get dressed. Better yet, I'll take you both to my house and cook steaks on the grill."

"I have to take a shower." The music ended and my students eyed us with interest.

"I'll wash your back," Ian offered, enjoying my discomfort at having such a personal conversation while my students watched. The fact that they couldn't hear a word didn't matter.

I scowled at him but I didn't mean it. "Stand here quietly if you're going to wait inside the studio. Don't distract my girls." And most especially, don't distract me.

After another warm-up at the barre, I called the girls

to the corner of the room. "*Piques* from the corner, three *en-dehors*, *pirouette*, followed by one *pique en dedans*, ending in *sauté arabesque* then a deep *plie,* holding the *arabesque* for a beat. Then move out of the way quickly so you don't get bowled over by the person coming up behind you."

Once they got going, four girls spun in a diagonal line from left to right, another four from right to left, creating a giant, motion-filled X. I looked over at Ian to see how impressed he was at my teaching finesse. But he wasn't looking at the dancers as they executed the complicated pattern.

He was looking at me, his eyelids lowered in a way that could only be described as sultry. Our eyes met, and I was sucked in, mired in the quicksand of his sex appeal. Not that I minded. Struggling against it didn't seem to be an option anyway.

"Miss Casey..."

I jumped. The music had moved on to the next selection and my students waited for me to tell them what to do next. "Everyone spread out behind me. We'll mark the step first. Starting right foot front, *croise. Coupe chasse pas de bourre* under...."

I danced every step along with my students without looking at Ian. At the end of class, we rose from the deep curtseys of reverence and clapped the traditional applause for a class well-danced. Each student came to me after class for a hug and a lemon drop from the candy jar I kept on the stereo cabinet.

The last girl in line hugged me and whispered in my ear. "Ooohhh, Miss Casey..." drawing out my name in the sing-song way girls use when teasing a friend. Then she licked her index finger and touched it to my shoulder, making a "tssss," sound like steam hissing on a hot skillet. I knew what she meant, and she was right. Ian was hot, and I was obviously hot for him.

"Don't you have homework?" I whispered.

She sent me a sly wink. "I'm going. You'll have him to yourself in just a minute."

"He's just a friend."

"Try harder, then," she suggested quietly. "I think you could hook him."

I herded her out the door after her classmates. "I'll see you next week."

"Love you, too, Miss Casey." She giggled, brushing against Ian on her way out.

"You didn't have to come up all these stairs to ask me to dinner," I told Ian as I locked the studio door behind us. "The phone works, you know."

"I wanted to watch you dance."

We started down the stairs. "What did you think of my girls?"

"I wasn't looking at them. I was looking at you."

"Did you draw any conclusions from your observations?"

At the bottom of the stairs, he pressed me against the brick wall. Lizzie settled down at our feet to wait. "Several." He kissed me, right there on the sidewalk in front of the newspaper office. "Would you like to hear them?"

"Ummm..." was as close as I could come to an answer.

"I concluded..." he spread a hand against my back in an exploratory way, "that you aren't wearing a bra." He ground his hips against mine. "Shall I tell you what that did to me?"

"I think..." I wet my lips with my tongue and saw his gaze drop from my eyes to my mouth. "I think I can tell."

"Did you know that your nipples stand out like little

raspberries when you do those big jumps?" He brought a hand up to touch my breast.

"*Jetes.*" I leaned into his hand.

He brushed a thumb lightly across my nipple, and my knees trembled.

I tried to find a coherent thought in the mush my brain was turning into. "You said something about dinner?"

"I did." He snapped his fingers to rouse Lizzie from her doze at our feet. She hopped into the back seat of his car as if she'd done it a thousand times, and I settled into the passenger seat.

I could get used to this. Leaving work together every evening, going home together.

The moon hung low, a glowing silver cradle suspended just above the road. A tender anticipation began to build in my stomach.

"Put in a CD?" Ian turned on the interior light and passed a leather case to me.

Flipping through the case, I noticed many of my favorites, but saw a few I'd never heard of before. I held one up. "Ry Cooder, *Bop Till You Drop.* Is it good?"

"Yes." He turned off the light. "You'll like it."

After a while, Ian slowed the car, then turned onto the gravel drive that was almost hidden by a wall of trees. Lizzie sat up in the back seat, ears pricked. Ian stopped on the circular drive in front of his house, ignoring a separate three-car garage that sat at a slight angle to the house. He got out, opening Lizzie's door first. "Come on, girl, we're home."

Lizzie hopped out of the car and followed Ian around to the passenger side, doing the helicopter-wag with her short little tail. Ian opened my door, extending his hand but saying nothing. I put my hand into his, feeling light enough to float away.

Inside the house, Ian gave me a little nudge in the direction of the master suite. "Go take your bath. I'll feed Lizzie and get dinner started, then come in to wash your back."

I didn't bother to ask about clothes. I knew that wouldn't be an issue for a while.

Chapter Twelve

IAN BROUGHT LIZZIE AND ME home on his way to work the next morning. I muted both phones and went straight to bed, wearing sweats and a T-shirt of Ian's. I might give the sweats back next time I saw him—they were hilariously big on me—but the shirt was comfy, soft from many washings, and it smelled like him. It was mine now.

I woke hours later, still carrying the sense of completion I'd brought home with me. With Ian's clothes keeping me warm, I started the coffee maker and checked my phone messages.

"Casey." It was Ben. There was a pause, then a sound of exasperation in the background. "Call me when you get this message."

I dialed his cell first, then the house.

"Hello." He sounded harried.

"It's Casey."

"Where have you been? Don't you ever take your cell phone with you? Never mind. Look. I need you to keep the kids. I'm going out of town for a few days. I'll be back Friday or Saturday."

"Ben, I'll be teaching. I can't—"

"Lois and Herb can help. They just can't do everything. Lois is having trouble with her blood pressure, and you know how Herb is."

No, I didn't know how Herb was. I had no idea how Herb was. "I guess if you bring them over—"

"Casey, can't you keep them at our house? They could stay in their own rooms…"

I could see the sense in that. "Okay, fine. When are you leaving?"

"I'm late already. My flight leaves out of Pensacola in three hours. Lois can get the kids from school if you'll pick them up and take them home when you're through teaching every evening. Can you do that?"

"Yes." Because I still don't get the difference between something I can do, and something I should do. "I can."

"You know where Melody always hid the house key." A statement, not a question. "Go ahead and make yourself a copy when you go shopping. I stuck some grocery money under a magnet on the fridge. But in case that's not enough, take Mel's debit card. It's in my desk drawer, all the way at the back under some papers. The PIN number is 0981."

"Okay, Ben." I was being a doormat, an easily manipulated doormat. I knew it, but I couldn't stop myself from caving in. My good mood had suddenly gone flat. Its deflated husk sprawled inside me, mocking my good intentions, my inability to say no, my stupid need to be seen as a nice person.

Was there a twelve-step program for people like me? Hi, I'm Casey Alexander, and I'm an approval whore. I'll watch your kids, wash your car, water your plants when you're out of town. The only thing I won't do is say no. Because apparently, I don't know how.

After a full day of teaching, I slumped down the studio stairs with Lizzie leading the way. She looked back at me, grinning, trying to get me in the mood for the walk home. I knew she wanted to bark hello to the lonely Pit Bull behind the chain-link fence of the red-brick ranch-style house, then pee on the crimson Mums by Mrs. Mercer's sidewalk, and maybe catch a cricket, or at least try to, if one happened to hop by instead of just teasing with their siren song.

I just wanted to go home, run a hot bath, and read a good book.

We stepped onto the sidewalk, and a tapping sound caught my attention. Ian stood at his office window—the one next to the front lobby—tapping his keys against the glass. When he noticed me noticing him, he motioned for me to wait.

A second later, he opened the office door.

"Lizzie." I put my hand out. "Stay."

"She can come in." Ian kissed me and invited Lizzie in with a snap of his fingers. "It's my newspaper. I can let a horse in here if I want to."

We followed him into his office. He sat in a tall-backed leather chair on rollers, and held his arms out. "Come sit. Just for a minute. Then I have to get back to work." His computer screen showed a document marked with red lines and comment boxes.

I sat in his lap and wrapped my arms around his neck. "I had a good time last night."

His arms tightened briefly around me. "Me, too. I could get used to having you around."

Shit. That reminded me. "I won't be home for a few

days."

"Oh?" He leaned back so we could see each other. Eyebrows lifted, he waited.

"I'll be keeping Melody's—I mean, Ben's—kids while he's away on business. I'll be staying at their house."

"Ahh." His face was thoughtful, but the expression wasn't very revealing. I thought he might say more, but he kept quiet. He brought his hand from its resting place on my knees, and touched my chin lightly with his index finger. He trailed that finger down my neck, over my collarbone. He lowered his lashes and dipped his head for a kiss. Soft at first, his lips on mine, then insistent, his tongue sleeking over my teeth and inside my mouth.

If this was an attempt to make me regret my decision to keep Ben's kids, it was successful. I touched his cheek, feeling the rasp of his beard coming in now that the day was almost over. "I'll miss you."

"You'll have your days free, with the kids at school? We could have lunch..." His hand roamed, caressing in a long sweep from knee to thigh before cradling my butt.

"Amy gets out of preschool at noon."

Lizzie gave a short, sharp bark. I reached up to thread my fingers through the short soft waves of Ian's dark hair. "Lizzie has been in the studio all day. She's probably desperate to find a patch of grass."

Ian gave my bottom an affectionate squeeze. "Go. Text me when you're home safe."

A quick check of Ben's fridge and pantry confirmed my fears—I'd have to do grocery shopping tonight, rather than waiting till tomorrow. I called Lois first, to make sure they weren't in a hurry for me to get the kids, then went shopping.

An hour later, with Lizzie waiting in the front seat and ice cream melting in the back, I ran into Lois's house. The entry hall looked as if it had been hit by a tornado. Correction—the twister was still whirling; backpacks, coats, shoes, and accusations being tossed in all directions.

"Grandma." Jake's voice was the high-pitched whine of an F-5. "I told you I had to bring five different kinds of moss to school tomorrow! Now, it's too dark."

"You should have reminded me, Jake." Lois's poodle-permed hair looked as frazzled as she sounded. "You could have gone on your bike to the canal after school. Amy, where is your red sweater?"

Maryann and Amy both stood silent, holding each other up in the storm, as far away as possible without actually leaving the room. Amy stuck her thumb in her mouth. Maryann handed the sweater over to Lois.

I started picking up backpacks. "Maryann, please help Amy put on her shoes. Jake, I have some Sphagnum moss at home. We can pick it up in the morning on the way to school. And there's Spanish moss in the trees by the Methodist church. We can get that in the morning, too."

"That's only two," Jake moaned. "And it's a test grade."

"When did your teacher give this assignment? I can't believe she'd only give you one day to complete something that counts as a test."

"Two weeks ago, but Daddy didn't have time to take me."

Lois made a sound of frustration. "Well, why didn't just you go to the canal by yourself?" She flung up her hands, flapping Amy's red sweater. "There must be a hundred kinds of moss down there."

"Melody wouldn't have allowed it," I told Lois.

The canal wasn't anything like you'd expect, certainly not a slow-moving waterway filled with picturesque boats. It was a twenty-foot-deep by twenty-foot-wide runoff trench carved into the town's limestone foundation. Sometimes it was nearly empty, a truant's playground of algae-slick tadpole pools and assorted wildlife. Other times, it was full to the brim with a torrent of brown water hurling itself mindlessly toward the river.

Melody and I grew up exploring it, as had all the other kids our age. But these days, parents were more careful, and for good reason.

"Well," Lois huffed, stuffing Amy's arms into the sweater. "That's the silliest thing I've ever heard. You girls went there by yourselves all the time."

"Yes, ma'am, we did." And we were lucky we didn't drown or get snake-bit.

I looked around the foyer. The storm had swept past, and the kids had most of their stuff together. "Jake." I handed over his backpack. "We'll figure out what to do about your assignment in the morning."

Two hours later, with bedtime rituals observed and kids tucked into bed, I went to bed myself, feeling as if I'd been nibbled to death by ducks. Lizzie stretched out on the floor and groaned. I had invited her to sleep in the bed, but she had been more interested in prowling the house and checking that all the doors stayed locked.

"Are you here, Melody?" I whispered, my voice sounding strange in the quiet. "Are you here?"

A long time later I fell asleep, still wondering.

In my dream, I was floating in a warm, clear pool. One of many hot-tub-sized limestone holes carved into the canal floor, slicked green with algae, full of rainwater and tadpoles. Overhanging roots tangled at the edges of the canal's rim, high above. Tall trees leaned toward each other, arching into a lacy canopy overhead. Dappled sunlight filtered through the shifting leaves.

Ian was there, the perfect silhouette of his body outlined in light as he stepped into the pool. Our limbs entwined, arms sliding around ribs, legs tangling together. We kissed...

"Casey." Ben stood above us, holding out his hand. "I need you."

Reluctantly I lifted my hand to his, and suddenly I was standing beside Ben in the cold air. A cold wind raised goose bumps on my skin.

I reached for Ian, but something held me back.

"Casey!" Jake's panicked voice penetrated the dream and woke me with a start. I ran to his room and found him hunched over, sitting on the edge of his bed.

"What's wrong?" I turned on the bedside lamp. He looked miserable, but not frightened or sick. "Did you have a bad dream?"

He shook his head no.

"What, then?" I sat next to him.

"I don't know." His voice was barely audible. "I woke up, and my bed is wet."

"Oh, baby," I said sympathetically. I immediately regretted my choice of words when he stiffened and pulled away. "Jake, you know I didn't mean that like it sounded." I put an arm around him and realized that his shoulders were higher than mine. When had this child grown taller than me? Never mind. Take care of business. "Did you change clothes?"

He jerked his chin toward the tangled heap of pajamas on the floor.

"It's not a big deal. Get clean sheets from the linen closet." He went to the hall closet and I pulled the wet sheets off the bed. They weren't very wet... In fact, I realized, there was only a small spot.... Not a soaked spot, but a smear of something kind of thick and shiny.

Then it hit me. Jake hadn't wet the bed. That wet spot wasn't urine. It was something else entirely.

I stripped the sheets, took them and Jake's discarded clothes into the laundry, stuffed it all into the washer, got it running, washed my hands. Finished, I raised my eyes to the white ceiling. *Melody, help me.*

Jake waited in his room with clean sheets, and we worked together to remake the bed. When we'd finished, I still didn't know what to say. I'd just have to wing it. I sat beside him and looked into his brown eyes that were so much like his mother's my throat almost closed up. "Jake, you didn't wet the bed."

"I didn't think so, but—" His voice cracked then trailed away.

"Has anybody ever talked to you about... about..." Get a grip, I told myself. Be blunt. Weaving around the subject will only make it worse. "Jake, have you heard about boys having wet dreams?"

Understanding flared in his eyes. "I think so." He still seemed embarrassed but relieved he hadn't wet the bed like a baby.

"Do you want to talk about it? Or do you want to wait for your dad to get home and talk with him?"

"I'll wait." The faintest glimmer of a smile faded almost before I saw it.

"Just so you know, what happened to you is perfectly normal. It may happen again. But it's no big deal. Just part of growing up."

"Yeah. Okay."

"Get under the covers and sleep fast. Morning comes earlier than usual, since we have to find a bunch of moss before school." I'd thought of several places we could go without venturing into the canal, but it would still take a while to drive to them all and gather specimens. I turned out the bedside lamp. "See you in the morning."

"G'night, Casey. Thanks."

I had just begun to relax into sleep again when a small hand touched my face. "Can I sleep with you? It's dark in my room."

"Sure, Amy." I pulled back the covers. "Come on. I'll snuggle you up."

It felt so right, holding her little body close to mine, absorbing her warmth and giving her a little of my own.

But if this was so right, why wasn't I happier about doing it?

Tuesday, Wednesday, Thursday, flew by. Not like an orderly arrow of ducks across the sky. More like a murmuration of Starlings going first one way, then the other, then in five different directions at once. Time seems to do that when you're over-committed and three steps behind.

Between my teaching schedule and taking care of the kids, getting them where they needed to be when they needed to be there, struggling through math homework Jake didn't understand and I didn't remember how to do, I woke up exhausted on Friday. Exhausted, but humming the Hallelujah Chorus because I knew Ben would be home the next day, and I'd be able to pass the torch back to him.

One day from freedom, I sat at Melody's kitchen table, sipping coffee and petting Lizzie with my slippered foot. The kids still dreamed in their beds, but in another fifteen minutes, I'd wake them up and help them get ready for school. Soon, I'd be free again, free to get back to my quiet life with a new appreciation of what it was like to be a parent.

Never again would I judge any of my ballet moms for being late, for forgetting to pay their kid's tuition, for not coming to meetings, or not reading the notes I sent.

Being a parent was hard, when it wasn't fucking impossible. Now, I knew first-hand about the day-in-day-out chores. The morning rush of getting everyone ready for school. The pride of watching the kids you loved and resented and felt inadequate to help as they shouldered backpacks and walked into school without a backward glance.

They're growing up so fast, Mel. In just these few weeks, they've grown so much. I wish you could see them.

I thought again of Melody's last request. This was exactly what she wanted me to do. Be here in her place. She couldn't be part of her children's lives anymore, but I could.

Did I owe it to her to experience the things she could never know again?

The sweet warm weight of Amy climbing into my lap in the morning.

The emerging beauty and grace and wisdom of Maryann.

The strength and resilience and stubborn hardheadedness of Jake.

They were all growing up so fast, extra-fast because Melody wasn't there. Did I owe it to them to soften the effect of her absence by being there myself? I didn't have time to wonder, because Jake stomped into the kitchen. "My phone is dead! It's been plugged in all night, but my charger isn't working. I told Dad to get me a new one, but he—"

Maryann was right behind him, drowning out Jake's complaints with her own. "The dryer cut off before my jeans got dry. Now what am I going to do? I'll be late, and—"

I was still trying to figure out whether my semi-clean jeans would fit Maryann when Amy screamed from her room. "Casey, I wet the bed!"

I slugged back my coffee, bundled peed-on sheets into the washer, handed out pop-tarts and herded everybody into the car. My jeans did fit Maryann, though not to her liking. I was still wearing pajamas and flip-flops, but at this point, I'd have considered going out naked.

Lizzie, wisely, declined to partake in the proceedings. She crept into the living room, leapt onto the couch and burrowed under the 1970s multicolored afghan Mel's mom had knitted a hundred years ago. Needing a cocktail before my morning caffeine had kicked in, I dropped Ben's kids off at school.

Then I did a happy dance, because Ben would be home tomorrow.

At three o'clock that afternoon, sitting in the pickup lane of the junior-high school with Amy dozing in her car seat and Lizzie waiting at Ben's house, I realized I'd started happy-dancing too soon when Jake stalked toward my car with a furious scowl. "Where were you?"

Maryann got into the back seat and tried to calm Jake with a hand on his shoulder. "Casey's not late."

He sent a daggered glare my way.

Here we go again. I entered the slow crawl of traffic

heading away from the school. I didn't want to ask, but I did anyway. "What's the matter?"

"Everything you told me on the math homework was wrong. I had to sit out recess and do it over again. Me and all the dummies."

"Oh, honey. I'm sorry." I'd never been a whiz at math.

"Mom would have been able to figure it out."

"Jake, hush." Maryann put her hand on his shoulder again. "Casey, he didn't mean it."

Jake slapped her hand away. "Yes, I did."

Amy started crying, roused from a light doze by Jake's loud voice. "Stop yelling, you're waking me up."

"Shut up, Jake!" Maryann started howling, too.

"Come up here and make me," Jake yelled. "Or sit back there and cry like the baby you are."

"Jake," I threatened, "Do I need to pull over and deal with you?"

"Do what you want," he replied in a voice full of loathing, as if I'd deliberately sabotaged his entire school career. "I don't care. You're not my mother."

I decided to take the path of no resistance and drove the rest of the way to Ben's without responding. Jake simmered with fury while both girls sat in the back seat and wailed. Their distress fed on itself until it reached epic proportions. He got madder, they cried louder, and I hunched over the steering wheel and drove. I pulled into the driveway ready to scream.

Ian's black car was parked in the drive.

I'd never been so glad to see anything in my life.

My desperation melted away at the sight of him getting out of his car, leaving in its place a quiet sense of rightness. He looked like a fallen angel, dressed all in black. A sexy-as-hell smile tilted up the corners of his mouth.

I parked next to Ian. Jake slammed out of the car and

threw his backpack down on the driveway. Maryann gathered her things, tears pouring down her cheeks. I took Amy out of her car seat, set her on her feet, and reached in to get the stuffed Benjamin Bunny that had fallen to the floor. Jake stormed up and snatched Benjamin, the car keys, and Amy's hand. "Come on, Amy. I'll take you inside."

Maryann slumped behind them, dragging her sweater on the ground. I stood alone with Ian in the drive feeling as if I'd just been mauled by a pack of hyenas.

He opened his arms to me and I slid my hands around his hard middle under his open leather jacket.

"Having a bad day?" Ian tightened his arms around me.

"I don't know what happened," I whined. "They all just exploded at once."

"Ahhh," he said, as if that explained everything.

"God, you smell so good." I pressed my face into his shoulder. "I've missed you so much."

"Mmmm." He laid his cheek against the top of my head. "I've missed you, too. When can I take you away from here?"

"Tomorrow sometime. Depends on what flight Ben can get. I wish he'd get the knack of planning ahead."

Wisely, Ian didn't respond to my whining complaint. "Call me when you get home." Ian tipped my chin up with a finger and kissed me, a long, lingering kiss that reminded me exactly what I was missing. "Save the rest of your weekend for me?"

"Mmmm." I kissed him, letting him know that I'd follow him home now, if I could. "I can hardly wait."

"Aunt Casey!" Maryann stood at the front door. "The computer's not doing right. I turned it on, but the screen won't do anything."

"I'll be there in a minute." I held Ian close one more time, inhaling one more infusion of his comfort and strength before heading inside.

"Do you need my help?" Ian offered.

I was on the verge of saying yes when Amy bolted onto the front porch, wrestling with the snap front of her jeans. "Casey! I have to potty! Hurry!"

Ian held his hands up in surrender, clearly deciding this kind of trouble was out of his league. He chuckled and turned me toward the front door, giving my behind a pat to get me going. "Have fun."

Chapter Thirteen

I WOKE SATURDAY MORNING WITH AMY'S arms and legs flung over me like a starfish on a rock. Sun shone through the bedroom window even though a steady rainfall pattered on the roof. The rich, chocolatey aroma of coffee called out to me. Easing myself out from under Amy, I padded into the kitchen. Ben stood at the counter, pouring coffee into a mug. Gilded by the rain-diffused light coming through the window over the sink, he belonged in a Maxfield Parrish painting.

After all these years, he still looked like the man I'd once fallen in love with.

It was I who had changed, and I wondered how much.

Lizzie sat at Ben's feet, her expectant gaze turned toward him. She pawed at his jeans-clad leg.

"Yeah, yeah, dog. I see you." He tore a chunk off the bagel he was eating and handed it to her.

I waited for the familiar feeling of guilty, reluctant attraction to grab me, but it didn't. Instead, and maybe even more disturbing, my heart felt like it had been filled with warm honey. I realized, with a flash of intuition, how Melody must have felt every time Ben came home from a business trip.

As if she somehow stood here, inside my body, showing me what I could have if I wanted, I felt my heart expand with the comfort and security of a deep, abiding love that had endured years of changes and come back stronger with each one. "Ben, you're back. When—"

"I got a late flight." His voice was gravelly from lack of sleep. "Got back around three in the morning. Slept on the couch."

Lizzie looked around at me and I scowled at her, stalling for time while I tried to absorb my strange shift in emotion. "Some watch dog you are."

She grinned at me briefly, then waggled her little stub tail and returned her attention to Ben. *I love you, but he has bagels.*

Too bad life isn't as simple for people.

Ben patted Lizzie on the head and gave her the last bite of his bagel. "She knows her people, don't you, girl?" He glanced over at me, looking almost the same as he'd looked when we were in high school. Taller, more muscular, but with the same handsome face I'd once loved. I could easily see how it might have been if I'd taken the other path, if I'd made the choice to stay in Angel Falls with Ben.

I knew, without a doubt, that I could pick up the thread I'd dropped and move on as if the missing chunk in the middle had never happened. Was that what I wanted? I didn't think so, not anymore. But Melody's voice whispered in my ear—this was a sure thing, while my infatuation with Ian could still go either way. As could his infatuation with me.

"Here's your coffee." Ben handed me a cup already doctored with milk and sugar, exactly the way I liked it. "Do you want a bagel?"

I shook my head and took a sip of coffee, still stuck in

a weird déjà vu twilight zone in which suddenly I had changed places with my doppelganger and begun living the life I'd left behind at that last, major crossroads.

Was my doppelganger now in New York, rehearsing for the next performance?

Ben sat at the kitchen table, unfolded the newspaper and shook it open to the front page. "How did things go?"

I pulled myself from the strange fantasy playing itself out in my head. "Interesting."

"Oh?" He turned down the edge of the paper to look at me, and raised one eyebrow in that way that hinted at a bit of devil hidden behind his angel face. His blue eyes sparkled in the watery light that poured through the window. "Tell me."

"Everything was fine, really." I moved to sit across from him. I felt comfortable with him, as if we'd been living together for the last twelve years. I took another sip of coffee, and looked out the kitchen window at the now-vacant bird feeder Melody had hung on the dogwood tree. Something real to anchor me in the here and now.

Ben shot an inquiring look over the top of the newspaper. "And?"

"Amy was wonderful, as always. Maryann has been wonderful, too. She's been helping out with the housework and the laundry, and getting Amy ready for preschool in the mornings." I paused, when I should have kept going. "Jake..."

"Was not wonderful," Ben supplied.

I regretted that pause. "He's having a hard time."

Ben made a sound of agreement. "Tell me about it."

"We had an incident you'll need to discuss with him."

"What did he do?" Ben and I knew each other so well,

I read all the unsaid things into those four words: I know he's a handful, I'm sorry you had to deal with him, I'll punish him and make him apologize.

"No, it's nothing like that." I hurried to correct Ben's impression. "He had a wet dream. He thought he'd wet the bed. I had to explain—sort of, anyway—that it was normal for boys his age." I waved my hand to close the subject. "You'll have to *really* explain it to him. I don't think I did so well."

Ben laughed, reaching out to cover my hand with his. "Poor thing."

"Yes, he was mortified."

"No. I meant poor you, having to deal with that."

"It was okay." It seemed that Ben and I had slipped right back into our old souls-bared way of speaking about anything without embarrassment.

Ben laughed. "Thank God it was you instead of Lois with the kids last night. I don't even want to think about how she'd have handled the situation."

Again, warm honey trickled into my heart. I guess I would always love Ben, one way or another. I shrugged. "We did okay."

"I can't thank you enough. But I could at least take you to dinner tonight. I'm sure Lois would keep the kids."

"Oh, Ben. That's sweet, but I can't."

"You can't?" Ben folded the paper down and peered at me. It must have been something in my voice. "What's up?"

"I, um... I have a date."

"Oh." He was clearly surprised I had a date. "We'll go Sunday, then."

"A weekend date," I clarified.

Ben's mouth dropped open. "You... have..." he enunciated slowly, "a weekend date. As in all weekend long, nights included. You're kidding."

I sat up, bristling. "Now why would you think no one would ask me on a weekend date?"

"That's not it." He put a hand on my shoulder. "I mean, it's just not like you, that's all. I didn't even know you were dating anyone, unless—"

"Well, I guess I am. You remember that time you were late and—"

Ben dropped all pretense of reading the paper. He folded it and put it back on the table, curiosity and... something.... in his eyes. "Not... Not Ian Buchanan."

My face heated, ramping up slowly but getting steadily hotter, until it was all I could do not to pick up one of the vinyl placemats and start fanning myself. I felt like a wife announcing her plans to commit adultery. "Yes. Ian Buchanan."

"You're joking." Ben laughed, looked away, then looked back again. When I couldn't stop blushing, his smile morphed into a look of amazement. Amazement, and something else. Jealousy?

"You're not joking. Casey, Melody told me you hated him. What was it you called him? The Newspaper Nazi?"

Had Melody told Ben absolutely everything? What other secrets had she told him about me? "I was wrong about Ian." I sniffed. "I didn't know him then."

"And you do know him now." A hard note crept into Ben's voice. "Just how well do you know him, Casey?"

"It's none of your business, Ben," I snapped. "Drink your coffee. Read your paper. I'm going home." I flounced out of the kitchen, but the effect of my exit was ruined because I still wore my chenille robe and fuzzy slippers, and because I'd have to get dressed and pack my bag before I could actually leave.

The serenity of my clean, quiet home welcomed me. I checked phone messages then took a long, soothing bath. With both phones muted so I wouldn't be disturbed by weekend telemarketers, I spread a towel over my pillow and indulged in a naked nap while my hair dried. I couldn't wait to see Ian, but wanted to be rested and refreshed when I did. I didn't want to look like the desperate woman he'd seen yesterday afternoon in the driveway.

A while later, dressed in clean jeans, with my teeth and hair brushed, I went to call Ian, only to find that he'd left a message while I was napping. My shoulders slumped when I heard his deep voice. "Lass, I'm so sorry, but I have to cancel our plans. Something's come up. I'll talk to you later. Bye."

I looked out the window at soggy gray skies that promised more rain. After a couple of hours of slumping around the house, I called my mom.

No answer.

I called Meredith Sutton, the ballet mom I'd visited with briefly at Ben's after the funeral.

"'Lo?" Her husband answered, in that soothing voice of his that was deep as the ocean but soft as a sigh.

"It's Casey. Is Meredith there?"

"She's at work."

"Oh." I'd thought she was a stay-at-home mom.

"She's working part-time at Murphy Realty while she studies for her realtor's license. Do you want that number?"

"That's okay. Just tell her I called. Bye." I felt like everyone in the world was out doing something except me and Ben. I dialed his number.

He answered on the second ring. Ben and I were, in fact, the only two people on the face of the earth at home on a rainy Saturday afternoon.

"Hey, Ben." I tried to sound nonchalant though I knew there was a forlorn note in my voice. "My weekend plans fell through. Could we still go out for dinner tonight?"

"Sure." Ben sounded pitifully eager, didn't even ask why I was suddenly available. I knew I'd latched onto a kindred spirit, another lonely soul who didn't want to be left alone with his thoughts. "Let me call Lois and see if she can babysit."

"You don't have to do that. We could take the kids somewhere. The park and then McDonald's, maybe. They'd like that."

"Oh, please." The grimace was plain in Ben's voice. "Please don't make me do that. I'll call Lois and then call you right back."

"Okay." I hung up and watched out the window as the skies started spitting rain. Again.

Now I'd be going out to dinner with Ben. Why didn't that make me feel better?

I slouched in the quilted reading chair, taking comfort from Chester's fat feline form in my lap. His nasal purr started up the moment I started petting him, and his ecstasy-inspired drool dripped onto my leg, darkening the denim. "You are a totally worthless cat."

Chester blinked his crossed blue eyes and purred even louder.

The phone rang. Expecting Ben to call, I picked up the receiver, still petting Chester's back with long, smooth strokes. "Hey, Ben."

Silence on the other end, followed by a low, throat-clearing sound. "It's not Ben."

Well, shit. It was Ian, clearly not happy that I was expecting a call from Ben.

"Um," I faltered. My gut felt like it was shrinking, curling up like a snail that had just been dosed with salt. "I wasn't—"

"Expecting me to call?" Ian finished my sentence smoothly, with a light tone that didn't fool me, not even a little.

"Well, no, I wasn't." My gut kept shriveling, but the rest of me decided to fight back. A smidgen of huffiness crept into my tone. I'd have been with Ian right now if he hadn't broken our date. "Not since I got the message you left earlier."

"As I said, something came up. I'm very sorry—"

"So I heard," I interrupted. I took a breath. My gut was recovering from the shock of hearing Ian when I'd expected Ben, and the rest of me had begun to calm down as well. "I'm sorry, too. I've been looking forward to seeing you all week."

Ian was silent for a second. So was I, and I had time to wonder why we were so stiff, so angry, so adversarial. Neither of us had done anything wrong.

"So," I tried to infuse warm nonchalance into my tone. "Is the something that came up over now, or still ongoing?"

Just for a heartbeat, I could have sworn I heard a woman's voice in the background, and my whole being went on high-alert. I almost decided I had let my imagination take over. Or at least, part of me did. The rest of me was busy imagining scenarios that didn't include me.

"It's still ongoing," Ian responded. "It looks like I'll be... unavailable... until late tomorrow afternoon."

"Okay," I said brightly, like he'd just offered to buy me a new car. "I'll see you tomorrow evening, then."

"Great. I'll call you."

Did that mean I'll call you, as in I'll-call-you-don't-call-me? What, exactly, was going on? "Okay, fine." My voice sounded unbearably chirpy. "I'll talk to you later. When you call me."

"Lass..." his voice was tentative, as if he wondered why I wasn't sounding like coconut-covered meringue on a sweet pecan pie. "Is everything all right?"

"Everything is super-fine." And fuck-you-very-much-for-taking-the-time-to-call. "Bye."

"Goodbye." His voice was quiet, resigned, as if he'd meant more than an ending to a phone conversation.

I put the receiver back in its cradle, and spread a hand over my belly, trying to soothe the ache. My gut had shriveled again, knotted-up over an innocuous little phone call, in which very little was even said.

The stuff that wasn't said sat at the bottom of my stomach, a heap of empty snail shells. The phone rang again, and Chester leapt down from my lap with an indignant sniff but didn't slay my thighs. Was Ian calling back to apologize and confess whatever he'd been holding back? Hope and despair battled over my vocal cords. I made myself answer, and came out with a wimpy, raspy, "Hello?"

"Hey, Angel," Ben said. "Are you all dressed-up?"

Did Ben think I'd been prettifying myself since he hung up, just in case we had a date? Did men think our lives revolved around them? I tugged at the ragged collar of my sweatshirt, peered at the bags under my eyes that I could see from a distance in my reflection in the living room window. "Hells, yeah. I'm looking like a million dollars right about now. Can't wait for you to see me."

"Good. I can't wait to see you, either. I've made a reservation at The Plantation."

The Plantation was an intimate, expensive restaurant on the far side of the neighboring town. "That sounds great, Ben."

"I'll pick you up in ten minutes."

"Make it fifteen, and I'll be ready."

I exchanged my slumming clothes for the velvet sheath dress I'd worn on my date with Ian, brushed my almost-dry hair, and put on mascara and lipstick so it would look like I'd tried. Wondering why I didn't just stay home by myself, I fed Lizzie, made sure Chester still had plenty of food, and topped up the communal water dispenser.

I could stay home by myself. I probably should stay home by myself. I was more-than-likely whipping myself into a frenzy over nothing, but couldn't stop obsessing long enough to rein myself in. Ian breaking our date just didn't feel right. There was something going on that he didn't want to confess. Maybe it was nothing, but if it was nothing, why didn't he just explain?

Barefoot with my stiletto pumps in one hand, I waited on the front porch. While I stood there, rain poured from the rooftop, drilling holes into the soft dirt below.

Ben pulled up in front of the house and opened his door to get out, but I waved for him to wait, ran down the sidewalk and got into the Cherokee. "No sense in us both getting wet."

"Wow, Angel. You look great." Ben leaned across the seat and kissed me on the cheek. "I'm lucky Ian stood you up."

I ignored Ben's comment. It cut too way close to the bone. I wondered again why Ian had broken our date, but made myself attend to Ben's chatter about the kids, Ben's work, and the weather, while he navigated the slick streets out of town then headed down the highway.

The local radio station spouted worst-case scenarios

about a flash flood warning, roads closing and neighborhoods flooding. It probably boosted their ratings, and good for them if so, but I wasn't concerned. Heavy rains went along with the autumn season here, just as they did in the spring. Rivers, creeks and ditches overflowed then receded just as quickly, and only out-of-towners took much notice of it.

During our conversation, it didn't register which direction we were driving. But when we hit the black highway, Ben started fiddling with the radio controls, and I was slammed by a strange, backward sense of déjà vu. I'd been messing with the radio that night, too, and looked up to see the truck coming straight at us.

"Casey...."

I heard Ben's voice from a far distance, as if I was sinking underwater and he was standing on a riverbank high above me, calling out my name.

"Are you all right?" He reached over and squeezed my hand. His hand felt burning hot against my icy fingers.

"No." I wasn't getting enough air, even though my lungs were squeezing and inflating way too fast, an accordion pumped by a monkey hopped up on speed. I gasped and gasped but I couldn't catch my breath as it raced away from me. "Stop the car."

"Angel, I can't pull over here."

Above Ben's voice calling me by the pet name he'd used when we were dating, I heard Melody's voice in my head, saying, "I can't pull over, there's nowhere—"

"Hang on. You're having a panic attack. Breathe slow and deep. I'll pull over as soon as I can." I still heard his voice from ten feet away even though I knew he was right beside me, holding my hand. But after that first, burning contact, I didn't feel anything. I only knew it because when I tried to pull away, I couldn't.

Like a horror-struck moviegoer who couldn't look away from the screen, I stared out the rain-streaked window, watching for the place we had run off the road. I knew I'd see churned-up earth, broken trees, skid marks. "Is this where—?"

But it had been three months now. Maybe the marks would be gone, the weeds grown back over the bare-scraped ground. My breathing slowed, slowed, slowed, and I could feel Ben's hand holding mine again.

"It's a little farther up ahead." Ben slowed to the speed of a Sunday drive. "Do you want me to turn around? We could go to The Riverboat instead."

"No. I want to see." I was finally ready, though I had avoided this road ever since the accident. I had started in this direction when I'd tried to follow Ian to Birmingham, but my car bummed out before I got this far. And I'd been so heated by anger and the desperate need to see Ian, I hadn't thought about this being the road...

"Here it is." Ben slowed the car to a crawl, and with no other cars in sight, gave me the time I needed to see the visual marks of the accident. Still here, after all this time. A silent language that testified to those horrible moments when everything changed forever.

"God, Ben." Panic filled my insides with adrenaline, urging me to run, to escape the accident I was about to relive again. I couldn't escape it, because the signs made everything clear. Short, choppy black smears on the pavement—shuddering tires pushed faster than they could roll. Swirling parallel rows of quotation marks—our backward spin down the highway. A deep furrow of dug-up earth—our descent down the embankment.

I wanted to vomit. I wanted to run. I wanted to somehow turn the clock back. "Pull over."

Ben pulled over onto a red-dirt-and-gravel verge just

wide enough to get the Cherokee off the road. "Are you sure you want to see this?"

"I have to. Can you?"

"I already have." He grabbed my clasped hands and twined his fingers through mine. "I came the next day. Watched them pull the SUV out and haul it to the police station. I followed the wrecker, looking at that twisted hunk of metal all the way there."

Poor Ben. I hadn't even thought about him, how he'd felt, what he'd done. "Was it... very bad?"

"Worse."

I squeezed my eyes shut and pressed my lips together. I would not cry.

After a minute, we got out of the car. It had stopped raining for the moment, but the very air we breathed seemed full of water. Holding hands, we crossed the road then walked down the damp highway. We stopped at the spot where twin ditches pushed past broken trees and mangled shrubs into the chasm. So far down.

A stout Cypress guarded the river's edge, skinned of its bark where the car had smashed.

If not for that tree crushing the driver's side, Melody might still be alive. But if not for that tree, we would've sunk into the river, been sucked down into the mud, and Melody and I might both have drowned. Covered by spindly reeds that lifted their arms up out of the narrow scrim of waterlogged limbs and dirty plastic milk bottles, we'd have been entombed while the river rushed by, relentless and uncaring.

It was a miracle Ian and Wilson and the rescue team had found us as quickly as they did. A miracle they'd found us at all.

Ben squeezed my hand. I squeezed back, and we stood together, looking down. Holding each other up by the strength of our clasped hands.

We didn't speak. Not then, not on the walk back down the narrow highway, and not as we got back into Ben's car. I could have asked him if he was okay. He could have done the same. But we already knew. Neither of us was okay.

Ben pulled back onto the road. The skies opened up again and hurled fat raindrops at the Cherokee as it gathered speed. "I drive past here all the time," he finally said. "On the way to the airport."

I looked over at him, wondering how we could be here, having this conversation, both of us dry-eyed.

"It's the drive back that's the hardest. Driving the same direction y'all were going. It's usually at night, and I can't see where you went off the road, but I always know when I pass by."

"I'm so sorry, Ben." The tears I'd denied earlier came so fast I didn't have time to guard against them. "It should have been me. Melody had so much to live for."

"Hush." Ben took his hand from the wheel long enough to wipe the tears from my cheek with his thumb, but his tenderness only made them flow faster.

I turned my face away to stare out the window but saw nothing of the rain-drenched view. "Just give me a minute."

Ben dropped his hand and let it rest for just a moment on my thigh before returning it to the steering wheel. "Do you remember that time you and Melody kissed me in Kindergarten?"

I gave a little hiccupping laugh. "I couldn't remember whether we got our turns."

"Yeah. You did. After you held me down for all the other girls."

"I'm really sorry about that."

"I'll bet you are." His tone was teasing.

"No, really." I wiped my eyes. "You must have hated it."

He chuckled. "I'm sure I was scarred for life."

I sniffed as quietly as I could and rubbed my hands across my cheeks to wipe away the last of the tears.

"Look in the glove box. I keep some tissues in there."

I dug through the glove box. "I must look hideous." I flipped down the lighted mirror on the visor. "Oh, God. I *do* look hideous." I repaired as much of the damage as I could with the Kleenex, spitting on a wadded end and wiping at the smeared mascara under my eyes.

"There's a hairbrush under the seat if you need it."

"If I need it. You're a master of understatement." I added a layer of fresh makeup from the kit in my purse. I might end up looking like a hooker, but that was better than looking like I'd been crying. I'd deal with the tangled mess of my hair in a minute.

A few minutes later, we pulled into the restaurant's parking lot and Ben parked under a big magnolia. When he cut off the engine, I turned to him. "Do I look okay?"

"Beautiful, as always." He leaned across the console and gave me a quick kiss. "Let's eat."

I started to open my door, but he stilled me with a hand on my leg. "I'll do that."

He came around the hood, took my hand, and steadied me as I stepped down from the Cherokee. This was how I'd imagined we'd be all those years ago, going out to dinner together on weekends while our kids spent the night with my parents, or his.

But Jake and Maryann and Amy weren't our kids. They were his kids. And this moment was nothing I'd dreamed of all those years ago, even though a snapshot photo would have looked exactly the same. Stuck again in a Twilight Zone of what-ifs, I followed Ben into the restaurant.

"We have reservations," he told the hostess. We followed the young woman to our table where Ben ordered my favorite wine without asking. We sipped the smoky Cabernet and talked some more about the kids, my studio, his job, and deer-hunting—a subject we'd always disagreed on. For long moments, I saw him as himself. Not Melody's husband, not my lost lover, not the man who'd betrayed me with my best friend. I saw him as Ben, simply Ben, his good and bad qualities all rolled up together.

For the first time in forever, I gave myself a little credit.

I could have gone all Jerry Springer when he left me for her. Instead, I had strangled my infant love for him and embraced his newly adopted relationship with Melody. Or at least, I'd tried. But that strangled love wouldn't die. Denied the right to grow and mature as it should, it became a stunted, misshapen monster. My best-friendship with Melody had become twisted as well. Paired with jealousy, it created a conjoined-twin love-hate relationship that made me hate myself more than I hated Melody for taking Ben from me.

"Madame?" The waiter leaned toward me to catch my attention. "Are you ready to order?"

"Oh, yes." I glanced down at the menu and blurted out the first thing that caught my eye.

We were just finishing our dinner when I looked up to see Ian talking to the maitre'd.

His hand rested at the waist of the most stunningly beautiful woman I had ever seen.

Chapter Fourteen

ALL DARK TONES, HONEY SKIN and wild black hair, the woman on Ian's arm could have been a Spanish Flamenco dancer. In a skin tight red dress and high-heeled red-soled fuck-me pumps, she stood only a couple of inches shorter than Ian.

Her painted-on dress left nothing to the imagination, but any man looking at her didn't have a working brain left in his head anyway. Her image, mixed with testosterone, would immediately liquefy any remaining gray matter and send it sliding south.

The bitch was tall, curvy, voluptuous. A centerfold in the flesh. Loops of black hair rioted around her oval face, emphasizing dark, almond eyes and a luscious red mouth. I couldn't help but compare my not-quite blond hair and tiny but perky boobs.

She leaned into Ian and whispered.

He bent toward her, listening intently. An intimate half-smile lingered on his lips.

Asshole.

Bastard.

Liar.

Still, I couldn't much blame him. What a woman. And

Ian was one of the few men on the planet who could hope to hold her attention for more than a day or two.

That strange phone call he'd made this afternoon made perfect sense. He'd wanted to tell me something, but couldn't bring himself to do it. Now, I knew what—or who—that something was.

Ben turned around to see what had me so transfixed. "Good God."

My thoughts, exactly. I slugged back the last of my wine and watched Ben's eyes widen.

"Oh, Angel..." His voice held a world of compassion.

I was about to need a truckload of it. I'd been kicked in the chest by a rodeo bull and was still trying to figure out how to get up off the dirt. I just hoped to God that Ian and his new girlfriend weren't about to be led to a table near us. I could get over being gored by the bull's horns, but I damn sure didn't want Ian to see me squirming in pain.

Ben put a hand over mine. "Let's go." He raised a hand to signal the waiter.

"Wait." I held my head down during a dicey moment when the hostess looked our way, then tapped the computer screen at her podium. Frantic on the inside, I sat rooted to the chair and considered exit options, which pretty much amounted to hiding under the table. But God was on my side in this, at least, and the hostess led Ian and his sex-goddess to the opposite wing of the restaurant.

My stomach decided whether to give up the meal I'd just eaten while Ben paid the bill. The next thing I remembered was him speaking to me as we drove out of the parking lot. "It might not be what you think."

I tried to laugh but it sounded like a wheeze. "Ben, I'm more heterosexual than any woman I met in New

York, and I'd have sex with that woman if she'd let me." She was that compelling, no kidding. "And Ian is a man. It's exactly what I think it is."

"Maybe it's just business." Ben sounded about as sure of that as I was.

I tried to take a steadying breath, but it shuddered on the way out. "Yeah, and I'm the Secretary of State."

Ben took his eyes off the road for a second and brushed gentle fingers across my cheek. "You really care about this guy?"

"Yes," I whispered. My throat tried to close up but I wouldn't let it. "I guess I do."

He put both hands on the steering wheel and returned his attention to the rain-drenched highway. "Do you love him?"

I watched the windshield wipers swish away a scattering of tiny, star-like raindrops as soon as they fell. "Well, that'd be pretty damn stupid, wouldn't it?"

Wisely, Ben didn't answer my question. He turned off onto a dirt road, one I remembered but hadn't seen in years. After a few minutes, the headlights illuminated a deserted, fallen-down house overgrown with Kudzu. "Remember?"

Ben and I had made love on the concrete picnic table in the back yard of this place more times than I could count. "I can't believe it's still here."

"Land doesn't tend to move around much." Ben put a hand on my thigh and squeezed, teasing just a little to urge me into a better mood.

"I mean, you idiot, I thought someone would've built something else here by now." A stone's throw from the river's edge, right across from Angel Falls, the landmark for which the town was named, this should be prime real estate.

Ben drove around back of the vine-smothered ruin. He parked on the last scrap of high ground, turned off the engine, turned out the lights, and plunged us into the past. We sat in the car and watched the fast-flowing river hiss past below. Across the river, the silver thread of Angel Falls slipped down the limestone cliffs and into the embracing arms of the Angel, an eerily lifelike formation complete with wings and a white robe shimmering from water that seeped through fissures in the limestone.

The moon peered from breaks in the shredded clouds above, drenching the angel's face in its pale glow. The light rain had turned to a soft, silent mist that settled on the windshield like dew. I opened my door and walked across the wet grass to the concrete picnic table at the edge of the river's sloping bank.

"Hang on a second." Ben took out the blanket I'd left in the back of his Cherokee so Lizzie could ride in the back without messing up Ben's precious leather seats when I used Ben's car to squire his kids around. He spread the blanket over the table. I took off my shoes and set them side by side on the bench seat, then climbed to the table-top and sat cross-legged.

Ben sat beside me, put an arm around my shoulders and hugged me close. "You're shivering. Wouldn't you rather sit in the car?"

"No." I watched the rain-swollen water ripple and shine, and made excuses for Ian's bad behavior. I had no right to be angry. Ian had never claimed to love me. He had never mentioned monogamy. My expectations weren't Ian's fault. He had never promised anything. The fault here was entirely my own. I should have known better than to expect anything from him just because we'd made love.

Correction; had sex.

Ben chafed my arms to help me stay warm. "I'm sorry you had to see him with another woman."

"He left a message on my machine this morning. Said, 'something came up.' Now I know exactly what came up, don't I?"

"I'm so sorry, Angel." Ben ran a hand down my arm. "I'm really sorry."

"Who could blame him? My God. Did you see that woman?"

"Oh, yeah," he said a little too heartily. "I saw her."

"You jerk." I balled up my fist and punched his shoulder. But he wasn't the one I really wanted to hit.

"Ow!" Ben rubbed his shoulder, being dramatic. I hadn't hit him that hard. "What did I do?" he said. "I'm not the one who—"

"Yes, you were," I snapped. Maybe I did want to hit him, after all. "You were the first one who jilted me for someone else. You just weren't the last."

And then I started crying.

"You're right. I'm sorry." Ben pulled me into his lap and wrapped his arms around me. "All men are jerks."

"And assholes." I tried to wipe my eyes without smearing my mascara. "Assholes and buttheads."

"Idiots," Ben supplied. "Idiots and imbeciles, the whole lot of us."

"What's wrong with me?" I wailed, falling directly into the pit of self-pity and wallowing there. "Why can't I find someone who will love me?"

"Everybody loves you, Angel." Ben rocked me gently in his arms. "You know they do."

"That's not what I mean." I gave him another thump on the arm. He'd be black-and-blue in the morning, and I didn't give a shit.

"Well, how about this, you little witch." His voice

turned rough, and so did his hands. He tangled his fingers in my hair and tilted my face toward his. "I love you. I always have, and I always will."

Then Ben kissed me the way he hadn't kissed me since Melody took him for herself.

I opened my mouth to his, learning again the taste and texture of his tongue. Strong emotions swirled together in a brew as heady and confusing as Long Island Iced Tea.

Ben laid me back, my dress rode up, and the rough blanket scratched my bare legs. The mist-heavy air slid cold fingers along my exposed skin. I let him kiss me, and I kissed him back, trying hard not to compare him to Ian, or to the Ben I'd known so many years ago.

Back then, I'd made the mistake of thinking I could maintain a relationship without giving up anything. With Ian, I'd made the mistake of thinking if I gave up everything—my body, my heart—the relationship I craved would follow.

I'd been so accommodating, hadn't I? Too accommodating.

Ben's long legs tangled with mine on the scratchy blanket. He was taller than he had been when we were teenagers. Taller, heavier, less rangy, more muscular. We didn't fit together the same way we had back then.

This was not the Ben I'd fallen in love with.

"No." I wedged my arms between us and pushed at his shoulders. "Stop."

Immediately, he pulled away. He sat up, ran his hands through his hair. I sat up, too, and reached out to smooth down the silky strands, but it was a lost cause. The humidity made the loose curls of his perpetually too-long hair tighten into little spirals.

"I'm sorry," we both said at the same time.

Ben covered my mouth with his fingers. "I shouldn't have kissed you, not tonight. Coming here was a bad idea."

I took his hand in both of mine and held tight. "I needed you to try, even if I did say no."

"I meant it when I said I still love you." His eyes were soft, his voice even softer. "I never stopped."

"I love you, too, Ben." I put my hands on his shoulders and looked him in the face. "Always have, always will." A vision flashed through my mind of the two of us as we'd been in the third grade, sitting cross-legged behind the alphabet chart stand, taking turns reading to each other. "But you're not the same person you were all those years ago. Neither am I. We can't take up where we left off. If we start anything, we have to start slow. I don't think either of us can stand another broken heart."

Ben pressed his forehead to mine. "Have you always been this smart?"

"I used to think so." I chuckled, though I wondered if I'd ever feel like laughing again during this lifetime. "But now, I'm fairly certain that I'm dumb as dirt."

The rain continued after Ben dropped me off at home, a persistent gray drizzle that perfectly matched my mood. The skies cried, and I cried along with them.

I was getting ready for bed when the phone rang. I had already convinced myself Ian wouldn't call. When he did, I didn't pick up. Partly because I was still mad, hurt, and grieving. Mostly, I didn't pick up because my nose was so stuffy from crying. I knew I'd sound horrible and I didn't want Ian to know how badly he'd hurt me. He left a cheery message in his damn Scottish accent, saying how much he'd missed seeing me today.

Arrogant playboy bastard.

I should have known he was out of my league when I first met him. Ian was no boy-scout. He probably didn't even realize he'd done anything wrong, and I wasn't going to be the one to inform him that it just wasn't right to keep two women on a string. No way would I let him see how much he'd hurt me.

I turned on the TV, watched an infomercial about vacuum cleaners, inhaled an entire party-size bag of Tostitos and killed what was left of yesterday's bottle of Cabernet.

Ian called again an hour or so later. I wadded up the empty Tostitos bag and hurled it at the phone. The message he left was less cheery, but he obviously had no clue. "Now you're worrying me, lass. I'd come check on you, but…" There was a slight pause, and I could hear him sigh. "I'll see you tomorrow."

I got into bed and tried to let the sound of the rain on the roof lull me to sleep. But how could I sleep with bed buddies like these—anger, hurt, betrayal, loss? They kicked and pinched and swirled inside me. I tossed and turned and searched for excuses to make what Ian had done okay.

Maybe I had jumped to a conclusion.

Maybe she was his long-lost sister who'd been abandoned at birth.

Maybe, despite all evidence to the contrary, Ian had a good reason to break a date with me and go out with another woman. I tossed aside the sheets and schlepped to the bathroom to pee. Relieving my bladder in the dark bathroom, I berated myself.

I should have answered the phone.

I shuffled to the sink, rinsed my hands, turned on the

unforgiving bathroom light, and squinted into the mirror. Why the hell hadn't I answered the phone? Because now, I was actually considering driving out to his place with my red-rimmed eyes, my swollen nose, my blotchy face.

Wasn't I an adult? An adult who owed it to Ian to at least give him the chance to explain? I should call him back. But no—I needed to see his face, so I could tell whether he was telling the truth, or playing on my desperate need to believe his lies.

I splashed my face with the hottest water I could stand and followed with a cold rinse. Visually unimproved but filled with purpose, I pulled on clothes, grabbed car keys, and headed out into a driving rain that soaked through my jeans before I got the car door open.

Ian still wanted me, or he wouldn't have called.

But why would he want me when he could have her?

I had no idea, but I needed to find out. Maybe giving Ian everything wasn't the wrong thing to do, after all. Maybe all I had to do was lay my soul bare and then give a little more.

It took an hour to make the twenty-minute drive to his house. I navigated flooded streets and detoured around an entire section of town where homes and businesses stood under a foot of water. Just before midnight, I turned onto his drive.

The big house was all-but dark. A dim light over the kitchen sink glowed through the mullioned dining room windows that faced the highway.

I turned off my headlights and stopped halfway down the drive, remembering. I'd once stood at that sink, sipping coffee, leaning against Ian, watching a pair of deer nibble at the gardenia in the back yard.

Should I go through with this? I looked like hell.

Maybe I should wait until Monday morning and go by his office.

I had just made the comforting decision to retreat when I saw her.

She emerged like a seductive ghost from the shadowed dining room into the kitchen, her hair floating around her in rich ebony waves. When she reached up into the cabinet over the sink, the black satin robe she wore pulled against ample breasts. She brought down a crystal tumbler, held it under the faucet, and gazed out the window into the dark back yard.

I knew the pure, flowing well-water would fill the glass in exactly the way she expected, just like everything else she'd ever asked for or wanted. She was the kind of woman who never had to wonder why anything happened—or why it didn't. Just like Melody.

I didn't worry whether the beautiful woman behind the window saw my cranky old car parked halfway down the drive. Even if she'd been looking in my direction, she couldn't see me. Even if she'd thought of looking past her own desires, the kitchen light would reflect against the dining room windows and throw back her own image.

She would never know that once again, I had come in second.

She would never know that once again, I was sitting on the outside looking in.

She would never know, and neither would anyone else.

I backed my car down the drive, and waited until I reached the main road before I turned on the headlights. I went home and tried to sleep, finally giving up when the sky lightened to a pearly gray. Then I walked to the river, so early in the morning that even Lizzie wasn't interested in coming along. I sat alone on the bench where I'd first kissed Ian, and watched the pale, insufficient sun rise over the water.

Chapter Fifteen

I MANAGED TO AVOID IAN ALL of Monday.

Once, he came up the stairs between classes, but I initiated a conversation with a couple of parents and waited for him to lose interest.

Maybe he had a great excuse for standing me up and then having dinner and a sleep-over with that sex-on-stilettoes woman. The sad fact was, he wouldn't need a great excuse. Or even a good one. I'd believe any old flimsy excuse he gave, because I was weak where Ian Buchanan was concerned. And until I could be strong, I had to stay away.

I wasn't even angry anymore. I was sorry I had let him get so far under my skin. Sorry I'd let my need for love blind me to the truth, and hadn't realized from the beginning that for him, it had only been about the sex. But at least now, I was crystal-clear about what I wanted.

I wanted marriage. I wanted a man who would love me—and only me—for the rest of our lives. I wanted more than Ian could give. Maybe I should give Ben a chance...

When I got home, I changed from my ballet clothes into jeans and a tee in two-point-nine seconds, and Lizzie and I left the house in case Ian decided to drop by. Because if I came face to face with him, I would cave in.

Ben had asked me to cook supper for him and the kids, and I knew Ian wouldn't show up there. I could take refuge with Ben until Ian got the message.

I'd been half afraid things would be strained between Ben and me after the Saturday kiss, but they weren't. Ben leaned against the kitchen counter, sipping wine and pretending to be interested in learning how to cook. Canned laughter spilled from the living room where the kids lounged on the couch in front of the TV.

I handed Ben a bag of rice. "Make yourself useful. Follow the directions."

While he measured rice and water into a boiler, I battered the chicken. We worked in companionable silence, like a long-married couple. I knew without a doubt Ben and I could be happy together. But would we ever again feel that magnetic pull of pulse-pounding, overwhelming lust? Had Ian ruined me, even for this?

"Shit!" Ben's voice blended with the hiss of water boiling over onto the stove. He plucked the lid off the rice pot and dropped it onto the counter with a clatter, then shook his fingers to dissipate the heat. "Why'd it do that?"

I turned the burner to low and used a potholder to replace the lid askew, leaving space for the steam to vent. "Didn't the directions say to turn it down once it started boiling?" I picked up a battered chicken breast. "Watch and learn." I showed him how to slide it gently into the pan of hot oil.

He snorted. "You're so talented. That must have been really difficult."

I wiped my hands on a kitchen towel and moved aside. "Let's see you do it."

He picked up a drumstick and lowered its butt end into the boiling oil. The sizzling sound made him jump—he dropped the drumstick into the pan, splattering hot oil. "Damn!"

"Not as easy as it looks?" I demonstrated again how to slide a battered chicken wing into the pan. "Do the rest, and I'll show you how to make biscuits and gravy."

As we stood at the stove, he put an arm around me and rested his hand casually on my hip. He took it away after a moment and commandeered the spatula, scraping the pan to keep the gravy from sticking. A calm certainty settled over me. Whatever happened, Ben and I would always be there for each other.

I came home that night half expecting to find Ian waiting on my doorstep, but he wasn't. He hadn't left a message. He hadn't called, at all. More disappointed than relieved, I supposed he'd given up.

Early Tuesday morning, Ben called. "Did I wake you?"

I cradled the phone between shoulder and ear, poured coffee into a mug, doctored it with sugar and milk. "No." I cleared my throat and sat down at my kitchen table. "I just haven't had my coffee yet. What's up?"

"Amy's sick. She started throwing up in the middle of the night."

"Poor baby. You want me to come take care of her?"

"No. We're doing okay. She's asleep now. I'm going to try to get some work done in a minute."

"Okay." I stroked Chester, who'd settled into my lap like a huge, puffy pancake. "What do you need me to do?"

"Could you pick up Jake and Maryann after school and keep them with you? If there's any hope of keeping them from getting what Amy's got..."

"Sure. No problem. Tell Amy I hope she feels better soon."

"Thanks, Casey. I don't know what I'd do without you."

"Good thing you won't have to find out." I hung up the phone, feeling a small glimmer of hope, and a slightly larger glimmer of determination. I loved Ben, and I loved his kids. Maybe it would be best for everyone if we wound up together.

But no matter what happened, or what didn't happen, between Ben and me, I couldn't continue teaching in such close proximity to Ian. Every time I passed his office, I would want to rush in, throw my heart at his feet, and apologize for not answering his calls. If I asked my mother's opinion, she'd say I should stay put, wait it out, and allow time to work its healing magic. But I didn't ask my mother's opinion, because I didn't want to wait that long.

I took a deep breath, picked up the phone, and called the realty office. Thirty minutes later, I parked my car outside the vacant building that had once been the scene of my high school romance with Ben.

In fact, until my junior year, it had been the scene of every high school romance in Angel Falls. A new high school had been built that year, and the old high school—this old building—had been abandoned. Empty and alone, it stood on a hard foundation of cracked red dirt, its vacant eyes put out by hooligans with slingshots and too much time on their hands.

I got out of my car and walked up the smooth-worn concrete steps to the padlocked double doors. Chipped brick walls served as billboards for graffiti artists, making the place look more like an inner-city ruin than the cultural art center the city wanted to turn it into. And so far, no one in town had shown any interest. But if the project had a chance in hell, I was more than willing to take the first leap.

Something moved in my peripheral vision. My heart lurched in desperate hope. Then I realized the car coming toward mine wasn't Ian's black sedan. Murphy Realty's big maroon land yacht bumped over the curb and tore into the beaten dirt surrounding the old building, sending a plume of dirt into the air—a giant orange exclamation point rising up behind the car.

Joan Murphy got out and slammed the driver door. "Hey, Hon." The noontime sun shone directly down on her, lighting up the short spikes of her red hair. It was an impossible shade I'd have thought fake if her kids' hair hadn't been exactly the same color, including her twin daughters who took ballet. The firecracker red hair was just an indication of their firecracker personalities.

Meredith got out the passenger side, looking like a runway model with her wild brown hair and lean, leggy build. I waited in front of the school's front doors, my hands shoved into the front pockets of my jeans.

Joan and Meredith came up the stairs, and Joan unlocked the padlocked chain wrapped around the doors' push bars. "Sorry we're late." She unwrapped the chain and dropped it in front of the door. "Richard was showing a house, and he had the key to this place so we had to wait for him to get back."

Joan Murphy and her husband Richard owned the largest realty office in town, so they stayed pretty busy. "I knew y'all would get here sooner or later."

The creaky entrance door swung inward. My heart

sank down into the dust that covered the old wood floors.
"Oh, Lord." Festoons of peeling paint draped from the
ceiling and hung down the walls, suspended in a matrix
of cobwebs. Dank mildew and black rot gathered in corners and crevices. I imagined I could see mold spores
teeming in the humid air. I could certainly smell them.
"This is horrible."

"I know it looks bad," Joan said. We entered the old
ghost of the building quietly, stepping lightly on the
dusty floors as if treading on someone's grave. "But if
you decided to take over some part of it for the ballet
studio, the city would send in a cleaning crew."

"It will take more than cleaning products to make this
place work." But hoping to be proved wrong, I followed
Joan and Meredith down the trail of footprints someone
had left in the wide hallway.

"As I told you on the phone," Joan said, "the Historical
Society—"

Meredith chuckled, and Joan shot her a look. Meredith
explained. "Cole calls it the Hysterical Society."

Joan hooted. "Whatever you want to call it, the society wants to preserve the building. At their request, the
city council has voted to allow any civic groups, clubs,
or what-have-you to adopt space in the building, rent-
free. The only catch is you'd have to do the renovations
for your space on your own dime. Here are the girls'
bathrooms."

The three of us followed the veering path of footprints
to the dark narrow bathroom on the first floor. The
place was flat-out scary—bad enough to inspire nightmares. We all crowded at the spider-webbed doorway
and peered in.

"I'm afraid to walk in." It was hard to believe this place
had ever housed rows of giggling teenage girls standing

in front of the mirrors putting on too much mascara, or coaxing the rusty tampon machine to cough up one of its paper-wrapped lifesavers.

Peeling paint, rusting sinks, wobbly plywood dividers separating cracked toilets. There was no way any of the little ones would consent to go in here. Nor would I want them to. "Fixing this bathroom alone would cost thousands."

"The city would fix them," Meredith said. "Right, Joan?"

"Right. They just want to know that someone will actually use the space before they do. And all the utilities would be paid by the city. Once you got your studio space fixed-up, you'd have a free place to teach from now on. Let's go look at the auditorium." Joan led the way, and Meredith brought up the rear.

I hurried to catch up with Joan. "Has anyone else agreed to use space here?"

"Cole says that Matthew's Boy Scout troop is thinking about taking one of the upstairs rooms," Meredith said from behind me. "They haven't committed yet, though. They haven't had enough volunteers to do the work."

"I can see why. This isn't looking very promising."

"I'm afraid I agree." Joan stopped at the heavy auditorium doors that stood almost as high as the twelve-foot ceiling. "But it's interesting to see the place again. Brings back memories, doesn't it?"

"Yes, it does." The day Melody made the cheerleading squad and I didn't, because even though I could dance, substandard cartwheels were the sum total of my gymnastic abilities. The day Ben pinned me to the wall outside the girls' bathroom and refused to let me go until I'd kissed him. The day a ballet company came from New York to perform, and offered local dancers the opportunity to audition for their company.

"This is what I thought you'd be interested in." Joan swung open the auditorium doors. The sloping floor was lined with rows of movie theatre type seating, about three hundred seats in all. The chair seats and backs were bare wood, with long strips of laminate peeled off. Hundreds of adolescents had carved initials in the soft wood. Somewhere near the front, my own initials were paired with Ben's inside a lopsided heart. I'd carved the initials, he'd added the heart.

Heavy blue velvet curtains still flanked the stage. The material would be rotted by now, held together by cobwebs.

Joan led the way down the aisle. "I thought you could use the stage for classes."

"But there's no place for mirrors, or barres..." I could just see kids running backstage, or hiding in the wings. "It's too open."

"You could use it for performances," Meredith suggested.

"At Ms. Daphne's last recital, people lined the walls of the high school gym, and it holds five hundred chairs. This isn't nearly big enough."

"Don't give up yet." Joan ushered us out of the auditorium. "Let's go upstairs and look at the classrooms."

We climbed wooden stairs worn down a couple of inches in the middle so each stair seemed to bow up on the ends. I knew this was a lost cause. Still, I followed Joan to the second floor, remembering. The wide-planked wood floors, the tall windows, the high ceilings. Ben sitting next to me in literature class, his long legs stretched out in front of him as he slumped in his chair.

I felt my lips curve into a real smile when I realized that the old memories of Ben had lost their bittersweet edge. Now, they held only sweetness.

I tried the tarnished brass knob on the first door. "This was Old Lady Carroll's literature class, wasn't it?" The knob moved freely, but the door didn't budge.

Joan came up beside me. "English Lit, and you had to be lit to sit through the whole class without sleeping. At least, that's what my brother said." Together, we pushed until the swollen wood scraped against the old wood floor, opening grudgingly to reveal the classroom inside.

"Oh, wow," Meredith breathed, her voice reverent. "This is perfect." Tall windows, tall ceilings, one long, blank wall for mirrors. This room was a dancer's dream.

The rest of the building was a nightmare. "I really wanted this to work, but I don't see how it can."

Meredith shook her head. "Too bad this room is attached to the rest of the building."

Joan nodded a wordless oh-well. "I guess we'll have to keep looking."

That afternoon, storm clouds gathered. Jake stood outside the school, laughing with a group of friends. I didn't see Maryann. I parked in the first place I could find. Leaving Lizzie in the back seat of the running car, I got out and waved to get Jake's attention. "Where's your sister?"

"She didn't come outside." He turned back toward his friends again. Cole and Meredith's daughter, Jennifer was in the group, her coltish long legs and wavy hair like her mom's. She smiled and waved.

I waved back, then walked toward the bank of metal doors that still belched out kids with backpacks slung over shoulders. Inside the school, a couple of sullen-faced boys sat on the bench just inside the office door, faces smeared with dirt and tears. One held a pair of smashed eyeglasses. The other pressed a wet paper towel to his swelling lip.

"I'm looking for Maryann Hansen," I told the blond, pixie-faced young woman behind the desk. "She isn't outside."

The woman clicked the computer mouse a couple of times and picked up the phone, holding it poised in her slender hand. "Whose class is she in?"

I answered her question, and she pushed a button on the keypad, twirling her stud earring between her fingers while she spoke into the receiver. "Mrs. Meyers, is Maryann Hansen still in the classroom?" She listened for a moment, said, "Ah-huh, thank you," and then looked up.

"Her grandmother picked her up about an hour ago. She went home sick."

"Oh." I wondered why Ben hadn't let me know. I guess he had his hands full. "Thank you for your help."

The woman raised a hand briefly and returned her attention to the computer screen.

When I walked out, Jake leaned against the wall just outside the doors. I patted his arm. "I guess it's just you and me."

He shrugged a who-cares shoulder. "Where's Maryann?"

"She went home sick." We crossed the street to the car. "Amy's sick, too. You're coming home with me until they get better."

"Awww." He tossed his backpack onto the back seat, barely missing Lizzie, who moved over just in time. "I was going skateboarding with Nicky after school today."

"Maybe you can play with Ray when we get to my place."

"He's just a little kid." Jake slammed the door.

"A whole year younger than you. Buckle your seatbelt."

He growled under his breath, as if I'd asked him to dig a ten-foot hole. He obeyed, but his expression made it clear he didn't plan to cooperate any more than he absolutely had to. He ignored me and looked out the window with the long-suffering expression of someone chained to the seat in a prison van.

"You wouldn't have been able to skateboard for long anyway. It's going to rain. You could take Lizzie for a walk before it starts."

Lizzie's ears pricked up at the mention of her name, but Jake made a noncommittal sound and slumped down into his seat. The storm clouds gathering overhead had nothing on his expression.

I pulled away from the curb. "We'll think of something fun for you to do."

"Whatever."

When we got to my house and piled out of the car, I thanked my lucky stars that Angela's son, Ray, was sitting on the front porch swing. A ginger-headed, freckle-faced Huck Finn wearing last year's grass-stained, holey jeans and a raggedy T-shirt.

"Hey, man!" Ray jumped up from the swing and hopped over the front porch rail, landing at the edge of my carefully tended azaleas. I didn't fuss the way I normally would, because today, Ray was my savior. I felt sure that given a little time and inattention, my problems as Jake's entertainment chairman would take care of themselves.

"Hey, Ray," Jake grumbled.

"I don't have any homework," Ray announced. "You want to hang out?"

Jake shrugged.

"You can do your homework later," I told him. "Y'all go ahead and play now, before it rains."

Jake cringed at the word "play," and I remembered that kids his age didn't play. They hung out. Assuming his agreement anyway, I went inside and left Lizzie and the boys standing in the front yard. I figured Jake would do better without me watching, since he wouldn't feel compelled to impress me with how miserable he was.

I straightened the house and started a load of laundry, occasionally glancing out the front window to make sure they were okay. After an hour, I tapped on the window to get their attention. The porch swing stopped banging against the side rail, and Jake schooled his expression into a mask of irritation.

"Are y'all hungry?" I raised my voice so they could hear me through the window glass.

"What have you got to eat?" Jake yelled.

"Apples, oranges, yogurt—"

"Nah," they said in unison.

"Can Jake come over to my house?" Ray asked.

"If it's okay with your mom. But don't go anywhere else without telling me, okay?"

Jake stood, and the porch swing bumped against the rail as both boys abandoned it. A second later, the door to Angela's apartment slammed closed.

I settled into my comfy quilted reading chair and was deep into the newest JoAnn Sky book, when someone knocked. My heart hammering in case it was Ian, I put my book aside and opened the door. Angela stood there, twisting her hands, a worried frown on her face. "Are the boys over at your house?"

I stood back so she could come inside. "They're not in the back yard?"

"No. And they've left the back gate open. Is Lizzie with you?"

"She was outside with the boys. I told Jake not to go anywhere without telling me."

"They've probably just gone for a walk." Angela sounded hopeful but not convinced. Neither was I, and fear billowed like smoke from my stomach to my throat. It wasn't the first time Ray had pulled a stunt like this. But knowing Jake's rebellious state of mind, I knew the blame couldn't be laid entirely at Ray's door. These days, Jake was an accident waiting to happen, and I didn't want it to happen on my watch.

"I'll go look for them." Rain was imminent, so I took my hoodie off the hall tree and put it on. "You stay by the phone." I grabbed purse, car keys, and courage—surely the boys were okay, just temporarily AWOL—then gave my cordless handset to Angela. "Here. In case Jake calls. I've got my cell. Call if you hear anything."

"Okay." Angela took my phone and went back to her duplex. I drove slowly along the streets with my windows down, calling out. "Jake... Ray... Lizzie..." I figured they'd all be together, but there was a slight chance the boys had left without the dog, and she had gotten out later through the open gate.

When the streetlights came on, panic shoved fear and irritation aside. The sky had darkened, and I realized I wouldn't be able to see them even if I drove right past. I came back home feeling as if a hard-edged brick was lodged sideways in my stomach.

Angela met me on the porch. "Any sign?"

"No. Ben is going to kill me."

"Come on inside. I was just about to make some hot

tea."

I followed her in and slumped into a kitchen chair. I picked up my cordless phone from her table. "God, I hate to call Ben and tell him I've lost his son."

Angela patted my hand. "Don't call just yet. Ben wouldn't be able to do anything but worry anyway."

"I can't believe Jake would just take off without telling me."

"Boys do this sort of thing every now and then. I can tell you from experience, it's not time to worry yet. They'll probably come walking in that door five minutes after it starts raining."

But I couldn't stand waiting around, doing nothing. "I should go back out."

"Drink your tea." Angela put a mug in front of me. "If they're not back by the time you're finished, we'll go together."

We sat in silence for a moment. Angela cleared her throat and looked up at me, in a kind of sideways, under-the-lashes, I-know-something-you-don't look.

"What?" I said, welcoming the distraction from my worry over the boys. At least Lizzie was with them, I thought. Hoped.

"A certain good-looking, dark-haired man sat on our porch for an hour yesterday evening, waiting for you to come home."

"He did?" My heart thumped a little faster for a few beats, a stone skipping over water.

"I sat with him for a bit. We had a nice talk."

"Oh?"

"Why you'd want to avoid such a perfect specimen of the male species is beyond me."

I bristled. "You don't know the whole story."

"Neither does he, apparently."

I looked down and pretended great interest in the handle of my tea mug. "What did he say?"

"He figures you're mad at him but can't imagine why."

I snorted. "I'll bet." I took a sip of tea and looked out at the darkening sky. "What else did he say?"

"Just that you'd know where to find him when you were ready."

I shoved my cell phone into my front pocket and stood. "I'm going out again."

Angela took a little pink flashlight from her junk drawer. "I'll come, too."

I plucked the flashlight from her hand. "Stay here in case they come back. If they do, tan their backsides, then call me."

This time, I walked down the sidewalk instead of taking my car. "Jake!" I called out, then paused to listen. Silence. "Ray!" Silence, again. "Lizzie!" I walked down one block, then another, then another. All along the way, I debated whether to call Ben or keep looking.

Then I heard it, a faint sound in the distance. "Yip!"

I started running. "Lizzie!"

"Yip!" The sweet, high-pitched sound came from half a block away, outside the old vacant high school.

I slowed to a walk, pulled the cell phone out of my pocket, and called Angela. "I hear Lizzie barking."

"Are the boys with her? Are they okay?"

"I don't know." The low cloud cover made evening twilight seem like true darkness, but I could see Lizzie's white coat shining in the gloom. "I see Lizzie." She was tied to a big oak tree with a length of light-colored rope. She was still barking—her front feet lifted off the ground with each yip. "The boys left her tied to a tree, but I don't see them."

"Where are you?"

"The old high school." I knelt down and untied the rope attached to Lizzie's collar. She swarmed over me, all happy licks and gratitude. I struggled to keep the phone anchored between shoulder and ear.

"I'm gonna kill Ray when he gets home." Angela's voice shook with fear or rage or a combination of the two. "I've told him not to go in there."

Were the boys poking around one of the scary bathrooms? Or in the basement I'd be afraid to go into, even in broad daylight? "You think they went inside?"

"Kids dare each other to go in there all the time. Ray knows better, but I doubt it would stop him now that he has a partner in crime."

"How do they get in?"

"Most likely, through a broken window."

"That doesn't narrow it down much."

Lizzie bolted from me. I ran after her, following to a shadowed corner of the building where two walls met. Lizzie sat beneath a small, chest-high window. It wasn't broken, but the sash was pushed up high enough for two skinny boys to slip through. "Angela, I think Lizzie is showing me where they got in. Hang on a sec."

I yelled into the dark, dank building. "Jake!" Only my voice echoed from the pitch-black void. "Ray!" Again, only the eerie echo of my voice bounced back. I took out the little pink flashlight and shone it into the room, but the beam illuminated my hand and not much more. I put the phone to my ear. "Angela, will Carl be home soon? I'm going to need some help."

"He's making an out-of-town delivery today." The phone connection crackled and skipped. "Should I call Ben after all?"

"No. He has his hands full with the girls." My heart sped into overdrive when I realized what I was about to say, and for the first time in hours, I felt that everything would be okay. "Call Ian. Tell him to come. Tell him to bring a flashlight."

"Okay, I will." I barely heard her voice through the static. Then the connection was lost.

Chapter Sixteen

I LOOKED AT THE CHEST-HIGH WINDOW ledge and the dark, gaping maw beyond the open window. I shoved my cell phone and the pitiful pink flashlight into my front pocket and hoisted myself up onto the rough granite ledge, shredding skin and fingernails. I got one knee up and slid a leg over the sill. With my toes reaching toward an uncertain landing spot, I fell inside.

The strong odor of mildew and dust coated the inside of my mouth with a sour taste. "Jake," I yelled, my voice shrill with fear and anger. Mostly fear. "Ray, where are you?"

I got to my feet, took the feeble pink flashlight out of my pocket and shone it around the first-floor classroom. Boxes. Broken desks. Turned-over chairs. A rotting mattress.

A mattress? A chill crawled up my back, and my scalp tingled. Some vagrant had slept here. Or lured children here, drugged and tied and gagged them… Sinister possibilities crowded into my mind, fed by my vivid imagination's reaction to the nightly news. What had Jake and Ray gotten themselves—and me—into?

Outside the window, Lizzie barked for all she was

worth. "Wait for Ian," I called down.

She wagged her stub tail and looked out at the road, as if she knew Ian was on his way. "Good girl. Wait for Ian."

Reluctantly, I turned away from my good dog. With the flashlight's uncertain beam probing the darkness in front of me, I picked my way through the humped shapes of indistinct objects and jumbled debris. If I ever got out of here, I vowed that I'd update my phone to one with a built-in flashlight.

At the door, I swung my flashlight's inadequate beam down the wide dark hallway. Open doors lined the hall, some still on hinges, others leaning drunkenly against the walls. Trails of dusty footprints went in both directions, sometimes veering into one doorway or another. Not just one set of footprints, but several.

The trail leading to the right seemed more distinct. "Jake?" Clenching my flashlight and my teeth, I followed the trail, calling the boys' names. "Ray?"

The flashlight's beam flickered and dimmed. I shook the light and was rewarded by a flare of renewed brightness. At the end of the hall, I had to make a choice. One dust-covered trail of footprints led up the stairs to the second floor. Another, newer-looking trail led down, into the basement.

The windowed classroom doors on the second floor glowed from a streetlamp outside. The basement yawned before me, pitch black. "Shit." I swallowed hard. Why couldn't they have gone upstairs? "Shit." With my heart galumphing like a herd of startled wildebeest, I started down the steps.

The flashlight's beam illuminated only a couple of feet in front of me. "Jake," I called out, my voice shrill with fear. "Ray!" I made it down the stairs and into the subterranean depths, where a constant drip, drip, drip splattered. A horrifying vision of dripping blood blossomed in my mind.

With my heart pounding a hysterical staccato in my throat, I swung the flashlight's weak beam from one side of the cavernous space to the other. No hallways here, just monstrous piles of shadowed objects lurking in the bowels of the old building. The footprints I'd been following disappeared, the dust consumed by the damp concrete floor. The bare brick walls emanated the cloying, sweet-sour odor of decay.

"Boys?" I held my breath, but heard only the scrabbling of rats scurrying from the flickering light. I walked slowly, staying away from the tall support pillars in case someone might be hiding behind them. Something soft whispered across my face; its sticky tendrils clung to my hair. I screamed—from surprise more than fright—then my flashlight went out.

Surrounded by complete darkness, I shook the dead flashlight. "Damn." Looking down, though I couldn't see my feet, I felt my way through the dark room, moving, I hoped, in the direction of the stairs. The darkness seemed less complete up ahead, and I shuffled toward the hope of light coming from an unseen stairwell.

A sound made me look up. Harsh light blinded me. Hard hands closed around my upper arms. A wall of unyielding muscle blocked my escape. I screamed, this time from pure terror, and held my pink flashlight up in defense. It wasn't much, but I fully intended to knock the vagrant's brains out with it.

"Sweetheart, it's me."

Relief took the starch out of my legs. "Ian." I sagged against him. I must have looked in danger of passing out, because he pulled me against his chest and held me tight.

"I haven't found the boys," I wailed. "I haven't found them."

Ian brushed my hair away from my forehead and ran his fingers through its length, gently sifting through the tangles. "Angela has them. They're all right." He pressed his lips to my temple. "Getting the scolding of their lives right about now."

"Lizzie—"

"Angela took her home. Lizzie was standing outside the window, barking like a maniac when I got here." Ian led me out of the basement and up the stairs with an arm around my shoulders, his heavy-duty high-beam flashlight showing the way.

"Where were the boys?" I huddled against Ian's side and clung tight, gratefully letting him lead me out of this hellhole. I'd think about being rational later. "How did you find them?"

"They were going out the window as I was coming in." He smiled, and I caught the glimmer of his white teeth in my side vision. "I think I scared the piss out of them. I hope so."

"So Angela—"

"Drove up as I was tossing the boys out the window. I told her to meet us here."

We reached the dark little room I'd first climbed into. I sniffed back tears. Now that the boys were safe and I wasn't about to be killed any second, my stifled emotions threatened to erupt.

"Let me climb down first." Ian handed me his big flashlight. "Then I'll help you."

When my Keds hit the red dirt below the window, I'd have crumpled to my knees, but Ian caught me. Adrenaline's strength had deserted me, so I let Ian lead me to his car and guide me inside. He reached across to buckle my seat belt and gave me a gentle kiss.

"Thank you," I whispered. The image of him with another woman kept me from saying more.

"Any time." He closed the passenger door and got into the driver's seat. An uncomfortable silence shimmered between us. With all my heart, I wished I could go home with him right now. I wanted to spend the night in his big bed and let his strength shelter me from the big bad world. But he had chosen someone else. Even if that betrayal had only been for one night, it was betrayal enough. Once again, I'd come in second with a man I loved.

And shit-fire, I realized what I had just admitted to myself. I loved the bastard.

For a moment, he looked like he was about to say something, but with a tiny shake of his head, he started the engine.

If I had any sense, I'd let him take me all the way home without saying a word. But a quiet little voice whispered inside my head. *If you love him, you have to give him a chance to explain.* "Ian."

"Hmmm?" He turned toward me, one hand on the steering wheel though the car was still in park.

"I saw you at the restaurant the night you broke our date. Ben and I were there, and we saw you come in with a woman. Do you want to tell me what that was about?"

Then we could deal with the fact that she had also gone home with him afterward.

Ian leaned against his closed door, as far away as he could get and still be in the car. "First, why don't you tell me what you were doing there with Ben? That's not the kind of place people take their kids."

"The kids weren't with us." I hoped to hell Ian felt half as jealous as I did.

He clenched his jaw. His face looked hard, like a stone statue of a Greek god. "I'm unsure why you're angry about seeing me with another woman, when you were obviously there yourself, accompanied by another man. I guess I'm just slow, but maybe you'll inform me—what's the difference?"

I couldn't believe he'd skirted the issue by putting the heat on me, when he was totally in the wrong. "Ian," I explained, trying to sound patient, "the difference is you broke our date. I wouldn't have been there with Ben if you hadn't."

"So..." he drew the long O sound out in a way I found incredibly pompous and irritating. "Anytime I'm not able to keep a commitment with you for whatever reason, you're likely to run to Ben for comfort before the day's out."

"Ian, this conversation is not about me and Ben."

"Oh?" His voice drew out the O sound again, deadly soft. "What's it about, then?"

"I went to your house that night, after you broke our date to go out with that woman. I wanted to talk, to give you a chance to explain. But when I drove up, I saw her standing in your kitchen, wearing a slinky black robe."

"Christ, lass, what am I going to do with you?" Ian's gentle tone made my hopes rise that he could explain all of this away. "The woman is a business associate, nothing more. If you hadn't been so busy avoiding me, you'd know that. This would have been so much easier if you had answered my phone calls."

"Well, sure it would," I snapped. My newly-risen hopes plummeted when he didn't immediately explain-away the woman's presence in his kitchen at midnight. "I'd have believed anything you said, without having to see with my own eyes what you were up to. Business associate, my hind foot. What kind of business associate spends the night at your house?"

"Casey." His voice was quiet. Sad. "I think it doesn't matter what I say. You've already made up your mind."

"Then change it! Tell me why you stood me up to go out with her. Tell me what she was doing at your house that night."

"Sure. Then you can tell me why your shirttail didn't hit your back before you asked Ben to take my place."

"Just forget it," I huffed, staring out the windshield into the darkness. I should have known he'd argue like a lawyer, going on the offensive to keep from dealing with the real subject of the conversation.

Thank God we'd used birth control. "Take me home."

Ian revved the engine more than necessary. "With pleasure."

Monday evening, Ben came up the studio stairs to collect a backpack Maryann had left after her ballet class. "How did Melody keep up with all this shit?"

"It wasn't easy." I handed over the backpack. "It never is." I looked at the room full of girls, some taking off ballet shoes and gathering their things to leave and others getting ready for class. Their harried parents rushed in and out, hoofing it from point A to point B and back again. "Kids are hard work."

Ben sighed. "I had no idea."

I patted his shoulder. "I'm sure Melody would be gratified to hear you say that."

"I didn't give her enough credit. Even though she didn't work—"

"Hey, Buster, she worked, she just didn't get a pay-check."

"I didn't mean that the way it sounded. I know Melody worked hard. That's exactly what I'm saying, isn't it?" Ben put an arm around me and leaned his head against mine, heedless of the roomful of kids and the few parents who still hadn't left. "How did this conversation get away from my complaints about being overworked and under-appreciated?"

"I'm sorry. I know you've got it rough, just like every other parent in the world."

"If I could just have one day a week off. One afternoon. A few hours. Anything."

The guilt-monster struck again. I could help Ben. It would mean giving up my Friday afternoons, but how could I refuse? I owed it to Mel, and maybe I owed it to Ben, too. "You mean," I asked, "if I pick up your kids from school every Friday, and keep them till dinnertime, I won't have to listen to you whine?"

"I'd be your slave forever." He looked so sincere, I worried that he might drop to his knees in front of me, but thankfully, he didn't.

"Okay, done deal. Tell Amy's school I'll pick her up at noon on Fridays. We'll spend a little time together and then pick up the big kids, and you can catch up on work, or sleep, or whatever you need to catch up on."

"Thanks, Angel. I really appreciate it."

"No problem. Now get out of here. I have a class to teach." I turned back to my class, shaking off the bit-tersweet realization that life had gone on, even with Melody's family.

Only a few girls were here, their pointe shoe parapher-nalia littering the floor. "Where is everybody?"

Keely, a carrot-topped munchkin of a girl, looked

up from ribbon-tying, her snub nose wrinkling. "Parent-teacher meetings. They'll be a few minutes late."

"Okay. I'll find some fun music for us to warm up to while we wait." While I scrolled through my iPod for inspiration, I glanced around and noticed Maryann's ballet bag sitting by the door. She'd sent Ben for the backpack because she needed it to do her homework, but she hadn't mentioned the dance bag, and probably wouldn't think about it till next week. I grabbed it up and headed out the door. If I hurried, I could catch Ben before he left. "Y'all get your shoes on. I'll be back in a minute."

I started down the long, narrow staircase. Loud, masculine voices carried up the stairwell on a draft of cold air.

"What the hell is your problem?"

I recognized Ian's pissed-off Scottish accent.

"You're my problem!"

I couldn't mistake Ben's voice, either, not at that decibel. I doubled my pace down the stairs.

"How the hell am I your problem?" Ian's Scottish burr was getting thicker by the second.

"You've got a hell of a nerve," Ben yelled, "taking advantage of Casey when you know how much she's been through."

"You're the one using Casey," Ian roared. "She's not free labor. She's not your kids' mother, and she's not their nursemaid, either. Have you thought of hiring somebody instead of calling her every time you need bailing out?"

"What Casey is to me or my kids is none of your damn business."

Lord God. Any minute they'd be punching each other. Right outside my studio. With more students due to arrive any second. I galloped down to street level.

Even the clattering echo of my wooden-soled winter clogs on the metal stairs didn't drown out Ben's voice. "Hurt her again, and you'll answer to me."

I made it onto the sidewalk in time to see Ian grab Ben by the collar. "Keep treating her like your personal servant, and I'll shove your teeth out your arshole." He released Ben with just a little force. Ben stumbled back, then leaped forward.

"Stop it!" I got between them and grabbed Ian's arm. He shook me off, a barely-noticed mosquito. I put my butt into Ian's crotch and shoved backward. I hurled Maryann's ballet bag at Ben. He had no choice but to catch it before it hit his face. "You're both acting like children."

A car pulled up to the curb, and a girl hopped out, swinging her ballet bag over her shoulder. "Hi, Mr. Hansen," she greeted Ben on her way up the stairs. "I'm late!" The girl's mother leaned across the seat to wave, then drove away, apparently too distracted to notice the imminent fight.

"Ben, go home to your kids."

Ben stalked toward his car, stiff-legged as a cur dog. Of course, just like a man, he had to toss the last word over his shoulder at Ian. "You stay away from Casey."

"The hell I will." Ian walked to his own car without even looking at me. "The hell I will."

On Friday, Lizzie and I took Amy to McDonald's then back to my house, where the three of us snuggled on the couch and watched cartoons until Amy fell asleep. She napped until it was time to pick up Jake and Maryann at school. Leaving Lizzie at home, the kids and I went straight from the school to the local movie theatre for the Friday Matinee. Free to kids twelve and under—the cinema made their money on concessions—this week's movie was a rerun of Disney's *Happy Feet*. In spite of my desire to support the community, I doubted the cleanliness of the soda fountain and popcorn machine, so I smuggled our own snacks in my biggest handbag.

Waiting in line to give money for my ticket and to show Jake and Maryann's school IDs to the gum-popping ticket taker, we shivered in our sweaters and light jackets.

"I'm cold," Amy whined. "Hold me. I'm tired of standing here."

"Okay, sweetie." I hitched Amy onto my hip, glad of her warmth and the camouflage she provided for the humongous shoulder bag that hid bottled water and Ziploc bags of popcorn.

"This is so lame," Jake complained for the thousandth time. "I can't believe you're making me go to a kids' movie."

I didn't respond to his attitude. I took a step forward as the person in front of me did.

"I want to see it," Maryann piped up. "Aunt Casey, you'll love it, too. There's lots of dancing."

"I hope none of my friends see me standing here." Jake looked around as if he'd just robbed a bank and cops lurked behind every corner. "Why couldn't I just wait for y'all at your house?"

I handed over cash for my ticket. "Because you disobeyed me the last time you were there. You're lucky your father didn't ground you for the rest of the school year."

Once in the darkened cinema, we made our way down

a nasty, squelching tongue of carpet that stank of spilled Coke and ground-in popcorn. We settled into our seats, with Amy on one side of me and Maryann on the other. Jake sat several seats away, pretending he'd come here alone.

The already-dim house lights went out.

Amy squealed in alarm and squeezed my hand. "Can I sit in your lap?"

"Sure." I hauled her over the seat's plastic arm and passed my handbag to Maryann, who dug out a Ziploc bag of popcorn. When the movie started, Maryann leaned against me. Even though I held Amy on one arm, I put the other around Maryann and snuggled her up. She looked so much like Melody, with her thick dark hair and brown eyes, but she hadn't inherited Mel's attention-getting gene. In fact, she seemed to be perfecting the art of invisibility.

Jake demanded attention by being hardheaded and difficult. Amy demanded attention by being loving and sweet. Maryann didn't demand attention, but I should remember that she needed it anyway.

After the movie, I took the children home to their house. We walked inside, welcomed by the savory aroma of spices wafting from the kitchen. We followed the enticing smell. The table was set with plates and silverware, and steam rose from a matching set of serving bowls and plates. Ben had cooked. An entire meal, vegetables and all.

"Wow, Ben, I'm impressed! Kind of unsure why you spent your kid-free day cooking, but…"

He handed me a glass of wine. "I thought I should thank you properly for giving me a full day of uninterrupted work time. Besides, I cheated. I cooked the meat on the grill and the biscuits are from a can."

I took the glass and hung my purse on the back of a kitchen chair. "That works."

"At least it's not macaroni and cheese," Maryann said. "Should I fix everybody's drinks now, Daddy?"

Amy jumped up and down. "I wanna."

Jake picked Amy up. "Come here, squirt."

Amy pushed at his shoulders. "I am not a squirt."

"Want to help me put ice in the glasses?" Jake made it sound fun by the inflection in his voice and the excited look on his face.

Amy bounced in his arms. "I can do that."

"I wish Melody could see this." I regretted the words the moment I heard myself say them. Thank goodness the kids hadn't heard. They were too busy helping each other.

Ben put a gentle hand on my arm. "I've thought the same thing a million times. You know what I think?"

"No, what?"

"I think she can see them. I think that maybe somehow, she's helping them get over her death and get on with living."

"I hope so." Tears pricked my eyes. "They still need her so much."

Ben pulled me against his side. "Know what else? I think Melody knows you're here for them when she can't be."

"Everything's ready," Maryann announced. "Come eat."

Ben and I sat next to each other with the kids around us at the oval table with seating for six. Amy was on my right in her booster chair. Then Jake, then Maryann. The extra chair was on Ben's left. I couldn't help looking at it and wondering if somehow, Melody was sitting there.

When I shoved that strange feeling aside, I enjoyed sharing a meal with Ben and the kids, but something vital was missing. I filled a hole in this family's life, but what about the hole in mine? What about my dream of having a husband who'd choose me first, not just as an alternate?

After dinner, Ben cleaned the kitchen. I supervised Amy's bath time and dressed her in Hello Kitty pajamas. Then Ben and I tucked Amy into bed.

Amy locked her arms around my neck and pulled me close. She whispered, filling my ear with her hot, damp breath. "I need you to snuggle me up while I go to sleep."

"Baby, I can't." Her toddler bed was exactly the size of a baby crib, though it was close to the ground and fashioned like a regular bed. "I can't fit in your bed."

"No," she clarified, louder this time. I knew Ben could hear her from where he stood, leaning against the bedroom doorway. "I want you to snuggle me up in Daddy's bed, like Mommy used to."

"Tell you what." I looked over to see the grin on Ben's face. "I'll give you another kiss now, and check on you in a few minutes."

She sighed, disappointed but resigned. "Promise you'll come right back."

"I promise."

Jake and Maryann had both retreated to their own rooms, under lights-out-at-bedtime orders. Ben and I went into the den and sat together on the couch, but not close. With his arm stretched across the back, his fingers touched my shoulder. "Casey, I've been thinking." He flicked his fingers in a fleeting caress.

"Oh, please don't do that," I teased.

"I want to sell this house. The kids and I need to live where memories don't tackle us every time we turn a corner. I loved Mel, but I need to move on."

He had my attention. I searched his face, waiting.

"Would you help me find the right place? It wouldn't have to mean anything about you and me." He looked over at me with a meaningful expression, then delivered the zinger. "Unless you want it to."

Had Ben sort-of-almost proposed to me? "Ben, I—"

"Let me finish." He held a hand up. "I want to have the kids out of this house by Christmas."

"Ben, there's no way. It's almost Thanksgiving."

"And—"

"But—"

"My God, woman! Would you let me finish?"

"Sorry, sorry." I barricaded my lips with my fingers to stop any more outbursts.

"I trust your judgment, and if I'm lucky, my house may be yours too, someday—"

Again, that sort of almost sounded like a proposal. My heart started fluttering, with fear or anticipation, or a combination of the two. "Ben—"

"Don't get all jumpy. I said the day may come, not that it will."

"But—"

"Will you stop being so damn difficult and let me finish?"

I clamped a hand against my mouth.

"On Christmas morning when the kids open their presents, I want it to be in a new place, where every moment isn't compared with the times when Melody was here. Will you help me?"

"Yes," I found myself saying. "I will."

Chapter Seventeen

O N MONDAY, I BACKED MY car up to the sidewalk outside the studio, hoping my helpers would arrive before I followed the urge to seek out Ian and throw myself at his feet. Today and tomorrow, I'd be measuring everyone for their recital costumes and taking money to place the order instead of teaching ballet classes. Two eight-foot folding tables I had borrowed from my parents covered the fold-down back seat and stuck out the back. I couldn't carry the tables upstairs by myself, but Victoria and Keely had promised to help, having gotten permission to leave school an hour early. But they were late.

I looked at my watch again. I trusted these girls. Besides, they knew that anyone who saw them slacking off was likely to notify me, or their parents. Absently, I stroked Lizzie's head and turned my face toward the cool breeze that wafted through the car's open windows. Nice weather for late November. Sweater weather.

In the rearview mirror, I saw Wilson, the young man who supervised the press runs, rush out of the newspaper office. His spiky blonde hair stuck out all over his head, again reminding me of a peroxided rooster. His build wasn't right for that analogy, though. His neck was too thick for that. Sensing he was coming out here on my account, I climbed out of the car and held the door open for Lizzie, who hopped out onto the sidewalk and shook herself.

Wilson barreled toward me with purpose. "Hi, Miss Casey."

"Wilson, what are you up to?" I hurried around the back of my car and met him halfway.

He only shoved me aside, gently of course. "Scuse me." A man of few words.

"Wilson, what are you doing?"

"I'm carrying your tables upstairs," he explained, as if I wasn't terribly bright.

"You are?" I moved aside, watching the tendons in his neck stand out while he pulled the topmost table out and put one end on the ground.

"Mr. Ian noticed your car sitting out here. He sent me." He hefted the table, tucked it under one arm, and started toward the stairs. "Good thing these here are the narrow ones. The wide kind, I'd have to get some help with."

It was nice of Ian to send Wilson out to help me, and I wondered what it meant, if anything. Though his "the hell I will" comment to Ben last week made me think he might call me, he hadn't. He'd left the relationship ball in my court. Sometimes I wanted to bat it back to him, but other times I knew better than to leap off safe ground with Ben into the unknown with Ian—who, let's face it, I didn't know all that well in spite of the fireworks between us. For all I knew, he was still sleeping around. So instead of making a decision, I lived in a state of anxious agitation and indecision.

"Wilson, wait." I hurried to catch up, reaching to support one end of the table, at least, as he carried it up the stairs. "I'll help."

"Nah." He gave the table a tiny little jerk, so I lost my grip. "I can do it better by myself."

I followed him up the stairs and squeezed past to open the door. Lizzie slipped by us both and took up her station under the studio's classroom windows.

Wilson huffed into the foyer and turned in a half-circle. "Where d'ya want it?"

"Right where you're standing will be just fine." He flipped the table over, set up the legs, and positioned it in less than a minute. Even with the help of the two girls, it would have taken us a lot of huffing, puffing and sweating to get that table up here.

Testosterone is apparently a necessary ingredient for some activities.

"Okay, then." He shot a surprisingly shy smile my way. "One down, one to go."

I couldn't help much, but felt obliged to follow and look appreciative. Coming down the stairs, we met Victoria and Keely coming up. Wilson smiled at them, and they clutched at each other, stifling giggles.

I gave them a 'what is wrong with you?' look, and followed Wilson down the stairs. When I trailed behind him as he carried the second table into the foyer minutes later, my supposed helpers had splayed themselves out in the center of the foyer, practicing the splits.

Showing off for my beefy-armed, rooster-haired helper.

I looked at him again. Was he what passed for cute these days? I guessed so. He was young, built, and blond. Brad Pitt's young country cousin on steroids. I couldn't pass judgment on the girls for showing off. Hadn't I done the same for Ian?

My conscience sniffed. At least I'd warmed up first.

Finished, he tucked his hands into the front pockets of his tight jeans. "Is that all you need?"

"Yes, Wilson. Thank you so much." I pulled a ten out of the cash box and offered it as a tip, but he refused, blushing and looking down at the floor.

"No thank you, ma'am. I was happy to help." He grinned at the girls who were still practicing their splits—wearing jeans, to boot—in the middle of the floor. Then he ducked his head, and went back downstairs.

"Miss Casey." Victoria twirled a lock of cinnamon-brown hair. "How many boyfriends do you have?"

"I like Mr. Buchanan best," Keely said. "I think Wilson is too young for you."

"Y'all are so funny. Go get the folding chairs out of the storage room and set them up along the walls." I set out the measuring tape, paperwork, and the collage I'd made of the recital costumes for each class.

I'd pored over costume catalogs for days, selecting the costumes for each dance. I'd spent hours with the calculator, adding prices, deducting discounts, calculating shipping charges, dividing by the number of students in each class. If I was any sort of business woman, I'd add on a little profit for myself. But unfortunately for me, I wasn't any sort of business woman.

With the cash box ready, I could make change for parents forking out frightening amounts of money to pay for costumes. Keely and Victoria measured, I handled the money, and students were free to go—in fact, encouraged to leave—as soon as we'd finished.

For my helpers' help, I paid for their costumes.

I had scheduled siblings together to simplify things for parents. Amy and Maryann ran in together, with Lois far behind, breathing hard. She paused to catch her breath. "I hope we're not late." Her thin, veined cheeks flushed crimson; her poodle-gray curls clung in sweaty strands to her neck.

"No, you're not late." I led her to a folding chair. "Are you okay?"

"I'm fine." She took a deep breath and let it out, then sat heavily, as if her legs had stopped working. "Ben wanted to bring them, but he got stuck in a conference call. He's doing most of his work from home now, you know."

I sat next to her. "You're not looking fine right now. Are you sure you're okay? Can I get you some water?"

"My blood pressure's higher than it should be. I have a doctor's appointment tomorrow."

"That sounds serious." I knew nothing about blood pressure problems.

Lois waved my concern away. "I'm glad we have a minute to talk. I want to thank you for all you've done for Ben and the children."

"Oh, Lois. You know I'm happy to help."

"I want you to know that whatever happens between you and Ben will be okay with me. It's what Melody would've wanted."

I glanced over at Victoria and Keely, who worked together to take Maryann's measurements and note them on the list. They weren't listening to us, and thank God there weren't any other adults around to hear this. Gossip in Angel Falls spread like butter on a warm biscuit. "Lois, there's nothing—"

"I know there's nothing between you and Ben... yet." She put a hand on the side of my face. "But I also know that you have a history. Maybe one worth repeating?" She patted my cheek. "You've been an angel, and I know my grandchildren and son-in-law couldn't find anyone better to take Melody's place."

I started to say something—I don't know what—but Lois stood and opened her purse. "What do we owe you for the costumes?"

That night, I counted money, wrote deposit slips, and fought myself over calling Ian. I should thank him for sending Wilson to unload those tables, my southern belle polite side argued against the sensible part of my brain that told me to keep my distance.

In a weak moment, I grabbed the phone and dialed his number. One ring, two... maybe he's asleep already....

"Hello?"

I had missed his sexy accent, the way he drew out the O sound in his deep voice. "Ian. It's me."

"Casey." His voice sounded tentative, like someone walking across a newly-iced pond.

"Thank you for sending Wilson to carry those tables upstairs."

"You're very welcome." His voice held a quiet reserve that made me think he might not be alone.

The words I didn't have the courage to say crowded up against the back of my throat.

Ian, I love you.

Ian, I want to talk about what happened.

Ian, why was that woman spending the night at your house?

"Well," I said. "Thanks again."

"No worries. As your landlord, I'm always ready to help if need be."

Ouch. That stung. "Okay. Well. Thanks again." How many times had I said that? Not too many, I hoped.

"Bye."

"Goodbye, Casey."

I hung up, wondering if his words were as final as they sounded.

Meredith came into the studio with her daughter Jennifer on Tuesday, another costume-fitting day. She handed me a manila envelope from the realty company. "I know you're busy, but Joan wanted me to give you the MLS listings for our area, with every house on the market in the price range Ben gave her. Y'all can ride by and take a look, then let her know which ones you want to see inside."

"Meredith," I kept my voice low and quiet. "You know I'm just helping Ben out... as a friend." Rumors could get started so easily in a small town, and I didn't want Ben's kids to be hurt by malicious, or even idle, gossip. "Can we talk about this later?"

"I'm sorry." Meredith lowered her voice. "I wasn't thinking." She glanced around at the crowd of students in the foyer. Most had arrived minus their parents, which made life difficult. They had just been sent up the stairs with a blank check for costumes. Now Victoria and Keely and I would have to spend our time keeping the girls out of trouble while they waited to be picked up. "Do you need us to stay and help?"

"Could you really?" I put my arm around Jennifer and gave her a quick hug. She was such a sweet girl, a little carbon copy of her mother. "I'll give you Jennifer's costume for free."

Meredith scoffed. "Not necessary. I'll just text Cole and

tell him to put a chunk of frozen lasagna in the oven."

"I'll babysit the little ones who are waiting to be picked up," Jennifer offered. "I can put a DVD on for them to watch in the studio."

"Thanks so much."

Meredith and Jenn gathered up a bunch of girls who were milling around the foyer, and my helpers and I were left with blessed silence and only one girl being measured while her mom wrote a check.

Joan Murphy burst into the silence like the firecracker she was, as sparkling and loud and attention-getting as fireworks. Her twins trailed behind, and a few more parents arrived with their kids.

"Hey!" Joan's voice was three times as big as her body. "I see Meredith brought you those listings. Let me know when you and Ben are ready to look inside some of the houses."

Victoria cut her eyes toward us, listening to the conversation while she called out measurements to Keely.

"Okay, Joan." I lowered my voice in the hope that she'd lower hers. "Thanks."

"I'm pretty free on Friday if you and Ben want to come by the office then."

"Okay. Thanks."

"No problem!" Joan wrote a hefty check for costumes and signed with a flourish. "Y'all let me know as soon as you make a decision on which houses y'all want to see!" She talked as if everyone around her was hard-of-hearing but needed to know what was going on. "I know you'll love one that isn't even on the list! We'll look at it once you've seen the others. Even though it's a little out of Ben's price range, it's a great buy! Someone else will snap it up for sure if you don't beat them to it! I can't wait to show it to you!" She glanced at her watch and whistled. "Girls, are y'all about done? We've got to fly to pick up your brother at band practice!"

They left like a whirlwind, leaving everyone in the room breathless. Meredith came back in and marshalled the kids waiting to be measured along one wall, then sat beside me. "So," she said quietly, "I'm confused about something."

"Yeah?" I was counting out cash, paper-clipping each bundle when I got to a hundred. "Rumor has it that you're dating the new editor, but you're house-hunting with Ben."

I stopped counting but didn't look up. "Wrong on both counts. Ian and I aren't together anymore, and Ben is just a friend."

Meredith made a humming sound. "I figured you and Ian might not be an item anymore, since he..." She cleared her throat softly.

"Since he—what?"

"Well, that big house he's living in is about to go up for sale. You know he's just renting, right? And he has first refusal but claims he doesn't want it, even though the owner just came down off the price by a substantial amount. His lease runs through the end of the year, but..."

Meredith's voice was drowned out by the clamor in my head. No wonder Ian wasn't interested in making amends. He didn't plan to stay.

"He's in negotiations to sell the newspaper, too. I know this is none of my business, and I'd probably get in trouble for telling you if anyone found out, but I wanted you to know in case... in case..." Meredith put a hand over mine.

"Thanks." I went back to counting money, while my heart crumpled like a used paper cup. "I appreciate the information, but it isn't necessary. Ian and I are old news."

I spent the next two mornings driving past houses. Even if the perfect house fell on top of our heads, Ben wouldn't be able to close a deal and get his family moved in before Christmas. Still, I looked. I came up with five possibilities and called Ben Thursday night.

"I can't go tomorrow," he said. "We're starting a new project with a company in Birmingham. I'll have to be there early in the morning to meet with the development team. I was just about to call you, to make sure you could take care of the kids."

"But what about looking at houses? Do you want me to move the appointment to Saturday?"

"No, no." Ben sounded distracted. I could hear him rattling papers in the background. "Look at them all and pick the best one. I won't be back until really late tomorrow night. We'll all go together on Saturday to check it out."

"Ben, one day is not enough time to find a house, for God's sake. These things take time. Maybe you shouldn't try to move until summer break."

"Do the best you can." He said it as if he was sending me to the grocery store for milk and couldn't figure out why I was having trouble with the assignment.

"Ben," I said, exasperated.

"Angel, I've got to go. You'll pick the kids up after school tomorrow?"

"Yes, I will."

"You can drop them off at Lois and Herb's if you need to, but they'd rather sleep in their own beds, if you're willing to stay with them."

"Fine, Ben. I'll keep them at your house."

I called Joan and set up an early morning appointment, since I'd have to pick Amy up at noon.

I went to bed feeling... I don't know... manipulated, unappreciated. I wasn't quite sure what it was, but I knew I didn't like it. I pulled Chester's furry bulk closer. "Come here, fat cat." Poor thing, he lived alone half the time while Lizzie and I stayed at someone else's home. "Let's go to sleep." And after a while, we did.

Friday morning dawned blustery gray, spitting a half-hearted drizzle that made the cold go all the way to the bone. I dressed in layers topped off with a rain slicker, grabbed a kiwi-strawberry smoothie from the fridge, patted Lizzie on the head, and left the house.

Joan's big maroon Cadillac was parked outside Murphy Realty, a squatty red-brick building in a row of others just like it. I parked in the empty space next to Joan's ostentatious land yacht, and saw her sitting inside. She honked the horn and waved to motion me in. I exited my car and entered hers in less than a minute, but the spitting rain hurled big fat drops like pebbles that pelted my face, soaked my hair and drenched the hem of my jeans in seconds.

"Lovely day you ordered." Joan backed out and pointed to the console. "I got us some coffee from Bo's." She pointed to the new restaurant at the end of the block. Close to a line of train tracks, the restaurant's front was built around a real boxcar. "Their coffee is actually quite good."

I picked up one of the steaming Styrofoam cups stamped with the logo from Bo's Boxcar Diner, and held it between my palms. Taking a sip, I decided that Joan's definition of quite good differed from mine. It wasn't

Starbucks, and it wasn't Jiffy-Stop, but somewhere in-between. Bottom line, I could drink it. "Thanks."

While rain showers came and went, we looked at all the houses I'd thought were likely choices. They all had their good points, they all had their bad. The one I liked best had a flooded front yard—good information to have, and maybe worth the trouble of house-hunting in the pouring rain. None were as perfect for Ben and the kids as the one they lived in right now, and I still had serious reservations about his plans to move. I knew he thought it would help them rebuild their lives, but it seemed too soon to me.

Ben would have to realize this was going to take a long time. His expectations would have to bow to reality. You can't just order up the perfect house and expect it to appear. And once they made it through this first Christmas without Mel, things wouldn't seem so bad.

Joan folded the MLS listing we'd been working from and put it aside. "I have one more that isn't on the list. The one I was telling you about on Tuesday." She sounded so mysterious a shiver of anticipation went through me. Or maybe it was just the raindrops drying on my skin. "This one had a sale pending, but the financing fell through. It has passed all the inspections, and the owner has already moved out. It's a little more expensive than the others, but I think the owner would come down off the price for a quick sale."

She pulled up in front of a gray brick Tudor-style house in an old neighborhood. Within walking distance of my house and the elementary school, the location was ideal. Ivy covered the walls, and with the overhanging oaks surrounding the house, it looked as if it had grown up out of the ground. A welcoming ray of sunlight parted the clouds to shine on the wet window glass and make it sparkle.

"It backs up to the canal. You'll have lots of birds and wildlife coming to your back yard."

"Ben's back yard, Joan. Not mine."

"Sure. I get it." Her tone implied that she didn't believe me. "Let's go inside."

The wood floors echoed as we stepped into the empty house. But even empty, the house had a warm, welcoming feeling.

"Oh, Joan," I whispered. If I spoke too loud—or even breathed too hard—would this mirage disappear?

"Wait until you see the kitchen." She led the way to a huge custom kitchen where delft blue and white tiles accented the eggshell walls and ceiling. An antique butcher-block island occupied the center of the brick tile floor.

The window above the sink looked out over a fenced back yard dominated by a huge dark tree with low-growing branches.

"That's a flowering plum," Joan said. "It's lovely in the spring. You can see it from the other side of the canal." I could imagine a tree house there for Jake, Amy's Little Tykes cottage huddled below.

Joan left the kitchen, expecting me to follow. "Let's see the bedrooms."

I couldn't believe it. The house was perfect. A long bank of windows in the downstairs master suite offered a glimpse of the canal through the trees. A small adjacent room would be suitable for an office. There were four rooms upstairs, two on each side of a central hallway, each pair linked by connecting baths.

"This is it." I was awed by the luck that must have been shining down on me, or at least on Ben, this rainy day.

"There's a half-basement, too," Joan said, "and a space

over the garage that you could convert into a studio. It needs some work, though. Come on, I'll show you."

I didn't bother to correct Joan about her assumption that I'd have any use for a studio at Ben's house. It never did any good.

We got back to Joan's office around eleven-thirty, and I walked in distractedly, eager to call Ben and conscious that I'd soon have to pick up Amy from school. Joan pressed the key into my hand. "Keep it for the weekend. Ben can drop it on Monday, after y'all have another look at the house."

"Thanks." I had that being-watched feeling, and looked up to see Ian standing there. He looked powerful and elegant in gray trousers, white shirt, gray silk tie, his gray suit coat unbuttoned.

She was right behind him, smiling and shaking hands with Joan's husband, Richard. Her glossy curls weren't just dark, they were ebony. Her curvaceous body was expensively clothed in a sweater-dress that had to be cashmere. I looked away from her to meet Ian's gaze.

No, his glare. He looked murderous, and that piercing stare was directed straight at me.

He turned to the woman. "Will you excuse me for a moment?"

He reached me in three strides, grabbed me by the arm, and hauled me out of the office. I had a quick impression of everyone staring open-mouthed at us before I found myself alone with Ian on the sidewalk.

His fingers squeezed my upper arms. "What are you playing at?"

"Playing?" Through the window of the real estate office, I could see Joan and Richard standing in the lobby with that woman. All of them stood like statues, watching the show we were putting on. "I don't know what you mean."

With a quick glance at the window, Ian hauled me by the arm again, this time to the edge of the building. He was seething, his anger barely leashed. The thunderclouds overhead looked meek by comparison. "House hunting with Ben? I must say, this happened mighty fast. Just a few weeks ago, you were under the covers with me. Having trouble making up your mind?"

His angry expression, his rough treatment, his mean words, turned up the heat on my simmering anger, making it flare out of control. I slapped his face. Needles of pain stung my palm, chastising me for hurting him on purpose, for being a bitch instead of the lady I'd been raised to be. My face flooded with heat. "Ian, I'm sorry. I shouldn't—"

He pulled me into his embrace.

The door to the realty office opened, and the woman drifted onto the sidewalk, a quizzical expression on her beautiful face. "Ian, I hate to interrupt." She glanced down at the bracelet-style wristwatch on her slender wrist. "I really should be going, or I'll miss my flight."

Ian buttoned his coat, smoothed his tie. "The car's unlocked. If you wouldn't mind…"

"Certainly," the statuesque beauty said. "But I do need to get to the airport soon. I told my husband I'd be on the next flight out as soon as we finished our business here."

"I'll be right there," Ian promised. His voice was cool, neutral, businesslike.

Had I been wrong? I felt horrified and relieved at the same time. The combination of feelings turned my knees to mush. He still hadn't explained why she was at his house that night wearing that sexy black robe. But it suddenly dawned on me with absolute certainty—I had been wrong, all along. "Oh, Ian. I'm sorry. I should've…"

"Trusted me?" A bitter smile twisted his lips. I reached up and laid my palm against the red mark I'd left on his cheek. He pulled away, just slightly, but enough for me to feel it. "Yeah, I guess you should've."

"Ian, you have to understand how it looked… how I felt when I drove up to your house and saw her through the window. I couldn't think of any explanation except the obvious one. I still can't."

He stood like a stone statue, arms crossed. My words poured off him like water off granite. Nothing I said made his expression soften.

I held my hands out, but didn't dare to touch him. "You can't blame me for taking what I saw at face value. You know you'd have done the same in my place."

"Maybe," he allowed, his voice low. "But I'd have given you the chance to explain."

"I did give you the chance to explain, when you helped me find the boys, but then you—"

"You want to go there now? Really?" He looked at me like he hated me. His amber eyes were cold, his mouth a hard slash in his stony face.

I saw with sudden clarity how finding out that I'd gone to dinner with Ben that night must have felt to Ian. I thought about everything Meredith had said, about Ian not wanting to buy the house he was renting. About him putting the newspaper up for sale. Had all that happened before, or after, Ian had broken our date and I'd gone out with Ben instead?

"You're right. I was being childish, and I'm sorry." I put a hand on his coat sleeve, and he moved back just far enough that I had to let it fall to my side again. "Ian, please. I know I was wrong. But I still deserve an explanation for that night, don't I?"

Ian took another step back and stood at the edge of the sidewalk with his hands in his pockets, looking out toward the street. When he turned back toward me, his closed-off expression made my heart flop over. "You know what, Casey? I'm through." He didn't sound angry anymore, just very, very tired. "I was married to a woman who did her best to suck me dry. She demanded more than I could give, then manipulated me by withdrawing when I didn't please her. I can't do that again. I won't."

"Ian, please. I didn't—I wouldn't..."

"Yes, you did. That's exactly what you did. I waited for you outside your house. I left messages begging you to call me. I felt like a goddamn stalker, the way I kept after you."

God, he was right. The realization went through me, a rollercoaster of regret that bottomed out in the pit of my stomach. "Ian..."

I stepped toward him, but he put up a hand to stop me. "Tell Ben I said hello." He turned and walked away, didn't even bother to look over his shoulder at me. He just got into his car and slammed the door.

The roar of the engine and the crunch of gravel under tires assaulted my ears. I didn't look up. I was looking down, imagining my heart at my feet, flattened as if it had been run over. I had no one to blame but myself and my stupid pride. I had thrown away something rare and precious. I stumbled to my car, fell into the driver's seat, looked at the clock.

"Shit." It was almost time to pick up Amy. I'd have to fly to get there on time. Past all those school zones. Shit.

Then, with a peal of thunder, a jagged fist of lightning zipped open the skies, and it poured rain.

Chapter Eighteen

THAT EVENING, I DID THE fifty-thousand things I had to do for Ben's kids, when all I wanted was to climb into bed with a bottle of wine and my dog and feel sorry for myself. But kids have a way of forcing you to get over yourself, so I stood at the stove, stirring the spaghetti noodles to keep them from sticking. Amy clung to my leg, absently patting my hip.

We got through dinner, word problems, and a science project proposal. I fed Lizzie, cleaned the kitchen, and tucked Amy into bed. When Maryann retreated to her room to read before bedtime, I climbed into Ben's bed with my wine, my dog, and the phone.

I wanted to call Ian, but I called Ben instead. Smoothing the comforter over my thighs, I leaned back against the headboard, waiting for Ben to answer his cell. I could just barely hear the bedtime music I'd put on for Amy in the next room. Other than that, the house was quiet. After a few rings, I figured I'd have to leave a message, but then he answered.

"Hey, Casey."

"Ben, I found y'all a house. Joan left a key so we can look at it tomorrow."

"That's great. But I won't be home until Sunday."

"Sunday? But you said—"

"I've been asked to stay and socialize. I kind of have to."

"Ben, has it occurred to you that I might have other plans beyond keeping your kids indefinitely?" As it turned out, I didn't, but he didn't know that.

Ben made a huffing sound of exasperation—as if *he* had any right to be exasperated with *me*. "Go ahead and show the house to the kids, and if you can't keep them after that, I guess you can take them to Lois and Herb's."

"I can watch them." Since I'd blown it with Ian for good, I might as well be taking care of Ben's kids. "I'll take them to see it tomorrow."

"Good. Then I'll see it on Sunday."

"Okay, fine." I sighed.

"Casey, you sound a little off. Is everything okay?"

"It's been one of those days."

"Except for finding the house."

I sniffed. "That was definitely the high point."

"Well, tuck the kids in and get some sleep. Maybe I can try to get home late tomorrow night."

"No. I don't want you driving on that road at night unless you have to. I'll see you Sunday." I hung up the phone and scooted down into my nest of pillows, then pulled the comforter up to my chin and waited for my body heat to create a warm cocoon. I had just started to get toasty when the bedside phone rang, jolting me out of a light doze. I managed to snatch the receiver up before the second ring.

"Hello? Ben?"

"It's Ian. You didn't answer your cell." His voice sounded strained, and I knew it had cost him to call me here, at Ben's house. But he'd called, so maybe it wasn't really over between us. Maybe I had another chance. He could still buy the house he was renting. He could still decide not to sell the newspaper.

"Hi." I stacked pillows at the headboard and leaned against them. "My cell is muted for the night. I'm glad you called."

"I just got back into town. I had to drive Bianca to the airport, and rush hour traffic in Birmingham was horrible."

Bianca. So that was the curvaceous beauty's name. It suited her. "Oh," was all I could think of to say.

Ian cleared his throat. "I called to apologize. I shouldn't have spoken to you the way I did this afternoon. You're not like Maeve, and I shouldn't have compared you to her. That was unfair."

"I was unfair to you, too, and I'm sorry."

"Is Ben there?"

"Of course not. I'm here because he isn't."

"I'm coming over. See you in twenty minutes." Then he hung up.

Still wearing my flannel nightgown, I went out onto the front porch to wait for him. Lizzie followed, taking the opportunity for a nighttime potty and patrol around the yard.

My heart rate tripled when Ian's car pulled into the drive. Butterflies flooded my insides when he killed the lights and stepped out of the car. They started doing backflips as he came up the walk. Everything about him made those butterflies flutter and swarm. His broad shoulders, gleaming black hair, the devastating smile I could just make out when he got closer to the porch light.

I opened the front door and stepped into the foyer. Lizzie scooted past into the dark house. "Come in. It's freezing out here."

"No wonder you're cold." He came in, closed the door, turned the bolt, took me in his arms. "If you were wearing something besides this..."

"It's called a nightgown, Ian. And it's more fabric than you've ever seen me in yet." I shivered against him, absorbing the delicious heat beneath his jacket for a minute, then pulled away and led him into the darkened den. I had closed the doors to the kids' rooms and the hallway. We would have complete privacy for our talk, unless one of the kids woke up.

I prayed that wouldn't happen, because once Ian's body pressed mine into the couch, we didn't do much talking. Explanations could come later. Right now, I wanted nothing more than to climb into his skin and inhabit his warm strength.

In Ian's arms, I felt a sense of rightness, of belonging, of blessed relief. I sent up a silent prayer of thanks. "I missed you." Sliding my hands around the muscular warmth of Ian's ribs and back, I kissed him with joyous abandon. "I've missed you so much."

He trailed kisses down my neck and murmured against my throat. "I've missed you, too."

His hands molded my breasts, skimmed my ribs, caressed my hips. His touch roused me to squirming, panting, gasping need, and I reveled in the electrical response of every nerve-ending. Through the combined layers of our clothing, his erection pressed into the aching cleft between my legs. Full, hard, insistent.

The thick folds of my nightgown wrapped around us both, and Ian tugged at the voluminous fabric, pulling it up though his weight trapped it between us. I reached down and tried to help, hiking up handfuls of cotton and lace to expose—

"Aunt Casey."

I sat up abruptly, banging my forehead against Ian's with an audible crack. I pushed Ian to one side of the couch and scooted out from under him. I held out my arms for Amy, who stood uncertainly in the doorway, outlined by the hall light.

Somehow, I made my voice work. "Hey, what's the matter? Come here."

Amy crept forward, clutching her security blanket, thumb securely in mouth, a wary expression on her face. Skirting Ian's outstretched legs, she climbed into my lap. "Who's that?" She pointed at him with her little finger without taking her thumb out of her mouth.

She'd seen Ian before. Probably knew his name. She just didn't know him in this context, in her house, lying on top of her babysitter-honorary aunt. "This is my friend, Ian."

"Hi, Amy." Ian held a hand toward her, but she only curled closer to me, and he dropped his hand onto his lap after a second. "Couldn't you sleep?"

"You were kissing my Aunt Casey," she accused. "You were *on top* of her."

Ian cleared his throat. "Well, Amy, we're..." his voice trailed away and he sent a desperate glance my way.

"We're really good friends," I finished for him. "We were kissing because we were glad to see each other."

She turned in my lap and cupped my face in her small hands. "You don't kiss my daddy like that."

I sent another silent prayer of thanks up through the ceiling. Amy, unknowing, had said exactly the right thing.

Ian stood and held a hand out. "Would you like a glass of water?"

To my everlasting surprise, she bolted from my lap and

took his hand. "Yes, please. I'm so thirsty. I dreamed I was living in the desert."

Ian took Amy's hand and cast another glance my way. I nodded toward the kitchen. Together, they left the room. "Was it a nightmare," he asked in a serious tone, "or only a dream?"

I sat on the couch, listening to their voices.

"It was a horrible nightmare," Amy told him. "There were prickly cactus plants, and big orange snakes that chased me all over the place."

Ian asked Amy where the glasses were. He chatted her up to the grind of the ice dispenser, and then at her direction led her back to her bedroom. Again, I listened to the conversation as he tucked her in, and started the bedtime music again.

He would be a wonderful father.

My foolish heart envisioned a future with him tucking our children into bed while I waited for him to come back and make love to me.

And I didn't even want children. At least, not yet.

Ian came back into the living room. "Thank God she got thirsty when she did, and not fifteen minutes later."

"I guess we'd better stick to talking." I patted the couch beside me.

"I was afraid you'd say that." Ian sat and took my hand in his.

"Okay." I took a breath and let it out. "Where do we start?"

Ian cut to the chase, completely skipping over Bianca's midnight-kitchen-appearance. "I'm selling the newspaper. Bianca and her husband are colleagues of mine, and as you've probably figured out by now, they're buying it. We had just signed the papers when I saw you at the realty office."

"Oh." My heart stopped beating, my lungs quit working, and I doubled over from what felt like a punch to the solar plexus. He wasn't just planning to sell the newspaper at some possible future date that might not occur. He'd already done it. "So that means..."

"Sweetheart." Ian stroked my back, but I didn't feel it, not really. "I never meant to stay. I buy failing newspapers, revive and flip them. Then I move on and repeat the process in another place. I've already bought another paper in South Carolina. I'm sorry."

I clenched my hands against my belly to keep my guts from falling out. A meaningless fling with the curvaceous Bianca would have been better than this.

He ran a hand down my back in a soothing gesture that didn't soothe me, not at all. "I never meant to hurt you."

"So, you're leaving." Why had he come here tonight and wrapped me in his arms like I meant something to him? Why had he called me sweetheart, and kissed me like he'd been starving for me? Why had he made me fall in love with him all over again when he'd been planning to leave all along?

"I had to break our date that night because her flight had been cancelled. She'd come to see the newspaper, and ended up staying at my house because—"

"Do you think that matters now?" I stiffened, pulled away, shut down. But he didn't seem to notice. He stroked my back as if I were a cat or dog who'd be grateful for any show of affection. "You're leaving. That's all that matters." Every slide of his magic fingers on my skin made me angrier than I already was. How dare he? How dare he treat me with such tenderness when all he'd ever meant to do was leave?

"Casey, please, this doesn't have to change—"

"Stop touching me!" I shoved his hand away.

He didn't try to touch me again, but let his hand hover over my back in a way I could still feel, damn him. "The deal in South Carolina closes next week. I usually move right away, but this time I'll stay in Angel Falls until the South Carolina paper is officially—"

"Move today." I jerked upright, stood and pivoted toward him like a wooden marionette who'd just had her strings pulled. "Leave as soon as you can."

"Casey, honey, please." His quiet, reasonable tone made me want to pick up the nearest sharp object and hurl it at his head.

"Please what?" I backed away from him as if he were holding out a poisonous snake. "Please let you fuck me even though you're planning to leave? Please admit that I've fallen in love with you even though you..." I choked on the words, and turned away before he could see the hurt I knew was plain on my face.

"Casey, honey, it's just business. It doesn't have to mean anything about us." He stood and came toward me but I kept backing up, always a step away from him.

"You meant to leave from the very beginning." I skirted the piano and edged into the entry hall. "You had a chance to buy the house you're renting, and you turned it down. I can't believe you'd suck me into thinking we had a relationship, knowing it was a lie, all along."

"Sweetheart, it was ne'er a lie." His Scottish brogue had deepened, the low tones reflecting the pain I felt, as if he felt it himself. But how could he feel pain over this? It was all his doing. It had been his choice from the beginning. Stumbling against the closed front door, I wrapped my fingers around the cold knob.

He put his hands on my shoulders and tried to pull me into his embrace. "Sweetheart, please don't do this."

I shrugged away, turned my back, rattled the damn doorknob that seemed to be stuck. "Why won't this stupid thing open?"

"We can still see each other on weekends." He hugged me from behind, and his heart hammered against my back.

My bones weren't connected anymore, and one deep breath would have me collapsing on the floor like a broken doll. "Why does God hate me?" I wailed to the ceiling.

"I'll drive here every weekend." Ian kept trying to wrap me in his arms while I squirmed away and fumbled with the deadbolt.

Finally, I yanked the door open, taking comfort from the blast of air that punched its cold fist through my nightgown. "Leave now, Ian. Leave now, before I say something really nasty."

"Casey, don't shut me out." He hugged me close in the doorway while the chill night air flapped and fluttered my nightgown against my legs. "Let's talk about this. We can figure something out."

I shoved him away, though all I really wanted was for him to hold me close again. "Oh?" My voice dripped sarcasm. I stepped backward onto the concrete porch, feeling its cold, hard surface scrape against the soles of my bare feet. "You mean, you'll change your mind and stay if I ask you? You'll back out on the deal you just made and buy that big-ass house you're renting? You'll marry me and stay here in Angel Falls to make babies and live happily ever after?"

He let go of me. "Lass, be reasonable. I'm only doing the job I came here to do. We can still see each other—"

"On weekends, yeah. I heard that part." I'd have been shivering from the cold if my anger hadn't been heating me from the inside. "We both know from experience how well long-distance relationships turn out, don't we?" I took another step back.

He stepped forward. "We can make it work if we want to."

"Wanting isn't enough." I backed to the edge of the porch. "You have to leave."

He stepped forward again, as close as he could get without touching me. "Please don't be this way. Let's—"

My throat tightened, as if he'd grabbed it with his long fingers and squeezed. But he wasn't even touching me. He seemed to know now that I was beyond his reach. I couldn't step back any farther, but I turned my face away from him. "Just go."

He walked down the steps and stood on the long side-walk looking up at me. "If I call you tomorrow, will you talk to me?"

"I don't know." I went back to the door and stood there, holding the knob. "I'll have to think about it."

He put his hands in his pockets, the gesture uncon-sciously self-protective. "Casey, I'm still trying to figure out what I want. I—"

"Don't waste your time trying to figure out what you want," I warned him. "You may not get it anyway." Then I went inside, shut the door, and slid the bolt home.

His car door slammed, he drove away, and I realized I still hadn't given him a chance to explain why that woman had been at his house late at night, wearing a slinky black robe.

And I didn't care, or at least, I shouldn't, because it didn't matter anymore. Ian was leaving me, just as I'd left Ben all those years ago. This time, I was finding out how it felt to be the one left behind. But I knew something I hadn't known back then. I knew the chances of making a long-distance relationship work were zero to nil.

I felt drained of emotion when I turned off the lights and went back to bed. Some part of me had died and gone on to another place, leaving a dry, empty shell. I crawled under the covers and closed my eyes, not caring whether I talked to Ian tomorrow. Not caring why he'd taken that woman to his house, or whether we ever got the chance to talk again.

None of it mattered, if he wasn't going to stay.

Chapter Nineteen

SATURDAY MORNING, MY FIRST WAKING thought was of Ian, but I pushed it away. Pushed him away. There was no point in torturing myself over him anymore. If he was determined to leave, I was determined to forget him as soon as possible.

I had more immediate, if much smaller, problems, such as how to get out of the little-girl-sandwich I'd woken up in. Amy backed up to me from the front, Maryann pressed against me from behind. I managed to wiggle out without waking them both by sliding out from the top like pulling a hand out of a glove, then crawling down the channel between their bodies.

Waking them wouldn't have been a serious tragedy, but at least I could have a cup of coffee in peace before the onslaught of children demanding breakfast. I walked past Jake's room and looked inside. He wouldn't wake until after noon without determined intervention. He lay sprawled under a heap of covers, extremities sticking out of the rounded pile like so many toothpicks from a marshmallow.

I turned on the coffee maker, tightened the sash on my robe and headed out to get the paper. I wasn't going to read the stupid thing, but I had to bring it inside to toss into the recycle bin. I should suggest to Ben that they get a parrot, so they could at least line the cage with newsprint. Now that the *Informer* was available online and even had its own Facebook page, I saw no earthly use for the printed version.

When I came back inside, the phone was ringing, and I snatched it up right away. If it hadn't already woken the kids, I didn't want it to. "Hello?"

"Casey, it's Ian. Don't hang up."

My heart flipped over and started beating way too fast, a flock of pigeons fighting to get out of my chest. "I won't hang up."

"When can we talk?"

"We're talking right now."

"When can we get together? I don't want to do this over the phone."

"Do what? What are you planning to do that you didn't do last night? You've already told me you're leaving. What else is there?"

A long silence stretched out, and I envisioned Ian counting to ten, hanging onto his temper by a thread. Good.

"Sweetheart, I know you're angry."

I snorted.

"You have every right to be mad at me. I should have told you from the beginning that I didn't intend to stay in Angel Falls."

I didn't say anything, which led to another long silence. I hoped he was pulling his hair out.

"When does Ben get home?"

"Tomorrow."

"What time?"

"Afternoon."

"I'll see you then."

"I don't think—"

But I was talking to myself. He'd already hung up.

"Okay, kids." I pulled into the driveway of the empty house by the canal and cut the engine. "You can open your eyes now."

"Whose house is this?" Jake asked.

"We'll talk about that in a minute." I unbuckled Amy's car seat. "Get out, everybody."

I carried Amy to the front stoop and set her onto her feet so I could unlock the door. Everyone followed me inside.

"Wow." Maryann's voice echoed off the bare walls. "This is nice."

Jake gave me a sidelong look. "Whose house is this?"

"Yours, if y'all and your daddy like it. What would you think about that?"

Jake scoffed. "You mean move away from Nicky and all my friends in the neighborhood? No way."

"Your friends are only a bike-ride away."

"But I love my room at home," Maryann whined.

Amy skipped across the living room floor and examined the pocket door between the living room and the dining room. "Look, it slides."

They wandered the first floor, peeking into doorways, looking out windows.

"Look, Jake," Maryann squealed from the kitchen. "The back yard is huge."

"That big tree looks good for climbing," I said. "Maybe your dad would build y'all a tree house."

"Tree house!" Amy shrieked, enjoying the echo in the empty rooms downstairs.

Maryann pulled at my sleeve. "Can I go upstairs?"

"Sure. Just for fun, why don't you decide which bedroom you'd like best?"

Jake pushed past her and rushed up the stairs two at a time. "I'm getting first pick!"

"No fair," she screeched, pelting up the stairs behind him. "You meanie, I get first pick."

I followed more slowly, holding Amy's hand. "If you and your daddy decide you want to move, he can help you choose which room you want."

Jake poked his head out the open doorway of the room he'd just entered. "I don't want to move."

"Me, neither." Maryann followed Jake into one of the bedrooms overlooking the canal. "But if we do, I want this room. Aunt Casey," she called. Amy and I made it up the stairs and joined them. "It's bigger than my room at home, isn't it?"

"Yes. Much bigger. And look," I opened the lid on a built-in window seat. "A toy box."

Jake went on to explore the rest of the upstairs. "I found my room," he yelled from across the hall. "Come see."

We followed his voice to the largest of the four rooms. It had a dormer window on the street side and another that looked out at the branches of a large magnolia. Across from the dormer window, built-in bookshelves filled the entire wall.

"Look at this." Jake opened a small door about three feet tall, revealing a crawl-space to the attic. "I could hide stuff in here."

"Which room do you like best?" I asked Amy. She'd been unusually silent.

Her answer was a shrug.

"I think I know which one you'd like best." I took her hand and led her to the second bedroom that faced the canal. It was connected to Maryann's room by a shared bath.

"It's almost the same as the one Maryann likes. See the window seat? It makes a good toy box. What do you think?"

Amy stuck a thumb into her mouth and shrugged again.

"We could paint the walls pink. You could put stars on the ceiling just like you have in your room now."

Amy took her thumb out of her mouth with a wet-sounding pop. "The very same stars?"

"Yes, the very same stars. We could take them from your old room and bring them here."

Amy sucked her thumb again for a moment, her fair brows knitted. "My toys, too?"

"We could bring everything in your house, if your daddy and y'all decide to live here."

Amy looked undecided, sucking furiously on her thumb. She tugged the hem of my shirt as if yanking the bell-pull of an old-time hotel. I knelt down and put my arms around her. She pulled my ear until I brought my head close to her mouth.

"But how will mommy find us when she comes home?" Amy asked in a small voice. "How will she know where we are?"

"Oh, sweetheart." I looked to see whether Jake or Maryann had heard. It seemed they hadn't.

"Can we go see the back yard?" Maryann asked.

"Sure. You two go ahead. Amy and I will catch up."

Jake started down the stairs. "I want to go in the canal."

"Me, too." Amy pulled my hand, her forlorn question forgotten for the moment, so we followed the two older kids down the stairs.

"We'll stand at the back of the yard and look down."
I had played in the canal as a child. So had every other
kid I'd known. It was a slippery, forbidden place dug
twenty feet deep and at least as wide, out of the limestone the town of Angel Falls was built on. Built for
drainage so long ago that no one I knew remembered
when, it snaked through the city and emptied into the
Black River. The canal is often a quiet, magical place
where birds flit through the leafy canopy overhead and
small animals drink from the circular pools dug by
decades of swirling currents of rainwater. Other times,
a maelstrom of white-capped waves pound through the
channel, charging toward release at the river's edge.

Amy and I joined the others, and we all looked over
the back fence together.

Most days, the canal floor would be visible here, pale as
chalk in some places, bright green with slippery algae in
others. But today, because of the unusually rainy fall season, the waters churned, high and brown with sediment.

Amy's question whirled in my mind like the rushing waters below. A question that would have to be
answered, but perhaps better answered by Ben. I wanted
to talk to Amy, to help her work though her questions
about Melody's passing. But maybe my willingness to
help enabled Ben to distance himself from his children
when they should be growing closer as a family.

"Look!" Maryann grabbed Jake's arm. "I see a snap-
ping turtle!"

"That's a Red-eared Slider, Doofus." Jake shook Maryann's hand off his arm.

Maryann stamped her foot. "I am not a Doofus!"

Seeking distraction from the brewing argument, I
walked back toward the house. "Come look at the climb-

ing tree. See that bunch of leaves there at the top?"

"Yeah, I know," Jake said, his voice bored. "It's a squirrel nest."

"Really?" Maryann asked, "Are there any baby squirrels in it?"

I put my arm around her shoulders. "Not now. But I'd bet this tree houses a new batch of babies every spring."

"I'm hungry," Amy whined.

I held out a hand to her. "Who wants to go to Bo's Diner and then to the park?" For once, Jake offered no opposition, and we locked the door on the empty house and piled into the car.

On Sunday, Lois took the kids to Sunday school and planned to keep them through the afternoon, so Lizzie and I headed home. On the way, I called Ben to tell him to pick up the kids at Lois and Herb's house when he got back into town.

"I'm almost home now," he said. "I left Birmingham at dawn, so you and I could look at the new house together while the kids are at church with Lois. You still have the key?"

I don't know why I suddenly wanted to crawl into bed and sleep for days. I suppose I was just tired of dealing with other people's junk. Even if it was good junk, I was sick of it.

"Ben, can't you look at it by yourself? The key is on your kitchen table."

"Where are you?"

"I told you, Lizzie and I are going home."

"I'm pulling into my driveway right now. I'll get the

key. Meet me at the new house."

I sighed. "Ben, please. I'm tired, and I need to do laundry."

"Come on, Angel." His voice was cajoling, sweet, boyish. The same one he'd used to convince me to take my bra off when I was sixteen. "I want us to talk without the kids around. I promise you'll be back at your house before ten a.m."

"Fine," I snapped. Parking in front of my house, I let Lizzie out of the car and marched across the morning-damp grass to let her into the back yard. "I'll be there in ten minutes."

I made it in ten, but Ben was already there. His empty car was in the driveway, its hood making pinging noises as it cooled. He had left the house door open a crack, so I went in. "Ben?"

"Up here." I heard a door close upstairs and then the sound of footsteps in the hall. Looking up, I watched him come down the stairs, wearing jeans and a travel-wrinkled T-shirt, a lopsided grin on his handsome face. "The house is perfect."

"I'm glad you like it," I said. "I thought it would work for y'all."

Ben met me at the bottom of the stairs and pinned me with his intense blue gaze. "This doesn't upset you, does it? The fact that I want to move out of the house where Melody and I..."

His voice trailed away awkwardly, and I knew why he felt strange talking about this. I had a history with Ben that didn't include Melody, but I also had a history with Melody that didn't include Ben. She was my best friend, and I might have felt outraged on her behalf that Ben was ready to abandon the home where they'd shared so many happy years together.

"It's okay." I put a hand on his shoulder. "I wasn't sure moving was the right thing for y'all at first, but I've come around. I think this will be perfect for you and the kids."

Ben sat on the bottom stair and drew me down to sit beside him. "What about you?"

I fiddled with the laces of my Keds. "What about me?"

Ben sighed, and leaned against me. "It's too early for me to be thinking about starting a relationship, but one of these days, I don't know when, I will be ready. And when that time comes, you'd be the perfect—"

"Stop right there." I held up a hand. "I refuse to be anybody's most convenient choice. Even yours."

"It's not that." Ben put an arm around my shoulders when I would have pulled away. "You know I love you. Like I said before. Always have, always will."

"I know you'll always love me. And I'll always love you. But it's not the same kind of love you had with Mel."

"It was, once. And it's more than a lot of people ever get."

"Well, I want more." I leaned my head on his shoulder and snaked an arm around his waist. "Don't you?"

"I've had more. I had more with you, then I had more with Melody. Maybe that's all I can expect in one lifetime."

"Ben, I don't think that's true." I squeezed his hand, and held him close with the arm I still had around his waist. "I was your first love, just like you were mine. But Melody was your soul mate. That doesn't mean you can't have another. I'd be really sad to see you settle for less. I'd be sad to see me settle for less."

"You're my soul mate, too, Casey. You've always been a part of me." Ben looked down at our clasped hands.

I squeezed his hand. "If I hadn't left, things would have

been very different, wouldn't they?"

"Yeah." He cuddled me close against his side, and I felt for an instant what it would have been like to have been sheltered by this man for all of my adult life.

"Ben…" I didn't want to ask, but I had to know. "If I had stayed here, would you have chosen me instead of Mel?"

He was silent for a moment, and I knew I shouldn't have asked the question. To even think it wasn't fair to Melody's memory.

"Angel…"

"I'm sorry." I drew my hand out of his grasp and placed my fingers over his lips. "That was selfish and stupid of me."

Ben clasped my hand and kissed my fingers. "I don't think Melody would mind if I told you this. I did choose you. I had already packed my bags to leave for New York when she found out she was pregnant with Jake. We'd gotten drunk together and consoled each other, just once, because we missed you. Jake happened, and I couldn't afford to look back. I had to make it work with Melody, no matter what my heart wanted."

I burrowed close against Ben's side and savored the comfort his lean body offered. I had already guessed as much. To have it confirmed didn't give the rush of vindication I'd expected, but I felt a warm flow of acceptance that events had unfolded exactly as they should. Maybe the things we'd wanted hadn't been the right things, so fate had intervened and helped each of us to follow the path that had been pre-ordained. "So you and Melody made it work."

"We did." Ben unglued his hand from mine and wiped his eyes. "If we hadn't, we'd have ruined our lives, and yours, and Jake's. We had to forget the past and learn to love each other as more than friends. We had to learn to be more than two of the Three Musketeers. We did what we had to do to stay together, and somehow we created something bigger than both of us. I guess we turned into soulmates, despite ourselves."

I leaned against his shoulder. "I wonder why you and I keep circling back to this place, when we're obviously not meant to be together."

Ben stiffened. "I don't know what's so obvious."

"Ben, I love you, and I love your kids, but I'd always feel like I was betraying Melody if we ever... you know."

Ben pulled me into a full hug, turning me toward him so he could put both arms around me. "You were never second choice with me. And if Melody had a choice, I know she'd choose you to take her place."

His words were so close to what Melody had said, a shiver skimmed along my spine. I hugged Ben, then pulled away. I loved Mel, and I loved Ben. We had been the Three Musketeers, once. But now, we had to move on and find our own identities, separate from each other, but maybe still connected in all the ways that mattered. "We need to talk."

Ben took his cue from me and put a little distance between us, leaning back on his elbows against the stairs. "About what?"

"I don't know if you've looked at the school calendar, but the kids have Thanksgiving break all this week."

"Yeah. Lois invited us to her house for Turkey Day. You too, of course."

I brushed the invitation away, a fly at my shoulder. "Sometime this week, you need to take the kids to get a Christmas tree. The best ones are at the tree farm in Ferndale. The grocery store trees aren't fresh. You'll spend all your time sweeping up dead pine needles."

Ben smiled, just a little upward curve at the corners of his mouth. "You are so bossy."

"I'm just telling you what Melody would want you to do." I leaned forward with my elbows on my knees and looked back at him. "Christmas will sneak up on you before you know it. Take each kid separately to buy gifts for the others. I'll babysit if you need me to. Go out for ice cream or some other treat while you're shopping. It's important that you spend quality time alone with each child. And I'm not just talking about this shopping thing. Understand?"

Ben nodded. He was beginning to look a little shell-shocked, but I wasn't done.

"I've made a list—top drawer of your roll-top desk—of who each child needs to shop for, in case you don't know. Teachers, best friends, relatives."

"God, Casey." He made the little "Tsss..." sound between his teeth that meant he was getting a belly full, so I hurried with the rest.

"Take Amy to visit Santa at the mall. Listen to what she asks for, and buy it as soon as you can. The stores run out of the most popular toys. Jake and Maryann won't do the Santa thing. You'll have to ask. But buy everything early, or you'll never be able to find it all."

"You are so mean," he teased, trying to lighten the mood.

"I'm almost finished." This was the hard part. I hadn't meant to say any of this, but laying my burden down on Ben's capable shoulders suddenly felt like the right thing to do. "You know I love you."

Ben leaned forward. "Of course I do."

"You know I love your children, and I would lay down my life for any one of you."

"Oh, Casey." He reached out to me.

I pushed him away. "If you or the kids ever need me, I'm there for you. But." I took a deep breath. "Y'all need to stand on your own feet. If I keep showing up, interfering, then you don't get the chance to grow together the way Melody would have wanted. I've sacrificed part of my life to allow you to be absent from yours."

"Angel." I heard all the words he couldn't say—I'm sorry, I love you, I'll always love you, I wanted you but I couldn't change what happened. "I didn't mean to take advantage."

"I know you didn't. Everything I did for you or the kids, I did because I wanted to. Because I love them, and I loved Melody, and I'll always love you, no matter what. "

He tugged me close, and this time I let him.

"Even though you're an idiot," I felt I had to add, "a lot of the time."

"Point taken." We sat there for a while, absorbing each other's energy. After a second, we moved apart. He leaned against the wall and I leaned against the stair rail. He nudged my knee with his, his blue eyes solemn. "Go on. I know you're not done."

I took a breath before the plunge. "The thing is, we all need to move on. And when you find someone to share your life, it needs to be because you love her more than you need her."

"I'm not sure I agree, but I'm listening." He reached for my hand, straightening out my fingers and stroking down their length the way Ian had done.

Ben's touch imparted cool comfort. Ian's had ignited passionate heat. "Ben, it's my turn to find my soul mate."

"You and the Newspaper Nazi?" Ben squeezed my hand.

"Don't you ever tell Ian I called him that." I scowled

and pointed a finger at his face. "I know people who'd murder you for fifty dollars and toss you into the canal. And some owe me money for their kids' ballet lessons."

"I won't." But his promise was made with a grin that looked a little too devilish for my liking.

"Anyway, it doesn't matter," I said. "Ian is leaving, and we all know how well long-distance relationships work out."

Ben took my face in his hands and pinned me with his intense blue gaze. "I was stupid back then, punishing us all because I couldn't have you in exactly the way I wanted. I won't be that stupid again." His hands slid from my face to my shoulders. "I understand that if you don't try with Ian, you'll always wonder what might have happened if you had. If he's what you want, I'll back off. At least for now. But if it doesn't work out, I'll be waiting."

Chapter Twenty

BACK HOME, BEFORE TEN A.M. as Ben had promised, I dumped my dirty clothes into the washer and started weekend house-cleaning.

I planned to call Ian later, but first I was going to take this time alone, scrubbing and vacuuming and mopping and thinking. I had already made my decision, but I still needed to make peace with it. My ego rebelled against my heart's choice, but I planned to offer to drive—Hell, I'd walk, if I had to—all the way to South Carolina on weekends. I was willing to work at building a lasting relationship. What I was not willing to do, was to be Ian's no-strings-attached weekend-fuck-buddy. He could take me or leave me on those terms.

The church bells down the street signaled the end of the morning service. I didn't hear the doorbell, but Lizzie's happy bark announced Ian's tall, broad-shouldered form standing behind the thick beveled glass door.

I'd been cleaning for a good hour and a half, so I looked like a dirt-smeared homeless person. I wrenched open the door and faced him with a belligerent yet hopeful stare. "Yes?"

He grinned a sexy, lopsided grin that was totally

unwarranted given the fact that we weren't exactly on speaking terms. "Hi."

I cocked my weight back on one hip and pretended I was wearing motorcycle leathers instead of slouchy socks and ratty sweats. "Your dime, start talking."

He shouldered past me, petting Lizzie on the head and breathing all the air in my living room. "Pack a bag for the night."

I drew myself up. "What makes you think I'm going anywhere with you?"

He strode down the hall, veering into the laundry nook to pick up the empty duffel bag I'd left in front of the washer. "I'm not asking permission." He marched into my bedroom and tossed the duffel onto the freshly-made bed. "I'll kidnap you, if that's what it takes to make you listen to me."

"You've had success with this caveman attitude in the past?" I trotted after him, hovering in my bedroom doorway while he opened my closet door.

"Where's that black velvet dress?"

"I have no idea which dress you're talking about," I lied, remembering his fully clothed body spread across my naked one.

"Ah, here it is." He took down a hanger and whipped off the dress, then wadded the velvet into a ball and stuffed it into the duffel.

"Wait!" I rushed forward and retrieved the dress, holding it against me to fold it properly. "You'll wrinkle it." Washable velvet didn't wrinkle easily, but he didn't know that.

"Underwear."

Turning toward my dresser, he opened the top drawer and took out the first scrap of fabric he touched, a tattered old pair of yellowed granny panties I reserved for the heaviest days of my period.

"Not those!" I snatched them out of his hand and buried them at the bottom of the drawer.

Ian backed off and crossed his arms over his chest. "You pack, then."

I brushed past him and took out black thongs, a lacy, high-rise pair with just enough spandex for tummy control. "Where are we going?"

He looked smug. "I'm not telling."

I eyed him. He wore a tan cotton sweater that draped deliciously over every ridge of his divine torso, and tight-enough faded gray jeans. "Do I get to change before we go?"

He eyed me right back, his gaze roaming over my sweaty, tangled hair and grimy, holey sweats. "Do what you want. You look fine to me."

It would serve him right if I didn't bother to change clothes. Whipping the sweatshirt off over my head, I tossed it aside and skimmed sweats, panties, and socks down in one smooth stroke. Enjoying his widened eyes and the slight flare of his nostrils, I stood before him naked. "Maybe I should go like this?"

He grinned. "I doubt we'd get far."

"Go wait in the living room while I take a shower."

I took the quickest cold shower in the history of the world. I had used up all the hot water doing laundry, but the cold water didn't dampen my mixed emotions. Crackling with energy, desperate hope, and sexual excitement, I drew the black dress on over my wet head and stepped into the sexiest black pumps I owned.

I stuffed the panties I wasn't wearing, the hairbrush I'd just used, and a change of clothes into the duffel. Yanking open my pajama drawer, I added a peach-colored silk-and-lace nightgown. Tromping into the bathroom,

I grabbed the still-packed toiletry bag and shoved it on top, then zipped the whole thing up.

"I'm ready." I threw the words out like the challenge they were.

"Good." Ian took the duffel. "So am I."

"We are not having sex again." I took a shawl from the hall closet and settled it over my shoulders, then let it slide provocatively down on one side. "I don't sleep with anyone unless there's the possibility of a permanent relationship." I hoped he would go crazy, knowing he had no chance of getting into my panties.

Especially when he found out I wasn't wearing any.

"Fine." He set the duffel by front door. Lizzie slinked forward inquiringly, and Ian stroked her head. "Sorry, girl. You don't get to come this time." He flicked an authoritative glance my way. "I've filled both food dispensers and put out fresh water. Are you ready?"

"Yes."

"Good. Let's go."

Why did I let Ian get away with his high-handed manner? Why did I go along with his plans without knowing what they were?

Part of it was curiosity. Part of it was the still-living hope that he would change his mind about leaving and give our relationship a real chance. Most of all, I had to trust him—even though I didn't, quite. Every plus had a built-in minus, every minus had a plus. He had baggage that might prevent him from chancing a permanent relationship, but he was struggling with the decision. He might balk at any time, but he wouldn't hurt me on purpose.

I settled into the passenger seat and fastened my seatbelt. Ian stowed my duffel in the trunk. He drove out of town on Highway Eighty, which meant he wasn't taking me to his house. It would be a hotel in Tuscaloosa. Maybe dinner and a movie. I'd been hoping to see the new Bradley Cooper movie sometime this week.

I took Ian's CD case from the glove box, and slid an Enya CD into the player. The words to the song about love and choices and uncertainty cut so close, I turned the volume down. "Ian, what are we doing?"

He glanced my way. "I wish I knew."

I'd been talking about more immediate plans—Bradley Cooper or Brad Pitt—but since Ian had opened the door to a more in-depth conversation, I decided to go with it. "What do you want from me?"

He reached across the console and caressed my thigh. "I want a chance."

I made a small sound of frustration. "A chance at what? Can you be specific? Exactly what do you want from our relationship? Do we even have one?"

"Of course, we do." He sounded offended, but wrapped his fingers around mine. "How can you imply we don't?"

"It's easy. If we had a relationship, you'd tell me important shit like the fact that you fucking well planned to leave here."

He lifted our clasped hands and ran his knuckle down my cheek. "Did you realize you curse whenever you feel threatened?"

I tugged my hand from his grasp. "Don't think you can change the subject."

He sighed and put his hand back on the steering wheel. "Okay. You want me to tell you what I expect from our relationship."

"Yes." I laced my fingers together in my lap to keep from touching him.

"I came here for business. Period. I wasn't looking to meet someone I'd want to spend my life with."

My heart kicked at those words.

"But then I met you."

I didn't say anything, didn't even look his way, because it took every ounce of energy to sit and listen to what he was saying without trying to guide his words.

"I have to admit that I don't know whether I'll ever want to get married again."

I swallowed my disappointment. "Okay. Well. Thanks for being honest."

He reached for my hand, but I kept my fingers clamped tight together and he had to settle for putting his hand on top of mine. "Casey, you have to understand. Maeve and I had the perfect relationship. Then we got married, and it all went to hell. It *was* hell. For both of us. We made each other miserable, and ultimately our decision to marry killed her. Can't you see why this is hard for me?"

"I'm not Maeve." My tone was wooden. I wanted to call Ian a coward for not wanting to try again. I wanted to lash out because his fears were more important than our love.

But neither of us had said yet that we loved each other. So maybe that was the problem. If he loved me, he'd take the chance. He wanted me, but a wide gulf stood between wanting and loving. A gulf he might never cross.

"I know you're not Maeve." He squeezed my clenched fists with his long fingers. "But I'm still the same—"

"Are you sure?" I chanced a look at his face. Sunlight through the windshield made his amber eyes sparkle though his expression was serious.

He shrugged but didn't answer.

"Maybe you're not the same man now that you were then. You just don't realize it yet."

His lips quirked up on one side, into an almost-smile. "Maybe."

God, he was so sexy and handsome, I almost smiled back, delighted over the sheer pleasure of looking at him. "I'm not going to have sex with you again. Not until you've decided you can commit to something permanent." Big words I'd just said. I hoped I could stick to them.

"Fair enough."

Then I realized, I hadn't said what I really meant. I wanted more than a permanent living arrangement. I wanted happily-ever-after, and I'd better not be scared to say it. He'd been honest with me, and I had to have the courage to do the same, not matter what it cost. "I want marriage, and until you can commit to that, you'll be keeping your hands to yourself."

This time he did smile, a full-out grin that melted my heart and my resolve all in one go. "I'll keep my hands to myself, if I can remember to. That's about all I can promise."

"Then I'll just have to remember for both of us." I hoped to hell I could.

"I'm still kidnapping you for the night."

"I'll still make you keep your hands to yourself."

Ian pulled into the parking lot of The Plantation. "I'm bringing you here for lunch, by way of apology for the night I broke our date."

"Apology accepted, but you're still not off the hook for the other thing." We both knew the 'other thing' was that woman standing in his kitchen long after midnight.

"We'll talk about that in a minute." Ian helped me out of the car, took my hand, and led me into the restaurant. The hostess looked up. Ian smiled his melt-your-heart smile. "We have a reservation."

The poor woman smiled back, her expression dazed as if she'd been blinded by a flash of light. I thought I might have to pinch her, but she snapped out of it. "Oh, yes. Mr. Buchanan. Your table is this way."

The hostess led us to the table and a waitress passed by to offer complimentary Mimosas before I'd even put my napkin in my lap. The Plantation's Sunday Brunch was legendary, but even that didn't explain the over-the-top attentiveness. Excellent restaurant service must be one of the perks of going out with a devastatingly attractive man. I didn't mind having people flutter around us in an effort to provide good service. But if anything ever came of this thing between us, I'd have to get used to being with a man other women wanted a piece of.

Ian leaned back in his chair. "Do you remember the weather that night I broke our date?"

Odd conversation opener, but I took a sip of my mimosa and followed it. "Yes. It was raining."

"You remember it flooded pretty badly in places?"

"Yes." When I'd driven out to Ian's house, I'd had to detour around flooded areas, and the roadsides had looked more like lakes than land.

"You remember that the motel, the only one in town, flooded as well?" He lifted his glass to his lips and watched me over the rim, waiting for the information to sink in.

Understanding dawned. "So, she was staying at the motel, but then her room flooded..."

"No, she had already checked out of the hotel downtown, and I was about to take her to the airport when she got the text that her flight was cancelled because of the weather. I tried to find her a place to stay for the night, but the motel was flooded, so the hotel was full. Even that scary B&B behind the Baptist church was full. I didn't think I had any choice but to invite her to stay in the guestroom at my house. I called you as soon as I knew."

I shot him a slightly-accusing glare. "And you didn't have any food in the refrigerator, but you did have a reservation, so you took her to dinner instead of me."

"If you had answered the phone, I could have explained everything, but you didn't. And I didn't feel I could leave her alone at my house, so I couldn't very well drive into town and force you to talk to me."

"I'm sorry, Ian." I fiddled with my butter knife and unburdened my soul. "I was an idiot. My only excuse is that my feelings were hurt. I thought you'd tossed me over for somebody else. Since that's happened to me before, I guess I'm a little sensitive about it. Maybe I overreacted."

"Apology accepted." Ian reached across the table and covered my hand with his. "I was wrong not to tell you from the beginning that I didn't plan to stay in Angel Falls. At first, I didn't think we knew each other well enough for my long-term plans to matter. After that, I was afraid you'd tell me to piss off if you knew I wasn't going to stay."

I turned my palm up under his. "Apology accepted."

We sat in silence for a moment, and the waitress arrived with our food.

"So now that we've forgiven each other," I ventured, "where do we go from here?" My heart wanted him to say that he'd stay in Angel Falls and we'd live happily ever after. My mind knew it wasn't that simple.

"I don't know." He cut a small piece of steak and speared it with his fork, then held it out to me. "Try this. It's very good."

I took the food into my mouth and chewed, but it tasted like mush because I felt like I was waiting to hear back from a dance audition. Would he choose me, and Angel Falls? Or would this long-distance relationship gamble leave us both empty-handed?

"It's good, isn't it?" Ian raised an eyebrow, waiting for me to speak, wondering, no doubt, whether I planned to act like a grown-up, or whether I planned to throw a childish tantrum and insist on getting my way.

I swallowed. The meat went down, along with my unrealistic expectations. "It is. Very good. Thank you."

Ian sat back, frustration clear in the way his eyebrows drew together and his lips tightened. "Are we ever going to get past this... this... whatever it is, and just enjoy each other's company?"

Chastened, I sat back as well. He was trying. The least I could do was try, too. His decision wasn't as black-and-white as I was making it out to be, and he wasn't going to decide overnight. I had to quit being so damned impatient and let things unfold as they would. Hadn't I learned anything from my experiences? Fate would have the last word, no matter what I wanted. If I had any sense, I'd enjoy the time I had with Ian and not insist on having everything or nothing. "I'm sorry. It takes me a little while to shift gears. I've been angry and upset for so long, it's hard to let go. I guess it's going to take some time for me to get used to the fact that you're leaving."

"My leaving is only geography, Casey." His expression softened the words. "Can't we take some time to see if our relationship develops into something?"

As far as I was concerned, our relationship *had* developed into something. I was in love with Ian, and that was all I needed to know. The rest was up to him. "I'll be okay with it," I said. "Just give me some time to adjust."

After dinner, Ian drove toward Tuscaloosa, just as I'd thought he would. Maybe he'd stop there, or maybe he'd keep going toward Birmingham. I didn't much care if we kept driving all the way to Kalamazoo, because we were enjoying each other's company so much. We listened to one CD after another, comparing musical tastes, or forgetting to listen altogether as our talk veered to other topics. I realized after a while, that we'd been so deep in conversation on the way, I hadn't even noticed when we passed the place where Melody's SUV had gone off the road.

Closing my eyes, I said a prayer asking Mel's forgiveness; for forgetting to remember her when we'd driven past the place she died, for making the decision to abandon Ben and her kids so I could build my own life, and especially, for being jealous of her happiness with Ben.

I woke hours later with a crick in my neck, as late afternoon sunlight knifed sharp rays through the windshield and into my closed eyes. I sat up slowly, careful not to let any abrupt movements escalate the sore muscle into an outright spasm. The highway we traveled wasn't the familiar one between Birmingham and Angel Falls. "Where are we?"

"Almost there." Ian reached across to caress my thigh. "Have a nice nap?"

"Um-hmm." I massaged my neck. "Where are we?"

"You don't get to know. I'm kidnapping you, remember?"

"Oh, yeah."

"Would you put in another CD? I'm getting fairly sick of this one."

I rifled through the CD holder and switched out the one playing for U2. Relaxing into my seat, I looked up and noticed a signpost. Exit to Columbia, one-half mile. We were just a stone's throw from Columbia, South Carolina, where Ian had just bought another newspaper to resurrect from the dead before he moved on.

Chapter Twenty One

I POINTED AT THE ROAD SIGN. "Why South Carolina?"

"There's something here I wanted us to see."

Treetops and buildings sped past as we winged our way onto an overpass. Ian's secretive smile spread as he took an off ramp that dumped us onto a grid of roads surrounded by tall buildings.

I sat up and wiped my eyes. "I don't know if I trust you while you're wearing that Cheshire-cat-grin."

Ian pulled into a parking garage. "Maybe you shouldn't trust me. I might just be trying to get into your panties."

"I'm not worried about that," I said with an airy wave. "I'm not wearing any."

"I knew that." He drove up the spiral parking deck to the second level, taking a hand off the wheel long enough to slide a finger along my panty-less waistline. "But you know it kills me to hear you say it."

I couldn't help the wicked giggle that escaped. "I hope it drives you crazy."

It was mean of me to tease him, especially since it soon became apparent that he'd gone to a great deal of trouble and expense to get orchestra-level seats at *The Nutcracker* ballet. Though we could've gone to Birmingham or Atlanta to see the balletomane's winter season classic, he had gone to the trouble to find a performance in South Carolina. Getting me used to the commute, I figured.

"Thank you," I whispered in his ear an hour later, as the Sugar Plum Fairy wowed the audience with the crisp perfection of her technique.

"You're welcome," he whispered back, giving me a quick buss on the cheek. "I'm glad you're enjoying it."

I was enjoying it, to my surprise. I had gone to one ballet performance since I broke my ankle and lost my dream job—not only my dream job, but my dream life, my dream of who I could be, my sense of who I was. I had cried through that whole performance, because the one thing that had always given me joy only brought sadness and regret.

Now, because of Ian, the joy had returned. I could watch someone else nail those thirty-two fouette turns and feel nothing but appreciation.

Appreciation, and arousal. Ian's warmth reached me, the faint spice of his aftershave, his unique combination of pheromones and testosterone.

Plus, my soft velvet dress caressed my bare bottom every time I moved.

I pretended to watch Mother Ginger onstage, but really, I just wanted to get Ian alone and rip off his clothes. Even though I had threatened to withhold sex until he realized he wanted to spend his entire life making love to me, my sensitized nerve endings didn't give a flip.

After the performance, we walked through the parking deck to the car. Still under the spell of the performance, we didn't talk. I couldn't imagine doing anything but checking into the nearest hotel and having my way with him. I sighed with the delicious contentment of being held close to a gorgeous man while cold air nipped at my face.

"Tired?" He pulled me closer.

"Content," I answered.

"Good." His voice rumbled, vibrating through his rib cage and into mine.

"What now? Are you kidnapping me to a hotel room?" A huge yawn took me by surprise.

Ian chuckled. "Ready for bed, are you?"

"Um-hmm."

We reached the car, and Ian unlocked the doors. "You're awfully quiet."

"Trying to decide whether to back out of my ultimatum." Maybe honesty was the best policy, talking about my feelings and conflicts instead of trying to finesse the outcome of something I had no control over.

His hand strayed to my backside, caressing through my dress. "I can help you with that decision."

I ignored his seeking hand. "I'm also tired. Please tell me you have a plan that includes sleeping in a warm bed soon."

"I have a plan, sweetheart." He ushered me into the car's cold interior.

Less than a half-hour later, he opened our hotel room door, flipped on the lights, and dropped our bags onto the floor. "You take the bathroom first." He launched himself at the bed and somehow landed perfectly aligned along one side with the remote control in one hand, the other hand pillowing his head. "I'll see if there's anything good on TV."

I took a quick, hot bath, brushed my teeth, and slipped on my nightie. The flowing apricot silk had stretch-lace insets in all the right places. I brushed my hair upside down, then tossed my head to settle the strands in a soft cloud around my face. Maybe I would let him talk me into having sex. I could always claim afterward that he wore me down.

When I came into the room, Ian looked my way, his face arrested for a heartbeat. "My turn." He took his toiletry bag off the dresser and moved past me. At the bathroom door, he turned back. "Here's the remote." He tossed it at me.

I caught it, climbed under the covers, turned off the TV, and closed my eyes. The shower came on and Ian started humming something off-key. Deliberately, I relaxed each part of my body, from my toes to the top of my head. I concentrated on slowing my breathing, so I could convincingly pretend to be asleep when he got out of the shower. I knew I'd give in, but I wanted him to have to work for it, just a little.

I relaxed myself right to sleep, and started to dream.

I was running down a black snake highway, chased by the big truck that had killed Melody. A dark wind pushed me from behind, set my hair flying about my face, obscuring my vision, stinging my skin.

Then Melody was clutching my arm, slowing me down, begging me to save her. "My children need me," she cried. The truck kept coming, right behind us now. Mel's fingers dug into my skin. "Casey, don't let me die."

All at once, I was lifted up off the black highway and into the sky. The strength and warmth of the arms around me became familiar and comforting. Ian's strong arms. His warmth surrounding me. "Shhh," he whispered, his warm breath close to my ear. "You're all right. It's just a dream."

I slid my arms under his T-shirt, seeking the comfort of his skin. He lay down with me and pulled me close, arranging me into the curve of his body. My head was pillowed on his shoulder, my hands under his shirt, curled against his chest.

I spread my fingers over the rough-smooth feel of his sleek, muscular chest with its covering of springy hair. Turning toward him, I opened my mouth to taste the delicious spot between his neck and shoulder, the clean, soap-scented salt of his taut, warm skin.

Then I moved up, and up some more, until my lips touched his. The inside of his mouth was warm, like the rest of him. His arms tightened around me. He ran his tongue over my teeth and sleeked it inside, stroking my tongue.

I pulled his shirt up as far as I could get it, but his weight had the fabric trapped under him. "Ian, please."

"Please, what?" He rolled me to my back. He sat astride my thighs, pulled the shirt over his head and tossed it aside. I slid my hands upward from the flat, ridged wall of his stomach to the bulging curve of his pecs.

"Kiss me."

His wide shoulders shadowed me as he claimed my mouth for another kiss. He caressed my face, sliding fingers along the seam of our kissing lips, down lower, skimming along my jaw, down to caress my breasts. I pushed down the waistband of his underwear, touching.

Grabbing my hands, he held them above my head on the pillow while his body covered mine. The hard heat of him beckoned through unwelcome layers of clothing. Teasing. Taunting. Torturing. I welcomed the pressure, but wanted more. I reached down again, trying to get rid of his damn underwear. "Ian, please."

"What happened to your hands-off policy?" He brought my hands up again but held them more firmly this time, one strong hand encircling both my wrists.

"I don't know," I admitted. "Maybe I was wrong."

He stole my words with a kiss, sucking, devouring. His free hand skimmed down a length of apricot silk, pressing hard against my pubic bone. I moved against his hand, seeking the fulfillment his body denied me. "Please," I said into his mouth.

"God, lass," he whispered against my lips, "what you do to me..."

"Ian, I want you inside me." I pulled against his restraining hold, but he held fast. "I need you there. Please..."

He let go of my wrists. Almost roughly, he pulled my panties down. I kicked them off then sat up a little so I could pull my nightgown up over my head. Ian took the scrap of silk and lace and tossed it on the floor. "Yes," I murmured. This was more like it.

With an arm around my naked waist, he hauled me farther down the bed. His body raked down mine, raining kisses in a burning trail until his mouth finally began to relieve the aching heat between my legs.

"Ahhh," I drew my knees back. Twined my fingers in his short, dark hair. "Ahhh, Ian, that feels so good... so good..." And yet, and yet. What I really wanted was the pressure of his body inside mine. I grabbed his shoulders, tried to pull him up.

He kissed a line up my stomach. His chest brushed against my belly as he paused to tease each breast with his mouth. He kissed my neck, my jaw, my chin. Captured my mouth with his lips, still holding the tangy taste of my body. I welcomed his kiss, dragged his underwear down, tossed it aside.

He stopped kissing me. His eyes searched mine. "What happened to no-sex-without-commitment?"

"I don't know. Tomorrow I may change my mind again."

His arms trembled as he held his weight above me. "Would it help if I told you I love you?"

My heart stopped. The blood in my veins stopped moving. Every cell of my body stood still, waiting. "Do you?"

"Yes, God help me." He kissed me once, hard. "I do. I love you."

"Oh, Ian." My heart expanded in my chest from the sheer joy of hearing those words. "I love you, too."

Back at home a few days later, I set aside my dog-eared copy of *Dragonfly in Amber* and dragged myself up off the couch. Even my imagination's conjuring of Jamie Fraser couldn't compete with my conflicted thoughts today.

Ian had brought me home on Monday then gone back to South Carolina alone the next day. All my doubts and insecurities had returned to take his place.

To have a relationship with Ian, I'd have to be willing to leave everything—my parents, the business I'd built—and follow him to South Carolina. Maybe I could, but he wouldn't be staying in South Carolina, either. For all I knew, his next move might be to Alaska.

Ian's nomadic existence of buying, selling, and moving on wouldn't allow me to have the sort of studio I wanted, where I could build relationships with my students and their families, and watch my students grow and learn and become proficient dancers. It wouldn't provide the stability to raise a family, and even though I didn't want children right away, one day I would.

My own children.

Mine and Ian's.

But unless he decided to stay, either here or somewhere else, I feared that Ian and I had no future together, and those maybe-children would never be born.

"Come on, Lizzie girl. We're getting too lazy." Days of rain had imposed laziness upon us, coming down with a vengeance without stopping until it was good and done. But now the sun was out, and any laziness from this point on would be self-imposed. "We need to go for a walk."

At the magic word, walk, Lizzie lit up like I'd plugged her in. She could hardly contain herself while I put on my hoodie. In two days, it would be Thanksgiving, but it was warm enough to go without a heavy coat. She hurtled down the porch steps and waited on the street corner while I locked the door.

We jogged toward the river, turned at The Riverboat, passed the tennis courts, headed away from town along River Road past the big old antebellum houses that lined the river bluffs. A few minutes later, Lizzie and I walked through the tall cemetery gates.

Melody's grave was almost all the way to the back, a shiny pink granite headstone topped with an angel statue. The angel's Madonna face looked down, her wings spread out to the back. I knew Melody wasn't lying under that pink marble marker. I knew she'd be with us all wherever we needed her.

She'll be with Maryann on her first date. She'll be with Jake when he goes out with friends and does stupid things he knows he shouldn't. She'll be with Amy at night, when she stares into the dark and waits to fall asleep.

"Melody." I rubbed Lizzie's ears back down when they pricked up from the sound of my voice. "I'm sorry, but I can't do what you asked me to." I stroked Lizzie's ears again, watching her eyes sparkle in the lowering sun.

"I've realized that the thing they need most is for me to leave them alone and let them find their own way. I did try to help. But with me there, Ben didn't have to be around. And it's him the kids need most. They all need each other now, without interference from an outsider."

As I heard myself say that word, I realized that was exactly what I was. An outsider. No matter how hard I tried to be what they needed, I would always be an outsider. I knew they loved me, and I loved them, but that didn't matter. I was still just an outsider.

The air cooled while I talked to my friend. The sun edged below the treetops along the river, turning everything yellow, then orange, then pink. "I should go, Mel. I just wanted you to know I won't be able to do what you asked. I'll still be part of your kids' lives, but I won't be there every day, or even every week, maybe. I have to keep my distance so they can work out their own way as a family."

Then I realized something I hadn't thought of before. "I'll stay here in Angel Falls, just in case they need me." I couldn't follow Ian to South Carolina. Thinking about giving up everything to be with him was one thing, but actually doing it would be impossible. Not because of the ballet studio. Not even because of my parents. Even living in the same town, we didn't see each other every week. But I had to stay close enough that I could come running if Mel's kids needed me.

Until Ben met someone who could take Melody's place in their lives, I had to stay here.

The thought felt like a weight on my soul, but another weight had lifted.

I knew now, as clearly as if Melody had said the words herself, that my jealousy hadn't caused her to die. I had sacrificed twelve years of my life wishing I could get back the man she'd stolen from me, but it hadn't hurt her at all. The only person I'd really harmed was myself.

But I owed those three kids something, and not only because I'd promised Melody to take care of them. Because I loved them.

I stood and put my hand against the cooling marble of Melody's headstone, then traced the letters of her name with my finger. "I'll be here for your kids when they need me, Mel. I'll cuddle them until they're too old to let me. I'll scold them when they've gotten too big for their britches. I'll pick them up when they call me from a party because they've had too much to drink and they're afraid to call Ben. I couldn't do what you asked. But I think I can do what you'd want me to do. I hope that'll be enough."

I sighed and shoved my hands into my pockets, wishing I'd brought a more than a light jacket after all. "I love you, Melody," I said, then turned to go.

I walked quickly, hoping the movement would warm me. The sky blazed violet and magenta along the horizon. The streetlights sent a circle of haze into the darkening sky.

Blue-day was the time of day my mama called it. The dusky blue of twilight just after sunset and just before full dark. As a child, I'd always been told to be home before blue-day. Woe be unto any child of my mother's who wasn't through the front door five minutes after the streetlights came on.

Several children ran screaming in a last-minute game of tag. Farther down the street, a crowd of sweat-shirted teenage boys played a rowdy game of basketball in someone's driveway. Life went on all around me.

No matter who died, no matter whose dreams died, life went on.

When Lizzie and I got home, I made hot tea and bundled into a fleecy robe and slippers. I had just put a frozen dinner in the microwave when the phone rang. I grabbed my tea and ran to the living room to pick up. "Hello?"

"Hi, love. What are you up to?"

At the sound of Ian's voice, I settled into my reading chair and drew my robe over my updrawn knees. "Waiting for the microwave so I can eat a starch-filled tasteless box-dinner by myself. What about you?"

"Feeling sorry for myself because I'm too far away from you."

Several good responses flitted through my mind. Well, it's your choice so live with it, or maybe, join the club. I went with, "Me, too."

"What are you planning for tomorrow?" he asked, keeping the conversational ball rolling since I wasn't helping much.

"Thanksgiving dinner with my folks." There was a moment of silence then I added, "What about you?"

"I was planning on going with a tasteless, starch-filled box-dinner."

"Oh." I had to laugh. "Good. I hope you enjoy it. Just remember that you could be at my parent's house, eating turkey and answering all my mom's questions about everything you've done in your life up until this point."

He chuckled. "I'm not sure if that would be good or bad."

"Better than a box dinner."

"Maybe I should just drop everything and drive down there."

I sat up. "Could you?"

"I really have too much to do here. The sale's a done deal as of today, and this long weekend is the perfect time for me to go through files and inventory. That way we can hit the ground running when everybody gets back to work on Monday."

"Okay. I guess I'll see you weekend-after-next, then."

"Definitely."

Yeah, unless something else comes up.

We talked for another fifteen minutes, but the whole time, all I could think was, there's no way this is going to work. We'd limp along for a while, making do with daily phone calls and every-other-weekend visits, until eventually the phone calls came only once-a-week, and the visits dropped to once-a-month.

It was only a matter of time until we had to admit there was no future in this relationship.

Chapter Twenty Two

CLASSES STARTED BACK THE MONDAY after Thanksgiving, and I was glad of the distraction. Days and nights without Ian moved slower than a salted snail, and I was so lonely that staying away from Ben and his kids became a constant effort.

A dozen times I stopped myself from picking up the phone just to be sure they were all doing okay. But I knew how bad it was to be second choice. I wasn't going to use them that way, no matter how lonely I got.

Coming up with new choreography for all the classes kept me busy—not busy enough—but at least remembering the new combinations provided a challenge, especially during the advanced class at the end of the day. Still, my students and I had the chance to talk to each other while everyone changed into their pointe shoes.

"Hey, Miss Casey," Claire said. "My Uncle Wilson said your boyfriend sold us down the river."

"You mean, Ian?"

"Yeah." Claire nodded, blond curls bobbing, eager to spill the juicy gossip. "My Uncle Wilson said—"

"Wait a minute," Keely interrupted. "Wilson... you mean Wilson who works at the newspaper office? He's your uncle?" Keely put both hands over her heart and sighed. "He's so cute."

Claire laughed at Keely's dramatic gesture. "Yeah, but he doesn't work there anymore. The new lady fired him, and then he quit."

"What?" I asked. "Why?"

"She's firing everybody." Claire made quotation marks with her fingers. "Reorganizing."

I couldn't believe Ian would sell to someone he knew would fire everybody. He had said Bianca was a colleague of his, but he must not have realized what she'd planned to do. "But, I thought she was going to be the new editor."

"Uncle Wilson said she and her husband own a lot of newspapers, but they don't run them. They send in their own team to hire and train new people. Anybody who wants to keep their job will have to interview for it, just like everybody else."

"Oh." I didn't know what to say. I felt somehow responsible. Ridiculous, but feeling responsible for the entire universe is something good southern belles, even modern ones, are raised to do. "I'll talk to Ian about it."

"Uncle Wilson already tried to call Mr. Ian. He hasn't called back."

I knotted the ribbon on my pointe shoe and tucked it in. "I'll call Ian. We'll see what this is all about."

As soon as I got home, I called Ian's cell. When he answered, I jumped in with both feet. "What on earth is your lady-friend up to?"

"Lady-friend?"

If he really didn't know who I was talking about, I was going to inform him before he got any older. "Your *colleague*." I made it sound like a dirty word. "The woman you sold the newspaper to."

Silence.

"Ian?"

"I'm here."

"Did you know you were selling out all the people who worked for the newspaper? Did you even care? Where is Grace Lambert going to get another job, as old as she is? She needs that job. And what about Wilson? Have you returned his calls yet?"

"Whoa, lass. Wait a minute. What calls?"

"Claire said Wilson tried to call you, several times."

"As far as I know, Wilson hasn't called me, unless he called the house in Angel Falls. I haven't checked those messages in a while."

"Well, you need to get in touch with him, because all hell is breaking loose here since you sold the newspaper to that bitch from hell. I thought you said you knew her. Is this what your friends are like?"

Ian sighed, a sound of frustration. "Sweetheart, I never said Bianca was a friend. She and her husband are colleagues, nothing more. We used to work for the same newspaper a hundred years ago."

I snorted at that one.

"They were willing to pay my asking price for the *Informer*. That's all I know."

"Did you know their modus operandi was to send goons down to fire everybody and then make them interview for their own jobs?"

"No, I didn't." Ian sighed. "All I knew was that they were willing to pay the price I set."

"I can't believe you would be so cold." My own voice was dripping icicles.

"Casey, I will look into this and see what I can do. I really don't have any power to change things, but I'll talk to Bianca, I promise."

"Okay. And call Wilson."

"I will."

For a heartbeat neither of us said anything. "I'm sorry I jumped on you," I said.

"I'm sorry about the newspaper. I didn't know they would fire anyone."

"Thanks for checking into it. You will do that tomorrow, right?"

"I said I would, and I will. First thing."

"I miss you," I whined. "Everything seems to take forever when you're not here. I used to think there weren't enough hours in each day, and now they drag on forever."

Ian sighed. "I know exactly what you mean. I miss you, too."

"When are you coming back home?" I realized my wording was a little off—this wasn't his home—but I didn't correct myself and he let it slide.

"Not for another week, sorry. It's no wonder this paper was going under—they kept horrible records, if they kept them at all. I'd invite you to come here, but I have to go through boxes and stacks and plastic grocery bags, God-help-me, before I can even meet with the bookkeeper. You'd be bored to tears. I'll be back weekend after next, for sure."

Already we were skipping two weekends at a time. "I guess I'll take what I can get." This relationship would be breathing its last before Christmas, and there was nothing I could do to revive it. "I'd better let you go. I'm tired."

"I promise my work load will ease up in a few weeks."

Just a minute ago, it was a couple of weeks. "Yeah, sure."

"Please don't be upset. I'll be standing on your porch

before you know it. Christmas holiday, for sure, if not before."

"Okay, fine." No way was I going to get drawn into a big phone conversation about this. I wanted to be face-to-face when we decided this wouldn't work out. "We'll talk tomorrow."

Defeated, I hung up.

The weeks between Thanksgiving and Christmas vacation limped along. The last day of the semester, Ben asked me to pick the kids up after school and take them to my house. He needed all his concentration to direct the movers in packing up the old house and moving to the new one.

Ray and Jake were good buddies now, so we'd hardly seen them since everybody piled out of my car at three-fifteen. Maryann had been more of a challenge, but I convinced her to take Lizzie for a walk. Amy curled up on the couch in Angela's living room, watching a Rugrats marathon on television. Angela and I felt there was hope for a quiet cup of tea, so she put a kettle on.

"Mom," Ray yelled, banging through Angela's back door. "Me and Jake are going down to the canal."

"You mean, Jake and I," Angela yelled back. "Come in here when you're talking to me. You know I hate it when you yell to me from another room."

Ray stomped into the kitchen, trailing mud and dragging a youth-sized rifle behind him.

"Don't you bring that thing in my kitchen," Angela screeched. "You take it straight back to your daddy's gun cabinet. You are not to use that rifle unless your daddy is with you. You hear? And carry it carefully." Angela looked at the rifle as if it could rear up and bite one of us. "It isn't loaded, is it?"

"No'm." Ray dragged the rifle into the living room where Carl's gun cabinet stood next to the TV. Jake slumped past, sending me a quiet teenage-boy grin.

"Hey, boy." I snagged Jake by his jacket sleeve. "Come over here. I don't care how old you get, you don't walk past your Aunt Casey without getting a hug."

Jake obliged, leaning over to hug me from behind. "What's up?"

"You and Ray better leave that rifle alone, you hear? That gun is not a toy, and you're not to have anything to do with it unless there's an adult right there with you. Got it?"

"Yes'm."

"Mom," Ray called from the living room, his voice raised above the sound of the gun cabinet being opened and then closed again. "Can we go to the canal?"

"I believe I mentioned something about you coming into whatever room I'm in before you talk to me." Angela waited until Ray peered around the corner into the kitchen with an exaggerated look of obliging patience on his face. Then she looked out at the window at the heavy gray clouds that promised another day of rain. "Not today, son. It's been a rainy season, and an even rainier week, so the canal will be dangerous. Y'all take your bikes out. Go for a walk or something."

"Aw, Mom. The canal isn't bad at all. It's already drained from last week."

"Aw, Ray," Angela mimicked. "Thanks for the canal report. I'm sure it has drained from last week, but now it's filling up again. Y'all go on and find something else to do. But be back by blue-day."

I smiled at my mother's familiar expression.

The teakettle whistled. Angela got up and took it off the heat then poured the boiling water into the teapot. Jake slunk past to join Ray in the living room. A second later, we heard the front door close. The sky had already started spitting rain. The poor kids wouldn't get much time to play outside before they'd be cooped up for the rest of the evening. "I guess Ray got that rifle he wanted for his birthday."

"Yeah. Milk and sugar, right?"

"Yes, please."

Angela put milk and sugar into our teacups then topped them up with the hot tea. "He's been dying for Carl to take him to the shooting range for target practice, but it's been so rainy." She brought our tea to the table. "How are things with you and Ian?"

I took a sip—ow, too hot—then set the cup aside. "I don't know, but maybe I'll find out later tonight. He said he's coming for Christmas vacation, but I'm not holding my breath."

Angela paused for a minute before she slipped in the trick question. "Has he told you yet that he loves you?"

"Yeah." But it didn't mean anything unless he was willing to stay.

"I knew it." She patted me on the hand. "I knew from the minute I saw that man sitting on our porch he'd be the one for you. Didn't I tell you?"

"Well, no, Angela. Actually, you—"

"Of course, it was obvious. The walls are pretty thin around here."

"What?" My face heated at Angela's implication. "What do you mean?"

"Well, you know." She looked under her lashes at me. "For a while, I thought you'd end up with Ben, after Melody and all, but... well, it's just... Like I said, the walls are thin." She pulled her chair closer with a scraping sound against the linoleum. "Ben comes over, we never hear anything but the TV or the stereo in the living room. Ian comes over, and, well... our bedroom backs up to your bedroom. If you know what I mean."

"Oh, Angela." I was mortified to the bone. "You never said..."

"What should I say? Landlady, you'd better not holler so loud when your boyfriend comes over?"

"Angela." I knew my face had turned three shades of red. "I am so sorry."

She laughed. "Don't be sorry. It's not a problem. I told Carl he should try to make me holler like that."

We were both hooting with laughter when Maryann came charging in, her clothes soaked, her hair a wet tangled mess hanging down her back.

"The boys went to the canal on their bikes, and they wouldn't let me go, too." She put her hands on her hips. "They said girls aren't allowed to go into the canal. That's not true, is it?"

I looked out the window. "Those little toads!" Surely they wouldn't actually go down there after we'd forbidden them to.

Angela jumped up. "Damn that boy! He's gonna get skinned alive. At least he didn't take that gun with him."

"Yes ma'am, he did," Maryann said with smug assurance. "I told him he shouldn't, but he said you wouldn't mind."

"Wouldn't mind," Angela steamed, "wouldn't mind, my hind foot! That little so-and-so. When I get him home safe and sound, I'm gonna kill him."

"I'll go get them, Angela." I knew I wouldn't be able to sit here and wait. "You stay with the girls. Maryann, do you know where they went into the canal?"

"No'm. But they said they were going past the new house."

"The bridge steps by the hospital." I sighed. "I know Ben has to be at the house to supervise the movers, but I should let him know what's going on."

Angela nodded. "You're going to need his help. I'll take the girls to the new house, and we'll supervise the movers." She followed me to the front door and watched while I pulled on my mud boots. "If Carl weren't making a run to Greensboro today..."

I put on my rain jacket and checked my cell's battery. Thank goodness, it was full. I squeezed Angela's arm to comfort us both. "I'll bring them back safe, then we'll tan their behinds."

I put my head down and ran through the rain, my heavy boots sloshing and sliding. When I got into my car, I called Ben, not sparing time for greetings. "Jake and Ray have gone down into the canal. They've got Ray's rifle. I don't know what kind of shape the canal's in right now, but..."

"I can see it from here. It's not bad yet, but it will be soon. Where do you want me to meet you?"

"My guess is the limestone steps by the hospital bridge."

"I'm on my way. Don't go in there without me."

"All right, I'll wait. But hurry."

I knew I'd guessed right when I saw the boys' bikes propped against the bridge rail. I parked on the wide gravel and grass verge that extended to the canal's edge. A second later, Ben parked beside me, and we both got out, slamming doors.

Muddy skid-marks from the boys' shoes marked the crude limestone steps someone had long-ago engineered into the canal's steep bank. Limestone tended to break off in flat slabs, and the big chunks looked like they'd been shoved into the crumbling, nearly vertical slope.

We looked down into the chasm. A fast-moving stream of white-capped brown water rushed down the center, snaking along the deepest cuts in the limestone. There was still space to walk along both sides of the stream, but it wouldn't stay that way for long. I cupped my hands and yelled. "Jake! Ray! Boys!"

Ben patted my shoulder. "They can't hear you. I'll have to go down after them."

At least it wasn't raining as hard here as it was at home. Yet.

"Angela's taking the girls to the new house to help with the movers. I told you Ray has his rifle? I don't know what they think they're going to shoot down here."

Hands on hips, a worried scowl on his face, Ben gave a short, distracted nod. I could tell he was figuring out the best way to proceed without either of us getting our necks broken. "Tin cans, most likely. The canal walls are soft enough to absorb any stray shots without throwing them back. I hope." Ben started the slippery descent into the canal, holding his arms out for balance as his tennis shoes skidded down the slope. "You stay here."

"No." Without waiting for discussion or permission, I began negotiating my descent. "I'm coming with you."

Ben paused on a ledge about halfway down and held up a hand to help me. "You never listen to anybody, do you?"

"Nope." I took his hand and let him steady me. Step by slippery step, we slid and skidded into the depths of the canal. When we got to the bottom, there were few firm footings. The torrent rushing down the center channel made the limestone floor slippery as owl shit. "I'm sorry this happened on my watch."

Ben held onto me, gauging the safest route before proceeding. "Not your fault. Jake's been headed for an ass-whipping for a while."

I could barely hear Ben now that we were in the canal. The rushing water echoed off the smooth limestone walls, drowning our voices. We walked hand in hand because it was so slippery, taking turns holding each other up.

We headed north, their most likely direction. The canal widened just south of the bridge where we'd entered. It flattened out there, spreading the churning water across the entire floor. It would have been almost impossible for them to have gone in that direction.

The sharp report of a rifle shot ricocheted along the high limestone walls. Then another, and another. We moved as quickly as we dared toward the sound.

"I hope to God they don't shoot us," Ben shouted. I barely heard him. Brownish water sloshed over the edges of the deep channel. Ben lost his footing on the slick floor. I grabbed his arm, and an instant later he held me up when I hit the same algae-slick spot.

Ben pointed up ahead, where runoff rushed over the walkway. "We'll have to jump," he said into my ear. "The only way is on the other side."

Yeah, until that one flooded, too.

"I'll jump it first then catch you." Ben backed up to the wall then took a running leap across the stream. His mud-slick tennis shoes slid, tossing him up against the opposite wall. He turned and held out his arms, ready to catch me.

In heavy knee-high mud boots, I took a preparation stance for *grand jete*, then cleared the trench with ease and landed lightly beside Ben.

"God, you're good." Relieved that neither of us had

been killed yet, he wrapped his arms around me and kissed me on the mouth.

I grinned. "You're not surprised, are you?"

He chucked me on the chin. "I've never forgotten."

Abrupt pops of rifle fire seemed to elicit a low rumble of thunder from the gray skies. I sent up a prayer of thanks that only a light drizzle was falling. For some reason, on this side of the trench, Ben and I could hear each other better. "I can't believe those boys would do something this stupid," I said.

Ben resumed our trek along the canal floor. "Don't tell Jake, but I did this and worse when I was his age."

"Oh?" I chanced a look up at him then regretted it when my moment of inattention almost pitched me into the muddy whitecaps. "I thought sneaking out with me was the dumbest thing you did in your youth."

Ben steadied me with his hands on my hips as we walked single-file along a narrow, crumbling ledge. "Angel, loving you was one of the few smart things I did."

"Ben..." I would've looked over my shoulder at him if I wasn't so preoccupied with where I planned to step next.

"Don't worry. I'm not driving at anything. I know you're in love with Ian." With a brief squeeze, he let me go when the path widened enough for us to walk side by side again. He took my hand and helped me around a deep, round pit that created a sucking whirlpool at the flood's edge.

"Ben, I don't want you to think... I mean, even if things don't work out with Ian, I wouldn't want you to..."

"I know, Angel. I had my chance, and I blew it. I can't regret any of it. Not our time together, and not my life with Mel. I guess things happened just the way they were supposed to."

We rounded a curve in the canal, and suddenly we could hear the boys' voices carrying clearly above the increasing roar of the water. We couldn't see them, but we could hear them. Bits of conversation floated towards us. "...so cool... look at... yeah, like..."

Calling their names, we hurried toward them through the pattering rain. We slipped on the wet limestone, we held each other up, we slogged through inch-deep water where before there had been none. Runoff poured from pipes set at intervals along the top of the channel, mini-waterfalls raising the water level in this death trap.

Damn. Would it never stop raining? With the ground so saturated, every drop poured right into this gigantic ditch. I was a good swimmer, but I didn't want to brave the frigid waves that would soon be churning down this chute. Let alone try it with two young boys in tow.

"Man..." They were closer now, the sounds of their voices coming towards us. Ray saying "...Mom's gonna kill me. These are new shoes." Jake's, "Yeah, my dad would have a cow if he—"

They stopped short at the sight of Ben and me coming toward them.

"Dad." Jake's voice cracked uncertainly. His Adam's apple bobbed in his throat as he swallowed. "What are y'all doing here?"

"Busted," Ray moaned.

"Busted is right," Ben said. "I hope you boys had fun, because it's the last fun you're going to have for a very long time." Ben jerked the rifle out of Ray's hands. He pointed it at the ground and cocked the bolt back several times. Cartridges splashed into the rushing stream at his feet. "Let's get out of here before this ditch fills up."

Ray stepped back and swallowed hard. The freckles on his pale skin stood out even more when he realized for the first time the danger we were in.

Jake's gaze darted from one pouring drain pipe to another. "Shit," he said without thinking, then clapped his hands over his mouth.

"Worse than that," said Ben. "Ray, can you swim?"

"Yes, sir."

"Thank God." Ben took Jake's hand and turned back the way we'd come. "Follow me. Stay close."

I grabbed Ray's hand, tugging him forward. The slick limestone floor we navigated was difficult at the best of times. Now, with water flowing ankle-deep in the shallowest places, it was treacherous. Ray slipped—his hand ripped from mine with surprising ease—and fell into one of the deep circular holes that pitted the canal bottom. He went under, sucked into the whirlpool for an instant before Ben hauled him up by the collar.

He took a moment to steady the boy, then took Jake's hand and trudged forward again. We passed another gushing pipe, and the flood rose higher, swirling to my knees. In no time, it was thigh-deep.

Up ahead, two more pipes spewed water into the deepening flow. We slogged on, avoiding the deep trench in the center.

Ben held the rifle out to me and reached for Ray's hand. "Casey," he yelled above the increasing roar, "Take the rifle and get out of here while you can. The boys and I will follow behind. If the gun's too much trouble to handle, ditch it. But it's not loaded; you may be able to use it for leverage."

"I'm a good swimmer," I yelled back. "You might need my help."

"No." He handed the gun over. "You're the smallest one of us. It would be too easy for you to get swept away."

And just like that, my feet slid out from under me. The rifle was snatched from my hands by a churning current that swept me along.

Chapter Twenty Three

"CASEY!" BEN'S VOICE SOUNDED FAR away. The wild torrent hurled me downstream, and I was helpless against a vicious tide, an evil, living thing determined to destroy me. I scrambled to stand. My feet skidded along the slippery bottom, then the water sucked me into a strong undertow.

The cold, dark water closed over my head. The current dragged me under and slammed me against the bottom. I fought to the surface, choking and sputtering, only to be sucked down again. I was a breath away from drowning.

I flailed up to the choppy surface, dragged in a breath, and tried to organize my panicked movements into something resembling true swimming.

Then I saw him.

Ian stood waist-deep just ahead of me, ignoring the punch of the waves that caught him in the chest. Ignoring the undulating curves of a water moccasin that popped its triangular head out of the water an arms-length away before submerging again.

I saw Ian, and knew I would be okay.

He stood in that churning, muddy water, his wet hair plastered to his head, jaw clenched with determination, waiting for the current to bring me close. He looked like some sort of warrior-god wearing a soaked T-shirt. I raised my head, gulped for air, and swallowed a mouthful of dirty water when a wave broadsided me.

"Swim to me," he yelled. "Kick hard!" He held out an arm and leaned as far toward me as he could without sliding into the deeper current that held me in its clutches. I kicked desperately, but the surge hurtled down the chute toward the river, taking me with it.

Keeping my head above the waves took so much energy, and I didn't have energy to spare. I held my breath and dove under, hoping to cut through the water toward Ian and safety.

I stretched my arms out, reaching blindly, and kicked for all I was worth. I hoped Ian could grab me before the tide carried me past.

Strong fingers gripped my wrist, pulling hard against a current that tried just as hard to suck me downstream. I grappled for his arm.

Finally, I closed my fingers around hard muscle.

He dragged me closer, grabbed me around the ribs and hauled me up against his chest. His heart pounded so hard I could feel it. "God, lass." He hauled in a ragged breath. "Ye scared the shite outta me."

I wrapped my legs around his waist and clung like a barnacle on a rock while water swirled around us, sucking, seeking to drag us in.

"Ben has the boys?" Ian was still breathing hard, his ever-warm skin cold, peppered with goose bumps.

"Still behind me."

"I'm too old for this." He carried me toward the steep limestone steps. "If ye'll swear to God never to do anythin' this dangerous again, I'll stay in this bloody town forever."

I rested my head on his shoulder, breathing in a single moment of pure joy that I would never forget. "I'll be good."

"Ye sure as hell need a keeper." Ian set me down in knee-deep water. "I might as well be it."

Shaking with exhaustion, I held onto his hard waist for balance, but slogged the last few feet under my own steam. I figured once the adrenaline had subsided he'd be backpedaling, but I was more than happy to go along and hope for the best. "You're right, I do need a keeper." I'd have been whooping with joy if I had enough breath to do it. I settled for patting him on the arm. "If you're up for the job, you're hired."

"We'll talk about my terms of servitude later." He grabbed my waist and hoisted me onto a limestone step. "I've got to help Ben."

I scrambled to my knees, and Ian gave me a boost on the rear. "Get up that hill so I don't have to worry about you." He turned and slogged back toward Ben and the boys.

"Hey!" Angela stood above me, a big bundle of rope in her hands. She made a quick loop around the bridge rail, tugged on it, then tossed the frayed end down. "Grab on!"

When I finally struggled to the top, she propped me against the hood of her old Volvo station wagon and wrapped me in a towel. "The boys?"

"Ben has them," I answered through chattering teeth. "Ian's gone back to help. They'll be okay."

"Thank God he showed up right after y'all left." Angela rubbed my arms with a towel. I was shaking from the cold air that buffeted my wet clothes.

"Where are the girls?"

"I asked Lois to take them to the new house so I could

come here in case y'all needed help." Angela draped the towel around my shoulders, and we walked together to the bridge rail to look down into the canal.

The water had risen another foot in just a few minutes.

"Shit." Maybe I shouldn't have been quite so confident. Ian was my hero, and Ben was no slouch, either, but they didn't have superhuman powers.

Angela hugged me tighter. "They'll get the boys out."

Just then, Ian rounded the corner with the back of Ray's shirt clutched in his fist. Ray was swimming at the edge of the canal's limestone wall, where the current wasn't as strong. Ian was walking, the water lapping at his armpits. Pretty soon, he'd be swimming, too. Ian gave Ray a push every now and then, but he never let go of Ray's shirt.

Ben and Jake were right behind them, not quite as close to the limestone wall. "They're too close to the center," I worried out loud. If they got caught up in it, they'd miss the steps leading out of the canal and remain trapped within its walls all the way to the river—if they made it that far without drowning.

"They'll be okay," Angela said without much conviction. We both knew how treacherous those waters were.

A stick floated past Ben. It bobbed along for a while, then got caught up in a whirlpool and sucked under. Angela clutched my arm and pointed to the group as they progressed towards us. "It's not as deep where they are now."

The canal widened and shallowed just before the limestone steps. Ray could stand now.

I held my breath until Ian and Ben hauled the boys to the safety of shallow water.

"Here." Angela tossed down the rope.

Ian made sure Ray had a good grip then shoved him

halfway up the stone slabs. Ray's soaked tennis shoes slid on the moss-slick limestone, but Angela grabbed his arm and pulled until he stood beside us on the muddy bank. "You're in a world of trouble, boy," Angela fussed, giving him a quick fierce hug and wrapping him in a dry towel.

I took the rope from Ray's cold fingers and tossed it down. Ian caught it, then gave Jake the rope and shoved him up the bank just as he'd done for Ray and me. Ian walked up the steep steps using the rope for balance then tossed it down to Ben.

I met Ian at the canal's edge, wrapped my arms around his waist, and hugged, hard.

He slumped against me. His exhaustion twitched in muscles pushed past endurance.

I held him close, our clammy T-shirts and jeans clinging together. He shivered, and I held him tighter, sharing what little warmth I had. "I have an idea," I whispered in his ear. "Let's go home and see who can get naked fastest."

Ian gave a weak laugh and brushed a lock of dripping hair away from my shoulder. "Lass, you've got a deal."

Somebody handed Ian a towel. He pulled out of my embrace to dry his hair and swipe at his saturated clothing. Ben brought Jake close, one hand on his shoulder. "You've got something to say to your Aunt Casey?"

Jake hung his head and nodded without looking me in the face. "I'm sorry I disobeyed you, Aunt Casey. I won't do it again."

I hugged him, both of us shivering. "I accept your apology."

Ben gave me a brief hug, then shook Ian's hand. "Thank you for going down there to get the boys."

"You're welcome."

Angela hugged Ian, then me. "Thanks for saving my hard-headed son." The sullen skies hurled a gust of cold raindrops at us. "We'd all better go home and get dry."

I patted my pockets—my car keys were gone. "Shit. I've lost my keys."

Ian put an arm around my shoulders. "We'll deal with that tomorrow. I wouldn't want to let you out of my sight anyway." We walked hip-to-hip toward his car. Once inside, Ian started the engine and turned on the heater.

I held my hands up to the vents. "You came home early. I wasn't expecting you till late tonight."

"I missed you." He backed the car out.

I latched onto whatever brain cells I could still claim. "Have you spoken to Bianca?"

"Umm-hmmm."

He kept his eyes on the rain-slick road to my house. After a minute, I realized he had no intention of elaborating. Talking to a man can sometimes be worse than talking to a toddler. "So? Were you planning on telling me about it sometime soon?"

"Umm-hmmm." He cut a sultry glance my way. "I thought I'd wait until you were in a position to be suitably grateful."

"That sounds promising."

"I think you'll like my solution."

"Tell me."

"I bought the *Informer* back."

I clapped my hands and bounced in my seat. I know it was juvenile and unladylike, but I couldn't help it. "Ian, did you really?"

"I really did." His tone was weary. "Lost a load of money."

"It's only money." I put a soothing hand on his damp

thigh.

He covered my hand with his. "Easy for you to say. It's not your money."

"Thank you, Ian. I love you for doing this."

"I thought you loved me anyway."

"I do love you anyway." I unbuckled my seatbelt and leaned across the console to hug him. "You wouldn't believe how much."

The car swerved for a second, then righted. "Lass," Ian scolded, though I could hear a smile in his voice. "Sit down and buckle your seatbelt."

I sat back and fastened my seatbelt, patting his thigh and grinning so big my cheeks hurt. After a few minutes of watching the scenery fly by, I asked the question that had been burning a hole in my brain. "Will you really move back to Angel Falls? For good? You gonna buy that big house, or move in with me?"

Ian gave a weak laugh. "You're relentless, aren't you?"

"Yes, I am." Happiness zipped and zinged through me like a million ping-pong balls. "You might as well give up now."   ·

Ian parked in front of my house and walked around to open my door. He pulled me to my feet and into his arms. "If I had any sense, I'd have given up the moment I first saw you. It would have saved me a lot of grief—and money."

My heart expanded with the promise of all the happiness we had ahead of us. "I promise you won't regret it, Ian. I'll make you so happy, and I know you'll love Angel Falls."

Ian scowled down at me then gave me a hard kiss to disguise the beginnings of a smile that ruined his fierce expression. When he lifted his mouth from mine, the smile he'd tried to tame tilted the corners of his mouth.

"You just never let up, do you?"

"Not usually." He might as well know the truth now. "But if you want me to, I'll try to change."

"No, lass." With an affectionate pat on my soppy-wet butt, he turned me toward the house. We went up the steps with his arm around my shoulders, my arm around his waist. "I'll take you exactly as you are."

Epilogue

Twenty years later…

WE LOADED THE LAST FEW bridal shower gifts into the back of my car, and I slammed the trunk. The candy-apple red of the sleek Cadillac convertible gleamed in the weak February sunlight. I might have bought a VW bug if I'd had any say in the matter, but the Cadillac had been Ian's idea of the perfect Christmas gift, and of course I was thrilled because it was another expression of his love for me.

A gust of wind fluttered the hem of my long skirt and blew strands of my long, silver-streaked hair into my face. Shivering, I put an arm around Amy's shoulders. "Let's go inside. I have something else for you."

Amy leaned her head against mine. "Aunt Casey, you're too good to me. You hosted the bridal shower, and you're letting us take your new car on our honeymoon. Enough, already!"

"This next gift isn't a big one, just something I wanted you to have."

"Something borrowed?" she asked as we walked up the steps to the house.

"No. This is for you to keep."

I held the door open for her and led her into the den, which still looked pretty much the same as the first day I'd walked into it. The leather furniture was a different set, but the hulking shapes and dark soothing colors were similar. The big oriental carpet underneath was different, something we'd found on one of our vacations and then had shipped home. I reached onto a high bookshelf and brought down the photo album, handing it to Amy.

"Something blue," she whispered, brushing her hand across the pale fabric cover.

I laughed. "I wouldn't recommend carrying it down the aisle. It is a little heavy."

Amy took the album to the couch and settled down on the thick cushions. Flipping open the heavy cover, she read the inscription out loud. "To Amy from Aunt Casey, with all the love in the world."

I sat next to Amy on the couch and put an arm around her shoulders. "Most of it is empty, for you to fill with your wedding photos. I took the liberty of starting it with a few pages of your family's wedding history. I hope you don't mind."

"Mind?" Amy's voice wavered, and she sniffed back tears. "How could I mind?"

She touched the plastic-covered photograph of Melody and Ben on their wedding day with reverent fingers, outlining Melody's face with one manicured fingertip. "She was so beautiful. I wish I could remember her."

"She loved you very much," I said quietly. "She would have wanted to be here with you today. I'm sorry she's not."

Amy gave a sad smile. "Me too." The photo album flopped open in her lap while she leaned to hug me. "But you're here, and you've been like a mother to me. I never felt deprived, not even before Dad remarried."

I returned her hug. "That's sweet of you to say, honey. I know it's not entirely true, but I appreciate the thought. And I'm so proud of you. You've turned out to be a wonderful woman, and you look so much like your mother. I see her every time I look at you."

I brushed a thick, silky lock away from Amy's cheek. Her face was a perfect mix of Melody and Ben, taking the very best of each parent and combining them into a stunningly beautiful young woman.

Amy leaned against me. "I love you."

"I love you, too." I hugged her, then returned my attention to the photo album. I turned the page.

"Oh." Amy lifted the album just enough to take the chandelier's glare off the page. "I didn't know there was more."

I pointed to the first photo. "Your mom's parents on their wedding day." I slid my finger across to the opposite page. "And your dad's parents on theirs. I had a hard time getting copies of these, I don't mind telling you."

"I can't believe you did all this, Aunt Casey."

"There's more." I turned to a photo of Ben and his wife of fifteen years.

"Look at me in that picture," Amy said with a touch of self-loathing in her voice. "I was so horrible to her in the beginning. I don't know why it took me so long accept her."

I kissed the tip of my finger and placed it on the image of Amy's scowling young face. "Because she wasn't your mother. Not yet, anyway."

Amy giggled, then stifled the sound. "I shouldn't laugh, but..."

"What?"

"Remember the Christmas I decorated the big evergreen outside our house with her underwear?"

I laughed. "Your father had a fit."

"And we had a big argument, and I came to live with you and Uncle Ian for months."

"Weeks, maybe."

Just then, my teenage whirlwind, Sara, burst through the front door, leaving clumps of mud on the carpet. She rushed through wearing her riding clothes and boots. "I left my riding crop on the table," she said breathlessly. On her way back out, she spared us an airy wave. "Daddy's waiting. I get to ride Tempest today. Hi, Amy."

When the door slammed after Sara, Amy and I shared a moment of silence, then our gazes drifted down to the album once again. "This is the last photo," I said, turning the page. "I couldn't decide whether to put it in, because we're not really family..."

"Bite your tongue. If you and Uncle Ian aren't family, I don't know what family is."

"Look at us." I admired Ian's handsome image and remembered how it felt to be sparkling with happiness. Actually, I still felt that way quite a lot of the time, so it wasn't such a stretch. "We thought we were so old, but we were just babies, really."

"You were so beautiful," Amy said, then sat up a little straighter when she realized she'd called me beautiful in past tense. "You still are."

I smiled serenely. "I guess we're always beautiful to those who love us."

"This is me, isn't it?" Amy pointed to a little imp wearing a hot-pink ballerina costume, her blonde curls decorated with pink silk flowers.

"Yes, honey. My very best flower girl at the head of the line."

Amy laughed. "I can't believe you had two hundred

flower girls."

"Why not?" I pretended to take offense. "They all had perfectly good recital costumes to wear to the wedding."

"People still talk about the parade y'all had around the town square."

"Hey," I huffed, "what's an outdoor wedding without a parade? We couldn't fit the wedding party into any of the churches, so our only option was to get married in the park. The streets were blocked off anyway, so of course we had to have a parade."

"I swear, Aunt Casey," Amy leaned forward to study the picture. "It looks like you had everything at your wedding but elephants and dancing poodles."

I pointed to my old dog Lizzie, wearing her Aussie grin and a sequined tutu. "The poodles couldn't make it, but we did have the world's best Australian Shepherd leading the parade."

Acknowledgments:

Thank you, thank you, thank you, to…

My wonderful husband, Hans, my own personal hero, who never, not even once, complained about burned (or forgotten) dinners when I got too immersed in my writing world to remember the existence of that other world in which people were hoping to eat dinner sometime soon. Even though he did sometimes remind me of what his mother always said: "Where in the recipe did it say to walk away from the stove?"

My children, who have brought such joy into our lives—and on the occasions they didn't bring joy, at least they gave me something to write about. Christopher, Tessa, Natalie, I love y'all unconditionally.

My Executive Officer of Operations, Mistianne Langston, who keeps my life running smoothly so I have more time to write.

Amanda Lee Borgstrom, for keeping us straight back in the day.

Sue Hadley, who took such good care of my parents—and the rest of us—when my parents were here.

My parents, who aren't in physical form anymore but still hang around sometimes. Daddy, I know you love to make the little dog bark, and that's okay. Mama, I hope the Church Ladies in heaven don't give you too much grief about the sex scenes. I couldn't bring myself to take your advice and "leave the s-e-x at the bedroom door."

Rita Gallagher, a founding member of Romance Writers of America, who tutored me in her by-invitation-only critique class. I know she's looking down from heaven, saying, "It's about time."

Haywood Smith, NYT bestselling author who took the time to guide and encourage an unknown writer like me. All her books are on my keeper shelf. http://haywoodsmith.net/

Geri Krotow, writing goddess and good friend, who was happy to read a chapter when I needed a fresh perspective. http://gerikrotow.com/

Margie Lawson, who teaches fantastic writing classes that I highly recommend. http://www.margielawson.com/

The talented team at The Killion Group, for creating a gorgeous cover and doing all the jobs I can't, like formatting, uploading, marketing... Kim, Dana, Jennifer, Shelly... So glad I didn't have to do all that stuff. http://thekilliongroupinc.com/

My daughter Tessa, who drew the logo for my publishing imprint, Tranquil Dragonfly Press.

My critique partners and writing support team,
The Plotting Wenches:

Jessica Trapp, whom I met at my very first RWA meeting in Houston. It was her first meeting too, and we gravitated toward each other because we were both dressed like hippies and wearing Birkenstocks. We started critiquing when her son and my youngest daughter were in strollers, and now they're in college. Our friendship has lasted longer than most marriages because we're both awesome. http://jessicatrapp.com/

Jo Ann Sky, fastest reader, writer and CP in the West, who somehow skipped fifteen years of dues-paying by becoming an accomplished novelist practically overnight. We'll be critiquing forever, too, I hope, because she's just brilliant. http://www.joannsky.com/

Faith Eides, who met my husband when they attended the same high school in Kinshasa, Congo. He knew that Faith and I were peas in a pod, so he introduced us, and I'm so glad to know her and to have her literary and editorial talent as part of my team. www.amazon.com/Faith-Eidse/e/B00IWT66YA

Kimberly Savage, author and playwright who also has an amazing blog. I bow down to her ability to keep up with it all. https://kimberlysavage.com/

Lisa Miller, who writes YA and teaches a fantastic class about plotting called Safari. Think of her as your own personal GPS when it comes to writing. lisawmiller.com

Past critique buddies who shared a
vital part of my writer's journey:

Cindy Miles, who actually mentioned me in the acknowledgments of her first book! That meant so much to me. Being thanked for my input by such a talented author gave me hope and helped me believe in myself. Finally, I get to thank her in return. http://cindy-miles.com/

Ann DeFee, one of the funniest people I know. We always planned to be sitting next to each other at RWA National book signing events, since our last names are too close in the alphabet to allow anyone to come between us. http://www.anndefee.com/

Kay Austin and Betty Pichardo, amazing writers and CPs.

Shana Galen (AKA Shane Bolks) who critiqued with Jessica and me back in the day. http://shanagalen.com./

PJ Mellor, who's known for writing hot and sexy contemporary romance. http://pjmellor.com/

Friends who gave me a reader's perspective of this and other manuscripts; Celia Lambert, Shelley Glass, Jenn Reed, and Lauren Whitley.

Contest judges JoAnne Banker, Genevieve Montcombroux, and many more—some who became friends, and others whose names I never knew—who offered feedback and encouragement.

Colleen Thompson http://colleen-thompson.com/ and Sharon Sala http://sharonsala.net/ for being so open-hearted and down-to-earth.

Friends, neighbors, and relatives who are always just a phone call away to give support, encouragement, and positive energy. Too many to name, because I'm so lucky (but you know who you are, and so do I).

And those few people who have acted as spiritual sandpaper, forcing me to learn the art of remaining positive in the face of negativity... Or when that's not possible, slice them into tiny (figurative) pieces and cobble those pieces together to make a multilayered antagonist that I can, if I choose, kill off at the end of the book.

Author Bio:

Photo by Andrea McDaniel

Babette de Jongh lives in L.A. (Lower Alabama), close enough to the beach to take the dogs there, but far-enough away to be able to hunker down in a hurricane. Her backwoods home, Dragonfly Pond Farm, is a magical place where everyone gets along with everyone else, even though its inhabitants include dogs, cats, ferrets, horses, donkeys, goats, sheep, geese, guineas, chickens, parrots, the local wildlife, and (last but usually not least) humans. When she isn't writing, she's gardening, making art, or working as a telepathic animal communicator. The dog in the photo is Jack Skellington, who forever retains the title of THE BEST GOOD DOG.

Please visit Babette at:

www.BabettedeJongh.com
or
www.HearThemSpeak.com

And connect with her on Facebook at:

https://www.facebook.com/BabettedeJongh.author
or
https://www.facebook.com/Italktoanimals/

Twitter: https://twitter.com/Babette_deJongh
Pinterest: https://www.pinterest.com/bestbabette/

62483426R00183

Made in the USA
Charleston, SC
16 October 2016